Praise for C~~a~~

"I began writing and directing films twelve years ago through my production company, Olive Ranch Road Productions. One of my first and absolute favorite stories was *Captain Fin*. I would eventually write and direct that story as a short film. The film was a big success in festivals, so I then wrote the feature-length script. But it wasn't until I was introduced to Amanda M. Thrasher years later that I would see the depths that this story could really go. Amanda has molded the lead character, Hannah, into a beautifully enriched soul with incredible layers. Amanda's novel goes so much deeper into the life that Hannah leads after so much misfortune fell upon her as a little girl. Her story takes us on a gripping journey as she weaves us through Hannah's unrelenting pursuit of her past. This is my second feature film script that has been written into a novel, and it is without a doubt my absolute favorite! Amanda's kind and caring soul is so deeply embedded in this amazing novel... it will touch people on so many levels."

Kevin James O'Neill
Writer / Director / Producer
www.oliveranchroadproductions.com

5 STAR REVIEW READERS' FAVORITE
Captain Fin is a work of young adult fiction penned by author Amanda M. Thrasher and adapted from a screenplay by Kevin James O'Neill. In this tale, we find our hero Hannah Gunner in a state of turmoil regarding the secrets unveiled about her life. Hannah doesn't really know the full particulars of who she is, and so she forms

a trio of inquirers with her boyfriend Cash and best friend Lindsay to discover the truth about herself. She must distinguish between memories and dreams to uncover reality, coming face to face with the ghosts of her past and the elusive Captain that haunts her still. This is a fascinating tale that certainly has much to offer its young adult readers, with likeable lead characters, hidden treasure and secrets, as well as important social issues about growing up, learning who you really are, and having that sense of self put to the test by the information and people you face in the wider world. Hannah is an endearing lead character whom author Amanda M. Thrasher makes very likable and relatable, and I enjoyed the unreliability of the memories and secrets she has to deal with. This enhances the overall plot with plenty of twists and suspense, making it all the more exciting when moments of real truth do emerge for us to put the pieces of Hannah's life together. Overall, Captain Fin is a strong work of teen identity, adventure, mystery and plenty of hijinks to keep its readers entertained.

Reviewed By K.C. Finn for Readers' Favorite

CAPTAIN FIN

Amanda M. Thrasher

Based On The Screenplay By
Kevin James O'Neill

RISING PHOENIX PRESS ®

Text Copyright © 2019 Amanda M. Thrasher

All rights reserved. Published 2019 by Progressive Rising Phoenix Press, LLC
www.progressiverisingphoenix.com

ISBN: 978-1-950560-01-1

Printed in the U.S.A.
1st Printing

Library of Congress Cataloging-in-Publication Data and on file with the Publisher.

Edited by: Jody Amato

Cover Photos: Young Girl, Stock Photo ID: 209064253, Copyright: 4 PM Production. Older Girl, Stock Photo ID: 127669838, Copyright: Ababaka. Pirate Ship, Stock Photo ID: 255479581, Copyright: Proslgn. Back Cover Letter, Stock Photo ID: 156087626, Copyright: Free_lancer. Photos used by permission.

Information from The American Cancer Society:
https://www.cancer.org/cancer/chronic-myeloid-leukemia.html

Book cover design by Kalpart.
Visit www.kalpart.com

Book interior design by William Speir
Visit: http://www.williamspeir.com

Acknowledgments

I want to thank Kevin James O'Neill for trusting me with his script and being patient throughout when it seemed as if time was never on my side, thank you! I immediately fell in love with the life that young and teen Hannah could have led, and I'm thrilled to have brought her to life.

Special thanks to Jody Amato, my editor; we have yet another book under our belt! I enjoy working with you, and I look forward to our next one.

To my family whom I adore: Mike, Zack, Krista, Lauren, my dad, Martin Mulroy, Jo-ann, and my beautiful grandchildren, thank you for allowing me the time to do what I love as an author and business owner. I know how it affects you all.

Remembering my mom, one of the most incredible women I have ever met, Irene Yvonne Mulroy; you are not forgotten. I miss and love you still.

To my business partner and friend, Jannifer Powelson, we made it another year and I look forward to many more! I'd also like to acknowledge and thank our Production Manager, William Speir; our Marketing Director, Galeo Johnson; and of course, our Webmaster and the person who keeps PRPP running behind the scenes, Matthew Gene; thank you all for everything that you do!

To Sue Nodler Hamideh, for your constant support! You have read my work since *Mischief in the Mushroom*

Patch, and I am grateful. Thank you to Cindy Nave and Caroline Dixon; you took the time to read the manuscript during the earliest days. I appreciate it.

Amanda M. Thrasher
March 2019

Table of Contents

This novel is dedicated to anyone who takes comfort in their memories or imagination. Find your peace!

Chapter 1
Hannah

Shattered Layers
Broken Dreams
Tattered Hearts
A Past Revealed
Twisted Paths
Shadow Dark
Out of Grasp
A Father's Heart
~ Hannah Gunner ~

"That's it, then!" Hannah whispered in a raspy voice. "She's really gone?"

Lindsey stared down at her lap, avoiding eye contact, not knowing what to say to her best friend, who was still in shock and so much pain. Tears had welled up in Hannah's eyes, and though she'd been fighting to hold them back, they threatened to flow uncontrollably down her cheeks. Hannah couldn't allow that, not yet, knowing that once the tears fell she'd lose it completely. The air had chilled, and she stood shivering, but Hannah didn't seem to notice. The oversized black sweatshirt she'd picked that day drowned out her petite frame. She looked like a little kid instead of a teen. Every now and then her arm reached up and swiped away escaped tears from her face, as if denying they were ever there.

Lindsey had been Hannah's best friend since they'd been paired together junior year for a chemistry project. It was a good match. They had more in common than the pair realized. Gossip, boys, music, both lacked fashion skills, which didn't seem to bother either of them at all, neither wore much makeup, and they both loved to write, especially poetry, and constantly carried a journal or had one close by. They practically lived in Vans, jeans, sweatshirts, Nike shorts and, of course, T-shirts. This day, this terrible day, was the hardest day they'd ever experienced together as friends. Lindsey opened the door of her gently used gold Toyota Corolla, affectionately named Silver. A joke, agreed upon by the two girls, which made them laugh every time they referred to her—except for today.

"Silver awaits. Climb in; it's freezing. I'm taking you home."

Ridden with guilt, Hannah felt conflicted. On the one hand, she didn't want to be with anyone, including her best friend or her boyfriend, and on the other hand, she didn't want to be alone. Reluctantly, she climbed into the car. As soon as the door shut, face buried in her hands, she sobbed without taking a breath. Within minutes a full-fledged panic attack set in, and she couldn't breathe. Lindsey pulled the car over to the edge of the road and opened the windows. The fresh cold air blew across the back of Hannah's neck, but it didn't seem to help. Gently rubbing her friend's back, Lindsey whispered words to help calm her down.

"Breathe. Calm down and breathe, in and out, slowly, but just breathe."

"I can't, can't breathe."

"Just calm down and take a deep breath."

Hannah's heart was racing and it felt like her chest was about to cave in. Lindsey continued to talk her down. Finally, Hannah's breathing returned to normal. Struggling to hold back tears of her own, Lindsey dabbed her friend's tear-stained face with her sleeve. Sitting in silence for a few moments, the two huddled together inside the car. No words of comfort were offered, none needed—they'd already been said, and Hannah knew that Lindsey was grieving as well.

"Are you ready?"

"Yes. And I'm sorry."

"No need to apologize."

Lost in thought as she drove, a slight smile crossed Lindsey's face.

"What is it?" Hannah asked. "Could do with a smile myself."

Lindsey proceeded with caution. "It was a memory." Glancing at Hannah, she continued. "Of the first time I met Gloria. Do you remember?"

Thankfully, Hannah smiled.

"How could I forget? My mom told us, even that day, we were bound to be double trouble." Hannah laughed, the first time she'd laughed in a while. "She also said we were going to be thick as thieves."

"Cause we are!" Lindsey grinned. "I'm so glad she moved you back here."

Hannah remembered the day her mom had asked her to move back to their hometown of San Francisco. After relocating more than a few times over the years, it made absolutely no difference to Hannah where they went next, which thrilled Gloria.

"You have no idea how much this means to me! We'll be with your Aunt Kathy again, and I can't wait for you to have a relationship with her, and we'll all be a family again," said Gloria.

Gloria had smiled and hugged Hannah longer than usual that day because she was so happy.

"Nothing wrong with just you!" Hannah had grinned.

"Thanks! But you know what I mean, right?"

"No," Hannah had smirked. "But I don't care; that's fine by me if we go back to San Francisco."

Rolling to a stop at a red light, the cool breeze blew through the open windows. Hannah caught wind of a terrible smell, her shirt. As the air shifted, the stench of the hospital, which was sticking to her like glue, made her gag. Hospital smells, so specific—sick people, bedpans, disinfectant, hospital food, body odors—all together a terrible combination. Hannah had been barely able to walk into the hospital lately without feeling violently ill herself, and now the stench was all over her.

Struggling with what had just transpired and the realization that half of her life had been a lie, Hannah sat in the passenger seat, shaking in absolute shock. There'd been a lot of lies floating around, apparently for the past, say, most of her life! In those few moments, she tried to process three things: what in the hell was she supposed to do now, what exactly was her mom thinking, and last, but not least, could she find the Captain? She pulled a tattered yellow piece of paper out of her sweatshirt pocket and stared at it.

"What is that?" Lindsey asked softly.

"Something I need, but not sure I want."

Hands trembling, she moved the worn-out paper, a faded handwritten letter, quickly to one side, so a massive teardrop didn't splatter it and ruin the letters that were hard enough to read already. The words that were faded and worn weren't the problem; the problem was that as she read them to herself, Hannah didn't recognize who had written them. The sound of the voice that reverberated back to her as she read the words from the letter in her hand seemed foreign to her; this man from the letter was a stranger. His voice didn't match the sound of the gruff but comforting, familiar voice of the Captain's in her head that had held her together for years—the man who had taken the time to read to her night after night and turned her bed sheets into sails so they could reenact her favorite story. And the man who had created make-believe ships and sailed them to Treasure Island, taught her that treasure could be found anywhere, even in the real world, but that she was his most important treasure. That man, the Captain, who lived in her head—he was dead!

Chapter 2
The Gunner Family

Tell Me a Story
No, I Lied
Let's Play a Game
The Pirate Kind
You're the Captain
I'm Your Crew
We're All We Need
Me and You
~ Hannah Gunner ~

"I'm not asking you not to go; I'm asking you not to leave yet."

Hank knew Gloria, his wife, understood that he didn't have a choice when it came to the number of hours he worked, but she was getting sick and tired of the union business taking up so much of his time as well. Tensions at the dock were running high as talks of strikes circulated. Hank, respected by both his peers and representatives from the International Longshore and Warehouse Union, ILWU for short, were smack in the middle of negotiations. Gloria was well aware of what that meant: late nights and very little time with her husband. Hannah, on the other hand, was oblivious to her father's dealings on the dock and had climbed out of her bed for the second time that evening. A mass of long unruly hair, big blue eyes, and wearing a Disney princess nightgown, the five-year-old little girl appeared at her daddy's side and wrapped her skinny arms around his legs. He looked down at her, and she peered up at him with big, sparkling blue eyes and made a request he could hardly turn down.

"One more story, please Daddy, just one more?" Giggling, she twirled around and around his legs. "I promise, only one."

Gloria sat back and waited to see what her husband would say, but she knew it was already over. One look at Hannah—union meeting before work or not—and he wasn't going anywhere for a while. Pleased he was staying a little longer, she admired her two favorite people in the world, who just happened to be standing in her kitchen. Kissing Hannah on the top of her head, placing a peck on Hank's cheek, she waved them toward the hallway and poured herself a glass of wine.

"Well, what are you waiting for? Off you go!" she commanded with a smirk.

The two of them brought out the best in each other, her stubborn husband and her ornery, beautiful daughter. They were, without question, her pride and joy.

Hannah's giggles echoed down the hall and bounced off the wall as Hank held her upside down and swung her to and fro by the ankles. Her long hair draped the floor as she wriggled and squirmed the entire time. Blood rushing to her cheeks, face beet red, her giggles continued until Hank threw her gently down onto her bed. The gruff but kind voice that now bellowed from her daddy's mouth could only mean one thing: the Captain had arrived!

"One more, and a quick one at that, do ya hear me, lassie?"

Jumping up, Hannah reached for *the* book and excitedly handed it to him, knowing full well that before they had finished the next chapter they would be acting out the story together instead. In her words, *the bestest story ever!* There was no point in pulling down any of the other beautiful books that sat on her shelf, even her beautiful picture books, since none compared to the one that he read to her each evening. All the other books were ruined because of one thing: a game her daddy had turned this book into, a pirate game! Reading less than a few minutes into the book, the two would play-act the story instead of reading it together. It had become a ritual night after night that Hannah, though she didn't realize it at the time, would cherish for years.

"Ahoy there, ya Son of a Biscuit Eater."

"What's a Biscuit Eater?" Hannah asked inquisitively. "Sounds awful!"

Hank laughed. "Nothing for ye to worry about, me Hearty!"

"But what is it?"

"Matey, I already told ye, it's nothing for ye to worry about."

Hannah pushed her long blond hair out of her face and stared right into the Captain's eyes. She wasn't satisfied with that answer. Matey or not, she needed a real one.

"Captain," she said firmly, fixated on his face, gruff

scowl and all. "That isn't a real answer now, is it?"

"How would you know if you don't know what it is?" her daddy responded, trying as hard as he could to end this line of questioning.

"Does the Son of a Biscuit Eater eat real biscuits?" Hannah asked.

Knees tucked under her nightgown, intensity written all over her face, she waited for an answer to her question or a real explanation. Hank, desperately wanting to laugh at his beautiful girl looking so serious over something so ridiculous, wanted to turn ship and bail, but he didn't dare. This pirate stuff was serious business! Glancing at his watch, he knew he didn't have much time, and she loved this pirate game. He had to abandon this line of questioning. Suddenly Hank stood up and jumped on top of the bed, startling her as he waved an imaginary sword in the air and spelled out her name. H A N N A H!

"Did you see that?" he asked.

"I most certainly did!" she responded, not quite sure what he was up to now. "Especially since you said each letter out loud as you spelled them."

"I did do that, didn't I?" Hank chuckled.

As quickly as he'd jumped on the bed, he bounced off the mattress and landed on the floor and pretended to splash around in a make-believe ocean. Unexpectedly, he gagged on saltwater and had to pull himself back to the side of the bed-turned-ship, spluttering the entire time as he did. Ruffling her, the deckhand's hair, he leaned up and kissed her on the top of her head, before quickly apologizing for doing such a thing.

"Sorry about that; grateful to be alive, almost drowned. What was the question again?"

In between her laughter, Hannah managed to spit out the question and this time Hank had no choice but to whip up an answer that would actually satisfy his inquisitive little girl.

"Matey, I can't get *anything* by ya, can I?"

Hannah shook her head and waited patiently for his explanation. He didn't disappoint and in his gruffest pirate voice, the Captain tried his best to explain.

"A Son of a Biscuit Eater isn't really very nice. In fact, that there is pirate talk that you're not old enough to use, and therefore I shouldn't have even said it in your presence. How about that?"

Hannah shook her head. "But what is it?"

"It's just not very nice; it's an insult, not really anything, but something you shouldn't ever repeat."

Pulling out an imaginary telescope, he scanned the vast horizon of Hannah's bedroom. Hannah copied him and looked through her imaginary telescope as well. The two of them scanned the ocean, her bedroom, for a few seconds and when Hank put his telescope down, Hannah followed suit. To reiterate how important it was for Hannah never to repeat that insult, Hank, instead of the Captain, took the opportunity to casually remind her never to use that term.

"So, just to be on the safe side, never say it in front of that one out there unless you want to get into trouble." He pointed to her bedroom door. "You know who I mean?"

Hannah knew exactly who he meant: Gloria, her

momma. As soon as he realized she understood whom he was referring too, Hank brought back the Captain's pirate voice.

"Do not, I repeat, do not tell that scallywag out there that I even mentioned those words!"

Hannah giggled and giggled, trying to contain her laughter she pointed at the door. "I'm going to tell her."

"What?!" bellowed the Captain as he tickled her tummy.

"Momma," Hannah laughed. "Momma is a Son of a Biscuit Eater."

"I will demote ya, Matey, and throw ya off this here ship if you repeat those words again!"

"Momma is a Son of a—." It was impossible to finish the sentence; she was laughing so hard.

"Ya can't say that about that scallywag out yonder! She won't cook for ya anymore, wash your clothes, make your bed, take ya to school."

Hannah's face was bright red, hair soaked with sweat, and when she could laugh no more, Hank scooped her up and tossed her in the air. He had no choice; it was time for him to go. Kissing her on the cheek, the Captain left, and her daddy tucked her in bed. Hank stood outside her door for a few moments and listened to Hannah as she talked to herself for a while as she lay in bed. Gloria walked up behind him and slid her arm around his waist. Kissing him on the back of his neck, they stood and continued to listen to their little girl as she recreated their adventure nearly word for word from that evening.

"That momma's a scallywag and a Son of Biscuit

Eater!" Hannah laughed out loud at herself before repeating it again. "Momma's a scallywag and a Son of a Biscuit Eater."

Her sweet giggles caused Hank and Gloria to try and contain their own laughter as they listened to their daughter laughing to herself. Moments captured like these were rare and nothing short of magical. Hannah would one day describe the Captain's stories and their magical effect on her as a child. Those stories, turned into games, would become a safe haven buried in her mind, comfort and peace for her soul when she thought she was losing a part of herself.

Chapter 3
Celebration

I See You, Captain, Watching Me
Pretending to Sail the Mighty Sea
A Pirate's Life Is Fun, You Say
Let's Play Until We Sail Away
~ Hannah Gunner ~

Hank struggled to contain his excitement. Nathan, his best friend, and his wife Sandra, whom they all called Sandy, were expecting their first baby. It seemed as if they'd been trying unsuccessfully for years and now they were finally having a boy! Forget friends; they were more like brothers, and Hank was determined to make sure they celebrated like family should. The Gunners would throw Nathan and Sandy a party to celebrate their fantastic news.

"No more talk of work, union meetings, or anything that's not related to your new boy." Hank flagged down the bartender. "One more round for me and my brother; we're planning a party!"

Nathan grinned and thanked Hank for the beer. He didn't dare look at his watch; if he had, he might have left, knowing Sandy was expecting him already.

"Gotta be kid friendly, though," Hank insisted. "Hannah would be heartbroken if she couldn't come."

Nathan didn't need to be told that, and Hank didn't need to make such a request. Nathan knew Sandy wouldn't want to celebrate unless they were all together, Hannah included. A celebration right now, with all the stress surrounding the docks, was just the distraction that everyone needed.

"Big freighter coming in this week. Did you see the docket?" Nathan asked before downing a big gulp of beer.

Hank took a sip of his and nodded. "Yeah, I did. But remember, the ILWU has called for a coordinated port shutdown. It's gonna affect more than that freighter coming in; they'll be backed up for sure! Gotta love it, gotta hate it."

Nathan, worried, ordered another round. "Two more when you get a chance, please."

"Hannah's been asking to come down and see the ships come in and all." Hank nudged his buddy. "And to see you! But I just can't bring her down to the docks right now; it's too unstable, the tension, the men are short with each other and at each other's throats. I can feel the division between them. Can you?"

Nathan nodded. "Yeah, I can, and it makes me nervous."

Patting Nathan on the back, Hank scolded himself. "Enough of that! Let's plan your party."

"I can't; Sandy's texting." Nathan threw a twenty on the bar and stood up to leave. "Man, she's hormonal right now." Shaking his head, he downed the last of his pint and stuck out his hand.

Hank shook his friend's hand, but before he let go, he pulled Nathan toward him and gave him a big ol' bear hug.

"Congratulations again, man. I'm truly happy for you, for you both."

"Thanks, Hank, I know you are and I appreciate it, but *laaaaawd* give me strength." Chuckling, he slapped Hank on the back. "I hope I make it through Sandy's up and down nonsense!"

Hannah pushed her mom's step stool over to the back door, stood on top of it, and pressed her nose against the cold square glass panels. It was dark, and her dad should have been home by now. Anxiously eyeing people who walked past their house, ruling them out one by one, she waited for Hank to return. It was as if she hadn't just seen him that morning. Her mom tried to help calm her down.

"Hannah, sit down. You'll wear yourself out!" Gloria suggested, knowing it wouldn't help.

"Why isn't he here yet?" Hannah quizzed her mom. "He should've been home by now."

Gloria tapped the tip of Hannah's nose, squatted down in front of her, and looked her in the eye. "You know he'll be here as soon as he can. He has to work. It's what daddies do; go to work, remember?"

Hannah jumped off the stool and grabbed a piece of bread and butter that Gloria had placed on the table for supper. Frustrated, she blew her long bangs out of her face. How come her momma didn't remember the simplest details?

"But it's not what pirates do! Pirates don't go to work; they plunder goods and treasure. Don't *you* remember?"

"Well, you got me there!" Gloria rolled her eyes and stood up. "But according to your dad, being a pirate requires hard work, as well."

"Yep, Momma, it does. But it's a different kind of work, and scallywags don't understand pirate stuff!"

"Excuse me!"

Gloria swatted Hannah on the rear as she ran past her, hopped back on her step stool again, and waited at the back door.

"Girl! Scallywag? Please. I'll be talking to your daddy about that, mark my words!"

Well, the Captain would take care of that, but Hannah thought it best she kept that to herself. The aroma of lasagna filled the kitchen, and Hannah was getting anxious and hungry. Gloria poured herself a glass of wine, and Hannah a glass of milk. They sat down at the table, but Hannah kept staring at the door. Finally, he walked through it.

"Wash your hands, and don't say a word except 'hello family.'" Gloria grinned, pleased he was home.

Hannah jumped up from the table and leaped into his arms. Throwing her over his shoulders while he washed his hands, she dangled over his back and asked him a million and one questions about where he'd been. Finally, she quit talking when he mentioned the word "party."

"We're going to a party?" Hannah asked.

"No. I'm going to ask Mommy if we can host a party."

Gloria's ears perked up as she served the lasagna. She had a feeling it must be for Sandy and the new baby, and yes, Hank could count on her! Giddy, Hannah started to think about the cake, party favors, and balloons.

"Is it a party for me?" Hannah asked as she prodded the lasagna on her plate.

Hank took a bite of his lasagna. "Mmmmm... this is good! And no, Hannah, it's not your party. It's a party for Nathan's and Sandy's new baby." Beaming, he raised his wine glass. "A toast. It's a boy!"

"Oh, that's wonderful, Hank!" Gloria squealed. "When did they find out?"

"Today."

Hannah didn't get it, but she didn't care. They were going to throw a party, and that meant cake. For now, all she wanted to do was to get through dinner, take her mandatory bath, and finally, go to bed and read. Reading meant a new adventure with the Captain. Fidgeting at the table, Hannah was finally excused and sent to get ready for her usual evening routine. Grinning, she pointed to her daddy.

"See you shortly, Captain Fin."

Refilling their wine glasses, Hank took a sip of the bold red and smiled. Pointing his finger at Gloria, getting ready to speak, he laughed out loud and took another sip of wine.

"What is it?" she laughed. "You're making me laugh; just say it."

"Hannah!" Hank grinned. "Captain Fin—sooooo funny!"

Chapter 4
Captain Fin

"Treasure is where you find it.
But, Hannah, the most important treasure is you."
~ Hank Gunner ~

Most kids loved to play in the bath, but Hannah couldn't wait to jump out of the tub and put on her pajamas. Gloria no longer disputed or felt envious of Hannah's demands that her daddy put her to bed instead of her. The ritual of tucking her in, reading her a bedtime story, and placing a kiss on her daughter's forehead had now been replaced with the joy that her daughter's laughter from the other side of her bedroom door brought her. Hank's way of making the bedtime stories come alive was a treat even for her, and couldn't be replaced, duplicated, or reinvented.

"Is it time?" Hannah asked eagerly. "To go to bed?"

"Good grief, girl! Who asks to go to bed every single night?" Gloria poked Hank playfully in the ribs. "I blame you for this nonsense!"

"I'm tired," Hannah whined. "You should be glad I want to go to bed."

"I am; let's go. I'll take you to bed tonight. Pick a

book," Gloria teased.

"C'mon, Momma. You know it doesn't work like that!" Hannah rolled her eyes and swatted her wet hair out of her face. "Captain *always* puts me to bed."

Hannah turned to her daddy. "Well, aren't you coming?"

Hank topped off Gloria's wine, kissed her cheek, picked up Hannah, and slung her over his shoulder like a sack of potatoes. Gloria sipped her wine for a few minutes before placing a chair in the hallway just outside Hannah's bedroom door. Hannah, as usual, had no patience for listening to Hank read a chapter of their favorite book first. Fidgeting, she tried to speed up the game.

"Where's the Captain?"

"Captain who?" Hank inquired.

"Captain Fin, silly," she giggled.

Hank chuckled and muttered under his breath, "Captain Fin, now that's funny!" A gruff voice indicated that Captain Fin must have finally arrived. Gloria closed her eyes, sat back, and took it all in.

"Can ye smell the wonderful sea air, Matey?"

Hannah took a deep breath through her nose and nodded. "Yes, sir. I can smell the salty sea air, and it's fishy, too." She laughed. "I added the fishy part myself because fish live in the sea."

Hank winked at his bright-eyed little girl. "You're a clever little lass, aren't ya!"

Jumping off the bed, Hank knelt down on the floor and ran his hands through the carpet as if searching for something. He motioned for Hannah to join him.

Beaming, Hannah realized this was where they were about to search for lost treasure in the sand, one of her favorite parts of the game. Eyes lit up and sparkling, she leaped off the bed, crouched next to him and, copying his example, ran her little hands in makeshift circles as if she were scooping handfuls of sand into buckets. Hank nudged Hannah, and together they watched the imaginary sand sift through his fingers. Watching his little girl, her blue eyes focused on each imaginary grain of sand that slipped through his fingers with such intensity, both impressed Hank and astounded him. She was so incredibly focused on the imaginary sand that if one did not know better, they might actually believe this little girl thought her bedroom floor truly was a beach and that she was sitting in the middle of a real sand pile. A child's imagination, his child's, was the most beautiful thing that he had the privilege to observe and be part of on a daily basis. His gift: his precious family!

"What's wrong, Daddy?" Her voice startled him. "I mean, Captain."

Snapping out of his thoughts, he pulled out an imaginary telescope and took a visual around the bedroom-turned-island, and in an elevated Captain voice belted out firm orders to his First Matey, Hannah.

"We need to board the ship right now or we're going to be shark bait!"

"To the ship!" Hannah repeated. "What, now?"

"Questioning the Captain? Yes, now."

Folding her arms across her pajamas, sticking out her pouty lips, fearing the game was over, Hannah planted herself crisscross-applesauce firmly on the floor.

"We haven't even found the treasure yet!"

Stepping off the bed, Hank sat down in front of his defiant little pirate. "Have you forgotten the unspoken pirate rule?" Hank whispered. "Have you?"

Hannah hung her head as if she'd done something wrong. "I think I must've, but I didn't mean to."

"Pirate rule, unspoken of course, is that treasure is always where you find it!" He tapped the tip of her button nose and lifted her head up by her chin to look at him. "But you, my precious little pirate, you, Hannah, are by far the most important treasure of all!" Hank kissed the top of her sweaty head and pushed a wet strand of hair behind her ear. "So you see, I've found my treasure and you can still find yours; it can be anything you want it to be, and if you look hard enough, it can be found anywhere."

"Well, I like lots of things, but my bestest treasure ever is my magical shell!"

"That is a magical treasure! Best to always keep that safe!" Hank picked her up and tossed her onto the bed. "Okay, one more thing before bed and it's a doozie!"

Puzzled, Hannah waited to see what he would say next.

Hank pointed across the room. "A squadron; see it?"

"Aye, aye, Captain Fin!" Hannah replied. "They're getting closer!"

"What say we do, Matey?"

"Me? I'm a little pirate." Hannah laughed. "You tell me, Daddy. I mean, Captain Fin."

"I say we offer ye up as a peace offering and go on board the stranger's ship and plunder their goods, and then blow the ship to smithereens," he said, looking at Hannah. "What say ye?"

"I think that's a terrible plan, Captain!" Hannah waved her imaginary sword. "They might not bring me back!"

"You'll be fine. Trust me!" He pointed to Hannah's teddy bear on his left. "Second Matey, here, just promoted; he'll watch your back."

"Very well." Hannah turned to her teddy bear. "Second Matey Teddy, prepare the cannon and blow up the squadron after I've been offered. If anything is left standing, target them one by one." Hannah picked up Teddy and kissed his nose. "I probably won't see you again, because Captain failed to see I'll still be on board when you release the cannon."

"Very nice!" Hank replied. "I couldn't have instructed him better myself." Smiling. "Oh, and I'll send backup to rescue you before we blow up the ship."

"Okay, it really isn't a good plan, but you are the Captain."

Trying not to laugh at how serious Hannah was, her pouty lips, and her big blue eyes staring right through him, Hank wondered how on earth he was going to put an end to the night's bedtime adventure.

Sound effects of all kinds suddenly traveled down the hallway: pirate commands, explosions, blasts, shots, and the sound of the bed creaking as Hannah and Hank jumped on and off the ship. Gloria wondered just how long Hannah's bed would last; even though Hank had reinforced it with plywood under the box springs, it didn't stand a chance. Hannah was beet red, drenched with sweat, and looked as if she could use another bath. Overly excited, she hardly seemed ready for bed at all. Hank finally insisted this time it really was time for bed. Fortunately, Gloria appeared at Hannah's door. Kissing Hannah's burning red cheek, she grabbed Hank's arm and yanked him out of the room. She'd never been able to pull off a nighttime ritual quite like Hank's and had given up trying.

"Say goodnight, Captain," she said softly. "And I mean it. Say goodnight!"

"See, the scallywag said it's over." Hank winked and kissed Hannah's cheek.

"One more thing," Hank walked toward Hannah's bookshelf, ignoring Gloria's scowl. "It will only take a second."

He pulled down her magical conch shell, the one he had given her, which had become her favorite gift. Sitting on the edge of her bed, he placed it in Hannah's hands.

"Close your eyes, sweetheart, press this against your ear and listen to the ocean as you drift off to sleep."

"I hear the ocean, Daddy; it's whispering to me."

Hank leaned closer. "Yes, it is; now, as you drift off to sleep, you can think about a beautiful beach, a deep blue ocean, and our pirate ship, with Teddy on board." Hannah grinned. "All from right here." Hank tapped her forehead. "Your mind's eye."

He had never seen anything so beautiful or done anything so right in his entire life. Quietly sneaking out of her room, he peeked back one last time to stare at her. Hannah still held the shell to her ear, eyes closed.

Exhausted, his little girl was already almost asleep.

Chapter 5
Nathan

Please don't wake me, let me sleep!
It's only then that I find peace.
I hear his voice and see his face.
And in my dream, the Captain's real.
~ Hannah Gunner ~

There would be no celebration, no baby shower, after all.
A knock on Sandy's door was the first indication that
something was wrong, and the terrible look on the
officers' faces standing on the doorstep was the second.

"Mrs. Nichols?"

"Yes."

The officer on the left glanced at Sandy's pregnant
stomach, and instinctively she glanced at his nametag.
Their eyes met briefly.

"I'm Officer Taggit, and this is my partner, Officer
Langley. May we come in?"

Officer Taggit shuffled from one foot to the other,
and it didn't take a rocket scientist to figure out that he
was incredibly uncomfortable. Nervously, heart sinking
with each passing moment, Sandy waited for one of them
to say something. Taggit spoke first.

"It's about your husband, ma'am. Mr. Nichols."

"Where's Nathan?" Sandy asked frantically. "Is he all

right?"

"Ma'am. May we come in and sit down?"

Trembling, she stepped aside and let the officers into her house. She pointed to a room on the left, the living room, and they indicated she should go first. She felt numb as she walked down the hallway, entered the room, and sat down.

"Was your husband scheduled to work this evening?" Taggit asked. But Langley, the second officer, didn't wait for her to respond. "Because we do not show him scheduled."

Sandy glanced from one officer to the other, looking for answers to questions she didn't know how to ask, and then shook her head. No. Nathan was not scheduled to work.

"Do you know why your husband was on the docks this evening, since you've confirmed that he wasn't scheduled to work?"

Nathan hadn't gone to the docks! He was with Hank. They'd gone for a drink to talk about work, yes, but also to talk about what they were going to do while the girls were at the baby shower Gloria was planning. They'd already said they weren't staying for the whole thing, couldn't stand all that girl talk. She'd remembered Hank and Nathan specifically joking already about having to get out of there! Sandy couldn't process what the officers were asking her; why did they care where Nathan was, and why the hell did they wonder if Nathan had been at the docks? Wrapping her arms around her stomach, she pushed down the nerves that were trying to escape her; she wasn't going to worry. Everything was fine.

"Sir, where is my husband?" she asked inquisitively. "What is this all about?"

Taggit's head whipped around toward his partner as if he were struggling and wasn't quite sure what to say. His partner looked at his feet, and Taggit knew he had no choice but to deliver the terrible news. Sandy, numb, waited for them to speak, having no idea they were about to deliver the worst news of her life.

"There's been some trouble," Taggit started, his voice shakily continuing. "On the docks."

"Nathan hasn't been on the docks tonight; he's with Hank, his best friend," Sandy interjected.

"Nathan and Hank were on the docks this evening, with several others from their crew, including multiple ILWU organizers and dock workers. Words were exchanged about a pending strike, those for it and those opposed," Officer Langley added. "Things got out of hand, no doubt liquor was involved, when a few showed up late this evening."

Color gone from her face, Sandy shook her head and jumped up to grab her phone. "Nathan wasn't on night shift tonight and yes, he was with Hank, but they weren't supposed to be at the docks. This doesn't make sense. I need to speak to Gloria."

"Not yet, Mrs. Nichols. There's more; please sit back down," Officer Taggit insisted.

"A group of men, pretty good size of 'em, supporting the imminent strike, were arguing with those who had shown up opposing it. According to witnesses, Nathan was caught in the middle of switching sides from not wanting to strike to walking out and striking with the others. Gunner was there, Hank, Hank Gunner. Reportedly he was trying to keep the peace between both sides."

Sandy nodded. "Nathan says Hank is known for that."

Taggit pressed on. "I have to ask a difficult question. Are you sure you had no idea this was going down tonight, the meeting on the docks about a pending strike? Had Nathan mentioned anything about it at all?"

Shocked, she shook her head; she hadn't picked up on a single thing! Realizing Nathan had lied to her, she felt anger and fear combined. Wanting to vomit, she pushed the wave of nausea to the pit of her stomach and hoped her husband was in jail. Did they make house calls for such things? Praying they did, she questioned Taggit.

"Do I need to bail my husband out of jail?"

As Taggit laid his hat in his lap, she could hold back her tears no longer. Shaking, she wrapped her arms around her unborn baby. Preparing to be escorted to the jail—or maybe the hospital—she took a deep breath, straightened up in her chair, and waited to find out what had happened to her husband. Her mind flashed to Gloria, and she wondered if Hank was in danger as well.

"Ma'am, we're sorry to inform you that not only was the argument heated, but it turned violent. Hank Gunner was unsuccessful at negotiating any kind of peace between the two sides, for or against the strike, and the representatives of the union. Someone pulled out a gun, and in retaliation, another man fired back. Both men were intoxicated, and both men have been

28

arrested." Taggit put his head down, took a deep breath, and looked Sandy in the eyes.

"It is with a heavy heart we're here this evening to inform you that Nathan got caught between the crossfire. His injuries were life-threatening, and he was immediately rushed to the hospital."

Scrambling to her feet, Sandy gasped. "What! Where did they take him?"

"They took him to St. Mary's."

Tears rolled down her face as she frantically searched for her purse and keys.

"Ma'am, ma'am. Please, please, sit down. There's more."

"I don't want to sit down. Tell him I'm on the way; he needs me. Is Hank with him?"

The officers shook their heads. "Protocol only allows family in the ambulance," Langley barely whispered.

"He's all alone! We have to go. What are you waiting for? Please, come on!" Sandy rushed to the front door and pulled it open, but the officers didn't move.

"What are you waiting for?" she shrieked at the top of her lungs. "Come on!"

"Ma'am, they did everything they could. Everything."

Sandy, as if suddenly understanding what they were trying to say, covered her ears. "Hurry up, please! Or I'll find someone else to take me."

"Ma'am, ma'am, please come back and sit down." Taggit walked to the door and held out his hand, but Sandy refused to take it. Seeing her hand on the door, head held down, and one hand wrapped around her stomach, Taggit took a deep breath and softly continued.

"Would you please, please, for the sake of your child, come back in here and sit down?"

Fearing the worst, Sandy shook her head. "How bad is it?" she whispered. "How long will he be at St. Mary's, because it doesn't matter how long it takes for him to healed, we'll get through it."

Taggit took another step toward her, but neither Langley nor Taggit said a word. Their silence terrified her. "How bad is it? Is he going to be wheelchair-bound? We can handle that, or are you worried he won't remember his family?" Sandy's voice cracked as she spoke. "Will he remember we're having a child?" No one spoke. "Damn it, answer me, please!" she screamed.

Taggit, voice cracking as he tried to speak, delivered the worst news of her life in the only sound that he could muster. His faint whisper and the veil of pity on his face would haunt her for the rest of her life.

"You have our deepest condolences, ma'am, they did everything they could, but your husband died en route to the hospital due to complications from his injuries." The officer's voice cracked as he delivered the news, and his hands were shaking. "Mrs. Nichols, though it brings you no comfort at this time, we will convict the man who shot your husband and the other men involved in the monstrous act that took your husband's life this evening."

Time felt as if it stood still. Sandy slid down the wall and collapsed to the floor. Langley, moving as fast as he could, barely broke her fall, catching her at the very last second. Wailing in such a way, grief pouring from her soul, was a sound that neither officer had ever heard or experienced before; her pain felt as if it was shooting right through them. Though they could not show it, they were sickened, and their hearts wept with her on the inside. They would have given anything in the world if the floor they were standing upon in her hallway had opened up and swallowed them whole! Watching a pregnant woman in such a state was the most heartbreaking scene they had ever witnessed in their lives—devastating for her, their unborn child, Nathan, who did not deserve to lose his life that night, their family, his family, her family, their friends... the list went on and on!

Finally Officer Taggit spoke. "Is there someone we can call for you, please?"

"Gloria. Gloria Gunner, please, and my brother. Call them now."

Officer Langley made the calls and afterward pulled Taggit aside. Gloria Gunner was on her way, and Langley thought she might have additional information if Hank had confided in her. Taggit agreed, but insisted they go easy on her in front of Sandy.

"Light questioning only; anything else goes downtown."

Hank had been at the docks that evening handling the peace talks. Maybe if they talked to Gloria without Hank, she could confirm that she knew the meeting was preplanned and was going to take place that night. Nathan had lied to his wife that evening, but had Hank lied to his?

"Perhaps, if we're lucky, Hank will be able to identify the shooters."

"That would be nice, but even under these circumstances, is he a narc?" Taggit wondered. "She mentioned her brother; track him down as well."

Gloria, frantic, arrived with Hannah, still in her pajamas, in tow. Sending Hannah into the kitchen as soon as she entered Sandy's house was a mistake. Gloria thought Sandy was sitting in the living room with the officers, but she was sitting at the kitchen table by herself. Barely able to contain her own tears as the officers drilled her, Gloria did her best to answer all of their questions, despite not knowing what in the hell was going on. She didn't have the full story either, and yes, as angry as she was in that moment that Hank had lied to her and told her the same thing that Nathan had told Sandy, she wanted to make sure that he was okay.

"Can you run through it one more time for me, please?" Taggit scribbled in his notebook as she spoke.

"Sure." Frustrated, Gloria repeated word for word what she had already told him. They were going to the Shamrock for a beer to talk about the strike, yes, but to also talk about what they were going to do the night of the baby shower she was throwing Sandy. The boys weren't staying for the whole thing, just like Sandy had said. Hank had never mentioned heading to the docks that evening, and if he were on call or if he had to check a freight, crew, or anything that could possibly take him to the docks, he would always say he was going on site. He had, just like Nathan, lied to her!

Angry, Gloria knew it wasn't the time, and she was scared. Hank had talked about taking Nathan to a ballgame while the women were at the shower and he needed to get tickets for the game. Neither of them, she or Sandy, had a clue that they'd be headed back down to the docks that night.

"Sounds like it was preplanned, the meeting between the two sides, for and against," Officer Taggit stated. "Especially since representatives were on site."

Sandy, shocked, couldn't talk. Hannah had no idea what was wrong with her "aunt" Sandy.

"Is the baby ready yet?"

Sandy didn't hear Hannah's tiny little voice.

"Aunt Sandy. Is that baby ready yet? 'Cause I made a baby gift, and Momma says he's going to love it!"

Managing to raise her hand and stroke Hannah's hair seemed to pacify Hannah. Sandy didn't dare look at her for fear of scaring her with her tears. No one was talking, smiling, or even trying to visit with her at all, and Hannah suddenly felt anxious and worried that something was terribly wrong. Police officers were still talking with her mommy, and that was strange. Tugging at her aunt Sandy's sleeve, she quizzed her about the policeman. Sandy tried to hide her tears, but Hannah had seen them.

"Are you sad?"

Nodding, Sandy pulled Hannah into her lap, held her close, and cried silent tears until Gloria appeared at her side. The sadness in the house was overwhelming, and Gloria begged Sandy to leave with her and stay with them, but Sandy refused.

"I have to go to the hospital and be with him. He can't be alone. Nigel can take me."

"Shock," Taggit offered. "She's in shock, but we'll

take her and she can meet her brother there; we'll let him know."

Gloria nodded. "Thank you."

"Someone's purse is ringing," Langley pointed to Gloria's bag.

Gloria dug through her purse and grabbed it right before Hank hung up. She hit redial.

"Where are you and are you safe?" she yelled.

"Yes, but Nathan is—"

He didn't have to finish; Gloria finished his sentence for him.

"I know. Come home."

Gloria bundled Hannah up and took her home. The tone was somber, and even Hannah knew that something was very, very wrong. She tried to make her mommy smile, but Gloria didn't have it in her, and it certainly wasn't the time or the place. Everything that Hannah said or did as they walked home bothered or got on Gloria's nerves at that moment.

"Can we sing our walking song, Mommy?"

"Not now, Hannah, please!"

The only positive thing about that evening was that Hannah thought her daddy was about to be home, and even though it was late, she was still awake! Maybe, just maybe, the Captain would put her back to bed. As they walked down the pavement, Hannah listened to the sound of her shoes hitting the concrete and started to count each time her foot took a step and made the thudding sound. Imagining she was walking the plank on their ship, placing one foot in front of the other, she finally reached the end of the plank and was forced to stare down into the deep blue ocean. Dawdling, apparently, her mom yanked her arm and yelled at her for not walking as fast as she ought to be.

"Hannah, keep up!"

Hannah didn't argue, but picked up the pace. Trying not to fall behind, she did her best to keep up, but for some reason, her mommy was walking faster than usual.

"When we get home, can Daddy tell me a story?" Hannah asked.

Gloria, suddenly livid, tore into her.

"How selfish of you, and no!" She stopped and angrily yelled at her little daughter right there on the sidewalk.

"Do you have any idea what has just happened?"

Hannah really didn't, except it probably wasn't very good since everyone ended up in tears and Uncle Nathan seemed to be hurt.

"How selfish! How dare you, Hannah Gunner, think only of yourself! What is wrong with you that you could be so self-centered, selfish, and stupid at the same time?!"

Shocked, Hannah froze, having no idea that she'd done anything that bad. Cheeks turning bright red, eyes narrowing, for a split second Hannah Gunner thought she might actually burst into tears and cry. Blinking and holding back the water in her eyes, remembering that the Captain had promoted her to his First Matey position, reminded her that she was stronger than a crybaby girl! This here scallywag, Momma or not, was way out of line. Hannah jerked her arm out of Gloria's tight grip, took a step back, blinked away her tears, and started to march quickly toward the house.

Horrified she was terrorizing her beautiful little girl for no reason at all, and that she had spoken to her in such an awful way, Gloria immediately felt nothing but shame and immediate regret. Catching up to Hannah, she stopped and bent down in front of her at eye level. Taking Hannah by the shoulders and pulling her toward her, Gloria's tears wet Hannah's cheeks. Stiffly, Hannah obliged, and that broke Gloria's heart. Grief had overtaken Gloria; defiance and anger had overtaken Hannah.

"Hannah, baby, I am so sorry! Mommy is upset and very sad about Uncle Nathan, and I'm worried about Aunt Sandy, and even your daddy, but I never should have said such horrible things. I am sorry, and I didn't mean them. It's not true, you are not selfish and, of course, you are brilliant!" She couldn't even bring herself to say the word stupid and was utterly disgusted and ashamed that word had spewed out of her mouth at all while screaming at her child. Kissing each one of Hannah's cheeks, placing one kiss on her right and one on the left, she whispered in her ear.

"Do you forgive me?"

Hannah looked at Gloria for a few moments, smiled sweetly, and wrapped her arms around her neck.

"Okay, Mommy; I will."

"I am so sorry, Hannah. I'm grieving, which means I am sad. But that doesn't make what I said right, and I'm so, so, so sorry."

Hannah was sad too, but now she was scared. Her mommy was crying, and she didn't understand why. Aunt Sandy was crying, and Uncle Nathan had been hurt so bad he was gone. Gone. Exactly what did that mean, anyway?

Chapter 6
Hank

Silence this madness; the voices in my head
Guilt talking back to me
Wishing I were dead.
~ Hank Gunner ~

Pending an investigation, a mandatory suspension with
partial pay had been dealt from the board until the final
judgment could be ruled upon regarding the
unauthorized meeting on the docks. Hank had too much
time on his hands; between the extra time, grief, and the
guilt he wrestled with since the death of his best friend,
he grew restless at home. Given the stress that they
were under—work suspension, death of his friend, and
the funeral—friction between Hank and Gloria was
inevitable. Despite their best efforts, the tension was
becoming evident to Hannah as well. Hannah learned to
stay out of the way, escaping to her imaginary world of
pirates, ships, beaches, and vast oceans filled with
adventure. Thankfully, Captain Fin was home and often
decided to join her! Fleeing aboard a make-believe ship
with his beautiful daughter to avoid what was becoming
routine confrontations with Gloria, whom Hank had

nicknamed the tyrant, was far more appealing than facing his own demons. Hank's new reality was tearing his family apart.

Hank knocked on Hannah's bedroom door and in his gruffest, yet kind voice, impersonated Captain Fin.

"Permission to enter ye quarters, Matey."

Ear pressed against the door, he waited for her giggle and attempt to project her best *pirate voice* and answer him back.

"Aye, aye, Captain. Enter."

Perched on her bed, fake sword in hand, Hannah waited for her daddy, turned Captain, to say something. Hank stared for a few moments at his innocent little beauty, stuck in the middle of his mess, not knowing if she should come out of her room to play or lay low in her bedroom as he was about to advise. How had it all gone so wrong? A week earlier they were planning a party; today, he was waiting to see if he still had a job and continually getting under his wife's feet. He had no idea it was about to get worse. No one did. Sitting down on the bed next to her, he gently tapped the tip of her button nose. Carefully he delivered the message, trying to convince her it was for her own good that she try and lay low at this time.

"Stay aboard ship, Matey, and quietly." He looked around her room. "You know what I mean? Out of earshot, sight, and trouble!"

"Aye, aye, Captain," Hannah replied softly. "Stay in my room, I mean quarters."

Ruffling her blond hair, Hank scooped her up and hugged her as tightly as he could.

"Tell you what, why don't you pull up the anchor, and we'll set sail awhile. Sound good?"

Beaming, Hannah wriggled out of her daddy's arms. "Right away, Captain."

"Well then, let's head out to Treasure Island and hunt for treasure!" Hank smiled.

Hannah's eyes lit up as she placed her hands, one in front of the other, pretending to pull as hard as she could on an invisible rope, hoisting up a huge anchor off the bottom of the ocean so they could set sail! Helping her, Captain Fin grabbed the imaginary rope out of her hands, hoisted the anchor one last time, and tied it in a secure knot to the side of the ship. Exhausted, the pair mopped their brows and continued to prepare the ship for their journey. Hannah jumped on the bed, off the bed, and scrambled back up again as she pretended to climb into the crow's nest, where she pulled out her imaginary telescope, looked all around her room, and spouted off fake coordinates. None of what she had said made any sense, but Hank, though he had trouble trying not to laugh, didn't dare act as if they weren't the most accurate coordinates in the entire world.

"Go North West 35 degrees and West North 50 degrees, Captain."

"Excellent coordinates, lass. First Matey, betting we'll find gold on those." He wondered how his beautiful little pirate came up with such coordinates in the first place.

Her blond hair sticking to her sweat-dotted forehead now looked like stringy spaghetti, and the smile that she wore, despite trying to look fierce, radiated across her face. This made Hank want to laugh, but he honestly didn't dare for fear of hurting her wild spirit. Watching her come alive in her make-believe world was a gift, and Hank couldn't help but wonder if all parents experienced this with their children. If they didn't, they were missing out. *Missing out.* Hank's mind flashed to Nathan, who would miss out on every single thing that his new son would experience. Tragic. Not to mention his unborn son; he would never experience the love of his father, and that sickened Hank. Nathan would have been the best! Riddled with guilt, Hank found it difficult to fake a smile and stay in character. It was just as well that Gloria burst into the room, startling both him and Hannah and breaking up their pirate game.

"Done playing pirate, because there's plenty of work to do around here." Her tone was irritable and cold. "Make yourself useful until you hear about work and help me out."

Hannah shrunk down on the bed; a fight was about to erupt, and she didn't want to be in the middle of it. Her instincts, for a little girl, were right! Hank jumped off the bed and pointed toward Hannah.

"I'll help you, no problem, but you could ask nicely." His eyes motioned toward Hannah. "There's no need to be angry all the time, and certainly no need to be rude!"

"Don't lecture me. You're playing, and I need help before I leave for work." Eyes icy cold, glaring at him, she opened her mouth to say something else, but stopped herself before the words slipped off her tongue.

"What?" Hank demanded to know. "Just say it; not here, out there," he pointed toward the door. "But spit it out. It will likely make you feel better!"

Spinning on her heels, Gloria left Hannah's room and stormed down the hall. Hank followed her.

"What did you want to say?"

"Nothing."

"Now that's a damn lie, and you know it! Get it over with so we can clear the air."

Frustrated, Gloria grabbed her purse and keys, and headed toward the back door. "I don't need to talk. I'm leaving for work, again, overtime since you're not working at all because of that bullshit stunt that you pulled on the docks that happened to get your best friend killed!"

As soon as the words flew out of her mouth, she wished she could take them back, but it was too late. Hank's heart jumped into his throat, and his stomach felt as if someone had just sucker-punched him. Furious, he slammed his hand down on top of the kitchen countertop as hard as he could. Gloria stopped in her tracks, and Hannah half-jumped out of her skin from her bedroom when she heard the bang.

"That's frigging low, Gloria, even for you!"

Taking a deep breath, embarrassed by what she'd said, Gloria tried to backtrack as fast as she could. "I didn't mean that, Hank. I shouldn't have said that about Nathan, and that's not what I meant about the meeting—"

Hank cut her off. "Yeah, I kinda think you did, all of it!" His hands were trembling, and his voice was shaky at best. "Pretty sure you've felt like this for a while, but this is the first time you've voiced it."

"That's not true. I meant to say the stunt that was pulled on the docks, not that you had pulled the stunt on the docks. Not just you." Setting her purse and keys down on the kitchen table, Gloria pulled out a chair and sat down. "Honestly, I really did mean to say collectively, and not just you. I know this isn't your fault."

Hannah jumped overboard the ship, her bed, landed in the make-believe water, and pretended to swim by herself all the way to Treasure Island—her closet—and locked herself in. Sitting in the dark, knees tucked against her chest, head buried on top of her knees, and hands placed over her ears, she hummed as loudly as she could to drown out the sound of her parents yelling at each other. Let the storm die down and hunt for treasure later, she told herself over and over again. Let the storm die down and hunt later. Storm die down and hunt later. Storm die down and hunt for treasure later!

"Hank, please, I'mmmm so sorry! It's been rough on everyone, but I really didn't mean that."

"But you said it." His voice was cold and monotone. "I asked you nicely for Hannah's sake, not mine, that we talk about it out here and not in Hannah's room." He pointed down the hall. "And you had to turn that into this!"

Frustrated, late for work and upset, Gloria broke down in tears. Head in hands, she begged Hank to listen to her.

"None of this is easy on anyone, Hank. Not you, Sandy, Hannah, and yes, even me. Sandy is my best friend, and she lost her husband, your best friend." Wiping her hand across her face, she smeared her mascara with tears. "But I shouldn't have said what I said. I was wrong. I am sorry, but I didn't mean it!"

Gloria walked toward him and held out her arms. "Are you going to forgive me or hold it against me forever?"

Pulling her toward him, Hank kissed the top of her head. "I'm going to hold it against you forever, but love you anyway."

Managing a smile, she kissed him. "You are such an ass! I'm going to find someone to cover my shift. I just can't tonight."

Hank nodded. "Good idea, but I need some air."

She didn't try to stop him from leaving; though she knew he had forgiven her, she had still hurt him and she knew he needed time to cool down. Gloria called Sandy and they visited for a while, confiding to each other their pain, regrets, and fears. Consoling each other as girlfriends do, they said their goodbyes and promised to check on each other within the next few days. As Gloria waited for Hank to come home, she couldn't stop her mind from racing; it was overloaded. Worried about her husband and fretting over his suspension at the docks, grieving over the loss of her best friend's husband, Nathan, and her husband's best friend. Worried about her best friend, Sandy, and the new baby. On top of all of that, she didn't know if Hannah was really dealing with any of it or how she was doing after their fight. Hanging up with Sandy, Gloria poured herself a glass of wine, changed into her sweats, and peeked in on Hannah.

"You must be starving, baby. You ready to eat?"

Hannah didn't answer. Gloria looked around the

room, but she didn't see Hannah anywhere. Gloria checked the closet and found her daughter tucked away in the corner—fast asleep. Trying not to disturb her, Gloria picked Hannah up and laid her on the bed. Covering her with a blanket, she kissed her forehead and whispered in her ear. "I'm so sorry, sweetheart." Hannah opened her eyes, murmured something, but closed them again. "Mommy and Daddy didn't mean to fight; we love you so much!" Stroking her long blond hair, Gloria bent over and kissed her cheeks, leaving her lips on her little angel longer than usual, left cheek and then the right one. A true combination of them both, Hank and Gloria, stubborn as her daddy, but a sharp wit like him as well, and everyone said she had Gloria's eyes. She looked so beautiful sleeping there on the bed that Gloria felt ashamed for finding her tucked away, afraid, in her closet.

"When you wake up, you're going to be starving," she whispered. Hannah didn't answer. "Wake me up if I'm asleep. I'll fix you your supper." Creeping out of her room, Gloria looked back at her one last time. *What were they doing to their little girl?* This nonsense, the bickering, it had to stop!

Gloria sat half-dazed at the kitchen table waiting for Hank; she was exhausted from the hours she'd already put in at work, fighting with Hank, stress over their current situation, not to mention worrying about why he still hadn't come home. He should have been back hours ago, and she couldn't shake the feeling that he never should have left that night. It had been hours since Hank had walked out the door, and it was already dark outside. Resisting the urge to call or text him, allowing him his space, Gloria felt as if she were about to jump out of her skin as her mind rehashed the events from earlier that day. The wine was good, but it wasn't enough; she still needed to relax. Running a hot bath, fighting back her tears, she wished more than anything in the world she could have a do-over day! What she would have given to have done things differently that day: if she hadn't burst into Hannah's room and broken up their pirate game, if she hadn't said such hateful things that she didn't really mean or believe to Hank, and most of all, if she hadn't agreed to let him leave but asked him to stay, have a glass of wine and talk it through, and even have dinner as a family with Hannah that night. Gloria knew with all of her heart that Hank loved his family and he would have stayed! *Why hadn't she just asked him to stay? Why did she let him walk out that door? And why wasn't he home yet?* Sinking into the hot bathwater, pondering the questions she had asked herself, Gloria had no idea that her gut instinct was right; she never should have let him leave that day. Her world was about to be turned upside down and the Gunners were about to be pulled into a nightmare they couldn't possibly have imagined. Hank, with Nathan's funeral still fresh in his mind, ended up at his local pub, the Shamrock, for a pint. Going out to clear his head that afternoon would be the biggest mistake of his life. That simple decision cost him everything!

"Pete, if you don't mind, I'll have a shot of Jameson with that next pint."

"Sure, Hank, think I'll join you. You know, Nathan wasn't just a regular, he was my friend, too. Plus, I'm the owner, as well as the bartender." Pete winked.

Hank nodded. Grateful someone was there to drink with him and who knew Nathan. Nathan didn't have to die, not like that, and with Sandy about to have a baby, the whole situation seemed a hundred times worse, not that it could possibly be worse than a young man in his prime being shot down for no reason.

"Well then, to Nathan!" Pete raised his glass.

"To Nathan!" Hank raised his glass, could barely say the words without choking up, and slammed back the whiskey. "Another one, Pete, please." He wasn't paying attention to the other patrons wandering into the bar. Minding his own business, lost in grief and regret, Hank had no idea that trouble had walked into the Shamrock.

A sharp voice shot right through him, quickly bringing him back to reality. Tom O'Halloron, a big guy—mouth and physique—had slipped into the bar unnoticed. He had worked for Nathan, one of his crew. Tom was argumentative all the time, purposely taking the opposite side of what the majority of Nathan's crew voted for or against, wanted, or said, and it made things difficult for Nathan and everyone around him. Tom wasn't afraid to cause a scene, talk too loudly, or be obnoxious in general. Nathan didn't like nor dislike Tom, but Hank didn't care for him on any level. Tom, on the other hand, liked Nathan, but everyone loved Nathan. Nathan was fair, kind, and always had a smile on his face. It was no wonder he was so missed by everyone who knew him. Raising his hand, Tom hollered across the bar to Pete, the bartender.

"A full round here, Pete, whiskey and pints. We'll have a toast for our Nathan!"

The sound of his best friend's name rolling off Tom's tongue made Hank cringe. Sitting at the bar, head down, sipping on his beer, Hank tried to block out the sound of Tom's loud mouth shouting across the room. The waitress set a shot glass and a beer in front of Tom and each one of his friends. Quickly, as if knowing he was going to be an ass, she turned and scurried away. Tom didn't disappoint. Making an ass out of himself was what he did best. As soon as Hank heard a bar stool scrape across the wooden floor, the banging of a hand on the bar, and that voice that cut through him like a knife asking for a moment to say a toast to *his* best friend, Nathan, Hank had to bite his tongue. Tom's loud public toast went on, and on, and on!

"I think most, if not all of you, in the Shamrock here tonight knew Nathan." Tom looked around the bar. "And if you didn't, you should have! He was one of the best, ah hell, let's face it... he was the best!" Cheers erupted. "Certainly one of a kind! I loved working for him. He treated all of us here right, all of us! He was fair. A genuinely nice guy, and he'll be missed. So if you'll join me and raise your glasses, let's have a toast for a man who was too good for all of us, and who was taken too soon! To Nathan!"

Everyone in the bar, except for Hank, raised their glasses. "To Nathan!"

Tom noticed Hank hadn't moved—didn't raise his glass and hadn't said Nathan's name.

"Hell, Pete, another round. I think some of us missed the first toast."

Drinks were doled out, and Tom repeated a short toast. "To Nathan."

Hank pushed his drink away.

"You don't wanna drink with us and honor Nathan? Too much trouble to lift your glass and toast him properly?" Tom's menacing voice came from behind Hank. "He deserves to be honored, and the least you can do is accept a drink in his name, lift your glass, and say his damn name."

Gritting his teeth, Hank refused to raise his head and acknowledge that Tom was addressing him. Wrapping his hands firmly around his glass, so he wouldn't be tempted to wrap them around Tom's neck, he continued to stare at the bottom of his pint glass. The bar became eerily quiet as everyone waited for Hank to raise his glass. Pete intervened.

"Leave it, Tom. We've had our toast, Hank and me, and you've lost a shift-lead, but he's just lost his best friend. Everyone in here is honoring Nathan, not just you, and in their own way. Now leave it alone!"

"Are you telling me and everyone else in here, Pete, that it's okay for that son of a bitch sitting right there to disrespect Nathan by not saying his name during a simple toast? That right?"

"Did you not hear me, Tom? Drop it!" Pete snapped across the bar. "Me and Hank, we've had a toast for Nathan earlier, before you got here!"

"He owes Nathan!"

Hank's eyes—filled with rage—narrowed; he didn't owe anyone an explanation and neither did Pete, especially in his own bar. He never understood why Nathan kept Tom around anyway; damn worthless troublemaker, arrogant ass at best, difficult, and didn't get along with anyone except those who were using him. Odd that Nathan kept him around at all, but again, everyone loved that about Nathan. He was kind, tolerant, and fair, even to crap people like Tom O'Halloron. Pete's eyes flashed toward Hank, and he knew immediately it was time for him to exit; it wasn't fair for Pete to continue to defend him anyway, and he knew Nathan wouldn't want trouble over him. Hank threw another twenty-dollar bill on the bar, thanked Pete, and stood up to leave.

"I don't owe you an explanation, Tom. I'm asking you as nicely as possible, for Nathan, leave it alone." Downing the last of his pint, he added, "Leave me alone."

Tom slammed another shot, and as the liquid rushed down his throat, the burn seemed to fuel his temper. His face already reddened, he walked toward Hank, ready to grab him, but Pete stepped in front of him.

"Tom, I'm not asking, I'm telling you to leave this pub now. You're not the only one upset about Nathan, hell we all are, but you're the only one causing trouble! Damn it, Tom, he was Hank's best friend, not yours. For the last time, leave it the hell alone!"

Hank stood up to leave, shaking his head as he pulled on his coat. "I'll leave, Pete, no worries. I don't want any trouble, not today, and you don't need any."

Digging his hands in his pockets, head down, Hank walked past Tom and avoided any kind of eye contact. It wasn't good enough for Tom, who slipped in front of Pete, grabbed Hank's arm, and pulled him around to face him, whether he wanted to or not.

"This is all your fault, you piece of shit!"

Hank didn't respond.

"You killed him. You frigging killed Nathan!"

Hank's facial expression still didn't change and his body, despite wanting to kick the shit out of Tom, didn't budge. His frame, now noticeably ridged, showed incredible self-control as Hank held himself back from throwing a punch.

Tom continued. "He wouldn't have been there that night, on the docks, if you hadn't guilted him into it. You bullied him into that impromptu meeting that nobody gave a damn about, except for you!" Tom snickered, but it wasn't real. The entire exchange was forced and painful to watch. "And you wanna know why?" Searching the bar to make sure Tom had everyone's attention, which he did, including Hank's, he went on. "So you, the man in the middle, could be the frigging mediator, peacemaker, and for what? Not a damn thing! It was an impromptu meeting; it never counted because it wasn't even sanctioned!"

Hank yanked his arm out of Tom's grasp with such force that Tom fell forward. Gritting his teeth, Hank reached for the door handle before he did something he'd regret. Rage consuming him, about to blow, he had to get out of there! Laying hands on Tom would be easy; walking away from him would not be as satisfying. Hank knew it was time to head home. Tom signaled across the room and before the bar door had swung open a large man jumped up and pushed his body against it, preventing Hank from leaving. Tom's onslaught of blame continued to infuriate Hank; it worked, his words cut deep. It was as if a knife had pierced him all the way through and actually punctured his soul; though he knew it wasn't true, Hank couldn't help but blame himself for some of the things that Tom was spewing. But true or not, the last thing Hank needed was to hear those kinds of statements spilling from Tom's mouth!

"Everyone knew Nathan was against a strike. He needed to work for Sandy and his kid. Nathan showed up on the docks that night to show his support for you, Hank Gunner! It wasn't even a sanctioned meeting. You did this. You got him killed. You are responsible for Nathan's death, but worst of all is that YOU know it!"

Hank pushed past the guy standing against the door, fists clenched in his pocket, Tom's words ringing in his ears, and stormed outside. The chilly air smacked him in the face just as Tom rushed him from behind, knocking him to the ground. Crowds of people collected around the door to see what all the commotion was about, but as soon as they saw Tom on top of Hank, fists swinging, they made their way outside. Pete pushed his way through the crowd, hollering over them.

"Damn it, Tom, I warned you! I'm calling the cops." Dialing the phone he called it in, yelling across a now-empty bar. "I warned you, Tom. I frigging warned you! What the fuuu—. Oh, sorry, yes, ma'am. I'd like to report a fight, and it's happening as we speak."

Hank's grief, rage, anger, and hate found relief in each and every punch that landed and made contact with Tom's body. So angry, Hank never felt the physical pain of Tom's blows in retaliation. Swing after swing with no idea where the punches were landing, the two found themselves tangled around each other fighting like wild animals, slipping and sliding on the icy road. A crowd gathered around them, egging them on, pushing them back and forth, from side to side from the edges of the circle that they had formed around them. One minute rolling around on the ground, another fighting in the street, and before they even knew it the crowd had moved with Hank and Tom as they made their way toward the footbridge over the river that ran next to the frontage by the pub. Freezing cold water below, snow on both sides, no one seemed to care that both men were dangerously close to the aging, already damaged railing on the far side of the bridge. The crowd, still circling the men, took the liberty of dishing out their own swings, jabs, kicks, and shoves as they continued to push the pair back and forth among themselves as the two fought. Hank, unable to gain his balance on the icy bridge, fell to the ground. Tom never let up. A hand reached down and pulled Hank to his feet, only to shove him back into the direction of a punch landing in his face. Falling backward into a wall of men, the entire group braced themselves against the aging rail. Cracking, the wood splintered, and several pieces of the railing hit the ground or fell over the bridge. Scrambling, the men regained their footing. The violence had escalated to such a degree that the sounds of punches, breaking skin, and the eerie sound of cracking wood falling from the barrier railing over the bridge echoed through the night sky, and no one seemed to care. Tom and Hank landed against the broken railing of the bridge for a second time, along with an entire group of men pressed against them as they fought.

Several of Tom's friends kicked, shoved, threw punches, and continued to lean on Hank while trying to protect Tom. For a brief moment, Hank and Tom made eye contact. Tom's eyes dark and hollow, Hank's filled with fury, gave Hank the second wind he needed. Kneeing Tom in the groin allowed him to punch him under the chin as he doubled over. Hank spun around and broke free of Tom and the tiring crowd. Face to face with Tom, Hank pulled his fist back to deliver his final blow, but just as his fist was about to strike, Tom reached out and grabbed Hank's arms. Shoved in the back from behind, Hank jolted forward with such a force that he fell into Tom and instinctively grabbed his shirt as the pair slammed into what was left of the railing. To everyone's horror, the damaged railing gave way, and the pair fell off the bridge.

Scrambling to find their footing, desperately trying not to topple over the edge, the rest of the men on the bridge stopped fighting in their tracks and pulled each other back from the railing. What seemed like an eternity was a mere split-second as Hank and Tom, free falling, plunged into the icy river below. As their bodies hit the freezing water, it was as if concrete hit concrete. It was true what they say: so cold it felt like needles piercing the skin, and too cold to even breathe. Hank thought his heart had stopped. The fighting ceased entirely as everyone panicked, looking for the men in the water below. They knew that Tom and Hank had fallen, but had anyone else?

"I heard one splash!"

"Nah. I heard three."

"No, man. I heard two. There were two splashes."

"Two went over."

"Are you sure? I swear I heard several."

Waiting to see who surfaced, they followed the fast-moving current downstream. Two bodies for sure were being dragged down the river, both bobbing up and down while being pulled under from time to time by the current. All eyes were glued to the bobbing bodies, and no one could determine if anyone was coming up for air.

The men gathered on the banks to try to help fish out the two men, but only one seemed to be staying afloat. Others gathered coats to keep the two warm until an ambulance arrived once they were pulled out of the frigid water. Laying on the cold riverbank flat on their stomachs and holding onto each other, the men made a human chain as they waded out into the icy water to drag in a body lodged between two rocks that they had sighted from the bank. No one knew if it was Tom or Hank. First responders had been dispatched, and everyone could hear the sirens; they were close. Eventually one body was pulled safely to the bank and taken away in an ambulance, but the man's identity wasn't disclosed. The second man hadn't been located. No one knew if the men were alive or dead.

Rumblings started among the crowd as the police

gathered statements. Several versions of the same so-called story were told, but which version was the truth? The search continued for the missing body, and the buzz and speculation spread regarding who had survived and been sent to the hospital.

"Who'd they pull out?"

"I don't know. Looked like Tom, but hard to tell."

A police officer interrupted. "No one leaves without talking to us. Is that clear? We need statements from everyone here. Start talking; hell, there's enough of you. Someone knows something." He grinned. "The real version, I mean." He took out his notepad and his phone to record. "No one leaves this spot until I have names and statements from every one of you."

Tom's buddy, the big guy who had stood in front of the bar door barring Hank from leaving, stepped up.

"I'll tell you exactly what happened!"

"All right, then. State your name, why you were here, and your relationship to this Hank Gunner and Tom O'Halloron. We seem to be able to agree, so far anyway, that the initial fight started with those two."

"Yes, sir. Jerry Jonson is my name. I was in here with my buddy Tom O'Halloron and our work colleague."

"Okay."

"We were having a drink." Jerry took a step forward, but the officer stuck up his hand.

"You're fine right there, son."

"A drink to toast our shift lead, Nathan Nichols. He was recently murdered."

"Sorry to hear that; my condolences."

"Thank you, sir."

"Go on."

"Yes, sir. Anyway, Hank Gunner, he pushed Tom O'Halloron off this bridge." Jerry pointed to the footbridge. "And do you know why?" The officer stared at Jerry, recorder in hand, but never said a word.

"Because he was getting his ass kicked in a fight for being disrespectful during a toast to Nathan Nichols inside the Shamrock!" Jerry shivered in the cold night air, wrapping a blanket he'd been handed tightly around his shoulders. "Oh yeah, while we're at it." Jerry, defiant, stared the officer straight in the eye. "Also, because Tom called Gunner out for being responsible for Nathan's death. That's right! Gunner got Nathan killed, and Tom called him out, Hank caused all this trouble! Right, boys?!"

Chapter 7
Chaos

"Families stand together; we'll stand together.
We'll get through this!"
~ Gloria Gunner ~

Days turned into weeks, weeks turned into months, and everything in Hannah's world had been turned upside down; nothing was the way it used to be since Nathan had died. Hank had been accused of involuntary manslaughter, and Hank and Gloria agreed to keep the explanations to their daughter to a minimum, hoping it would soon all go away. Hannah pushed her Cheerios, one by one, under the milk and waited for them to bob back up to the surface of her bowl. It was a school day, yes, but her momma said she wasn't going today. Things were getting weirder, and where was her daddy? Pouring another cup of coffee, Gloria tousled Hannah's hair as she hurried past her and out of the kitchen.

"Where's my daddy?" Hannah hollered after her.

"He's at the courthouse, remember?" Gloria stopped in her tracks and turned around. "But if you hurry up, you might—not promising—might be able to visit with him a little bit today before they get started."

Jumping down from the table, Hannah peeled off her pajamas as she raced toward her room. Gloria followed behind, picking up her trail and tossing them into the hamper.

"Clean your teeth, and there's underwear, socks, and a dress on your bed. Pick out your shoes, dress or tennis, I don't care, but we have to get a move on!"

"Why are you making me wear a dress? I hate dresses!" Storming into her bedroom, Hannah stared at the dress in disgust. "I don't like that one; I'm not wearing it!"

Frustrated, Gloria swung open Hannah's closet door. "Then pick another one! I don't care which one, but pick a dress and get ready. You have to wear a dress inside the courthouse; it's a rule so that everyone looks nice for the judge. We don't have time for this today, and I've already explained the reason you have to wear a dress!"

Folding her skinny arms across her chest, puckering up her lips, Hannah pulled at the dress laid out neatly for her on the bed.

"Why do I have wear that again?"

"Because, sweetheart, it's important that we look our very best for Daddy today. The trial, remember, because daddy was fighting, is today."

Scared to death to leave the safety of her home, fearing the unknown, Gloria forced herself toward the front door, wondering how to explain to a five-year-old the rules of no talking while court was in session. Another thought crossed her mind, one that she hadn't allowed herself to think about until just that second for fear of jinxing Hank. A judgment, the worst-case scenario possible. Having a judge who didn't take into consideration that it was Hank's first offense, and probation was off the table. Hank, worst-case scenario, might actually have to serve some time. Shuddering, she wondered how in the hell she was going to explain to a five-year-old that her daddy wasn't coming home. Picking up her phone, she reread the text from Sandy.

Sandy: I have an appointment first thing for the baby, but I can cancel if you need me to. Or I can come straight from the doctor's office and pick Hannah up from the courthouse. Whatever you need; I'll be there!

Gloria held back her tears and kicked herself for having responded: Pick up Hannah from the courthouse when you're done with your appointment. *What was she thinking? She should have asked Sandy to cancel her appointment. Hannah didn't need to be there!*

The courtroom was bland, browns and tans, and there were strange people everywhere who were whispering as Gloria and Hannah walked by. Police officers were present, and Hannah didn't know if she should be scared or not, especially since they were holding her daddy somewhere, and adding to that factor, Gloria kept tapping Hannah's legs every few minutes, telling her not to swing them for fear of her kicking the back of the bench in front of their row. What a rotten day off school this had turned out to be!

"Where's Daddy?"

Gloria put her finger up against her lips and shushed her daughter. "Sssh, soon."

"Daddy!" Hannah squealed as soon as she saw a guard bring Hank into the courtroom through a side door and sit him down at a table with his attorney. Putting her tiny hands over her own mouth for fear of being asked to leave, she almost broke into tears when Hank looked her way and winked at her, just like the Captain did, right before he sat down.

Gloria slipped Hannah's hand into hers for safe measure, and they waited patiently for the trial to begin. The bailiff announced that Judge Gordon would be presiding and asked everyone to be seated. This was the final round of the case, which had dragged on for months. Judge Gordon addressed the courtroom.

"In our trial today, the defendant has decided to testify. No one can force a defendant to testify, but if the defendant chooses to testify, the prosecution is allowed to question the defendant." Staring at Hank, the judge addressed Hank's attorney. "Does the defendant understand this?"

"He does, your Honor."

"Swear him in, Clerk Baker, please, and let's begin."

"Please stand. Raise your right hand."

"Dad—"

A gentle but firm hand cupped Hannah's mouth before she could finish calling out to him. Whispering in her ear, Gloria slid her hand off Hannah's mouth. "Remember, we can't say a single word in here; we must be very, very quiet, for Daddy. Very quiet." Hannah nodded, but Gloria held Hannah's hand in hers for the entire trial, despite her daughter trying to wriggle her little fingers out of her grasp.

"Do you promise that the testimony you shall give in the case now before this court shall be the truth, the whole truth, and nothing but the truth, so help you God?"

"I do," Hank responded, hating every second that Hannah was in the courtroom.

"You may be seated."

During his testimony describing the events that night, Gloria's heart sank, blaming herself for forcing him to feel as if he had to flee their home for his own peace of mind. She glanced at Hannah, who had no idea of the severity of the case, the real reason they were there that day, or that they were nearing the penalty phase. Gloria noticed that Hannah continued to grow restless.

"Can we go now?" Hannah tugged on her momma's sleeve. "I'm thirsty."

"Sssh," Gloria whispered, wishing once again she'd asked Sandy to reschedule her doctor's appointment that morning. Silently praying for forgiveness for thinking such a thing, Gloria checked herself, again. She'd been doing that a lot lately. Feeling selfish, she whispered in Hannah's ear and begged her to be patient a little longer. Hannah laid her head on her mom's shoulder and for a minute took herself to an island with the Captain, and forgot for a second that she was sitting on a hard wooden bench.

After the attorneys cross-examined Hank, closing arguments by the prosecution and defense were presented. The judge spoke to the jury. "Ladies and gentlemen of the jury, I am now going to read to you the law that you must follow in deciding this case."

Gloria slipped out of the courtroom with Hannah as

the judge instructed the jury on what they were supposed to do. In the corridor outside the courtroom, they found Sandy. She reached out for Hannah's hand as she leaned into Gloria, who wrapped her arms around her and kissed her cheek, before bending down to kiss her beautiful new baby, Nate.

"I didn't want Hannah to come here today; thank you for picking her up." Seeing her friend trembling with fear, too choked up to say much more, Sandy pulled Gloria as close to her as she could, separated only by the baby carrier. "Sorry. I would have cancelled my appointment."

"No, please, don't ever apologize for such things!"

Sandy pulled Hannah toward the elevators. "Let's go get a burger."

"And French fries?" Hannah's eyes lit up.

"Well you can't eat a burger without fries!" Gloria heard Sandy say, and Hannah agreed. Such a normal conversation on any given day, yet here they were minutes away from finding out what hand fate was about to deal her husband.

The sentencing phase for Gloria was absolutely brutal. Despite the persuasive argument that Hank's attorney had laid out, it took less than an hour for the jury to convict Hank of involuntary manslaughter. It had not been premeditated, true, but several witnesses had testified and accused him of being the one who had pushed O'Halloron over the railing. They also claimed, despite Hank's attorney's objections, that Tom was the one who had hung onto Hank's clothes as he fell over the siding that day, forcing Hank to fall with him into the icy river, and not the other way round. Stunned that the accounts were so different, Gloria held her breath as the judge addressed Hank and the courtroom.

Though the judge sympathized with Hank, he emphasized that a man was dead, and someone had to pay. That someone was Hank Gunner. He received the maximum sentence for involuntary manslaughter, four years, but as his attorney pointed out, it could be reduced for good behavior. Struggling to grasp the reality of the situation, the number of years issued during the punishment phase hadn't quite sunk in. Desperately hoping for probation or a lighter jail sentence, the four years—forty-eight months—seemed like an eternity. Hannah would be nine years old by the time he got out. Nine. *What was she going to do? What was she thinking?! Get your shit together!* Gloria told herself. *We'll appeal the length of the sentence, anything to help, or he will get out earlier, if nothing else for good behavior! We're a family! We need to be together; but more importantly, families stick together!* Wiping her tears away with her hand, trying not to let Hank see her cry, she took a deep breath and asked the attorney if she could speak to her husband. *"We'll get through this together!"* she said to herself as she powdered her nose.

"What, babe? What did you say?" Hank hollered across the rows of seats separating him from his wife, a bailiff by his side.

"Bailiff, please, can we give him a minute to say goodbye to his wife?" His attorney waved Gloria over to them. Separated by a rail, she was inches away from Hank and barely holding herself together. Pouring her a glass of water, the bailiff handed it to her and asked her to sip it slowly.

"You've both been hit with quite a shock today. Sip this slowly. You look as if you're a about to pass out."

Hank, choking up, started his goodbyes. "I'm sorry, so terribly sorry about all of this! I love you, and I'm sorry! Please, please, please tell Hannah I love her, and I'll be home soon."

Numb, tears now pouring down her cheeks and dripping off her chin, Gloria tried to speak but could barely get the words out. "I'm sorry too, Hank. I never should have made you feel as if you needed to leave that day; we're a family, families stick together, and we'll get through this!" They started to direct him to a door to escort him away. "I love you, Hank. I love you!" One nod of his head, assuring her that he had heard her, and they took him away. As they reached the door, panicking, Gloria yelled across the courtroom as loud as she could, startling people who were exiting. "Oh God, please, Hank, please, please, please control your temper in there! No fighting. No FIGHTING! Stay out of trouble." A glance over his shoulder as they led him away, Hank made eye contact before the door closed and yelled, "For you and Hannah, I promise!"

Drained, Gloria plopped down on the hard wooden bench in the now-empty room. Shaking, she buried her face in her hands and sobbed. What in the hell was she supposed to do now, and how was she supposed to look her daughter in the face and tell her that her daddy went away?

Sandy and the baby were sitting on the couch waiting for Gloria to get home. Relieved Hannah was nowhere in sight, Gloria reached for the baby, snuggling him as close to her face as she could, and smothered him with sweet kisses. Fighting through her tears, she managed to get out the words, "It's bad, Sandy. Bad."

Sandy patted the couch and Gloria plopped down next to her. Kissing the top of the baby's head again, Gloria whispered, "Nate, your daddy would be so proud of you!" as the tears finally broke loose and trickled down her cheeks.

"I can't tell you how grateful I am that you picked up Hannah for me today!"

"No, don't. I know you would have done the same. What happened?"

Images of Hank being taken away flashed through Gloria's mind. "Four years. They gave him four years! I don't know what I'm going to do. And I don't know what I would have done if Hannah had seen them take him away like that; it was awful." Tears continued to spill over her eyelids and though she wasn't ready to give up loving on the baby, she had to hand him back to Sandy and brush her tears away just in case Hannah came into the room. Choosing her words carefully, Nathan's loss still fresh on everyone's mind, Gloria tried to contain her grief. "What will I tell Hannah? How will I tell her?"

"You'll just do that mom thing you're so good at and figure it out."

"Good at, me? I don't think so."

"Don't be so hard on yourself; you're a great mom, and at least Hank will come home." Sandy bundled up the baby and made her way to the front door to say her goodbyes. "You've got this! It's not going to be easy, but you and Hannah can still talk to him and visit if you like—that counts for something, doesn't it?"

"You're right, and I'm sorry for sounding so selfish. We'll get through this; it won't be easy, but we'll do it." She couldn't help but wonder if Sandy was still in shock. She was so pulled together despite her grief; maybe having Nate and being exhausted and busy was a good thing right now, instead of bad timing. He was keeping her sane. "Text and let me know you made it home!" Gloria yelled after her. Sandy waved, and Gloria closed and locked the door.

Lightly knocking on Hannah's door, Gloria waited for a response; there wasn't one. Dreading it, she entered the room. Hannah's usual things were scattered around the floor: the book her daddy read to her each night, her fake sword, teddy, a piece of paper with what looked like a hand-drawn map on it—Hank's handiwork no doubt— and princess jewelry. Treasure, of course.

"Hannah. Sweetheart. Can I talk to you for a minute?"

Hannah didn't respond, but did pop up from the other side of the bed. Her blond hair was a wild mess, and her blue eyes that usually sparkled were dull. She looked solemn, knowing that something wasn't quite right, and Gloria hadn't even tried to discuss that their lives were going to change yet. Testing the waters, her little girl started to ask the usual questions.

"What time will Daddy be home?" Hannah bounced up on her bed. "It's getting late, and he should have been here by now. He promised the Captain would board the ship."

"Can we talk for a minute, about your daddy and not the Captain?" Gloria asked. "You're shivering; why don't you put your warm pj's on and get out of your pirate outfit?"

It was as if Hannah hadn't heard a word her mom said, but Gloria recognized immediately that Hannah was choosing to ignore every word that she was saying. Gloria sat down on the edge of the bed and pulled a reluctant Hannah into her lap. Struggling to get away, Hannah forced herself to stay in her make-believe world.

"Captain runs a tight ship around here; but he says you're a scallywag, so you might not know that." Flushed cheeks and pouty lips, Hannah continued to lash out at her mom as she tried to get out of her arms, but Gloria's grip tightened around her. "Sometimes he says you're a tyrant."

Forcing a laugh, Gloria responded softly. "You don't even know what a tyrant is."

"Do too!" Hannah objected.

"Oh, yeah. How so?"

"Captain told me!"

"Is that right?"

"Yes he did, and you're a tyrant."

Frustrated, but glad Hannah was talking, Gloria prompted her again for an explanation. "So what is it, a tyrant, if I am one and all?"

The wheels started turning in Hannah's head. Gloria was witnessing Hannah's mind at work as Hannah's eyes focused on her mom with such intensity so she wouldn't cry. "You're a mean tyrant. Bossy. Always ruling us, me and the Captain, that's what you are... a tyrant!"

Why hadn't the Captain come home already, thought Hannah, *and dismissed this scallywag-turned-tyrant, so they could eat supper, and she could take her bath, and then she could go to Treasure Island with her dad before bed? No, that wasn't right. She had meant that she could go to Treasure Island with the Captain before bed! Where was the Captain, and why was her mom holding her so tightly? Why hadn't the Captain come home? And where was her dad, anyway?* It had something to do with that terrible place that they were at earlier that day, Hannah just knew it, but nothing was making sense and the questions in her head weren't coming out the way she wanted to ask them, and her head hurt anyway! Hysterical, she let out a wail that Gloria had never heard from her daughter in her entire life. As a mom it pierced her heart with sadness, and scared her to death at the same time.

"Where **IS** my daddy?" Hannah wailed. "What did they do to him?" Her little cheeks flushed bright red as hysterics and anxiety set in. Thrashing around, Gloria struggled to hold her down.

"Can we discuss this, please, Hannah?" Gloria begged. "I want to explain what's going on with Daddy." Wrapping her arms around her, holding her tightly and trying to calm her down, Gloria continued trying to talk

Hannah down. "Hannah, listen to me. It's going to be okay. Daddy is going to be okay." Tears turned into gasps for air, the thrashing continued, and Hannah melted down. Reasoning with her seemed impossible before the conversation had started; now, it wasn't even worth trying to discuss the facts with her at all. "Hannah, we'll talk about Daddy when you calm down."

Tantrum in full swing, Hannah lashed out. "What did you do with my daddy? Where is he, and why isn't he coming home?"

Shocked, Gloria could barely respond. "What have *I* done to him?" She hadn't done anything; this mess was all Hank Gunner's doing!

Chapter 8
Cruel to Be Kind

"For my family I can do anything!"
~ Hank Gunner ~

Adjusting to prison life hadn't been easy; missing Hannah's milestones, holidays, and sixth and seventh birthdays had been brutal. Talking to her on the phone wasn't the same. Hannah, like most kids, was bored within minutes, and since the rules wouldn't allow them to video chat or FaceTime, he felt as if slowly but surely he was losing the close connection that he once shared with his little girl.

"She's forgotten about me," Hank complained during a prison visit with Gloria.

"Honestly, she hasn't. She talks about you all the time, plays the pirate game—your role and hers—and sleeps with the shell you gave her every night."

"But it's not the same, is it, I mean really." Hanging his head, he knew it was impossible for it to be the same while he was locked up in there, and he had no one to blame but himself. Hesitating, he chose his words very carefully. Reading his face, knowing he was struggling, Gloria encouraged him to speak freely.

"What's on your mind?"

"Well, ah, you're not going to like it." Hank struggled for the right words.

Gloria fidgeted in her seat. Being in that place made her uneasy. Even if she was pleased to see her husband, she was always ready to leave as soon as she walked through the door. The prison, with its dark concrete walls, cameras pointed at you from every direction, less-than-desirable inmates, armed guards everywhere you looked, rules and more rules, creeped her out! "Spit it out." Forcing a smile for her husband, she added, "I'm listening."

Hank grinned. "It's gonna piss you off!"

"Then maybe you should keep it to yourself."

"Why won't you bring Hannah to see me? Other parents bring their kids here all the time." Boldness in his voice, he forced the issue. "She's forgotten her own father, for God's sake!"

A lump formed in Gloria's throat. This discussion was getting old. She thought they'd put it to bed once and for all the last time he'd brought it up.

"We've talked about this a hundred times!"

"Well, I wanna talk about it again!" Hank, on the opposite side of the table, facing Gloria, sat up straight in his chair. "She's my daughter, and I have a right to see her!"

"Again, Hank, we decided together it was best if Hannah didn't come here, remember? Or did you conveniently forget?"

"Damn it, Gloria, I've changed my mind!"

Uncomfortable with his tone, people staring at her,

Gloria gathered her things and prepared to leave. "Lower your voice, relax, and we'll talk. If you don't do that, and right now, I'm going home."

"Talk!" Irritated, Hank waved his hand toward her. "What is there to talk about? You know it isn't right, you keeping her way from me. It's not right!"

"I don't know that!" Folding her hands and taking a deep breath to calm herself, Gloria reminded him that they'd discussed this time and time again. "Do you have any idea how many times we've discussed the possibility of bringing her up here? Do you? Look around you. Look at you! Is this how you want your daughter to see you? Do you want her to come here, to this Godforsaken place, and visit you?" She leaned closer to whisper to him, but as soon as she did a guard quickly stepped toward her, reminding her there would be no private conversations.

"Don't lean over the line marked on the center of the table, please."

Leaning back in her chair, Gloria continued her plea. "You're wearing inmate clothes, so you all look alike; how do I explain that? That's what bad people wear, criminals—what do I say? People make mistakes, and only some people in here are bad, but some are nice. How does she process that? What do I tell her about some of the shady characters you can clearly see are in here? Hank, this is a state prison! Guards with guns walk around while people visit, kids included, yes, but you want your seven-year-old daughter subjected to this?" Fuming inside, Gloria didn't let up. "And let's not forget about the building."

"What about the building?" Hank snapped

sarcastically. "It's a prison. It's not the Hilton."

"Exactly! It's a concrete compound, barbed wire, armed guards, bright lights, not to mention security checkpoints." Taking a deep breath and rolling her eyes, Gloria asked, "Hank, are you telling me you're so selfish you want Hannah to go through multiple security checks, sit in an environment not conducive for a child, so she can visit with her idol across a table for a couple hours? Wouldn't you rather continue to speak to her on the phone, as her daddy, who she knows and loves? Or even as the Captain?" She brushed away a single teardrop that had rolled down her face. "Hank, look at you... examine yourself and where you sit; do you really want her to see you like this?"

Frustrated, Hank clenched his teeth and folded his arms over his chest, just the way Hannah copied him every time she was upset. "I don't like it, but I know you're probably right. Clearly I'm embarrassing and a disgraceful father to our daughter."

"Hank, don't be like that." Gloria sighed. "We've just gone this long without having to subject her to this, half of your sentence is over, and you're up for a parole hearing soon. Is this really what you want? Do you really, really—and take your time before you answer me—want me to talk to her about coming up here to see you when I go home?" Gloria softened her tone, pretending to talk to Hannah. "What did Daddy say? Um. Let me see. He'd like to know, sweetheart, if you'd like to visit him in prison. Would you like to do that?" Gloria half smiled. "Hank, of course she's going to say yes. But it's not a good idea, and we both know it."

The silence between the two was deafening. Knowing Gloria was right, hating her for it, but loving her at the same time, made the situation extremely difficult for them both. An alarm went off, and a red light came on; visitation time was up, and visitors began to say their goodbyes. Trying to lift his spirits before she left, Gloria told him how much they loved him. He didn't respond.

"I'm not trying to be cruel, Hank, and I know you know we're right to stand by this decision that we've made. Sometimes we have to be cruel to the ones we love in order to be kind." Turning to walk away, she whispered, "I do love you."

With a heavy heart, Hank nodded. "I get it, but I feel as if a piece of me is dying each time I talk to Hannah on the phone, and she doesn't want to talk to me. I love you too."

"Baby, she's seven. She doesn't want to talk to anyone on the phone. She wants to play and do her thing; it's honestly not you." Instinctively her hand reached out to him before she quickly realized what she was doing and pulled her hand back before a guard corrected her. "Do what you're doing: lay low and stay out of trouble. Your parole hearing is right around the corner!" For a split second, Hank's eyes lit up. "This is good, baby, so good! I'm positive that you'll get out early, and your attorney says it is possible you could be released within actual hours of that hearing, the same day even, based on time already served and good behavior, and soon we'll be a family again!"

Hank nodded. "I know, babe, and you're right, about everything! I'm sorry. It's this place. I just miss you,

Hannah, and our life. I love you, babe. I really, really love you!"

"I love you too! Trust me, it's going to be okay. Your hearing will be our lifesaver!"

Saying their goodbyes on a good note made Gloria feel better about leaving him there. Hank, escorted by a prison guard, went back to his cell, and Gloria made the long drive home.

Lying low and trying to stay out of trouble drew unwanted attention to Hank.

Unsociable, rude, asshole, freak, dickhead. Hank had been called a lot of names since he'd been in prison. Doing his best to stay away from other inmates had backfired and made him a target. He was provoked on a daily basis as he refused to take the bait and engage in fights, banter, or trouble of any sort. Parole hearing in sight, Hank tried to stay out of trouble as best he could, but that didn't stop the other prisoners from having a go at him. Bets were continually placed among inmates to see who would be the first prisoner to get Hank to initiate a fight. Being a murderer on the cellblock—involuntary manslaughter or not—didn't help his plight as inmates lined up to show Hank he was nothing that any one of them, on any given day, couldn't handle. The bounty on his head, to prove he was nothing at all, increased by the day. Between unreported beatings, his cell had been ransacked on numerous occasions and his personal items, what few there were, and commissary goods stolen. Hank had a target on his back since he arrived, and no one cared that he had had no intention of killing Tom O'Halloron.

It took a while, but finally the day came. Pushed too far, backed into a corner, and Hank came out swinging. There was one major problem: it wasn't a typical fight, and with wagers so high, there was to be only one outcome. Out of nowhere, a prison shank was shoved into Hank's left side before the inmate ran off. Two other inmates jumped in and started punching and kicking Hank before he fell, so no specific inmate could be blamed. Several would take the fall. Scrambling to his feet, wobbly at best, Hank managed to throw out a single wailing punch to try to defend himself. Unknowingly he struck a prison guard trying to break up the fight before once again falling to the ground. Assaulting a guard, regardless of the circumstances, was a charge he could not deny. The charge not only had to be addressed, but the warden insisted Gunner be made an example of in front of all the other prisoners. *No one, regardless of the situation, strikes a prison guard or causes a guard to be struck.* As Hank was rushed to the medical unit, all his privileges were taken away on the spot, immediately, before he had even made it out of surgery.

Standard procedure was enforced, and letters were written to the parole board from the warden himself. No hearing would be needed; assaulting a guard, no matter the reason, resulted in an automatic denial of parole. Hank received additional time on his sentence for assaulting a prison guard and for being in a prison fight.

Deemed a danger to society, he wasn't fit to leave prison early. Hank wouldn't be coming home for a long, long time.

Gloria could hardly thank the attorney for the call. It had not been a pleasure speaking to him, but she found the strength to thank him for taking the time to call her personally and deliver the news himself.

Soaking in a bath, tears streaming down her cheeks, Gloria submerged herself under the hot, soapy water and held her breath for as long as she possibly could. She reemerged, head pounding, and even the sound of Hannah's laughter seeping through the walls brought her no comfort at all. Drying her body as if in slow motion, Gloria ran through the words that she would say to her daughter about Hank's fight and his injuries. Should she even mention it at all, the stabbing? On the one hand, it was her duty as a mom to protect her child and sugarcoat the truth, and Hannah was too young to understand anyway; on the other hand, maybe Hannah had a right to know. Her conscience was divided. Wrapped in her worn terrycloth bathrobe, she sat on the edge of Hannah's bed.

"Can I talk to you for a second, Hannah? It's important."

Hannah stopped playing and plopped down on the bed next to her momma. Her legs were swinging back and forth, and Gloria wondered if her kid could ever sit still.

"It's about Daddy."

Hannah's eyes lit up. "He's coming home?" she asked excitedly.

Gloria forced a smile across her face and reached over to squeeze Hannah's hand. "Noooooo." Pinching the tip of her nose, basking in the sweet giggles of a seven-year-old, she forged ahead. "He was in a terrible accident today."

"Accident?" Hannah's legs quit kicking the bed. "What kind of accident?"

Hannah's beautiful blue eyes staring up at her as she waited for answers, Gloria stumbled around awkwardly, wondering what to say. "Well, he fell, and he's hurt. He's in the hospital, and they're doing surgery on him." The pressure of the situation and the uncertainty of Hank's outcome were too much. Gloria was scared to death she'd break down and scare Hannah. Gloria stood up and walked toward the closet door. Opening it, she flipped through the hangers, sliding clothes from side to side, and pulled out an outfit for Hannah to wear the next day. "He's in surgery, and the doctors are going to take care of him. But right now you need to jump in bed." Her voice was calm and soothing, void of anything that would indicate she was as worried as she felt inside. In control again of her emotions, she walked back over to Hannah's bed, pulled back the bed covers, and patted the mattress.

"Time for bed, little lady, or are you a pirate today?" Hesitating, she whispered, "You know, it's okay if you've outgrown the pirate game."

"That's silly, Momma." Hannah climbed into bed. "Who outgrows that game? It's a story; it comes from a book." She giggled. "Daddy said his daddy read it to him, and that's why he reads it to me." She started to laugh, knowing they barely cracked the book open. "But we never read it." Flopping backwards onto her pillow, she asked her momma a question she'd asked her a hundred times or more. "When will Daddy come home?"

Tired of disappointing her, Gloria dodged the question yet again. "Go to sleep, baby. It's late."

"But when?"

"When what, Hannah?"

"When will Daddy come back, here, to live with us?"

Feeling utterly defeated and lost for words, Gloria struggled. Where they lived? It had always been where they had all lived. Their family, their home. *Tell her the truth*, a part of her told herself. *Don't do it*, another part insisted. How do you say to a kid something like that? *He was up for parole, and he blew it; instead of coming home, he's staying in longer!* Tired. She was tired of not knowing what the right thing to say or do was, and tired of tripping over her own words. Sickened at the thought of trying to explain to a child what was going on, she forced a sentence out of her mouth that she hoped would pacify Hannah for a little while longer.

"Right now, little pirate, all we want is Daddy to get well, don't we?"

Hannah nodded.

"Why don't we make him a lovely card tomorrow and send it to him; a get-well card. How about that?"

Sleepily, Hannah agreed.

In the kitchen, Gloria sipped a glass of bold red, her head reeling as she waited for Hannah to fall asleep. Creeping into Hannah's bedroom on the way to hers, she stopped to cover her up and watched her sleep for a moment. Hannah looked so peaceful; one would never know she had a father who had been convicted of involuntary manslaughter, stabbed and in critical condition, and had immediately lost his chance for parole and early release. Topping that, he had been given a longer sentence. For all they knew, he might not even make it through the night. Bending down, she kissed Hannah's cheek softly, twice—once for her, and once for Hank.

"Why did you do this to us?" she whispered as she lay in bed that night, crying into her pillow. "Goddamn it, Hank Gunner, why the hell did you do this to us?!"

That night Gloria couldn't sleep, tossing and turning, worrying all night. Hurt, angry, and sad, mind racing, struggling with what she knew she was about to face, she made a decision that would haunt her for the rest of her life.

Chapter 9
Moves in Motion

"Leave me alone; I can't take anymore!"
~ *Gloria Gunner* ~

One by one the bills piled up, and each time the phone rang Gloria avoided answering it. Debt collectors calling nonstop about bills she couldn't pay was a problem. Picking up as many extra shifts as she could still wasn't enough to cover everything that was due, and no matter how hard she tried, she couldn't keep up. Every time the phone rang, it was a number she didn't recognize, unavailable, please call 1-800-423-8795, extension something, case #27659A or whatever, and to call immediately! Gloria hit decline or turned off the phone. It was inevitable; they were going to lose the house. Foreclosure notice after foreclosure notice arrived, and finally the knock on the door she'd been expecting and dreading came in the form of a large, disgruntled man who apparently hated his job; couldn't say she blamed him.

"Mr. Gunner here, please?"

"Who's calling?"

"Well, at this point it really doesn't matter, now, does

it? But if you insist, my name is Mr. Andrews, I'm with
SF Community Bank, and I need to speak with Mr.
Gunner in regards to a foreclosure notice. How's that?"
His tone was uncaring, and he had a nasty smirk on his
face.

"You condescending asshole!"

"Ma'am, you don't have to shoot the messenger. Is
Gunner available or what?"

Gloria snatched the paperwork out of his hand. "He's
detained; I'll see he receives these, now please leave."

"Gladly." The guy turned and walked down the path.
"You have a nice day!"

"How long?" she yelled after him. "Do we have before
we need to leave?"

He never looked over his shoulder or glanced back in
her direction, not even once. "Sixty days; then the bank
owns it. Goes up for auction, unless miraculously you get
caught up, which at this point I doubt. Sixty days start
from today!"

Fucking asshole! she whispered under her breath,
disgusted he'd brought her to such language. Grateful
Hannah was at school, she rushed over to visit Sandy to
vent and for comfort.

"What are you going to do?" Sandy asked.

"I don't know. I just don't know anymore. Move, I
guess, obviously."

"You know you and Hannah are welcome to stay here
with us, at least until to you get on your feet. Hannah
loves Nate, and I'd love to have you here."

Gloria hugged her and scooped Nate up into her lap.
"You have no idea how much that means to me."

Squeezing Nate close to her, kissing the top of his head, Gloria finally voiced the words she'd been thinking about but had been afraid to say out loud. "As terrifying as the thought of this is, I think we need a fresh start. Move. Not too far, but far enough away that we can have a clean slate."

"What about Hank?"

"He's not going anywhere. Right now they say he's critical but I can't talk to him, and they won't let me see him." Setting Nate down on the floor to play, she picked her mug of coffee off the table and took a sip. "I guess I'll start looking for houses and job transfers, but I think it might be good for Hannah. Don't you?"

Sandy shrugged her shoulders. "Honestly, as much as I would miss you, and I would miss you, I don't think it would hurt."

It took a few months, but Gloria was able to transfer into the same position with an affiliate hospital in a neighboring town. Sandy and her brother, Nigel, helped load the last of their things into the U-Haul. Gloria's heart sank as she said goodbye to their home and their friends. This was not how she had planned to leave their family home!

Playfully grabbing Hannah's ankles, Gloria tugged Hannah's legs and pulled her toward the edge of the bed. "You're going to be late for school."

"I don't want to go to school. Can't I stay here with

you?" Hannah hesitated. "I hate school."

"Already?" Gloria tapped the tip of Hannah's nose. "I didn't expect that kind of talk until you were at least a few years older. Besides, you said that about your last school. Give it a chance. Remember what I told you: make it your own adventure."

"I keep having that same dream, the one about the pirates and me on the ship with the Captain. Was my dad a real pirate, a captain of a ship for real?"

Gloria smiled, remembering the game Hank and Hannah used to play every night. There were times she honestly thought Hank enjoyed it as much, if not more, than Hannah.

"I've told you this, what seems now like a hundred times: your dad used to play that game with you nearly every night. Instead of reading a story, he would act out the pirate game, and you would play along. Sometimes, if he were home, you would play the game with him just to play it. It was one of your favorites." Gloria looked at her daughter, puzzled. "Why are you asking about this now?"

"Cause I dreamt about it again last night, and I dream that same dream a lot!"

"I'm not sure why you're holding on to that particular memory so much." Hesitating, as if wondering if it were the right thing to say, Gloria quickly added, "You really should be outgrowing that by now; you're a big girl!"

Hannah gave her the oddest look, insulted that she should throw her memories, dreams, or whatever they happened to be out the window just because she'd turned eight. It was the first time in her young life that Hannah inadvertently felt ashamed for loving the pirate game. Maybe it was a dumb game for little kids; she'd never thought about having to outgrow it before. From now on she'd keep her daydreams, dreams, and whatever was left of her memories and secrets to herself. Gloria, sick of the subject, turned her attention back toward the issue of school.

"Again, please hurry up and finish getting dressed."

It was Hannah's third school since they'd first moved away from their hometown. With each move Gloria had increased her wages, and even earned a promotion, allowing them to move into a better neighborhood with better living accommodations, which was high on Gloria's list. Her main priority was to keep Hannah in a safe environment, where she could play and meet other kids her age, and she didn't have to worry as much as if they lived in a bad part of town. Hannah had turned from the adventurous little girl who used to play pirate and take charge commanding her make-believe crew on her make-believe ship, to an observer as she continually tried to adjust and fit in. Making friends for Gloria was easy; she was well liked no matter where she went and fortunately often moved to locations where she knew at least one or two coworkers from previous hospitals or had received recommendations from such. Hannah wasn't so lucky; each time they packed up their things and moved, little by little she started to shut down. Gloria assured herself it was nothing more than an adjustment phase, and Hannah would bounce back to her usual outgoing, adventurous self in no time at all.

Pointing to Hannah's backpack, she rushed out of

the room. "Grab that and hurry up, or we're both going to be late."

Hannah didn't care if she was late. She didn't care about anything these days. Eight years old and already trying to figure out how she could ditch school and stay home instead of going to third grade.

"I bet the Captain wouldn't make me go to that horrible place every day," she complained.

Gloria pretended she hadn't heard her, but Hannah's words made her smile. Defiant. Stubborn. Always having to have the last word; Hank's kid through and through! It weighed heavily on her that Hannah hadn't adjusted to school yet, and Hannah's sly comments didn't help ease her conscience. Hannah would make friends and enjoy learning new things soon. *Sure, she was having trouble because this move was so close to the last,* Gloria told herself, *but Hannah will come around.* Dragging her out the door by the hand, Gloria couldn't help but notice Hannah's big blue eyes were no longer shiny, but dull. Time. The kid just needed time, that's all!

They walked the same route every day to school, and each afternoon Hannah rode the bus home. The first few times Hannah had boarded the bus, she was scared to death that she'd miss her stop, but the bus driver had kept an eye on her. Sally, a coworker and friend, worked third shift, three days on and two off, lived in the same apartment complex, and always met Hannah at the bus stop to walk her home and let her into the apartment. It wasn't an ideal situation, but Gloria was grateful Hannah wasn't a typical latchkey kid. At least someone walked her home and checked inside the apartment first.

That afternoon the air on the bus was sticky as they rolled from stop to stop. Hannah laid her head against the cool window, and the muffled sound of the kids chatting faded as she nodded off and soon began dreaming. Struggling to see who was with her, a familiar voice broke through her hazy dream, but whose face did the voice belong to? The cool sand sifted through her feet, and Hannah visualized herself looking down at her feet, digging her toes into the sand. Seagulls were circling and squawking above her, as gentle waves rolled to the shore, and if she wasn't mistaken, she could smell the distinct odor of the salty sea air. His voice, the Captain's, was vague, and for a second her heart raced in fear. Was it possible that she was beginning to forget who this person was supposed to be? Her memories, turned into reoccurring dreams, were familiar and comforting, and for the first time it occurred to the kid standing on the beach that she needed this never-ending dream. Startled as the bus driver gently shook her shoulder and woke her up, Hannah struggled to regain her surroundings and catch her breath.

"Wake up, sleepyhead; Hannah, you almost missed your stop."

Without saying a word, she gathered her things and walked toward the front of the bus. Sally stood nervously wondering what was taking so long for Hannah to appear; the relief she felt when the mass of blond hair suddenly walked toward her was written all over her face.

"Fell fast asleep, this one," the bus driver grinned. "I had to wake her up."

Amanda M. Thrasher

"Thank you! I appreciate you looking out for her, and so will her mother."

"No problem. Hannah, you go to bed early!"

They waited for the bus to pull away before walking home. Sally let her into the apartment, gave her a snack, and locked the door behind her. Gloria arrived shortly after, but Hannah couldn't have possibly been prepared for the news her mom delivered that evening. Nervously Gloria set her keys down on the hall table, walked into the kitchen, and poured herself a glass of wine. Slamming down half of it immediately, trying to calm her nerves, she sat down just as Hannah ran into the kitchen to greet her. Rambling about her day, how she fell asleep on the bus, and how she was starving, Gloria raised her hand and interrupted her daughter.

"Hannah, please, stop for just a minute."

"But it was the weirdest thing, Momma, I was on the beach and then the bus driver was shaking me, and I couldn't remember where I was, and what are we having for dinner?"

"HANNAH!" Gloria snapped. "Please, stop talking!"

Stunned, Hannah stared at her mom, who was visibly shaking. "Are you okay?" she asked.

Gloria's hands reached for Hannah's, and though she held her daughter's hand tightly in hers to steady herself, Hannah could feel her mom's hands trembling.

"What's going on?"

Taking a deep breath, tears filling her eyes, Gloria tried to explain. "I received a phone call today at work."

"Who was it?"

"Your daddy did not recover from his injuries; he has

passed."

All of the color rushed from Hannah's face. She had heard those words somewhere before, but what exactly did they mean? "What is that? Passed?"

Gloria took a swallow, not a sip, of wine. "Like Uncle Nathan, sweetheart. He's joined Uncle Nathan."

"But Uncle Nathan's gone!" Hannah yelled, tears forming in her eyes. "Daddy's gone?" Her heart was racing and she felt as if she couldn't breathe. "I didn't see him." She pulled her hand out of Gloria's. "You said I could see him!"

"Sweetheart, he was hurt during the fight. You couldn't see him." Gloria's voice cracked, her heart was in her throat, and she tried to grab her daughter to hold her, but she fought against her touch. "He loves you so much; loved you so, so, so much!"

Burying her hands in her face, dropping to the floor, Hannah sobbed uncontrollably. Every time Gloria reached out to hold her, Hannah pulled away. It killed her seeing her daughter in such a state, and whispering how much her daddy loved her didn't ease the pain her daughter felt. Hannah's sobs turned into wails, and she barely could catch her breath.

"I want my daddy; the Captain can't be gone, he's a pirate!"

Gloria held steady as best she could. "You'll be home from school for a few days. It will take time, but you will heal, and have fabulous memories of your daddy, and the Captain."

Hannah jumped to her feet, ran to her room, and grabbed the conch shell that her daddy had given to her.

Placing it next to her ear, she sobbed herself to sleep.

A few days later the argument with Hannah and going to school started all over again! This time Hannah was defiant and her eyes were empty.

"I hate that place; it's dumb!"

"It's an elementary school, Hannah. Have fun. Make friends. Enjoy yourself. You've got a long way to go!"

Kissing Hannah on top of her head, Gloria said her goodbyes and left her standing helplessly in front of the line teacher. *She'll adjust,* the teacher said. *Just takes a minute.* During recess, Hannah organized a group of kids into a pirate crew. Bossing them around, she gave each of the kids chores on her ship.

"You can be the boatswain; check all our supplies."

"But I was that last time. I want to be the Captain."

"You can't be the captain. I'm the Captain!" Moving right along, she pointed to a red-headed little girl with big green eyes. "You can swab the deck."

"Oh, brother—again?"

"Always complaining. Yes, again. Ships have to be clean; it's a pirate rule."

"Well, I'm going to the crow's nest to look for other pirate ships," a little boy named Seth chimed in. "And I don't care what you say, Captain or not."

Hannah looked at another blond-haired girl standing next to Seth. She wasn't offering anything up, and Hannah didn't think she seemed interested in playing the game at all. She was right. "I'm tired of this game. Can't we play family instead?"

"That's a dumb game!" Hannah insisted. "Who wants to play baby games when we can play pirate games?"

"I don't like this game anymore either; you're always the Captain."

"Cause it's my game; of course I'm the Captain."

"It's a stupid game," David Moore said in a snarky tone. "Let's play war. I want to be in the Army, like my dad."

"It is not a stupid game!" Hannah snapped. "You're stupid!"

"I'll only play if I'm Captain. You're always Captain and never let anyone else play."

"You can't be the Captain!" Hannah yelled. "I'm the only one who can be the Captain; it's my game. Besides, you don't even know how to be a Captain!"

"That's dumb. It's not your game; it's just a game."

"You're dumb!" She waved her pretend sword in his face. "And if you don't stop asking to be Captain, I'll make you a prisoner instead of a pirate 'cause you're so dumb!"

"You can't make me a prisoner if I'm not playing!" He turned his back on her. "And I'm not playing this dumb game anymore. It's stupid!" David turned to the others. "Do you want to play Army?"

And that was that! Most of her pirates quit, and the rest Hannah fired from their posts for being rebellious. Hannah decided she didn't want to play with any of them anyhow. She hated that school, and she refused to join in their games when the teacher noticed what was going on and attempted to mend the bridge between them all. Hannah happily alienated herself from all of the other kids and took refuge in the comfort of her own head.

After recess, the kids went back to their classroom

and sat in a circle. Disgusted with her classmates, Hannah sat outside of the group, and each day she purposely isolated herself a little bit more from the things that the other students were asked to do. When the teacher called out her name, twice, Hannah jumped. Lost in daydreams or her memories? It was apparent, even to Hannah, that she couldn't decipher what they were anymore; real memories or beautiful dreams, it didn't matter. Being anywhere, imaginary or not, was better than where she currently sat.

"Hannah, would you please join us?" the teacher asked sweetly.

Hannah froze. Join them where... in front of the class with those two other kids?

"No," she replied firmly.

"I'd really like you to stand by me, if you don't mind."

She did mind, very much so; no one wanted to be stared at. Hannah shook her head as her cheeks burned bright red.

The teacher walked over to Hannah, reached down for her hand, and tried to pull her gently to her feet. Hannah tugged her hand out of the teachers grasp, but the teacher continued to tug and try to coax her to join them.

"I promise it will be fun."

There was nothing about being stared at by a huge class that resembled fun! Hannah continued to refuse and was about to burst into tears. Recognizing that Hannah wasn't going to budge, the teacher smiled, gave her a hug, and moved on to the next child. Hannah never once looked anywhere but at her feet.

The bus ride home didn't bring Hannah the usual daydreaming escape that she quite enjoyed. About to experience her first bout of public anxiety, Hannah suddenly felt confined, as if she were stuck in a giant tube, and she struggled to get enough air into her lungs. Her palms became sweaty, and so did her brow. She needed fresh air and to get off of that bus! Her heart was racing, and she burst into tears. As soon as the bus pulled up to her stop, she bolted toward the door and leaped off the step into Sally's arms. Having no idea how to describe what was wrong, Hannah continued to struggle to breathe. It took less than a few seconds for Sally to recognize something wasn't right.

"What's wrong?" Hannah could barely talk. "Just calm down. Deep breaths. Breathe in and out. In and out," Sally instructed. "It's okay. Breathe. Just breathe. In and out, in and out, look at me."

Focusing on Sally's voice, locking eyes with her mom's friend, Hannah's breathing returned to normal. Her heart quit racing and feeling as if it were about to jump out of her chest. Sally tried to explain to Hannah that she thought she'd experienced a panic attack, and promised to talk to her mom about it as soon as she got home. Not understanding, but feeling weird, Hannah wanted to go straight to her room.

"Not yet. Eat this PB&J and drink this milk first. I'll wait for your mom. Okay?"

Embarrassed, Hannah nodded as she nibbled on the sandwich. Excusing herself from the table, she ran down the hallway to her room. Catching sight of her conch shell that sat on her bookshelf, she walked over to it and held in her hands. Placing it against her ear, she listened as the sound of the ocean swirled around and around the shell. It immediately brought her comfort. Grabbing her favorite book, she flopped down on her bed, the shell still placed against her ear. Hannah never once opened *the* book, but held it close to her chest. Struggling to see the image of the Captain's face, she desperately willed herself to remember him. His voice seemed stronger than ever as it echoed in her head. Straining to visualize him in her mind's eye, she allowed herself to disappear in her head.

"Watch from the starboard, Matey."

His gruff voice clearly instructed her, and for that comfort she was grateful. Squeezing her eyes shut as tightly as she could, she listened for his voice again. She couldn't hear him at first, but the sound of the sea in the shell gave her hope that it would return. Straining to listen to him again, she patiently waited. Casting her thoughts to her time aboard ship, her old bed in her old room, she listened for his voice to return and, to her relief, it finally broke through.

"Batten down. Storm's a-brewing!"

She watched herself running on deck. Her blond hair whipping across her face, because yes, the winds were getting stronger and the waves indeed were lashing over the side of the ship! Her hand reached up and brushed her hair to one side while the other hand grabbed a thick rope to secure the hatches. The Captain smiled at her, and she smiled back, knowing she'd made him proud. He pulled out his telescope, looked through it, and then handed it to her. At one point he bent down and scooped her up, throwing her over his shoulder and throwing her on the bed. Bed? What?! Surely it was a ship; it must have been the bed in the cabin. Forcing herself to drift off, she watched herself place one hand on top of the other as she climbed the rope ladder to the crows' nest; storm's a-coming, they needed to prepare.

Her bedtime stories that had turned into games became more and more extravagant in her head as she added details to keep her dreams going. She couldn't remember the exact way that her daddy, Hank, had acted it out with her, and that mortified her. By the time Gloria came home and walked into her bedroom, Hannah was fast asleep.

Why did such a beautiful child have to deal with so much? Surely Hannah's panic or anxiety attack was a result of the decisions that Gloria had made over the past few months. Doubting herself and her decisions—all of the moves, not taking Hannah to visit Hank in prison, the different schools—made her wonder if she had brought this on Hannah. Every decision Gloria had made, she thought, was to protect her daughter, and now she felt as if she'd done the complete opposite. Sally laid a hand on Gloria's shoulder and, as if reading her mind, reassured her that she had done the best that she could, but Gloria felt like a terrible mom. Guilt, regret, remorse, anger, and sadness consumed her.

"She's going to be fine; it was a panic attack, and kids outgrow those all the time." Handing her a glass of wine, Sally pointed toward the living room. "Let's sit a while. You need a break as well."

"I hope so, Sally!" Gloria kissed Hannah, covered her

up, and closed her bedroom door. "You're right, it's going to be fine. I'll get her through this; she's going be all right. She has to be!"

Chapter 10
Not Again

Don't make me go, let me hide!
I'd rather hide or flat-out die
I hate it there, can't you see?
No one there is quite like me!
~ Hannah Gunner ~

"Now, about this school thing you keep making me do. Can we talk about that?"

"What is there to talk about? Every kid goes to school; it's the law."

"But I'm not a kid," Hannah smirked.

"Oh really!" Gloria snapped jokingly. "And what exactly are you?"

She was about to say a First Matey, but reminded herself that her mom was a *pirate hater*, so went with the big kid thing that her mom had been going on and on about.

"You said I was a young lady, and that's not a kid, and young ladies don't go to school with third graders."

"Look, tomorrow will be better, and the day after that will be better than the day before, and so on and so on. I promise. You just need to adapt, that's all. School is fun!"

Gloria couldn't have been more wrong and was

shocked when she received a phone call demanding that she attend a parent teacher-conference concerning her child. She sat opposite the teacher, perched in a chair that was too small for any adult. Ms. Davis introduced herself and sat on a tabletop in front of her.

"I apologize about the chair. Would you like mine?"

Gloria shook her head. "I'm fine. Really."

Ms. Davis got straight to the point. It had been months since school had started and Hannah didn't fit in with the others at all; worse, she was making no attempt to try and acted as if that was fine by her. Isolation didn't seem to affect Hannah, and that was concerning to Ms. Davis and the other school officials. It was as if she purposely isolated herself from everyone at any given opportunity. She wouldn't participate in any group projects or even try. She refused to answer questions out loud, join in fun activities inside or outside, or participate in anything that involved group activities.

"Mrs. Gunner, it's unusual for a child this age to respond in such a way. Usually they enjoy at least some interaction with their peers."

"Is there anything she likes to do at school? Subjects, recess, lunch, anything?" Concerned, though not surprised, Gloria persisted in her line of questioning. "It hasn't been easy for her lately, but there must be something she enjoys. She's eight, for crying out loud, just a kid." Softening her voice, she apologized. "I'm not upset with you; I'm sorry, but I am worried about Hannah."

"I understand; we're all concerned. Hannah seems to enjoy art; she plays well outside, though mostly by herself these days, loves that pirate game, and I'm sure she must play it at home. She participates in P.E. but doesn't seem to enjoy it, and we think it's because she's forced to be a part of whatever the class is doing."

Pulling out a tiny chair to perch upon next to her, Ms. Davis proceeded with caution. "I can't stress enough that she's not in trouble here, meaning she's not disrespectful, causing problems, or doing anything wrong. But it is concerning that she will not participate in any group activity at all. Even when I purposely try to have her, say, be partners with me, she'll still object."

Stone-faced, Gloria continued to listen. At home, Hannah didn't hide her dislike of school, but she had no idea that her daughter was struggling to such a degree that she had alienated herself from her classmates. Granted, she recently had a panic attack, but it was only one, and of course she was monitoring the situation. An awkward silence filled the room, and then the inevitable dreaded question was posed.

"I have to ask, Mrs. Gunner, is there something going on at home that we should be aware of, anything that you would like to discuss or share with us?"

Horrified, Gloria tried to gather her thoughts; she was unprepared for such a question and had no desire to fill them in on the abominable details of their personal lives.

"Well, as you know, it has been incredibly difficult for Hannah these last few months—the moves to help pay our bills and her father's death." She hesitated before continuing, desperately trying to figure out how to brush over certain details—no need to mention the prison part —yet inform the teacher that much of what was happening to Hannah wasn't her daughter's doing. "Hannah was very close to her father and she misses him."

The teacher handed Gloria a tissue as her eyes watered and her voice cracked, a combination of embarrassment and sadness.

"For argument's sake, she's lost her father and made several significant moves that she hasn't accepted nor adjusted to just yet. Granted, each move increased my ability to support our family and was supposed to give her a fresh start, but clearly Hannah didn't see it that way. She should be mingling and enjoying herself and she isn't. I didn't expect it to be this bad for her. I blame myself!"

"Don't beat yourself up so badly! Let's focus on how we can help Hannah."

Gloria nodded, but the voice in her head wondered how she was going to discuss the issue at hand with Hannah without making the situation worse. They chatted for a while and devised a plan to help Hannah adjust. She'd sit with the school counselor at least once a week, just talk, about anything she wanted to talk about. After a few weeks, Gloria wasn't surprised to find out that most of the notes the counselor took were about the Captain, her dad, and the pirate game.

Later, Gloria stood outside Sally's door, a bottle of wine in hand, and told Hannah she could knock. Once inside, Sally poured Hannah a glass of soda and gave her a candy bar. Hannah was thrilled.

"Nice, she'll be up all night!" Gloria smiled and set

the wine on the table as Sally grabbed two glasses.

"What's the occasion?" Sally asked.

"Desperation!" Gloria replied.

Grateful she had a friend to talk to, Gloria confided in her. Regrets, mistakes, and fear were dictating most of the decisions that she had made and continued to make for her and Hannah.

"I've made a mess of things, and keep making them worse. I'm really not sure this school is the best fit for Hannah, but I can't afford private school." Taking a sip of her wine, she announced, "This is killing me. One bad decision after another."

"You can't live like this; the stress will eventually *kill* you."

"I agree! I was starting to get used to it," Gloria whispered. "But I know now that it's a terrible way to live, especially for Hannah, getting used to settling for all the wrong things."

"You have to decide, right here and now, to stop it! Make decisions based on new beginnings, for you and Hannah. A life filled with adventure and hope; you both deserve it."

Wiping her nose with her sleeve, Gloria topped off their wine and raised her glass. "You're right! We do deserve it." She took a sip of her wine. "I don't know what to do! Maybe I need to face my past and go home." Staring off into space, she added. "You know, my sister still lives there—Kathy. I don't know; I guess it's something to think about."

"Well, you're stuck with me so it doesn't matter what you decide—move, stay, makes no difference. Give yourself some time. Hannah might turn it around, you don't know yet." Sally grabbed Gloria's hand and squeezed it. "You and Hannah do deserve some peace and a new beginning, but take your time and think about it. Don't rush into anything; Hannah's been through enough."

Gloria lifted her glass. "To new beginnings, adventure, and hope!" Smiling. "One day, maybe not tomorrow, but one day I'll get this mess figured out."

"New beginnings, adventure, and hope!" Sally repeated.

Little did she know that evening that Sally was right. Hannah did eventually settle down and though she kept her circle small, she did have a few friends. They wouldn't move again for several years, and when Gloria approached Hannah with the subject about possibly making a move again, Hannah had just turned sixteen.

"So, I've been thinking," Gloria announced over dinner. "How about one last adventure?"

"Adventure." Hannah grinned. "Code word for move!"

Chapter 11
A New Adventure

Tormented Mind
Sorrow Weeps
Bitter Feelings
Wounds Are Deep
Rise Above
Head Held High
New Approach
Clearer Eyes
~ Hannah Gunner ~

It was to be the last move; her mom had promised. But the truth was, Hannah didn't care; she looked at moving as a brief adventure. That's what Hannah told herself: *Don't get too settled, and don't get attached to anyone or anything; you'll be off on another adventure again soon enough!* It worked; she kept to herself, laid low, made more acquaintances than friends, and when they did move, it wasn't such a big deal to Hannah. Looking back, that theory was likely linked to the separation of her dad more so than moving, but it took a while for Hannah to connect the two. Gloria was ready for a change, but this time there was something different about her delivery regarding the move. She addressed it as if it really were, this time, a permanent move for the pair.

"I'll be making more money," Gloria hollered from

the kitchen. "It's a promotion, and I'm thrilled about that, but the best part of all..." She quit talking and suddenly appeared outside Hannah's bedroom door.

"Yesssss," Hannah dragged out playfully. "What's the best part of this move over the last, say what, five?"

"Very funny, although you could be right." Gloria pulled out a chair by Hannah's desk. "This move is actually one you may or may not be familiar with." Hannah looked puzzled. "Okay, what I mean is we're going back to our hometown. You were little, but do you remember living in San Francisco?" Hannah had a blank look on her face. "Do you remember visiting Aunt Sandy, well she wasn't really your aunt, but we called her that because she was my best friend? And, you know Aunt Kathy of course; she lives there."

Hannah nodded. "Yes on Aunt Kathy, the Christmas presents, and not really, vaguely, maybe, I don't know, on the other one, the Sandy lady."

"Well, it's not important. I just think it's time we moved back closer to home, closer to family, Kathy." Gloria laughed. "It will be a good move for both of us."

Shaking her head, Hannah shooed her mom out of her room. "Whatever, I don't care. As long as I'm out of school for a few days, we'll label it another adventure and move on." Grinning, she handed her mom a dirty cereal bowl. "Can you take this to the kitchen on your way out, please?"

Gloria reached for the bowl, but not without giving her a dirty look and playfully rolling her eyes.

Over the next few weeks, Gloria and Hannah packed up their belongings.

Wrapping what few personal things she owned and placing them carefully into cardboard boxes, Hannah's eyes caught sight of her prized conch shell that sat on a makeshift bookshelf. The times she'd pack that thing away and moved it with her, only to unwrap it, check it for cracks, and place it carefully in yet another safe place had been too many times to count. Faded memories of the Captain, and that horrific afternoon when her mom delivered the devastating news of her father's death came flooding back to her. Hannah remembered hearing the words, but couldn't process them properly at the time. Gloria's explanation of her father's death brought Hannah little comfort; he'd been gone for so long anyway, but her strongest memories, memories of the Captain, managed to bring her peace. Her shell, a gift from the Captain, was a memory that she hadn't forgotten and counted as her most prized possession to date. Picking up the shell, she held it in her hands and remembered the gruff sound of the Captain's voice. Holding it to her ear, she listened for a few moments to the swirling sound of the sea and smiled, remembering her dad's words before wrapping it in a newspaper and placing it once again in the box. Hannah had asked about him a while back after picking up a photo that Gloria always set by the side of her bed. It was a photograph of the three of them, a family, and they looked happy. Hannah was in the middle, Hank on one side of her, and Gloria on the other.

"What happened to him?" Hannah had asked. "I know he died, but how?"

"They called it a shank. Kinda like a homemade knife."

Snapping out of it, Hannah looked around her room. She always packed the same way; working from the outer edges inward. Bookshelf, closet, chest of drawers, bedding, and that was about it. They didn't own much, so packing was a breeze. Walking through the apartment one last time, they locked the doors, turned in the keys, said their goodbyes, and hit the road. Pulling into rest stops and *making do for the night* meant they'd sleep in the car. Hannah pretended she didn't care, but she did. She wanted a shower, a clean bed, and real food. Cranky, tired, and sick of driving, she needed a hit of nicotine, her JUUL. They'd driven for fourteen hours straight, stopping only for gas, snacks, and to use the restroom. Finally, Gloria pulled into a rest stop and parked the car for the night. The air was hot and sticky, making it impossible to get comfortable in the tiny Honda Civic. The U-Haul Gloria was pulling weighed the car down, and between the trailer, the beat-up Honda, and the pair of them, they indeed looked and felt homeless.

"Once we arrive, we'll spend time with Aunt Kathy and check out the new place." Gloria took a sip of coffee. "You might not remember Kathy very well. Cards, presents, and phone calls are a lot different than being with someone in person, but she adores you and always has."

Hannah didn't care; anything beat where they were right then. The windows were cracked, but there was hardly enough air, and Gloria refused to roll them down all the way due to *stranger danger.*

"It's not safe with the windows down. Oh, I hate this." She turned to Hannah. "We're parked at a rest stop; we should keep going and try to find a hotel."

Hannah shook her head. "You can't drive; you're whipped. And I don't have my license yet. As much as I hate it, and I do hate it, we'll get through."

Gloria blew her a kiss. "Thank you! By the way, Kathy's picked out two apartments for us. One for sure is promising. And I have my entrance interview, paperwork, and whatnot on Tuesday at SF Memorial Hospital. Hannah, I promise, this move is going to be good for us!"

Hannah laid back on the seat and propped her feet up on the dashboard. A can of soda in one hand and a bag of chips in the other, but all she wanted was a hit of her vape. Gloria unwrapped a soggy PB&J and handed it to her. Hannah turned up her nose.

"Oh, hell no!" she responded. "I'm not eating that; it looks gross."

"Wrong answer, and watch your mouth!" Gloria tapped her on the leg. "I won't tell you again."

Shoving the sandwich in Hannah's lap, she unwrapped another for herself. It might not be the finest meal, but her kid was going to eat. Peanut butter was nutritious, and she'd cook her a real meal as soon as she could. Against her will, Hannah picked at the sandwich. Desperately needing fresh air and to stretch her legs, a break from the car, she couldn't stop fidgeting. Knowing that she couldn't vape, and her mom wouldn't let her stretch her legs, the only thing she could do was try to go to sleep. The sound of her mom's voice helped her drift off to a secret place in the corner of her mind. White sands and a blue ocean awaited her, along with a ship floating offshore manned by a few scrappy scoundrels and, if she was lucky, the Captain.

A young girl's giggles echoed in Hannah's head, a younger version of herself, as her mind drifted into sleep and she followed the laughter of a little girl until the image of the girl appeared running toward the water's edge. The waves were tickling her toes, and Hannah observed the Captain watching over the girl as she played, and just like that she had drifted off into a lovely dream where the seagulls circled around her, the waves danced at her feet, and she didn't have a single care in the world.

A smile crossed Hannah's face as she slept and Gloria could tell she was dreaming. It was impossible for Hannah to say if any of her memories were real; games that she'd played with her daddy or stories he'd once told had turned into dreams. All she knew was that the recurring dream, whatever it was, brought her a beautiful escape. That escape had become a crutch that Hannah had learned to lean on for years.

Chapter 12
Last New Beginning

Fresh Perspective
Dreams Anew
Hearts Not Broken
Feelings True
Solid Path
Ground Laid Out
New Direction
Life's Re-Route!
~ Hannah Gunner ~

Kathy was thrilled to have them! It had been too long,
she'd said, and it was about time they'd come home to
San Francisco. Their new apartment, if they chose the
one she was hoping that they would, was less than ten
minutes away from her house. Gloria was thrilled, and
Kathy was confident that once they'd seen the
apartment, they'd take it on the spot. It was ideal and
available immediately—a huge plus—and because Kathy
knew the landlord, the deposit had been waived. Plus, if
they took it he would allow them to sign an extended
lease, locking in the rate he'd discussed with Kathy.

"It's a great deal for a beautiful apartment, great
building, and of course you can't beat the location!"
Kathy bragged. "If I don't say so myself."

"I'm sold! Show me where to sign." Gloria grinned.

"Seriously, it sounds ideal, and I'm sure that will be the one we take."

The building was in a safe part of town, and the apartment itself, though small, was clean and had new appliances, fresh paint, wood floors, a vaulted ceiling, and a fireplace, which Hannah loved. Gloria agreed with Kathy; it was perfect and they didn't need to look at the other apartment she had picked out as a backup.

Wrapping her arms around her daughter, happy, she kissed her on the cheek and told her to pick a room. "Pick your room; any one, I don't care which."

"Well, in that case," laughed Hannah, "I'll take the master with the bathroom attached."

"Have at it!" Gloria laughed. "It's all yours."

As much as Hannah would have loved the larger bedroom with the bathroom, she immediately declined. "I was kidding. You take it. Really."

Gloria shook her head, but Hannah insisted. She wouldn't begin to feel at ease in a room that wasn't rightfully hers.

"I might not have a bathroom in my room, but at least I have my own bathroom, and the closet isn't too shabby either! Did you check it out?" Hugging Gloria, she steered her toward her closet. "This is great; look at the size of this thing!" Slinging one arm over her mom's shoulder and looping one arm through her aunt Kathy's. "Aunt Kathy, if you only knew what I could have done with a closet this big when I was a kid."

"Isn't that the truth!" Gloria pointed toward the door. "Let's get unpacked and moved in; this will be our last new beginning."

Kathy brought over coffee, food, and toiletries to get them through the first few days and helped put marked boxes in the rooms that they belonged. She noticed immediately how organized everything was; Gloria had moving down to a science. They ate soggy pizza, and Kathy and Gloria sipped a much-needed glass of wine as they talked about the people Gloria once knew and had left behind.

"I've already spoken to Sandy; she knows I'm back."

"You've stayed in touch over the years with her, though, right?"

Gloria nodded, but with a mouthful of pizza she couldn't answer right away. "Yes. Not as much as I would have liked, but over the years we have stayed in touch. Nate should be ten, almost eleven by now."

"I see her every now and then, not very often, but she always asks about you. Nate, he's lovely, and he does look just like Nathan."

Hannah ate her pizza as she listened to their conversation. She had few expectations about the people she'd likely meet in her so-called childhood town. She didn't remember much of anything about being there. She'd been too young, and what she remembered revolved mostly around childhood play. The thought of the necessary pending introductions at her new high school gave her anxiety. She hated those—on the spot, here's the new kid, and everyone stares. Gloria's wine, sitting on the countertop, was too easy a target as Hannah walked by. Helping herself to a mouthful as she walked toward her room, she knocked back the wine and pushed the thoughts of her first day of school out of her mind.

"I'm going to take a shower."

She allowed the hot water to run over her naked body. Hannah had always been thin, but as she washed her arms, she realized she had become too thin. Maybe her worrying about the move—or her mom's promotion, or the new school—had likely taken its toll without her knowledge. Her arms looked too skinny, and she realized she probably should eat a little more than she had been lately.

"Skin and bones" popped into her head, a voice from the past that startled her.

Did I actually hear that, or was it just a memory in my head? I'm either hearing voices, or I'm exhausted, she thought. She went with the latter.

Slipping into an oversized shirt, shorts, and a pair of socks, Hannah got ready for bed. As she unpacked some of her boxes, she came across her prized personal box. Gloria waltzed by, stopped, and stuck her head in Hannah's room to check on her.

"Everything okay?" she asked. "Unpacking coming along?"

"Yes, but I need some shelves."

Gloria nodded. "I'll add that to my list. We can hang them together; figure out where you want them, and we'll mark the spot."

"Fabric softener as well," Hannah yelled as Gloria walked out of the room. "Those towels, no good, rough as can be!"

"Got it," Gloria hollered back. "And remember when you check in at school tomorrow, remind the office that you're a transfer student. They're supposed to be expecting you, and your classes should already be assigned."

If looks could kill, Gloria would be a goner. "Do I have to go tomorrow? Couldn't you tell them we were delayed a day?"

Gloria shook her head. "I've got paperwork to fill out for my new job and you, my dear, well, you've got school."

Turning around, Gloria walked back into Hannah's room and sat down on the bed next to her. She was always uneasy when starting a new school. Hannah, although she'd learned to get on with it, still didn't like it.

"You okay?" Gloria asked. "I mean, about going to another new school?"

"Yeah, I am. Just tired, I guess. One more day to myself to get organized and settled would have been nice, that's all," Hannah assured her. "It will be fine. Promise. And you do know I love you, right Mom?"

Gloria's eyes filled with tears. Tired and overwhelmed herself, Hannah's words and support were exactly what she needed.

"I love you too, girl! Come here!" Pulling her daughter into her arms, she hugged her as tightly as she could, and Hannah hugged her back. "It's different this time, I promise. This really is the last time we'll ever move. It's our last new beginning!"

"That's what you keep saying!" Hannah laughed. "But I'll do the awkward first day of mandatory meet and greet the new people." Groaning, Hannah flopped on her bed. "I do hate that part!"

"You want to know another great thing about this move and my new job?"

"Yeah, what's that?"

"Aunt Kathy got us a deal with the apartment, and between that and my promotion, I only have to work one job."

"You know I can always get a part-time job. I'm old enough now," Hannah offered. "Besides, it might be good for me to earn some spending money."

"Let me think about it, but it couldn't affect your grades." She winked at Hannah, pointed to the bed, and walked toward the door. "I don't know where the time has gone. It seems like yesterday you were just a little girl, and now you're talking about getting your first job."

Hannah shrugged her shoulders. "I do love you, Mom."

"And I love you too, Hannah. I don't deserve a great kid like you, but I sure do love you!"

Exhausted, Hannah fell asleep as soon as her head hit the pillow, without any dreams. Gloria kept tossing and turning. Being close to Hannah was the only thing that gave her comfort. Tiptoeing into Hannah's room with a blanket and pillow in hand, she lay down on the floor next to Hannah's bed. Hannah stirred but didn't wake up, and Gloria knew she'd be up and out of there before Hannah woke up. It worked; within minutes Gloria drifted off to sleep.

Chapter 13
Welcome

Don't be nervous
Just be you
You'll blend right in
Write, draw, sing, and dance
Never leave life to chance
~ Hannah Gunner ~

A blue pair of ripped skinny jeans, converse, paired with an oversized grey sweatshirt, and light makeup completed Hannah's look for her first day of school. Desperately wanting to blend in, she hadn't realized focusing on such drab colors had the opposite effect. It had a way of making her natural features stand out. A beautiful little girl, Hannah had turned into a stunning young teen. Dull colors accentuated her striking features, and people couldn't help but wonder why she'd chosen such drab colors in the first place. Her long wavy blond hair fell loosely around her shoulders, just as it did when she was a child. Filling her coffee cup, grabbing her backpack, and shoving a note from her mom into her pocket, she hesitantly walked out the door.

The high school, less than ten minutes away, was thankfully a straight shot. Take a right out of the complex; turn left on First, and you couldn't miss it.

Daniel Martin High School was the ugly grey building on the left. Hannah knew the drill. Go to the attendance office, introduce herself as the new transfer student, and wait until they had time to deal with her. Depending on the staff, she'd either receive a warm welcome or they'd make it clear to everyone standing in the office that she was a massive inconvenience that had to be dealt with anyway. *Let the games begin,* she thought, as she made her way down the sidewalk. Admittedly over the years, the warm and fuzzy vibe that she exuded toward others had worn off, which inadvertently caused any first impressions that she made to be questionable at best. She'd been called rude, distant, detached, and her favorite—a snob—over the years, none of which she felt described her at all. Tired of being prejudged, rejected, or disappointing the people she met, she'd learned to lay low, keep to herself, focus on what she did like about school, and remind herself they'd be moving again soon anyway... except for this time. Time would tell regarding that promise, she reminded herself. It dawned on her for the first time ever that it was possible she could be stuck with the same people until she graduated. If that were indeed the case, she promised herself to make an attempt to be friendly and at least try to socialize to the best of her ability. That was truly the best she could do.

Ear buds in, head down, Hannah walked down the corridor toward the admin office. It was often the same in most schools: find the main entrance, follow the glass trophy cases, and eventually you'd run into the administrative office. No need to ask for directions. And if she didn't end up running into the office, she'd be the one kid walking the hallway after the bell rang, and inevitably spotted and asked, "Where are you supposed to be?"

Daniel Martin, fortunately, was laid out like the typical high school and she found the hallway leading to the office as soon as she walked in. A lovely middle-aged woman standing behind a counter was directing kids and answering the phone as she scribbled out hall passes. She smiled at Hannah and mouthed, "I'll be right with you." Patiently, Hannah waited her turn and decided it wasn't going to be a bad day after all.

"Yes. What can I do for you?"

"Hi, I'm Hannah Gunner, a transfer student. I think you're expecting me. I'm here to pick up my schedule." She knew they were expecting her, but it didn't hurt to act as if she was unsure and needed a little help. It worked. The lady's eyes softened, and she smiled the sweetest, *oh, hang on a second and I'll help you* smile.

"Welcome, and if you give me a moment to clear out these kids, I'll be happy to pull that for you."

Hannah nodded. "Thank you."

Her schedule was going to be tough, but Hannah purposely took as many AP classes as they'd allow, helping to keep her busy. New town, she didn't know anyone, and it was something that assisted with her career plan and occupied her time. She was smart, but any distraction was vital, and studying helped do that. Hannah's one indulgence was art; it was her favorite class. Losing herself in art and words had filled her empty evenings and weekends for years. Her love of drawing had developed after she received a gift of

Derwent pencils and a sketchpad from her mom on her ninth birthday. She didn't know what kind of pencils they were, but Gloria had told her that they were special tools that artists used, and they'd allow her to sketch out her feelings instead of talking about them, if she'd like to do that, and it might make her feel better. Hannah would learn later that a child therapist had given her mom the advice after all of the issues with Hank, the moves, dealing with loss, anger, frustration, and anything else kids couldn't articulate. Admittedly, it had worked to some degree, and after that Hannah discovered her love of art and words. Journaling had also helped, and that's when Hannah fell in love with words, especially poetry, and jotted down random poems and short stories on a daily basis.

Physics, her first class, wasn't something Hannah particularly minded. She was pretty good at math and science and often finished her work in class. The room was loud, and no one seemed to care that a new girl had slinked into the back. Nothing stood out as alarming or concerning to Hannah. It was another day, in a new school, supposedly in a town that she'd already been a part of but couldn't seem to remember. She found an empty seat at the back of the room and sat down. Earphones in, music off, she listened to as many conversations around her as she could. A few comments were made about the new girl who was sitting in the back of the room, but nothing rude or out of the ordinary. A group of boys that had gathered around a nearby table was instructed to take their seats. The teacher finally spotted her and introduced himself, and then brief introductions to the class were made. Hannah's cheeks flushed, but she managed a slight smile and glanced around the room before lowering her eyes toward her desktop.

"Headphones off and phones put away, or they become mine until the end of the school year. Oh, and I don't care if your parents call me. School rules. Not mine!"

Mr. Lambert dove right into his lesson. He didn't bother checking to see if Hannah understood what they were working on or if she could keep up. Fortunately, she could. She'd been studying a chapter on kinetic physics at her last school. It was shocking she could keep up at all with as many moves as they'd made, but somehow she'd managed. As soon as the bell rang, everyone poured out of the room. Hannah checked her schedule, gathered her things, and made her way to her next class. The usual classroom introductions were made and pairings for a group project begun. Hannah didn't have a partner, but neither did a tall, slender girl sitting on the opposite side of the room.

"Lindsey, partner with the new girl, Hannah."

The tall kid didn't object, but stood up and made her way toward Hannah. *Plain but pretty is the best way to describe her*, thought Hannah, as she waited to introduce herself, but the tall girl beat her to it.

"Hey, Lindsey Rawling." She stuck out her hand and waited for Hannah to reciprocate.

Who shakes hands in high school? Hannah wondered as she awkwardly extended hers. *That's not embarrassing at all!*

"Hannah." She hesitated. "Hannah Gunner."

"Cool name. Where ya from?"

And that was that. Their friendship started right then and there with an awkward handshake and Lindsey making small talk and offering to show Hannah around. Hannah agreed, though it was too early to tell if Lindsey would get on her nerves. She did have a habit of flipping her auburn hair—a lot—but Hannah didn't care and couldn't help but notice that when Lindsey's hair was out of her face, her green eyes jumped out against her pale skin and reddish-brown hair. Cool feature! Her personality was kinda quirky, and she made Hannah laugh without realizing it. It seemed as if Hannah hadn't really had a good laugh in quite some time. Refreshing.

Lindsey was liked by the other students, and she took the time to introduce Hannah to someone new every chance she got. Hannah—an observer and a quiet teen by nature—took everything in and appreciated the time that Lindsey spent with her. Hannah found it amusing to listen to someone talk about her, in front of her. Funny!

"She's super sweet, a tad shy until you get to know her, but you'll like her!" That was how Lindsey described Hannah to her friends.

Hannah had never thought of herself as shy before; detached, maybe, but she guessed that could be perceived by others as shy. It was more of a self-preservation thing for her, a necessary action to protect her feelings. If she didn't make friends, she didn't have to lose them every time they uprooted and moved.

But moving wasn't going to be an issue anymore,

Gloria kept reminding her, *because this was their last move.* Hannah wasn't getting her hopes up; she'd believe it when it actually happened and her mom threw away all of their packing materials.

Hannah couldn't remember the names of all of the people Lindsey introduced her to, but one guy she'd crossed paths with stood out. Sandy brown hair, dark brown eyes, medium build, taller than her, hot, but he had the weirdest name. As soon as Lindsey introduced them to each other, Hannah insulted him, wishing as soon as the words tumbled out of her mouth she'd kept her trap shut!

"That's a weird name." Hannah grasped for words. "I meant strange name; no, I didn't mean that either. Unusual. That's an unusual name!"

Lindsey started giggling, grabbed Hannah's arm, and pulled her toward a group of girls filing into the art room.

"Damn, brutal!"

"Stupid, you mean," Hannah laughed. "What possessed me to be so freaking rude?!"

"His hotness!" Planting herself down on a bench seat that stretched down the center of the room, Lindsey patted a spot next to her for Hannah. "Sit here; no assigned seating."

The room filled up quickly as students piled in and found spots on the bench seats around the two tables that were centered in the middle of the art room. To Hannah's horror, the hot kid walked in and nodded his head and smiled at Lindsey. She grinned, poked Hannah, and whispered. "Oh, yeah, I forgot to mention he's in our art class."

Hannah noticed that as soon as he walked up, people made room for him around the table. He chose a spot two seats down from where they were sitting. Leaning forward in front of the other students, Cash waved his hand to get Hannah's attention. He didn't need to do that; he already had it.

"Grayson. Grayson Parks."

"What?" Hannah asked nervously.

"My name, it's Grayson Parks, but my friends call me Cash. I'll tell you all about it sometime if we're ever friends, or Lindsey can fill you in." He grinned. "We're friends."

Cheeks flushed, Hannah shook her head and raised her hands. "That was rude. It's not weird. It's different, and being a nickname, it makes perfect sense. Sorry about that." Flipping her hair out of her face, struggling for anything else she could possibly say in such an awkward moment, Hannah fidgeted in her seat. "Again, no harm meant, and I'm betting Lindsey will fill me in."

Cash smirked. "Just giving you a hard time."

Moving seats with his friends, he sat next to Lindsey. "So, new girl, what's your name?"

"Hannah. Hannah Gunner."

"Cool name. The Gunner part; Hannah's not bad either." Glancing at the front of the room, making eye contact with the art teacher, he smiled and dipped his eyes as if he were making adjustments to a sketch he'd been working on already.

The art teacher spotted Hannah and darted toward her to introduce herself. Making an announcement from

123

where she stood, she also introduced Hannah to the class. Hannah couldn't wait for her day and all of the official introductions of the day to be over. The class assignment was given, and the class was told to work in silence. Grayson's explanation was going to have to wait. As soon as the bell rang, everyone, including Grayson, flocked out of the room.

Lindsey waited for Hannah to gather her things. Her first day was over, and it hadn't been that bad. Lindsey had made it easy. Lindsey pulled out her phone and took a picture of them both. "Smile!" She added it to her story. The caption read *My New Best Friend!*

"How *did* he get that name?" Hannah asked. "Go ahead and tell me or it will drive me crazy."

"Something about if his friends needed money because their lunch accounts were low or if they wanted something they weren't supposed to have, you know, like ice cream, he always gave them the extra cash. He was the kid who always had money on him. It became a thing, as in, 'ask Grayson, he's always got cash.'" She took another pic. "That turned into just 'ask Cash.'"

"Did he ever say no or did he always just lend it to them?"

Lindsey looked puzzled for a second. "I've never been asked that question before, but I guess he always did. I can't remember anyone ever saying that he didn't."

"Um," Hannah responded. "Generous kid."

Lindsey's fingers tapped away furiously on her phone as she added Hannah to all of her social media accounts and Hannah did the same.

"So where do you live?" Lindsey asked.

"About ten minutes from here."

"You want a ride home?"

"Sure. If you don't mind."

"I don't mind at all. I'm glad you moved here, Hannah!" Lindsey hesitated. "How do you feel about people who smoke?"

Hannah burst out laughing. "Seriously! It doesn't bother me a bit, although I did switch from cigs to vapes."

Lindsey nodded. "Same. Vape mostly, every now and then will go back to old habits and buy a pack. But my parents, for obvious reasons, hate both. Or I should say my mom hates both. My parents are divorced, and I quit doing the every-other-weekend thing with my dad years ago. I really only see him on holidays and special occasions. What about you?"

"Me?"

"Yeah. Your parents still together or are you part of the group?" Lindsey pointed to her car. "And there's my car."

"Deceased."

"Oh my God, I'm so sorry!"

"Nah, don't be. I was little, and I don't really remember that much about him anymore. He was gone a lot. Honestly, what I remember more than anything is a game that we used to play, a pirate game, based on a book that he used to read to me. I think the book was his favorite because his dad used to read it to him, and he wanted me to love it like he did. It became my favorite when he read it to me." Hannah laughed and climbed into the car. "Because he never read it. He always played it, turning it into a game, a pirate game." Hannah thought about what she was saying for a second. "I think over the years I hung onto that game, maybe remembered it as better than it really was, to keep his memory close to me. I don't know. But I do know that game helped me sleep when I couldn't, entertained my mind when I had no friends in new schools, especially when I was little, and made me feel like he was still around. The problem was that I felt closer to the Captain than to him."

"Well, that game must have been fun to have made such a lasting impression for all these years."

Lindsey turned the key to her gently used golden Toyota Corolla, opened up the sunroof, found her favorite playlist on her phone, and plugged in the aux. Almost at the same time, they inhaled, and the sweet smell of vanilla and cherry filled the car from their JUULs.

"Here's to the Captain. Captain Fin!" Hannah grinned as she put her tiny JUUL up to her mouth again. "Not sure he'd approve of this, but..." Laughter filled the car.

"Your dad is Captain Fin?"

Hannah laughed. "Was, yes. Now, let's see if the tyrant's home. She's gonna love you!"

Chapter 14
Settling In

Feeling sad
But I don't know why
Fake a smile
So I don't cry
There's nothing wrong
So that makes it worse!
Pick myself up and pretend to rehearse
~ Hannah Gunner ~

Hannah spent three weeks putting in job applications anywhere and everywhere she could think of that hired teens with no experience. Lindsey graciously ran her around so they could hang out while she looked. That evening a call came in for an interview, and even though Hannah wasn't thrilled about the actual job, she agreed to the meeting.

"I don't like this, Hannah," said Gloria. "A convenience store, they're dangerous. I don't want you doing it."

"I don't even have the job yet," Hannah objected. "Let me just see what they have to say. Plus, it's right down the road. I could walk, so I don't have to worry about getting a car anytime soon, and I may just work on the weekends. I don't know until I go."

Gloria shook her head. "I just don't like it. Can't you

please keep looking? The mall, maybe?"

"Not unless you want to support my shopping and spending habits." Hannah poured two iced teas. "Most parents are thrilled when their kids get a job. You're giving me a hard time. What's with that?"

Gloria stared at the young lady who stood before her, no longer her little girl. Where had the time gone? Hannah had gone from being the cheeky pirate, continually trying to insult her, to interviewing for her first job. Her mind wandered to a place it hadn't gone in a long time. *What would Hank think?* Hannah noticed the distress written on her mom's face in the form of scrunched-up lines across her forehead.

"It's just an interview for a job that I haven't been offered yet or accepted." Walking behind her mom, wrapping her arms around her neck, she kissed her cheek. "If it means that much to you, I'll call and cancel."

The touch of Hannah's warm lips still lingering on her cheek brought Gloria back to reality. She couldn't protect her forever, and it was, after all, just an interview. About to tell herself not to listen to her fears, Hannah beat her to it.

"Don't be so worried, Mom; it's just an interview. I thought you'd be proud of me."

"Hannah Gunner, not a day goes by that I'm not proud of you. I just worry, that's all. Let me know how it goes."

The QuickMart was exactly seven-and-a-half minutes away from the house on foot. They'd stopped and shopped there for gas and miscellaneous items dozens of times since they'd moved back. It was well lit at night, and Hannah noticed security cameras installed everywhere. Working too many hours, or late for that matter, during the week wouldn't be an option because she was a minor, and Hannah had already decided that she didn't want to give up both her Friday and Saturday nights and felt the manager wouldn't hire her based on that alone. Either way, she was grateful for the interview and thought she'd use it for practice, get some experience for the next one.

"Is Ed Greene available, please?" Hannah asked the lanky guy standing behind the counter. She was nervous, but he either couldn't tell or couldn't care less.

Nodding, he told her that he'd be back in a second and walked through a door behind him. He reappeared, pointed to where he had just come from, and instructed her to go on back.

"Connor, by the way."

"Hannah. Nice to meet you."

The office was small and crowded with furniture that was too big for the room. Calendars, posters, and photos were pinned to the walls, and the desk was overflowing with paperwork. Hannah couldn't help but notice a half-filled coffee cup sitting on a desk that looked as if it had seen better days. Ed, the manager, was a large man with a gut that hung over his pants. His hair was greasy and thinning, his glasses kept slipping off his nose, and he acted as if he'd been through this interview process one time too many. Hannah stood awkwardly in front of him.

"Hello. I'm Hannah Gunner."

He nodded and pointed to a chair in front of his desk. Bashfully, Hannah squeezed between the desk and the chair and sat down.

"Ed Greene. Manager. Nice to meet you."

He wasted no time firing questions at her. She felt like she was interviewing for a high-paying, important position, not for a part-time cashier clerk at a convenience store. Her favorite question was one she was sure every employer must be required to ask.

"Why do you want to work at QuickMart?"

I don't. I need a job, thought Hannah. "Several reasons. It's close to home, and I don't have a car, so walking most days is mandatory. And I'm looking for a job that will accommodate my school schedule. I'm wondering, actually, if this one would, but if that's not possible, I totally understand."

"Typically we don't allow employees, especially new employees, to tell us what they need in regards to scheduling, but I'll make an exception since the hours that we're offering are minimal. Fifteen to twenty hours a week; Connor needs a little help."

He took a sip of the nasty cold coffee on his desk. His face, though he tried to hide it, reflected the same thing Hannah had felt: it had seen better days.

"What hours are you looking for and why?"

Hannah gave him a reasonable explanation. He nodded, wrote down her request, and told her he'd be in touch.

She took her time walking home and enjoyed a new flavor she'd bought for her vape. She promised herself each time she exhaled that she would try to quit soon. As soon as she walked in the door, she hollered out to her mom, force of habit. The apartment was silent, and it was then that she remembered Gloria had worked the night shift the night before and was probably sleeping. Sure enough, Gloria was now stirring in the chair, the same place Hannah had left her a couple hours ago. Hannah's phone vibrated in her pocket. Darting into her bedroom, she answered the phone.

"Hello."

"Hannah?"

"Yes."

"This is Ed Greene, manager down at the QuickMart. I'm calling because I'd like to offer you the part-time cashier's position. However, it does come with one provision."

Hannah grinned from ear to ear. "Wow! Thanks! Yes. May I ask what is the provision?"

"Certainly. Though I will do my best to accommodate your request regarding the schedule, alternating every other Friday and Saturday night, starting at 5 p.m. and getting off at 10:00 or 11:00 depending on how busy we are, and working Tuesday and Thursday the same hours, from 5:00 to 10:00 p.m. There will be times you may have to work out the schedule with Connor, whom you met today, and our other part-timer, Lacey. It's not often, but sometimes there are conflicts if they have something to do and now we're adding a third person. It's usually resolved if you switch schedules among yourselves if need be." He took a deep breath and continued. "It doesn't happen very often, but sometimes I make the schedule and people do have personal activities, and since we're a small outfit, we just have to learn to work together." Pause. "Is this acceptable to you, and if so, do you want the job?"

Before she could think about it, she answered. "Yes, it is, and thank you so much, Mr. Greene. It's perfect!"

"Great. Call me Ed. Everyone calls me Ed. How about you start next Tuesday. Come in for training and fill out the necessary paperwork?"

"Absolutely. I'll be there!"

"Great. I'll put you on the schedule. You'll have to come in early that day because of the paperwork and all, so come in at 4:30."

"Perfect. And thank you again!"

Excited, Hannah took a photo and posted it on her story right away. Caption: Guess who got the job?!?! Right after that, her fingers tapped away on her phone as she texted Lindsey to make plans to celebrate.

Chapter 15
Gloria

Sunshine
Crisp cool air
Light airy feeling
Lost the despair
But for how long?
~ Hannah Gunner ~

While standing at the sink washing dishes, Gloria suddenly became lightheaded. She stopped what she was doing and held onto the countertop to steady herself; Hannah rushed toward her.

"Are you okay?"

Gloria nodded, but Hannah noticed her mom was trembling. Being a nurse, Gloria calmed her daughter down.

"I'm fine, really. My blood sugar must be low. I haven't eaten yet, since I picked up an extra shift late last night, and I've just walked in. I thought I'd do these dishes before I ate and laid down." She smiled. "Guess that was a mistake. I should've grabbed a bite to eat first." Slowly sitting down, she grabbed Hannah's hand. "Would you pour me a glass of orange juice, please? That'll fix me right up."

"I was going to do those dishes, you know."

Hannah set the orange juice down on the table in front of her. "Guess what?"

"Whaaaat?" Gloria answered, dragging out her response as if she were scared to find out.

"I got the job down at the QuickMart. But don't worry, it's going to be perfect!"

"Reaallly. How so?"

"The hours are insanely ideal, I can walk, plus the people I met seem really nice." Hannah handed her mom a peeled banana. "Eat this. Honestly, it's a perfect part-time job."

"Well, I'm proud of you and happy for you. But I do want you to be careful!" Gloria took a bite of the banana. "Call your Aunt Kathy and tell her; she'll be thrilled for you!"

"Will do! Well, if you're sure you're okay?" Hannah smirked. "I guess I'll go ahead and go to Lindsey's."

Gloria nodded. "Aunt Kathy's on her way around; get out of here, and tell Lindsey hello for me."

As soon as Hannah turned the corner, she pulled out her little pink vape. So tiny you could hardly tell she had it in her hand. The rechargeable device with the sweet taste of vanilla and cherry was her answer to not smoking Marlboro Lights. Pushing out her mom's warnings of the devices damaging her lungs, she inhaled, exhaled, and once again lied to herself. *I'm going to quit any minute; I am, but not yet.* Knowing her mom despised the fact that she smoked at all weighed on her. She took one more hit and shoved the vape back down into her jeans pocket and pretended she hadn't done anything wrong.

As she walked down the street, her mind drifted to, of all things, the recurring dreams that she used to have as a child. Searching for treasure with the Captain on a beach with the whitest sand while a great big flagship bobbed up and down in the waves nearby. A smile crossed her face as she tried to force some of her memories of the dream to come back. Reminiscing for a few minutes, Hannah allowed herself to imagine the warm sand sifting between her toes, the imaginary smell of the sea air, which she remembered the Captain always loved, and the cackling sound of the seagulls that sat upon the deck of the make-believe ship that was floating offshore. The Captain. Damn, maybe she missed him, the man, more than she thought she did! Pushing him out of her mind, she texted Lindsey.

Hannah: Be there in a few.

Lindsey: Great. Meet ya outside.

Lindsey had Silver, *her gently used gold Corolla*, started, passenger door open, waiting for Hannah to arrive. Waving to each other as if they hadn't seen one another in a long time, the two behaved like little kids instead of teens.

"Where we going?" Hannah asked.

"I'm hungry. You?"

"Yep. Always!"

"Go eat?" Lindsey suggested.

"Sounds good!"

Music turned up, and the sunroof opened, the girls took off. Hannah realized as they drove through the drive-thru that she finally felt content. Settled. Lindsey was rambling on and on about a guy in chemistry she thought was hot, and a pair of shoes that she just *had* to have, and Hannah felt for the first time in her life, she had a real best friend. They had clicked right away, and been inseparable ever since they'd been forced together on a project.

"Buy the damn shoes already! If you don't, I'm going to buy them for you with my first paycheck just to shut you up!"

Laughing, Lindsey agreed. "You're right. I should bite the bullet. I'm not going to want the knock-offs because they suck!"

They ate in the car, bantered with the boys who pulled up next to them, laughed, talked girl talk, shared secrets, drove around, shopped, and gossiped all day long. Hannah was happy! Grateful this was their last move and counting on her mom meaning it.

"To be honest, though, I'm glad your mom moved you back."

"My turn. To be honest, though, you are truly my best friend. In fact, I really think you're my first real best friend."

"Why, thank you. To be honest, I think I'm honored to hold that position in your life!'

Hannah was dying. "Damn, that's a lot of honesty." In between giggles, she asked, "You wanna stay over tonight?"

"Yeah. Let me text my mom."

Lindsey's mom: Yes. It's fine. Text when you're in for the night.

Lindsey: K.

Gloria sipped a mimosa while she waited for her sister to arrive. Kathy let herself in, hollering Gloria's name as she walked into the apartment.

"That looks good!"

"Care to join me?"

"Absolutely!"

Kathy poured herself a mimosa. "Didn't think I'd like mimosas this late in the day, but it's not bad." She took a sip and stared at her sister.

"You look terrible," Kathy said.

"Thanks, sis. Nice to see you too!"

Refilling Gloria's glass with champagne and orange juice, she sat down beside her sister on the couch and made herself comfortable.

"Well."

"Well, what?" Gloria played dumb.

"Don't do that; did you get your results back?"

Gloria's eyes were empty. She looked out the window and then fixated on her beautiful little First Matey, a photo of Hannah in a pirate costume for Halloween. She must have been about five years old when the picture was taken. Full of fire, like her dad, ornery, she could tell in the picture that Hannah was holding her dad's hand, but Gloria had long since folded the Captain, Hank, out of that particular photo.

"It's as we expected, Kathy, not good."

Kathy's hands were shaking, but Gloria looked stoic.

"What can we do?"

"We're already doing it," Gloria responded. "We'll have to wait and see if anything we're doing helps, but it's not likely." She took a sip of her champagne. "You know I knew that the odds weren't good when we moved back here, but I'd hoped that I was wrong."

Kathy walked into the kitchen to make some tea. Tears flooded her eyes even though she pretended that they hadn't. Clattering around the kitchen, buying herself time, Kathy finally let out a sob that she could no longer contain. Gloria appeared at her side and reached out, held her in her arms, and whispered in her ear.

"It's going to be fine. You're going to be fine. But you have to promise me one thing."

Kathy nodded. "You don't even have to ask. Anything. You know that. Anything. Name it."

"I'm begging you, Kathy. Please, please, please, I'm begging you, please watch over my daughter." Looking her square in the eye. "Protect and take care of Hannah."

Kathy wiped her tears with her sleeve and nodded. Sniffing, she tried to catch her breath. She could barely breathe, let alone get the words out to ask her sister the next question.

"Does she know?"

Gloria shook her head. "No. No, she doesn't. I wanted to be sure, and now I am. I wanted Hannah to have some normalcy for a minute."

Gloria walked back into the living room, and Kathy followed her. Flopping onto the couch, she pointed to a treatment information folder that she'd been reading. It was full of everything they needed to know, treatment-wise and options. She could continue to work as long as she felt up to it, though for the first few months of treatment it was possible she might not feel well enough. She was going to try to work as long as she could, and thankfully the hospital had agreed to work with her.

"I have some savings, and the hospital will work around my treatments. They said I may be able to work through them, on the rare occasion some people can, but if I'm at risk for infection, I'll wait for a bit."

Grabbing Kathy's hand in hers, she opened her mouth to speak, closed it again, thought about her choice of words and then finally spoke.

"If I'm given a little while longer, just until Hannah graduates, honestly that's all I want, that alone would be such a gift!" Looking down at the brochure so she wouldn't lose it, she added, "To see my little girl, the beautiful young lady that she has become, walk across that stage after all we've endured, would be my dream come true. I can't imagine a greater gift than to witness her starting her life as a young lady, ready to conquer the world, before I have to leave."

"If you don't tell Hannah and she finds out, she's going to be furious with you."

Gloria nodded. "I know." Grabbing her sister's hands in hers and squeezing them, she added, "but if I tell her, she'll stop doing the things she needs to do to prepare for her senior year and make it to graduation. Not to mention, Hannah should enjoy her senior year." Gloria let go of her sister's hands, stood up, and walked over to look out the window. "I don't want her to stop living because of me. I want her to enjoy every second of her junior and senior year. It's only fair. It's the right thing for her to do. Not to sit and worry about me."

Kathy knew that Hannah would be furious if she found out that they had kept such news from her, but she wasn't about to defy her sister, especially at a time like this.

That kid still had enough of Hank Gunner in her to be stubborn and to spit poison if she felt hurt. Gloria knew that Hannah didn't mean the cruel words that she was capable of spewing when she was angry, but she might not have enough time for Hannah to cool off when that day came.

"Whatever you want, sis, I'll do it. Just tell me what you need, and we'll get it done."

Gloria wrapped her arms around her stomach; queasy from the pre-meds for the treatment she had been taking. Chemo had not yet started, but they had implanted a port. Working at the hospital, she had a clear understanding of what to expect and how to handle it. She considered herself lucky in that regard. Her doctors agreed to implant the port while she was at work, hiding it from Hannah, and to wait until she could make all of the necessary arrangements regarding her schedule before starting treatment. If all went well and as she hoped, she could return to a light shift while on chemo. If too ill or at risk for infection, she could not. Her treatments would take place on her days off, and her schedule had been altered to accommodate the recovery period needed between treatments. The hospital had agreed to play it by ear, but Gloria was more concerned about keeping everything from Hannah. A little teamwork, a compassionate boss, and Gloria was going to do her best to keep her condition from Hannah for as long as she possibly could. Keeping secrets, that task, was becoming a beast of its own!

Chapter 16
Cash

Intrigued
Yes, he has my attention!
~ Hannah Gunner ~

As soon as the black Jeep Wrangler pulled up to the pump, Connor stopped what he was doing and nudged Hannah.

"Look at that!"

Hannah looked up from the magazine she'd lifted off the rack and stared across the parking lot to pump number seven.

"Looks like a Jeep," she said playfully.

"Trust me, they don't all look like that."

Connor started going on and on about the silver trim, killer wheels with the slight lift, the badass sound system, and how he'd give anything to drive a Jeep like that! Hannah, half-listening, hadn't paid much attention to the Jeep, but she sure had noticed the kid driving it. Standing up straight, ditching the magazine, and jumping behind Connor, Hannah watched him approach the store. She'd had a class with him and even had a brief conversation with him once, but hadn't talked to him since. She was certain he wouldn't even remember meeting her at all.

"Man, nice Jeep," Connor said as soon as the kid walked up to the counter to pay.

"Thanks." Cash smiled and threw down two twenties. "I'd wished I could say I bought it myself, sounds better than it was a gift, but I'd be lying. It was a gift."

"Dude, *hell of a gift!*"

"Right!"

Taking Hannah off guard, the kid turned his attention to her, tipping his head slightly so he could see her around her coworker as he spoke. "I didn't know you worked here."

Embarrassed, Hannah forced a smile and stepped out from behind Conner. "I just started."

"Cool! Now I know where to find ya." He turned and walked toward the door. "Later."

"Bye," Hannah replied, grabbing her phone so she could text Lindsey.

Connor never once took his eyes off the black and silver Jeep, while Hannah watched *him* walk out, jump up into his vehicle, and leave the lot. He'd looked taller than Hannah had remembered from their first introduction; in class, he was always sitting down, and cut out early before she had a chance to even get near him. His dark eyes were intoxicating, especially combined with his dirty blond, messy but cute hair. His clothes of choice weren't anything out of the ordinary: jeans, Vans, and a heavy plaid shirt over a black T-shirt. As soon as she couldn't see his Jeep anymore, her fingers started tapping away on her phone.

Hannah: Damn!!!! Cash came in, looked freaking hot, and he even remembered me!

Lindsey: He is hot! You should so go for him. He must like you, to remember you.

Hannah: You think? Likes me, I mean. Go for him? LOL... What does that even mean?

Lindsey: You're hopeless; never mind. And yes, why else would he remember you? He's got girls chasing him all the time.

Hannah: Thanks! Not sure I need someone like that... know what I mean?

Lindsey: They chase him; he doesn't chase them. He and his girlfriend broke up. Not too long ago, but he is available. ☺

Hannah interested Cash, and girls rarely caught his attention in that way. He'd been watching her since she'd arrived at school, and had asked around about her. Now he knew where she worked. Commanding Siri to call Donavan, he waited for his friend to pick up.

"Hey, what's going on?"

"Not much."

"What do you know about the new girl, the one who hangs with Lindsey?"

"She's hot, that's about it. Why?"

"Just ran into her; she works at the QuickMart."

"Oh, really! Guess I know where I'll be buying gas from now on!"

They both laughed—boys, amused by the simplest things at times.

"She's kinda hot, *no*?" Cash asked, as if double-checking his taste in girls.

"Is that a real question? She's really hot. Why, she off limits now?"

Cash started laughing. "I don't know yet. I'll let you know." They laughed again. "But I think she's hot and there's something about her, I don't know what, but I think I'd like to hang out with her."

"Well, shit! You pulled the *there's something about her* card and not the *I'd like to hook up with her...* they're different."

"What?! What the hell's that supposed to mean?" Cash grinned. "Nah, man, I just, I dunno, she seems different, that's all." He turned down his music. "I guess because she's just moved or something. She's probably really just like everyone else."

Donavan didn't care. He had a girl and was quite amused that Cash hadn't started the conversation with *I'd like to hook up with her.* "Guess it's a good thing I've got a girlfriend. She'd never go for me over you. Go for it!"

Laughter ended the conversation. Cash did like Hannah, but did she like him? He needed an excuse to see her. He started to text his friends to find out what was going on that night. Jackson texted him back almost immediately: Party tonight, my house, parents gone.

Cash: Bringing a couple friends.

Jackson: Cool. Anyone I know? BTW, my brother's supposed to be housesitting and watching me. LOL. He's going out. Standard rule: no damage.

Cash: LOL. Danny. Love that dude! See ya later, and it's a maybe on you knowing them.

Lindsey had known Cash since grade school,

acquaintances, but not exactly from the same crowd. He didn't know her well enough to invite her to a party, but he knew someone who did. Kennedy Hanson. Lindsey and Kennedy used to be best friends, but Kennedy drifted once she started dating Adam Davidson, and now Lindsey and Hannah seemed to be close. He'd flirted on and off with Kennedy for years, and she still liked him. It had become a game that they both knew would never end, but at the same time, it would likely never go anywhere. Cash, unfortunately, just didn't see Kennedy like that—especially after she dated Jackson, and that pissed him off! Little sneaky, but he didn't care; Cash had a plan. He'd get Jackson to ask Kennedy if she and Adam wanted to go to his party, and all she had to do was invite Lindsey. Lindsey inevitably would drag along a friend, and that friend would be the Hannah girl. Cash made the call to Jackson.

"Got a favor, and I'll owe you big time." Explaining his plight, Jackson resisted for a second, citing that his current girlfriend would kill him.

"Blame me. Tell her why. I don't care."

"I don't know. Kennedy's crazy!"

"But she's with Adam now, and it might be funny to watch those two together, but seriously, it's either that or call Lindsey direct." Cash threw in the friend card. "Man, I'd do it for you if the roles were reversed. You don't have to have anything to do with her, just ask her to invite Lindsey for Zack, don't say me; I sure don't want that to get around the Hannah girl."

"Cash, I would! But she is CRAZY. She will honestly think I really want to see her. You don't get it. She'll think I want to get her back, break her and Adam up. She thinks that crazy shit! Then, if I ask her to bring friends, she'll go nuts, jealous shit, 'cause she's crazy. I'm telling you. C-R-A-Z-Y!"

Cash started laughing. "I get it! No problem. But you're not off the hook. Tell her the damn truth. Tell her I want to see the Hannah girl, and she'll only come with Lindsey. Damn, that is the actual truth!"

"I've got to admit I'll to do it just to see you make a fool out of yourself. I've never seen you act like this... *you're* acting crazy! Have you ever spoken to this girl?"

"A couple times, but just small talk. I'd just like to get to know her."

"Damn. This isn't like you, but you've got to call Joslyn and tell her why I'm inviting this crazy girl to my party, so I'm not in trouble over you!"

Cash responded immediately. "Done!"

Satisfied they would be there that night, and picturing Hannah's face, Cash was excitedly nervous about seeing her that evening. It was her eyes. They were a beautiful shade, though maybe not even a perfect shade of blue, yes, but they seemed so eerily distant, detached somehow, and that made her attractive and interesting to him. He couldn't quite put his finger on it, but the curiosity it stirred within him was a feeling he hadn't experienced before. For some reason, the way she broke one stick of gum in half before shoving it in her mouth, and flipped her hair out of her face with her pen when she thought no one was looking was cute.

Twenty minutes later, Cash received a text from Jackson. As soon he read it, he smiled.

Jackson: She's coming, but if I get stuck with Kennedy you're DEAD!!!!!!!!!!!!!!!!

Cash: I owe ya!

Jackson: YES, yes, you do!

Lindsey showed up at 8:30 to pick up Hannah for the party. Gloria, feeling ill, was relieved for the first time ever that her daughter wasn't coming home that night.

"Call me when you get back to Lindsey's from the party." She pulled the blanket over her. "Where did you say it was?"

"We're going over to one of my friend's, Kennedy's. Hannah has met her before, *and then* we're going over to her friend's house for a small get together. His name is Jackson, and his older brother will be there as well, housesitting, while his parents had to do something."

Lindsey rushed the last part of the sentence, but Gloria quizzed them a tad more anyway. Once she was satisfied, she gave them the usual rundown. No drinking. No smoking. No drugs, and NOOOOO sex!

"OMG, Mom! I can't believe you just said that!" Hannah screeched.

"Be in by midnight," was her last demand. "Text me or call, please."

"Got it!" The girls said in unison, laughed out loud, and headed out the door.

Hannah's long, dark blond hair hung down her back in gentle waves. Her makeup was on point and her attire included jeans, a big cream sweater, and brown boots, basically an understated casual cute look. It was a perfect look for a party at the house of a person's she barely knew. Spritzing her favorite perfume on her neck and wrists, she glanced in the visor mirror one last time.

"How do I look?" Hannah asked.

"Like you always do. Amazing!"

"Me?"

"Beautiful as usual. Let's grab Kennedy. Do we want to drive with her or follow?"

"Honestly, your call, you're driving and Silver is alllll yours."

"Let's follow, then if the party's lame, we can leave." Hannah agreed. "Great idea!"

They followed Kennedy to Jackson's house. He lived out in a nice neighborhood, and by the time they'd arrived, the party was well underway. Hannah spotted Cash's Jeep. It was parked right in front of the mailbox.

"Oh my God!"

"What's wrong?" Lindsey asked.

"Nothing's wrong. Look." Hannah pointed to Cash's Jeep. "He's here. Cash. Cash is at this party."

Lindsey grinned from ear to ear. "Well, that's not a bad thing; maybe you'll get a chance to get to know him."

"Yeah. Maybe."

Hannah didn't see him immediately, though her eyes scanned the room that they stood in. Someone walked over and she wondered if he was the host, Jackson, but he introduced himself by another name.

"Hey, welcome. I'm Josh. There are snacks and drinks in the kitchen, help yourselves, standard rules, no damage, and most people are hanging out in the game room." He turned to walk away, then turned back around and added a semi-disclaimer. "Oh, hey, by the way, just so you know, you don't have to participate in the drinking, it's totally by choice. Trust me, no one here cares either way; there's no such thing as peer pressure at any of our parties!! We don't care what you choose, if you do or if you don't, it's one hundred percent up to you. And of course, it goes without saying, everyone these days knows not to drink and drive. Catch a ride, or crash on a piece of carpet."

"Thanks, and nice to meet you. I'm Lindsey, and this is Hannah."

Lindsey pulled Hannah into the kitchen, where the usual stash could be found. Beer in the fridge supplied by Jackson's older brother, a variety of liquor, no doubt stolen from parents' liquor stashes, sodas, and the usual snack foods including a variety of chips, pizza, crackers, cookies, and random packets of things, some opened and some still in plastic shopping bags.

"Do you want a beer?" Lindsey asked.

Hannah shook her head. "I can't stand the taste. But I'll take a tiny bit of that," she pointed to the vodka, "mixed with Sprite."

Lindsey started to pour the vodka. Hannah stopped her. "Just a tiny bit. I'm not a big drinker. It's more for show." Both girls laughed.

"I get it. Wish I didn't like beer." Lindsey pulled out her vape. "Do you think anyone will mind?"

Looking around, Hannah spotted others vaping in the house. "Well they are..."

"True. I think we're good. Let's scope out the house."

Cash was in the game room. It was huge! Ideal for any party, complete with its own bar, card table, pool table, multiple gaming consoles, a big-screen TV, even an old PacMan ghost machine, and a dartboard on the wall! Hannah had never seen such a room inside a private house. She spotted Cash, but he hadn't seen her yet. Poking Lindsey, she pointed to him. They hid behind several people and watched him unnoticed for a while.

He was hot, for sure! Surprisingly, he didn't act cocky like some of the guys Hannah had met over the years. Lindsey had given her some additional information about the infamous Cash. Grayson Parks, his given name, was the shortstop for the varsity baseball team. He was a good ball player, making varsity his freshman year, and had been offered a full ride to multiple universities, including out of state schools as far away as Texas. He was often surrounded by his friends, girls and boys, but wasn't loud, obnoxious, or conceited, considering how popular he was.

"Oh, and remember he and his girlfriend did just break up."

"Not sure I want any baggage issues," Hannah responded to her last statement.

"True. But I don't think so. I heard it was mutual. The relationship had kinda run its course."

Hannah raised her plastic Solo cup, and Lindsey raised her beer can.

"Cheers to that!" Hannah giggled.

"What would you do if he asked you out?" Lindsey whispered as they continued to watch his interactions with the other people in the room.

Hannah grinned. "I don't know. It's too soon. I don't even know him."

"Well, I could be wrong, but I'm sensing this whole

thing was a set-up."

"What?"

"This. The invite to this here party has got set-up written all over it!"

"What are you talking about?" Hannah laughed. "You're crazy!"

"Seriously, think about it!" Lindsey took one last drink of her beer before setting it down on the bar countertop. "I don't hang out with her anymore, Kennedy, we don't even really speak, not to mention why would Jackson ask her here? He has a girlfriend!" She laughed. "I'm betting this has something to do with you!"

Hannah giggled. "Girl, you've lost your mind. I don't know why all that went down! But I am glad we're here." She took a sip of her drink. "Damn, look at that boy!"

"Speak of the devil," Lindsey whispered. "Here comes Kennedy."

Kennedy rolled her eyes. "C'mon you two; let's get on with it."

"Get on with what?" Lindsey asked.

"Introductions."

"Told ya!" Lindsey whispered.

Kennedy marched right over to Jackson's group of friends, Cash included. In the most monotone voice, she did her duty.

"Hey, this is Hannah and Lindsey. This is them," she said and spun on her heels and walked toward Adam, standing awkwardly by himself in the far corner.

"See what I mean. Freaking CRAZY!" Jackson laughed. "Nice to meet you. Have you met this loser?" Jackson punched Cash in the arm.

"Yes, she has, sort of. We have a class together."

Trying to look confident and at ease, Hannah's cheeks flushed bright red instead. Lindsey smiled and said their hellos on behalf of them both.

Smiling, Cash complimented Hannah. "You look nice, by the way,"

"Thanks," she replied.

"What's your poison?"

"What?" Hannah laughed. "Who says that?"

Cash handed her a beer. "Absolutely nobody! It's an ice breaker; did it work?"

"I guess," Hannah answered. "It made me laugh."

"Do you drink beer?"

"I do. Thank you." Hannah reached for the beer he handed her; talk about caving into absolutely zero peer pressure... *what was that all about?* Stupidity at its finest, but she didn't even care! Happy to be engaged in conversation with him, she hadn't a clue that Lindsey had slipped away to give them space to talk semi-privately in a crowded room. *My gift, and thank you!* Lindsey had thought.

Hannah sipped the beer while Cash proudly introduced her to his friends, and she couldn't help but notice he never once asked her to hurry up and drink the beer she held in her hands, nor offered her a second one. In fact, she held onto the same one practically all night. That was something Hannah noticed and appreciated— no pressure to keep up with his drinking. Lindsey appeared at her side from time to time, but she was laughing and playing games with Donavan, Jackson, Kennedy, Adam, Rachel, and several others. Pleased

Lindsey was having fun, just like her, Hannah didn't feel guilty for spending time with Cash.

"I don't want to gross you out or anything, but if you're going to get to know me, you've got to take the good with the bad."

"Oh, yeah?" Cash looked at her, surprised. "What's the bad?"

"I've got to step outside for a smoke, well, a quick cherry-vanilla, actually, vape. Sorry."

"Ya know they've proven that's just as bad as for your lungs, right?"

Hannah laughed and shrugged her shoulders. "You sound like my mom, she's a nurse, and I know. I plan on quitting, but not today." She pulled her tiny device out of her pocket. "Now, you coming or staying? Makes no difference to me."

Her confidence surprised and impressed him; laughing, he grabbed her hand and pulled her toward the back door. The air was chilly, but the outdoor fireplace was lit, which helped take off the edge as several teens gathered around it chatting, laughing and smoking as well. Cash introduced Hannah, and it was as if she'd always fit in.

Shivering, Cash put his arms around her shoulder and pulled her closer to him. Hannah didn't mind, and her smile assured him everything was okay. Conversation and laughter around the fireplace was pleasant and light, and Hannah found out that most of the kids went to her school. Turning to Cash, Hannah began to quiz him.

"So where do you live?"

"Actually, not far from here, about twenty minutes."
He grinned. "I'd tell you, but you wouldn't have any idea
where it was anyway."

Hannah laughed. "True."

"Do you like it here?" he asked. "I mean, being new
in town and all... not right here... at this house."

Giggling, Hannah thought about his question before
answering. She did like it, but she was so used to having
to pack up and move again each time she had finally
settled in, that not moving was going to be an
adjustment.

"I know what you meant, but that was cute! To
answer your questions, yes, so far I really do. I just hope
this is really our last move."

"Do you think you'll be moving?" Cash sounded
alarmed.

"No. We're not supposed to be moving. But I can't
count how many times over the years we have moved."
Staring at her feet, Hannah continued. "My mom swears
this is the last move, and I'd like to believe her. I guess
it's just hard at times for me to trust her when it comes
to her saying something like that, that's all."

Cash watched her inhale, and though he wouldn't
admit it, the sweet smell of the cherry combined with the
vanilla was quite nice. She caught him staring at her
and immediately thought it was due to her smoking.

"Sorry! I'm going to quit, really."

"No need to apologize to me; it's your body, your
lungs."

Rolling her eyes, she added, "Man, you and my mom,
which by the way, she would kill me if she knew I was

still doing this."

Holding the tiny device, which brought her such comfort, in the palm of her hand, she stared at it. It looked so pretty. Pink, trimmed in black.

"What can I say, it's a crutch for right now. Gets me through the sad and stressful times."

Cash's deep brown eyes darted toward her. Sad and stressful times? He knew it! *Leave it alone, Cash,* he told himself. But at least now he knew he was right! Her big blue eyes were empty and distant because this beautiful girl was sad, and there was something about those eyes, her eyes, that absolutely tormented him!

Chapter 17
What's Going On?

Nervous speech and gentle kisses
He lifts me up but doesn't know it
Butterfly stomach
I'm a wreck
Just pretend and you'll forget
~ Hannah Gunner ~

Hannah and Cash had been talking and hanging out for a few months, long enough that the official dating thing had taken form, though not officially addressed until now. Cash, leaning against his jeep, pulled her toward him. Hannah didn't resist. His arms wrapped around her waist as he leaned in and gently kissed her. Her lips were soft and melted into his, and the speech that he'd played over and over again in his head suddenly disappeared. Sweeping her hair out of her face, Hannah playfully punched him on the shoulder.

"Having any doubts about hanging out with my mom tonight? Are you scared to spend the evening with us?"

He shook his head.

"No!" Grinning. "It's not like I haven't met her before, and besides, I feel as if I know all about her already, since you talk about her so much."

Hannah looked surprised. "I do?"

Cash nodded and laughed. "Yes, yes, you do!"

"I didn't realize that. What's wrong then?" Hannah laughed, and for a split second, he thought he caught a glimpse of a sparkle in her eyes.

"Um, well, there's no easy way to say it, so I guess I'll just lay it on you."

Hannah's heart sank, and the smile she wore disappeared. Any hope of keeping that sparkle in those beautiful blues was gone, as Hannah prepared herself for the worst.

The look on her face told him he'd screwed up. Wrong way to start the conversation and portray what he was trying to say. Hoping he hadn't ruined the entire thing, he grabbed her hands in his.

"Wait a minute, it's not what you're thinking. Let me start over."

"Well, you don't know what I'm thinking," Hannah replied nervously, trying not to look as worried as she now felt.

"True, but let me start over anyway."

Cash cleared his throat.

"We've been hanging out for a while now, and I really like you, and you like me, or at least I think you do."

Hannah waited on pins and needles. Was this the dreaded breakup speech or something else? Her eyes darted toward the ground just in case it was a break, not a break up, but the dreaded break, which always worse than an actual breakup because there wasn't ever a reconnect after a *break*!

"I just think we should officially say, that you know, we're now exclusive." He pulled her closer and lifted up her chin so she could look him in the eye. "Hannah, I don't want to date anyone else." Giving her a quick kiss on the lips, he added, "And I don't want you to date anyone else."

Hannah didn't respond at first, and nervously Cash asked her what she was thinking. Balling up her fist, she slammed him in the shoulder as hard as she could!

"That's it. That's what you had me scared shitless about?!?! I thought you were breaking up with me or ending this... this thing, here, that we have!"

"What are you talking about?" He laughed. "Are you crazy—ending it?" Playfully grabbing her head, he ruffled her hair, and for a split second the sensation of that feeling of her hair moving under someone's hand in such a way on her scalp brought back a memory, a flashback, but she couldn't remember where or why.

"I guess I'm just terrible at this stuff. Sorry. But anyway, what say ye?"

Hannah's head whipped up as soon as she heard him say those words.

"What did you just say?"

"What say ye?" He chuckled, knowing he had her undivided attention. "Those crazy pirate stories you always tell me about."

Her face dropped as she remembered her dad, or was it the Captain, ruffling her hair as a kid as they played.

"Why are you looking at me like that?" Cash asked. "I pulled a Hannah; you know, that thing you always say. *What say ye.* It's kinda cute, not gonna lie, a little weird, but cute in a weird girlfriend sort of way. See there, I said... girlfriend!"

"Do I say that, really, *what say ye*? I swear, I hadn't even noticed!"

Cash looked puzzled. "Yeah, you do, but like I said, it's really kinda cute. I guess it's from your pirate days as a kid."

Embarrassed, Hannah placed her hands over her face. "Yeah, I guess. I just didn't realize I said it around you; but I *love* that you just said those words to me here, right now." Hesitating, she added, "They were pretty special back then, and yes, I'll be your girlfriend!"

She leaned her head on his chest, and he wrapped his arms tightly around her again. Her hair smelled like strawberries, and he figured she must have used some fruity shampoo. But her perfume, the one that he loved, lingered on her skin. He inhaled the scent and kissed the top of her head. Standing on her tippy toes, she kissed his cheek. His deep brown eyes drew her in and made her feel safe and loved. She hadn't seen eyes quite like that before, and she realized right then and there that his eyes were one of the things she loved about him most. Cash felt the same way about her blues, except hers somehow had a hint of sadness in them that taunted him, forcing him to want to find out what had happened that made her eyes sometimes seem empty or not present.

"I don't know why, but those words startled me for a second."

Cash held her hands in his.

"Sorry about that; but you said yes, correct? You're in, exclusive, like just you and me?"

Was that even a real question? Hannah was thrilled!

Her feelings for Cash had only grown each time they'd hung out or talked. He made her laugh, listened to her, let Lindsey tag along with them without complaining a single time, and he hadn't once judged her or pushed her too far in regards to questioning about her past. Though, admittedly, Hannah had yet to understand how Cash could be so hot, nice, and attracted to her at the same time; she didn't inadvertently want to screw it up. Now here they stood, planning their date for that evening and when they'd officially tell her mom they were a real couple. Hannah didn't often take guys to meet her mom. Kissing him longer than usual, she finally gave him the answer he'd been waiting for.

"Yes, absolutely! Count me one hundred percent in!"

Cash kissed her a little longer, and she noticed a tad harder when he said goodbye. "I'll see you at seven, correct?"

She nodded. "Yes. I think we're having pasta, not sure, but that's usually our go-to meal."

"Love me some spaghetti!"

"Never said it would be spaghetti, maybe a version of something like that," Hannah laughed, waving goodbye, and before his Jeep was out of view she was already FaceTiming Lindsey.

"Y'all are so cute! But it's not like you guys haven't been exclusive for months anyway. I mean, really, I guess nothing's changed except y'all have just confirmed it with *the words*."

"True. But the way he asked me, you should've heard him, so damn sweet." Hannah giggled. "I must admit, something he said kinda freaked me out at first, the way he pays attention to what I say, I mean, more than I realized."

"Oh yeah, what happened?" Lindsey asked.

Hannah hesitated.

"Well, it's weird. Cash said that I say this thing that I used to say as a kid, 'What say ye?' But I didn't even realize it." A smile crossed her face. "Especially around him, so dumb, or that I said it often enough he'd notice!" Hannah laughed at herself. "The Captain, I guess my dad, hell I'm not really sure anymore which one used to say that." She laughed out loud and Lindsey laughed with her. "I think he was my dad, but the Captain, in my pirate dreams, would always say it."

Lindsey interjected. "I think it's safe to say the Captain was your dad. You've said it before that you thought that you remembered playing a pirate game with him, or him telling you amazing stories about pirates. He must have been quite the storyteller for you to remember those things so vividly for all these years. I'm betting you're just confusing the two, the stories and your dad."

"I guess," Hannah replied. "I'm honestly not sure if it was him or just a dream; but I think you're right, it probably was my dad. How cool is that... my dad... was the Captain. Well, if only in my dreams."

As soon as they hung up, Hannah ran into the apartment to help prepare for Cash's dinner with her mom. Gloria had been trying to sit down with him for weeks, but Hannah had kept putting her off. They were only friends, Hannah would say, no need to single him out and embarrass him. Now they were more than friends, and Hannah knew she couldn't put her mom off any longer. Gloria sat in the recliner in the living room, pale, unable to get up to greet her daughter.

"What's going on?" Hannah asked. "Are you all right?"

Gloria nodded, but Hannah didn't believe her.

"You look terrible. Are you sure you're up for company?" Hannah sat on the arm of her mom's chair. Even Hannah knew her mom wasn't up for company, let alone cooking a dinner for a guest. "Mom, Cash doesn't have to come for dinner tonight. We can go out and do this some other time. Promise!" Picking up her mom's hand and squeezing it, she added, "You look terrible, no offense."

Gloria shook her head and forced a fake laugh. "I'm fine, really. I've been a bit under the weather, but I'm feeling much better. In fact, I've got everything prepared. I really just need to heat everything up, and with your help, we'll be done in no time at all." She winked. "Trust me, I'm not about to miss dinner with your boyfriend, I mean so-called friend."

"Well, about that," Hannah grinned. "I guess you and I need to chat."

Gloria hung on to every word her daughter shared with her. Smiling, she nodded and squeezed Hannah's hand. Her first outpatient treatment had been that morning, but she'd yet to tell Hannah the truth about the diagnosis. The treatment was supposed to have minimal side effects, but it hadn't gone as well as she'd hoped. It had taken a toll on her, and until her body was accustomed to the toxins that they were prescribing to help her, she'd have to acclimate herself as best she could to the treatment she needed and get through the recovery period. One thing was clear: Gloria certainly wouldn't be going to work the next day, she felt too weak. A little white lie about a shift change, and she could hide the truth from Hannah a bit longer. Fearful she couldn't keep the truth from Hannah too much longer, she worried about how and when she would need to come clean and tell her daughter how ill she really was. But not today, not tonight, and not when her daughter looked so happy. Gritting her teeth, Gloria put on a smile, and insisted that despite how she felt, dinner would proceed. Scrambling for a reasonable excuse for her predicament, she came up with one that Hannah might actually believe.

"I did the stupidest thing today," she said. "It's all on me!"

Hannah sat down on the couch opposite her. "Oh yeah, what's that?"

"I took the wrong prescription for my blood pressure, accidentally got in a hurry and mixed it with the correct one, and between the combination of the two they made me violently ill." She wiped her nose. "I'm doing much better now, but it was rough for a minute."

Faking a smile, she reassured Hannah that she was truly on the mend. "A little 7-Up, some crackers, a break, thus the recliner and blanket, and I'm on the mend. I'm really looking forward to having dinner with Cash, officially visiting and chatting with you both, and pasta is easy-peasy to cook." She pushed her hair behind her ears, sat up straight to reassure Hannah that she was fine, but in truth the thought of cooking made her nauseous. Between the nausea and exhaustion, the thought of cooking was overwhelming, but the thought of eating was even worse. Gloria, white as a sheet, shook her head and took a deep breath.

"Mom, really, I'm not sure you can pull off dinner." Hannah crouched down on the floor in front of Gloria's chair. "Are you?"

Adamantly, Gloria insisted she was fine. "Don't dismiss me like a kid, young lady; I'm fine." Standing up, Gloria pointed toward her bedroom. "Time to freshen up." As she walked feebly down the hall, she hollered back at Hannah. "Put snacks out; Cash will be here soon."

Slipping a nausea pill under her tongue, Gloria splashed cold water on her face and sat on the edge of the bed, waiting for the medicine to kick in. A fresh set of clothes, a brush through her hair, and a swipe of lipstick was all she could manage. Hannah didn't seem to notice that the rest of her makeup was incomplete, and surely Cash wouldn't either. He arrived on time and brought a bouquet of flowers for Gloria.

"Suck up," Hannah teased, kissing him on the cheek for being so thoughtful.

Gloria did her best to entertain, making small talk through dinner, before casually dismissing the teens to do their own thing.

"Well, I'm sure you kids have got better things to do than sit here all night with me!" She stood up, hugged Cash, and tried to end the evening as politely as possible. "It was so lovely visiting with you this evening, Cash, and thank you again for the beautiful flowers."

The two teens stood up as well, and Hannah started to clear the dishes.

"No. Leave those! You two get out of here!" Turning to Cash, Gloria said, "Please have Hannah home by midnight, and have fun."

"Yes, ma'am," he replied, grabbing Hannah's hand as they said their goodbyes.

Hannah kissed her mom on the cheek, and though Gloria usually would have walked them to the door, she simply couldn't manage it. As beads of sweat formed on her forehead, and fearing she'd throw up if she moved, she couldn't get them out of the house fast enough. As soon as the door closed behind them, Gloria ran to the kitchen sink as the vomit rushed up her throat. Painful dry heaves followed, and she felt as if she were dying right then and there. Her ribs and stomach ached as her body violently shook with each hurl that produced nothing but bile. Finally able to inch away from the kitchen sink to the bedroom, she collapsed onto the bed. The dishes would have to wait. Taking deep breaths, she took another Zofran and tried to sleep off the sick feeling that had consumed her. For the first time in her life, Gloria didn't wait up for Hannah to come home or even check her phone for a call or text that evening. The moment she realized what had happened, her heart broke! It was getting close. She had no choice; she would have to tell her little girl, turned young lady, the truth soon. She was on borrowed time and she knew it.

Chapter 18
Time Is Ticking

Anger
Sadness
Helplessness and despair
Deception is lingering in the air!
Heart is breaking
And now I'm scared
Panicking as I lay in bed
~ Hannah Gunner ~

Time wasn't on Gloria's side, and for the first time since her diagnosis, she felt it. Hesitantly, she picked up her cell phone and called her oncologist. A brief conversation with the doctor confirmed her fears; she was running out of time and had no choice but to tell Hannah what was going on. It didn't matter anyway; it was inevitable that she'd figure it out soon enough. It was best to come from Gloria herself. Picking up the phone, she called her sister. As much as she knew she owed Hannah the truth, she couldn't do it by herself.

"I'll be there, don't worry."

"Yes. I just don't think I can bear to look Hannah in the face and deliver this news. She's already been through so much over the years."

"I'll be there shortly, unless you need me right now?"

Gloria shook her head but realized Kathy couldn't

see her. "No. Hannah's at work anyway," she managed to say as the tears that had welled up in her eyes spilled over her eyelids and ran down her cheeks.

Why now? Why couldn't it be in a year when Hannah graduated? The doctor had said it was possible, stranger things had happened, even though it was unlikely that she'd last that long.

Hannah was working until 10:00 that night. It was the first time Gloria didn't fuss at her about the late hour. Over and over again she repeated the words that she wanted to say in her head, but nothing sounded right.

"Don't worry. You'll be fine. I'll be fine. It's okay. I'm not scared, and I feel fine."

She wasn't fine—she was terrified! She was angry! And she didn't want to leave her daughter! She felt terrible all the time, was in pain, and physically nauseous more times than not. How in the hell was she supposed to abandon her daughter after all they'd been through? What was Hannah supposed to do? Her head was spinning, and to make matters worse, she broke out in a cold sweat. Clammy, shaking, and sick to her stomach, she called Kathy, who had just arrived, into her bedroom.

"I can't do it. I don't know what to say."

Kathy took her sister by the arm and helped her into the living room. She curled up under a blanket on the couch, and Kathy cradled her in her arms. Gloria looked like a shell of herself, and as if she'd aged ten years overnight.

It was 10:15; Hannah would be home any minute.

How would she even begin? And maybe she was making a mistake telling her this late at night. Second-guessing herself, Gloria asked Kathy what she should do.

"Should I wait until tomorrow morning to tell her about this mess? You know, let her have a good night's sleep?"

Kathy held her distraught sister's hand.

"I think that's a good idea, actually; let her have a good night's rest. We'll tell her she's staying home tomorrow so she can sleep in, and that we need to talk to her."

"But she'll know something's not right if we tell her not to go to school," Gloria insisted.

"She's going to know something's up if I'm spending the night," Kathy responded.

Gloria knew she was right.

"Besides, I'll handle the school part," Kathy added. "You go on to bed. I'll wait up for Hannah. I'll tell her what we've already discussed, and you can get some rest."

Gloria didn't put up a fight. Feebly she walked back down the hallway to her room, climbed into bed, and drifted off to sleep. Hannah arrived at 10:30. Kathy was sitting at the kitchen table. Alarmed, Hannah asked where her mom was.

"Hi ya! What are you doing here?" Realizing how that sounded, Hannah quickly apologized. "I didn't mean it like that. Where's Mom? Is she sick again?"

Kathy tried to force a smile, but she couldn't hide the fact that she was trembling. Patting the tabletop in front of her, she pointed to a seat at the opposite side of the kitchen table.

"Join me a second, will you?"

Hannah sat down, eyes searching her aunt's face for answers to questions she hadn't asked yet.

"What's going on?"

Kathy reached over the table and held Hannah's hands in hers. "We have some news that we'd like to share with you, but it's your mom's news to tell, and it does have to do with her not feeling well lately. In fact, she's resting now. So, good news for you! You can sleep in tomorrow, spend the day with us, and we'll chat in the morning, yeah?

"Is it bad? Should I be worried?" Hannah asked nervously.

Kathy tried to lie, knowing time was ticking, but she wasn't very good at it. "You know as much as me. I don't know, but your mom will fill us in tomorrow." Half smiling, she walked over and kissed the top of Hannah's head. "Let's look at this as a girls' day in! Sound good?"

Hannah nodded, but worry swept over her. Lying in bed that night, Hannah FaceTimed Cash.

"Something's up, and I'm not sure what, but something's definitely wrong."

"I'm going miss seeing you tomorrow, but if it's not your idea to take off, can you still go out tomorrow night?"

Hannah laughed. "Seems reasonable to me, assuming everything is okay. All I can say is, if she throws another move at me, after she promised this was the last move, I'm going to tell her that I'm staying here."

"You can stay with me," Cash offered, already knowing that was impossible. "I hope that's not it, but glad you have options to stay."

"Thanks! But I'm pretty sure Aunt Kathy will let me stay with her; she has an extra room, and I'm working. I could pay rent if necessary."

She looked worried, and Cash didn't think he had the words to make her feel better, but he was wrong. Right before they hung up, he said something he'd never even hinted at before.

"Hey."

"Yeah."

"I do love you, you know. It's going to be okay, whatever it is."

Taken off guard by the words he'd just said, Hannah's stomach filled with butterflies. She'd had those feelings for him for some time, but had never mentioned it to anyone, including Lindsey. Her palms were sweaty as the excitement that she felt rushed over her. Cheeks red, she repeated what he'd said.

"Well, you know I love you, too."

Laughing out loud, Cash nodded. "Well, I'd hoped so. But I guess I do now, know you love me, that is!"

Their goodnights were sweeter that night than they'd ever been, which was just as well, because the next morning was going to be hell. Hannah reached for her journal, jotted down a few lines, and lay in bed with the sound of Cash's voice saying those incredible three words, *I love you*, running through her head.

Chapter 19
Fix It

This is wrong, damn it!
Just wrong.
Fix it and make it go away!
~ Hannah Gunner ~

Tossing and turning all night, Hannah felt as if she hadn't slept a wink. But as the smell of fresh coffee wafting down the hallway and into her bedroom woke her up, she realized she must have drifted off at some point. The last one out of bed, she entered the kitchen, and to her surprise, her mom and Kathy seemed in good spirits. Surely that was a good sign; maybe she'd worried all night for nothing? Wishful thinking, perhaps, but Hannah was running with that. Scrambling eggs and buttering toast, Kathy asked if she'd like some breakfast. Hannah shook her head. No appetite; the thought of eating did not appeal to her at all.

"No, thanks."

"Eat something. It's not often we all have breakfast together," Gloria insisted. "Look, we're all at the same table."

Hannah shrugged and sat down opposite her mom. Kathy poured another cup of coffee and sat it in front of her.

"Cream?"

Hannah nodded.

"Sugar?"

She declined.

Curious why they'd asked her to stay home but scared to bring it up, Hannah waited. A text from Lindsey made her smile.

Lindsey: Did the bomb drop yet?

She answered it quickly—no—and put her phone away, but not before responding to a text from Cash that made her light up from the inside out without realizing it.

Cash: Hope everything goes well. Love you.

Hannah: Thanks. Love you, too.

Her smile was noticeable, but no one asked what was going on. Hannah needed something in her life that made her smile, and Gloria was happy to let her have a moment. Giving her some space regarding the text seemed like the least they could do. In all honesty, Gloria and Kathy were tiptoeing around each other, trying to figure out how to approach the elephant in the room: Gloria's condition.

"Was Kathy still up when you came home last night?" her mom asked. "I laid down and was out before you came home."

Hannah nodded. Her mouth filled with egg and toast, she took a swig of coffee and answered.

"Yes. She said we're having a girls day in today."

Kathy was picking at her food, and Hannah noticed that her mom still had the same amount of food on her plate as when they had sat down to eat. Hannah seemed to be the only one eating at all, and she wasn't even hungry! Not being able to stand it any longer, Hannah broke the ice and asked the question that they were dreading to answer.

"So what's going on? Why am I home from school today?"

Gloria opened her mouth to speak, but Kathy interrupted.

"If you're done eating, I think we should move into the living room, don't you?" She turned toward Gloria for approval, who didn't object. "It's a tad more comfortable for the type of conversation we're about to have, don't you agree?" Once again she glanced at her sister, and Gloria nodded.

Reluctantly, both Hannah and Gloria walked into the other room. Hannah sat in the large recliner in the corner, and Kathy perched protectively next to her sister on the couch. Hannah suddenly felt scared, especially when Gloria reached over and held her sister's hand tightly in hers. It was the first indication that something was terribly wrong. Kathy looked into Gloria's eyes and, without saying a word, Gloria knew she was asking who should speak first. Gloria responded by squeezing Kathy's hand and lowering her eyes.

"There's no easy way to say this, sweetheart," Gloria started. "So I'm going to do my best to explain what's going on without upsetting you."

Hannah noticed that Kathy was trying not to cry, and suddenly panic set in.

"Just say it; you're killing me here," Hannah snapped, and immediately felt terrible for being so angry.

"I've not been feeling well for some time." Gloria took a deep breath. "In fact, you might have noticed I've been tired, nauseous and well, to put it best, not quite myself."

Hannah's heart skipped a beat. "Well, go to the doctor!"

Gloria half smiled, knowing Hannah knew that she'd had many doctor visits, and the way she said it, so matter-of-factly, sounded just like something Hank would immediately have said. It made her think of him. *Well, get on with it!* Before Gloria could say another word, Hannah jumped in with another response.

"Whatever's going on, get a second opinion, or a different doctor if what they're doing isn't working." She stood up, walked over to her mom, and sat down next to her. "Wait, what is it?" She stopped herself. The look on her mom's face told her she wasn't in the mood for small talk or petty responses. Her mom was worried!

"Mom," Hannah asked nervously. "What's wrong with you?"

Kathy glanced over at Hannah as Gloria mumbled the words out loud.

"I have Chronic Myelogenous Leukemia, commonly known as CML."

Hannah, stunned, had no idea what that was, but knew enough to know it didn't sound good! Her line of questioning, more like an interrogation, began.

"What is that, exactly?" Taking a deep breath, Hannah whispered, as if she daren't say the words out loud. "Is it a type of cancer?" She took another deep breath. "Are you saying you have cancer?"

Gloria nodded. "Yes. It's the type of cancer where a mutated gene starts producing contaminated or diseased blood cells. Automatically." Her hands were shaking, but she tried to explain to Hannah what the illness was, an illness that felt more like a death sentence.

"I know you've probably noticed I've been more tired than usual and have had trouble eating because I feel nauseous." She hesitated. "I haven't been completely honest with you about why, up until now, because I didn't want to worry you, but the medications they're using make me feel sick at times."

Hannah stared at her blankly. "Medications? You mean, like, chemo?"

Gloria nodded again. "I couldn't even wait up for you to come home the other night and ask about your date with Cash." Smiling. "You know I wanted to hear all about that, or as many of the details as you would have shared."

Hannah couldn't think; her mind was racing ninety-to-nothing. She'd had a feeling something wasn't right with her mom, but she had *no* idea it was this. Gloria looked as if she was about to break down, so Kathy, fighting back her own tears, graciously stepped in and continued.

"Hannah, your mom started treatment as soon as they finally diagnosed her. You can't tell, but she has a port already surgically implanted. Right now she's also taking oral meds; they're constantly adjusting and switching them around, and that's part of the reason she feels sick."

Gloria unzipped her oversized sweatshirt and

revealed the port. "It's not too bad, really. This way, the nurses don't have to stick me over and over, and the doctors can request blood tests, administer drugs, give me fluids, all kinds of things right from here without having to stick me all of the time." Forcing a smile, she added, "Despite what it looks like, it's a good thing."

"Does it hurt?" Hannah asked meekly. "The port?"

Gloria shook her head. "I promise, sweetheart, it doesn't hurt."

In shock, Hannah felt as if the walls were closing in around her. Gasping for air, she tried to breathe. How had she not known? A million questions she needed and wanted to ask, but not knowing where to start, she struggled for the words. Tears welled up in her eyes, and when she could hold them back no more, they poured over her lids and streamed uncontrollably down her cheeks. Without saying a word, Gloria reached for her daughter and pulled her into her arms, cradling her, rocking her, and stroking her hair as Hannah sobbed uncontrollably. Crying and crying, barely catching her breath at times, right then at that moment, on the couch in the living room of their two-bedroom apartment, their whole world stood still as it fell apart!

"Are you going to be all right?" Hannah whispered. "As horrible as this is, it's curable, right?"

Kathy stared at her sister as if looking for an answer as well. Gloria's eyes were watery as she struggled for the right words to say. Kathy once again jumped to her sister's aid and helped her out.

"They're doing everything they can. Your mom has started treatment in an outpatient center. It's close to home, and they've switched her chemo, for now, to an oral drug. Plus, she's taking a drug that blocks the tyrosine kinase protein secreted by the BCR-ABL gene." She took a deep breath. "They think they've figured out one drug that she can handle without making her as sick as she's been, but it will still take your mom some time to get used to." Proceeding with caution, as if waiting for a reaction from Hannah, Kathy continued explaining Gloria's treatment plan. Hannah, stunned, sat in the chair motionless. "The meds are strong, and your mom is definitely weaker than she's ever been, but we do know that the other pills they had her on were making her ill. So the new prescription, once she adapts to it, will really be better for her."

"FIX IT!" Hannah suddenly blurted out. "Do whatever needs to be done, but just make them FIX IT!"

Gloria forced a grin. "I'll do my best—you can count on it!"

Hannah, despite her best efforts, started crying again, but this time Gloria and Kathy cried with her. Too weak to stand, Gloria raised her arms and Kathy rushed into them. The three, cradled together, comforted each other, but no one noticed that Gloria cried in silence.

Lying in her bed that night, Hannah held the conch shell close to her ear. The sound of the ocean drowned out her thoughts. Exhausted, she slipped away to *a forever time ago* as a little girl walking along the water's edge. The Captain followed close behind, and of all things, in her dream, her mom sat on a chair in a hallway sipping a glass of red! Surely, she was losing her mind. Reality and her dreams combined, and at that moment it brought her peace as she drifted away to her memories of a pirate, a girl, a beach, and a scallywag that she swore must have at one time been her mom.

Chapter 20
Hannah

My heart is breaking; I have no words
~ Hannah Gunner ~

Cash opened the jeep door, and Hannah climbed in. Her eyes were swollen, and her long hair hung loosely around her shoulders. Oversized sweats and a pair of converse were all she could manage. Normally he would have commented on how cute she looked, casually thrown together and all, but at that moment it didn't seem appropriate, and even Cash knew that.

"Are you hungry?" he asked.

Hannah shook her head.

"Coffee?"

She nodded. "Please."

As he drove, he reached over and placed his hand on top of hers; support without words, and though he had no idea, the simple gesture couldn't have been more perfect. Fearful of saying the wrong thing, offering words of comfort that did not come readily to him anyway, he allowed the silence to consume the Jeep. Relieved they'd finally arrived at their stop, he pulled into the first parking spot he found outside the coffee shop.

Pointing to a table in the corner, Cash directed

Hannah to sit down. She didn't argue. He placed their order and sat down with her. Small talk, pointless and awkward at a time like this, he waited patiently for Hannah to bring up her mom or say something first. He didn't have to wait long.

"I can't believe I didn't know she was really ill. Like, this sick."

Choosing his words carefully, he answered her as kindly as he possibly could. "How could you have known? Between school, studying, and work, you're as busy as your mom. Not to mention, she said she was feeling better."

"But I should have known," she snapped back.

Cash didn't respond, but the look on his face told her she was angry with the wrong person.

"I'm so sorry! It's me, not you."

"No worries," he whispered. "It can't be easy to hear that kinda news under any circumstance, let alone out of the blue."

Hannah rolled her eyes. "Tell me about it!"

A high-pitched voice called out their number and Cash jumped up to retrieve the coffee. Pointing to a piece of lemon cake sitting behind the glass, he smiled and added it to his order.

"Can I get that too, please?"

Setting it in front of Hannah with his hands raised before she could object, he stressed, "You don't have to eat it, but I'm betting you haven't eaten today."

He was right. Hannah hadn't been able to stomach anything since the news, and the thought of food made it worse. Neither had her mom, despite her aunt Kathy's attempts to make her eat something before she took her meds. Cash's dark brown eyes darted down toward the plate. The cake didn't look bad, and Hannah picked at it before finally taking a nibble. The sweet and tart flavor made her mouth water, but as good as it tasted, she couldn't manage more than a few bites. Sips of coffee washed the lemony sponge cake down and, for a few minutes, her mind drifted from her mom's illness, which she didn't understand. The distraction Cash provided from her sadness was just what she needed; leaning forward, she kissed him on his lips. His smile indicated that he was pleasantly surprised, and certainly not complaining.

"Thank you! Just wanted to say thank you," Hannah whispered.

"With a kiss, which was great," he added, the cutest smile crossing his face.

Cash listened as Hannah poured over the details from the night before, but purposely offered little in regards to advice. Asking if she or her mom needed anything, Hannah shook her head. She didn't need a thing except for maybe a hit of her JUUL, highly inappropriate at a time like this, but her mom, on the other hand, needed a miracle. The research Hannah had done since she'd heard the news had been grim. Sticking in her mind were the words *unfortunately, in many cases, CML is not cured, and the patient eventually dies.* But she loved Cash for listening and saying that *he'd be there by her side if she needed anything,* and for not judging her about her own habit concerning her addiction to nicotine. As she described the treatments, her heart sank. Targeted drugs, which Gloria had already started. Chemo. Bone marrow transplant, dangerous, and not necessarily successful; biological therapy, whereby the body's own immune system is encouraged to fight cancer; and trials, which her mom wasn't eligible for. Saying those things out loud drove her need for nicotine through the roof. Cash sipped his coffee, listened without complaint, and held her hand in his when she'd let him.

"I think I should go home now, but you can come with me and hang out." She hesitated. "Can I smoke before we leave? I know, not in your Jeep, but before we head back?" She looked at her feet, embarrassed, wanting to quit and feeling guilty and ashamed, wishing now more than ever that, at least for her mom, this wasn't her crutch.

Cash gathered up the trash, threw it away, grabbed her hand and pulled her to her feet. Not once did he say a negative word, but kissed the top of her head and held the door open for her to walk outside. "I don't want to impose," he responded. "I understand you need to be with your mom, and if she's up to it, I'd love to come in and hang out with you if you're sure she doesn't mind."

Hannah smiled, a real smile, one that he hadn't seen in days and it reminded him how beautiful she was.

"No imposition. Mom likes you, and it might even cheer her up."

He put his arms around her and pulled her next to him as she smoked. Softly placing little kisses on her cheek, he even managed to make her giggle as she swatted him away from her a time or two. Hannah needed all of the distractions that she could get, and even if he were playfully irritating her, she'd take it. Not thinking about what was going on for a few minutes was bliss. Cash, having absolutely no idea how happy it would make Hannah, asked if she'd like to invite Lindsey to hang out with them.

"We could visit with your mom for a while, and then when she rests we could all go for a drive. How does that sound?"

Surprised he had even given Lindsey a second thought, she nodded and her face lit up. "That would be wonderful, and thank you for thinking of her!"

Guiltily, he smiled. "Well, to be honest, as you would say," he laughed, "I was thinking of you, but I'm glad you like the idea."

Hannah immediately pulled out her phone, texted Lindsey, leaned into Cash and kissed him tenderly right there in the parking lot as they leaned against his Jeep. "Thank you, babe. I really need this!" Cash opened the door, and Hannah climbed into the front seat.

"Do you think we should take your mom some of that lemon cake?" he asked.

Hannah shook her head. "She won't eat it; thank you for asking, though." Watching him turn the key, she reached over and grabbed his hand. "And thanks for today—coffee, cake, listening, and especially for inviting Lindsey to hang out with us. Having my best friend and boyfriend with me is exactly what I need."

Gloria was sitting with Kathy when they arrived, and except for looking a tad tired, seemed as healthy as could be. Thrilled that Hannah had some color back in her cheeks, no doubt from the Jeep ride, the two sisters drilled the teens about where they had been. Hannah fussed over her mom, checking the temperature of the apartment, making sure she had a blanket next to her in case she felt a chill, and poured her a glass of tea. Gloria tried to make jokes, but no one was laughing.

"Maybe I should make an announcement like this more often!" Grinning, she added, "Feeling quite spoiled these days."

"Very funny," Hannah replied sarcastically. "Now, really, do you need or want anything else?"

She didn't. She needed to be left alone, like she'd usually spend her regular Saturday afternoons—alone. That way she could doze off in the chair at will, grab a snack if she wanted one, watch mindless TV, read a book, or do absolutely nothing at all. All of the fussing that Hannah was doing made her feel anxious and nervous. Knowing the road ahead of her could be long, she wanted Hannah to get on with living and enjoy herself. Gloria was sure she could smell the sweet scent of vanilla on Hannah's clothes when she had walked in, but one more fight about that disgusting vape habit would require more strength than she had in her right then. Knowing Hannah knew how she felt about it, that those devices still put holes in lungs, angered her but another fight about that would have to wait. Right now, seeing her daughter with color in her cheeks, a smile on her face, and her friends surrounding her was like receiving a free gift for that day.

"Lindsey, you can stay over if you like, and Cash, you can stay until midnight and watch a movie with us if you'd like to do that." Gloria adjusted herself on the couch. "I mean, when y'all get back."

Knowing she likely needed to rest and was trying to get some peace and quiet, Cash responded. "Thank you, ma'am. If you're sure you don't mind, that would be great! We shouldn't be too long."

Gloria nodded. "I'm going to watch crap TV, take a nap, and we'll order pizza tonight. Kathy's coming over as well."

Grinning, she turned to Hannah. "You two are a great-looking couple. Go have fun!"

Cash turned bright red, Hannah gasped, and Lindsey burst out laughing.

"Yeah, they're sickening. Boyfriend goals!" Lindsey laughed.

"Love you, Mom. See you later."

"Love you too! And guys, no drinking, smoking, drugs, or anything I might have missed!"

Hannah kissed her mom on the cheek, told her she loved her again, begged her not to worry, grabbed her wallet, and barreled toward the door. Cash, not wanting to purposely lie, just in case they did something wrong, didn't respond. A smile, a nod of his head, and he made his exit at the same time he said his goodbyes.

"See you later, Mrs. Gunner."

"Bye, Mom," Lindsey grinned.

All three piled into the jeep, the top rolled back, music cranked up, and pulled away from the curb.

"Where to?" Cash asked.

Lindsey leaned forward in between the seats.

"Let's go to the lake, drive around. I heard Danny's

group might be having a party over at Tigers Trail. Let's check it out. You know Danny, right?"

"Yep. I have two classes with him," Cash answered.

Cash glanced at Hannah for approval. Shrugging her shoulders, digging her hands into her pockets, she laughed and motioned with her head. "Let's roll."

For a few hours while hanging with her friends, Cash's arms around her, Lindsey acting like a fool, everything felt totally normal again. Lindsey downed a couple of beers; Hannah took a few sips and did her usual holding onto a beer until it was hot. Cash declined because he was driving, and took pleasure in watching his girl, Hannah, smile and laugh in such a way that he hadn't seen in quite a while. That night, for just a little while, they were teens hanging out, doing what teens shouldn't be doing, and hoping they didn't get caught. But at that moment, being a teen meant all was well for just a minute in Hannah's world, and she needed that!

Chapter 21
Complications

Slow it down
Please, listen to me
Don't take her yet
I'm begging you, please!
~ Hannah Gunner ~

Hannah's heart sank when she heard her name over the intercom requesting that she report to the principal's office. She hadn't been caught smoking on school property, so that couldn't be it, and she hadn't been in trouble in any of her classes. Fear set in, followed by panic, knowing something must be wrong at home.

Running down the hall, the teacher on hall duty, Coach Darwin, hollered at her to slow it down. "Where's the fire young lady? Walk!"

Hannah nodded but didn't respond. Walking as fast as she could, getting to the office seemed to take forever! The administrator behind the desk was talking to another student, so despite the hurry, Hannah had to wait anyway. Her eyes inadvertently stared at those standing in the same room, but thankfully no one made eye contact with her. Impatiently, she waited for the teacher to address her.

"Can I help you?"

"Yes, ma'am. I'm Hannah Gunner. I was called to Mr. Brown's office."

The administrator's facial features noticeably softened and her voice sounded sweeter. "Ah, Hannah. I'll let him know you're here."

This alone heightened Hannah's fears. Something was wrong. She was right.

"Mr. Brown will see you now," the administrator announced, pointing to his office door.

Nervously Hannah approached his office, knocked on the door, and waited. His voice responded with one word: enter. To her surprise, he handed her a note. Her eyes started to scan it, but all she saw was a three-digit number written in red ink.

"It's a room number; um, hospital room."

Hannah froze.

"Hannah, your aunt called. Your mom collapsed and was rushed to the hospital. Your aunt will meet you there, but you need to go immediately. Do you have a car, can you drive, or would you like a ride?"

Hannah tried to answer, but no matter how hard she tried to spit them out, the words would not come out of her mouth.

"Never mind. We'll arrange for one of our staff members to drive you; that's probably the best thing to do anyway."

Mr. Brown picked up his phone and started making arrangements for her dismissal and transportation. Hannah, totally numb, followed his directions in a complete daze. Hardly remembering whose car she climbed into, she barely remembered opening the door and stepping onto the pavement outside the emergency room. Charging through the wide automatic doors, her mind flashed to Cash. Should she text him? But she never pulled out her phone. Rushing up to the desk, she requested to see Gloria Gunner. The girl sitting behind the computer tapped away at her keys, read the monitor, and finally spoke.

"And you are?"

"I'm her daughter, Hannah Gunner."

"Mrs. Gunner has been admitted. They're preparing her room, but if you like you can wait with her until they take her up."

Hannah nodded her head. "Yes. Please."

The girl pushed a button under her desk and the two large doors behind her opened onto another hospital corridor that Hannah didn't even realize was there. Temporary holding rooms were on one side, separated by curtains, and examining rooms on the other, complete with real doors. Hannah glanced at the piece of paper still in her hands. Room 228 was on her left. She didn't knock but merely barged right on in. Kathy was sitting in a chair in the corner of the stark room, and her mom was lying in bed. She looked pale and scary, hooked up to all kinds of hospital equipment that Hannah didn't recognize. Monitors were beeping, nurses were drawing blood, and tubes seemed to be in odd places that Hannah didn't think they should be.

"What happened?" Hannah asked as she walked into the room.

She leaned down and hugged her mom, laying a kiss on her cheek. Gloria managed to raise her arms, but dozing in and out of consciousness, she hadn't recognized Hannah's face at that moment but thought she'd heard her voice.

"She's on pain meds and other drugs right now," Kathy explained. "I'm not even sure what they're all for, but her organs were struggling, and she was having breathing complications related to her illness." She paused. "She's been coming in and out since they gave the meds to her. They're pretty strong. But they're taking good care of her."

Hannah sat down on the edge of the bed and placed her mom's hand in hers.

"What are they going to do?" she asked her aunt.

"Try to stabilize her, and if possible, once that happens, when she's strong enough or if she's strong enough, perform a bone marrow transplant."

Kathy hesitated. "If she's up to it. But if her kidneys start to fail, they won't do it. She'll be on dialysis until... until its time."

"Time for what?" Hannah asked.

Kathy didn't respond.

The words *if she's strong enough* stung Hannah like hot needles pricking her bare skin. Why on earth wouldn't her mom be strong enough or regain her strength? Wasn't it too early in the illness for her to be so weak? And her kidneys—failing? What had happened? Gloria came to again for a few minutes and realized Hannah was in the room. Trying to speak but having difficulty getting out the words, Hannah spoke for her.

"Causing trouble again, I see—you trying to scare me?"

Hannah's smile melted her mom's heart and brought her a comfort she couldn't explain. Her hand reached up and pulled the oxygen mask off her nose and mouth as she tried to mouth the word, *sorry!* Hannah replaced the mask and hid the sadness she felt that her mom needed to apologize for being ill. *Sorry.* Why would she even say that?! Glancing at her aunt who sat close by, she received some of the answers she needed regarding the extra oxygen.

"It's to help with the low oxygen levels that she had when she came in." Standing up, Kathy wrapped her arm around Hannah.

"It's a precaution. It takes the burden off her lungs and allows her to breathe easier, since she was struggling with shortness of breath."

Hannah didn't question her aunt; not knowing for sure what was going on was more comforting than having all the facts. Watching her mom struggle to breathe was a lightbulb moment for the teen. On the one hand, she wanted to reach for her JUUL to settle her nerves, and on the other, she could see her mom struggling to breathe and never wanted to touch the tiny device again. What was happening in that room didn't have anything to do with vaping and yet the visual that she had of her mom struggling to breathe suddenly clicked with her mom's words and what she'd been preaching for years. It was staring Hannah in the face. Watching someone, someone you love, fighting to breathe, regardless of the reason, was shocking. Struggling for air. Even gasping at times, Gloria's chest heaved up and down, even with the extra oxygen. Kathy was wrong. It wasn't a precaution. Sick to her stomach, frozen in fear, silently Hannah vowed right then and there that the next time her mom called her out, she'd look her in the eye and truthfully be able to say that she, Hannah Gunner, one hundred percent wasn't smoking! White as a sheet, Hannah stood by her mom's bed and held onto Gloria's hand. Gloria dozed in and out of consciousness. Another doctor with a nurse by his side examined her. Making notes and writing orders, he started her on a strong round of antibiotics for fluid in her lungs, better known as pneumonia.

"Likely from within the community or passed on through her line of work, she's in health care, and it is pneumonia," he remarked. "Usually she would have been fine, but her immunity was already damaged, and that made her susceptible to the illness. Being stage three at diagnosis and now moving into stage four," the doctor hesitated. "Well, it isn't good."

He continued to examine Gloria, making notes and giving directions for her care.

"We're going to keep her here and stabilize her, get her through this. I really want to see how these kidneys are going to hold up, and for that reason we'll bring in our nephrologist for a consult." He paused. "Any questions?"

Any questions? Hannah had barely understood a word. Stunned at hearing the words *stage four* for the first time. How did her mom go from resting at home to being admitted to the hospital and organs starting to shut down? What in the hell had just happened? Kathy looked as shocked as Hannah; white, pale as a ghost, she stood at her sister's side by her hospital bed. Hannah, panicked, pulled out her phone and reached out to Cash.

Hannah: So sick right now! Fill you in soon. Luv ya

Cash: Do you need anything? And luv ya, too.

She never responded.

"Honey, do you want to talk about it?" Kathy asked. "Hannah. Hannah!"

As if in a trance, Hannah jumped when she heard her name.

"You were a million miles away. It's a lot to take in. Do you want to talk about it?"

"Stage four?" Hannah croaked. "That's not good."

Kathy's eyes darted toward Gloria, and she raised a finger to her lips. Hannah nodded, understanding that she didn't want to upset her mom. Stage four. Shocking. How? When? Too many questions, no answers, and surely not enough time!

Hannah sat down on the crisp white sheets of her mom's bed. The crinkling sound that they made forced her to look down and feel them with her hand. They were softer than she thought they would be given the crunching noise they'd made. Her mind was focusing on the most mundane things: the color of the walls, the steel sink in the corner, the disinfectant containers on the walls, rubber glove holders, and how many nurses came in before the doctor transferred her mom to another room on a different floor. Gathering her mom's things, she followed the gurney and equipment down the corridors. They stopped in front of two large steel doors, and Hannah didn't realize until the doors opened that it was a massive elevator. Rolling her mom's gurney inside, they made a space in the corner for Kathy and Hannah.

"There's room, y'all, come on in," a young nurse assured them as politely as she could, given the circumstances.

Gloria had never looked so frail in her life. She was pale, and all of sudden seemed way too slim. Little. Skinny. Hannah hadn't realized that before; her heart started to pound, and she couldn't think clearly. The elevator doors closed and her mind drifted back to a simpler time. Her mom was sitting at the kitchen table, the Captain was chasing her down the hall, and they were laughing hysterically. They ran into her bedroom for a bedtime adventure. Gloria's voice bounced off the walls after them. It was so clear. She was telling them to keep it short, and the Captain was making faces from the other side of the wall that made Hannah laugh. The sound of dishes clanging against each other told them Mom was cleaning up after supper. A second warning was about to come; that's how it worked. It was clear the Captain had always been there, and her mom was a part of that life they all loved. Go back to that time! Right now—why couldn't they just go back!

"Ahoy! All hands on deck, Matey," the Captain had boomed.

"Not too late, Hank, now you hear! She has school in the morning."

"Does kindergarten count?"

"Hank!" Gloria had snapped. "School is school, and we agreed, start her off right."

"You mean *Captain*, Momma."

"That's right, Matey."

The elevator moved slowly, and Hannah could see herself in her mind's eye, giggling. "And *you* mean First Matey, 'cause you done did promote me, remember?"

Hannah's heart jumped into her throat, realizing for the first time, in a long time, that her dad was the Captain and had been there, with them, in that house where she was a little girl, the one that Gloria had loved before he'd died. He had been real, and not just part of her imagination, which she was starting to believe and had purposely convinced herself of at times because it was easier than letting the memory of the Captain go. Thinking about the three of them while she rode in the elevator both pleased and momentarily stunned Hannah. She knew her dad had died. She knew she played with the Captain in her dreams, and she knew she had forced herself to forget that they were one and the same. But why on earth was she remembering all of that now? Panic set in as she realized one thing. Loss. She was fearful she was going to be confronted with losing her mom as well as her dad.

Trying to focus on her mom, she pushed out of her mind the images of Gloria packing up boxes containing her dad's things after she'd received the terrible news of his death. It was neither the time nor the place for those memories, but her mom's words flooded back to her mind. There had been a fight; he had died. Stop. Stop thinking about that now, she instructed herself. Kathy placed an arm around her shoulder, and thankfully Hannah was brought back to reality as the cold steel elevator doors opened up in front of her. For the first time in her life, as they wheeled her mom out of the elevator on the hospital bed, Hannah wished she hadn't always insisted that her dad act out her bedtime stories and put her to bed. For just once, she wished she had reached out and asked her mom to read her a story, any story, instead!

Chapter 22
My Closet

"Forgive me; I'm begging you."
~ Gloria Gunner ~

Sleeping peacefully, Gloria had no recollection of being moved to another room. Drifting in and out of consciousness, she mumbled and talked as she tossed and turned. Hannah sat on the edge of her bed, listening to words that she couldn't quite make out as she watched over her like a protective daughter should. Kathy sat with them for a while, noticing that Hannah suddenly looked so grown up, before stepping outside for some fresh air. The air was chilly, cooling down as the night moved in and robbed the day of the sun. Fighting the urge to scream at the top of her lungs, anger consumed her. Deep breaths, one after the other, Kathy tried to calm herself as she held back the tears that threatened to roll down her cheeks. Wrapping her arms around herself as tightly as she could, she paced back and forth, trying to forget momentarily how critical the situation was as she attempted to stay warm. Flashes of memories, laughter, and tears, pain, and struggles, she seemed to remember everything about her sister all at once. Using her sleeve to wipe away the tears that she could no longer contain, Kathy slid down a cold retainer wall outside the hospital doors and sobbed. Minutes passed—which seemed like an eternity—before Kathy managed to pull herself together and walk back through the sliding glass doors, to the elevator and back into her sister's room. Nurses, with pleasant dispositions, waltzed in and out of Gloria's room, making light and polite small talk with Hannah as they went about their duties. Hannah's fingers ran over her phone as she scrolled through her texts. Cash's words of comfort made her smile, and knowing she could count on him brought her a sense of internal peace that she hadn't experienced before. Offering to come and sit with her, she declined, but his offer meant as much as his presence. As much as Hannah loved him, she didn't feel secure enough to hide her fear of the seriousness of her mother's condition. And the relationship, to her, felt new enough that she should do that; Cash would have been disappointed had he known that she felt that way and that alone crushed her. Lindsey's texts were frantic, worried about her friend and her second mom. Hannah replied with as many details as she could, though, honestly, she didn't understand the entire situation herself.

Lindsey: Do you want me to bring you anything?

Hannah: No, but thanks.

Lindsey: If you change your mind, just text.

Hannah: K.

Hannah slipped the phone back into her pocket.

"How's she doing?" the doctor asked.

As if Hannah had a clue. She forced a smile. "She

hasn't really been awake yet; been restless, but she hasn't really woken up properly since she's had all of the pain meds."

Dressed in the usual scrubs with a stethoscope around his neck, the doctor nodded and went about his business. Hannah couldn't help but wonder if he really cared that the person lying in front of him was so special to her. That person, her person, was her whole world! Did he know that? So matter of fact, nonchalant, and suddenly it dawned on her. To him, this doctor, maybe not every doctor, but most doctors, this was merely another day.

"That's to be expected with the meds we gave her. Plus we gave her something extra for her pain." He pointed to his scribe and added a note on his chart. "The side effect of the two meds combined, it's normal, the drowsiness, but let's monitor that and adjust accordingly if necessary."

Hannah hung her head. "I didn't really know she was in pain. I mean, that much pain."

Looking up again, she asked him a question he heard often. "Has she been in pain for long?"

"Well, I'm not her regular doctor, so it's hard to say. But if I had to guess, I would say some days are likely better than others. In other words, yes. She's had some rough days being she's this far along, the CML, according to her doctor's notes, that is."

Alarmed, Hannah's mouth dropped open. "This far along—how long has she been sick?"

The doctor didn't answer at first; he kept checking out her mom. Kathy snuck back into the room and stood at Hannah's side. Without saying a word, she slipped her icy-cold hand into Hannah's and squeezed it tightly as the doctor continued.

"The complications that your mother is experiencing right now are due to the secondary infections because of her damaged immune system; that's what I'm treating." He checked the monitor. "This, of course, originally all leads back and starts with the CML. I'm not her oncologist, but I think it's safe to say one never knows how these types of infections originally develop during the treatments that we provide. It's hard to say because each individual patient responds differently to treatment. Her oncologist will treat the CML, and right now I'm going to treat what brought her to the E.R. in the first place."

He went into full doctor mode as he examined Gloria and went over her monitors. The scribe, at his side, tapped away on her laptop while the nurse in the room administered additional fluids through Gloria's IV. Directing his attention back to Hannah and Kathy, the doctor explained what he was doing and why, and asked if they had any questions or concerns. *Questions or concerns; yes, many of them,* Hannah thought, but had no idea where to start.

"Her doctor will check on her in the morning and decide what his next course of treatment will be for the CML, but right now, we've got to get her through this pneumonia."

He signed a med order, and the nurse and scribe left the room.

Five minutes ago, Hannah had a million questions.

When asked, she couldn't think of a single one.

"I should get you home, Hannah. You need something to eat, a shower, and some rest."

"I don't want to leave her, and you need to rest as well."

Kathy looked around the room. Gloria had a bathroom, and it had a shower. The room also had a large recliner and small couch that could pull out into a makeshift bed.

"I'll run to the house and apartment and grab a change of clothes for you and me, plus something to read, toothbrush, and few toiletries. Can you think of anything else that you need?"

Hannah shook her head. She didn't need a thing except for her mom to get well. Kissing Hannah on the top of her head as she gathered her things, Kathy left the hospital.

Perched in the corner, sitting crisscrossed in the chair, Hannah played CandyCrush on her phone and chatted with Cash via text. It helped pass the time, until her phone was nearly dead, and it was only then that she wished she'd asked her aunt to bring back her charger. Her mom had looked peaceful as she slept, but was finally starting to stir. Carefully, hoping not to disturb her, Hannah sat on the edge of the bed. Gloria managed to reach out and put her hand on top of Hannah's.

"Hannah."

"I'm right here, Mom."

Gloria looked pale and appeared weak, but that didn't stop her from becoming agitated and anxious. Hannah assumed she must be concerned about being admitted to the hospital and tried to ease her fears.

"Everything's fine, Mom. They've admitted you because you have pneumonia, but they've already given you antibiotics and something to help you rest."

Hannah leaned down on the bed and kissed her mom's hand.

"You're already getting better, and don't worry, we're not leaving you. We're staying right here, me and Kathy, no arguments!"

Gloria tried to pull Hannah closer toward her, but her shaking hands had no strength in them. Noticing, Hannah whispered words of reassurance.

"I'm right here, Mom; I'm not going anywhere."

Gloria's mouth was moving, but her words were barely audible. Hannah pleaded with her to rest, assuring her that they would talk later, but Gloria wouldn't have it. She had something urgent she wanted to say, and she needed Hannah to listen to her. Struggling to spit out the words was frustrating her.

"I'm listening. Go slow. It's the meds that are making you slur," Hannah said softly. Worried, she offered to call for help. "Shall I call the nurse?"

Gloria shook her head and became even more irritated.

Hannah, terrified that something was desperately wrong, begged her mom to calm down.

"There's something you need to know."

Hannah squeezed her mom's hand. "It's okay! I'm here, and I'm not going anywhere."

Tears filled Gloria's eyes, before a single one spilled over and left a single glistening trail on her cheek as it rolled down her face. Hannah began to panic.

"I'm getting the nurse."

"Stop, Hannah, please stop." She reached for Hannah's hand. "It's Hank."

"What?" Hannah didn't understand her and couldn't make out what she was trying to say.

"*Haaaank,*" Gloria repeated, dragging out the name.

Hannah stroked her mom's hair and kissed the top of her head. It pained her to see her mom in such a state. She missed the idea of her dad at times, but though she'd never admit it, the loss of the Captain hurt more. She never thought about her mom missing her husband; evidently he was on her mom's mind. Not knowing what to say, Hannah didn't say anything. Her eyes flashed around the room to see if by chance her aunt Kathy was back or a nurse was in the hallway and could help calm her mom down. No one was around.

"Your box," Gloria whispered. "Get the box."

"What?" Asked Hannah. "I'm sorry, Mom. I'm not sure what you said. What did you say?"

"The box."

Eyes closed, she pointed to the door as if shooing Hannah out of the hospital room to send her on her way. Where was she supposed to go? This seemed more like a game than her mom telling her something about Hank, her dad, and then Hannah realized her mom must be stuck in a loop; Hannah was still a little girl and Hank, her husband, was missed. Hannah had been guilty of the same type of memories on the elevator. The box undoubtedly was likely filled with photos. She'd seen her mom pack them tons of times over the years with each and every move; maybe they held her wedding photos or something sentimental to her that she needed.

"Box, Mom? What box? A photo box?" Hannah leaned closer to her mom. "Do you need me to find you a special box?"

Gloria tried to lift herself out of bed and pull herself up into a sitting position, but Hannah placed both hands on top of her shoulders and gently laid her back down.

"No need to get up. Just tell me where it is, and I'll find it for you."

"Get the box!" Gloria snapped and then apologized. "Sorry."

"Yep. I'm going to get the box." Hannah covered her mom back up. "Just tell me where it is; no problem."

"Get the box, Hannah. The box!"

Disturbed to see her mom so distraught, not knowing for sure if it was the drugs, a memory, or the illness that was plaguing her mind at the time, Hannah could play along no more. Against her will, she burst into tears.

"I don't know what box, Mom. When we moved? The boxes from my room, your personal boxes, photo boxes? What box?"

"Your box."

"My box?" Hannah asked. "The box belongs to me?"

Gloria ever so slowly nodded her head. The overly white hospital pillow crunched beneath her, and another tear trickled down her left cheek. Recognizing that finding the box was truly important to her mom, Hannah assured her she would find it if it existed.

"Tell me where I can find the box, Mom."

Gloria mouthed the word c l o s e t.

"Which closet?"

Gloria repeated the word, **c l o s e t**. Hannah continued to ask questions, hoping her mom would be patient with her a tad longer.

"There's a box, in a closet, and it belongs to me. Correct?"

Gloria nodded again.

"What's in the box?" Hannah asked.

"H a a a n k." Gloria managed.

"Oh my God! What?"

Hank is in the box? His ashes? Well no offense, but no thank you! He could stay in the closet, in the box, Hannah thought. She was in no hurry to find him. Urn. No thank you!

Frustrated, Gloria grabbed Hannah's sleeve and shook her arm as if she understood what Hannah was thinking. Hannah, against her will, forged ahead.

"Okay. What closet?"

Raising her hand, Gloria pointed to herself. "My."

"Your closet? Okay." Hannah smiled. "Hank, my dad, is in a box, in your closet."

Kissing her mom's hand that she now held in hers, she smiled, and sighed with relief.

"Why don't we leave him there? He's safe and all, and now that I know where he is, which is what you wanted, right, we're all good!"

Gloria actually managed a slight smile and found a whisper of voice from within her. "It's for you."

But Hannah didn't want him, not like that, and her face showed it. Frowning, she didn't know what to say except to agree and pretend that she'd take the urn.

Gloria sensed what Hannah must be thinking, that the box was something that it wasn't, and tried to explain why she needed her to retrieve it. Taking a deep breath, almost gasping for air, Gloria tried to explain why Hannah needed the box.

"It's for you; open it. It's on the top shelf, back of my closet, under a pile of sweaters."

Wanting to appease her mom, Hannah agreed to look for the box.

"I'll find the box. Do you want me to bring it to you?" Hannah asked.

Gloria shook her head and turned away. Tearfully she started whispering words over and over that Hannah at first had trouble making out. Once she understood them, Hannah didn't understand why her mom would say them in the first place. Walking over to the other side of the bed, Hannah listened carefully to her mom to be sure she had understood the words Gloria was repeating over and over. She had, but they didn't make sense.

"Sorry, Hannah. I'm sorry, so sorry!"

"Do you need a nurse, Mom?"

Gloria didn't answer. She once again turned away from her daughter as if in shame. Confused, Hannah continued to try to calm down her mom.

"Forgive me, Hannah," Gloria mumbled. "I'm sorry, Hank. So sorry, Hank. Hannah, I'm sorry."

Puzzled and concerned that the drugs were causing her mom to lose her mind, Hannah panicked, and without her mom's knowledge, pressed the nurse's button.

"How we doing in here?" the perky nurse asked as she bounced into the room.

"Not so good," Hannah responded. "I think my mom's delirious. Something's wrong, very wrong; she's talking crazy!"

Chapter 23
The Tattered Box

Memories
Dreams
Confusion
Turn into utter chaos
And dissolutions.
~ Hannah Gunner ~

Hannah wandered aimlessly toward the elevator, tapping away on her phone. The first text she sent was to Lindsey. Yes, she was hanging in there, didn't need anything, but thanks for checking. She hesitated before responding to the second text, which was from Cash. Desperately wanting to see him, she was torn between not wanting him to see her looking the way she did, like crap, with a tear-stained face and worn out, and responding to his text and asking him to pick her up so she could go home and shower in her own shower instead of the makeshift hospital shower in her mom's room. Her heartache over her mom's downward spiral, the need to see him, and the task now at hand, finding the mysterious box, if it even existed, had worn her out.

Hannah: Hey there, you busy?

Cash: Nah. Waiting for you to answer my text.

Hannah: Sorry about that, been crazy here.

Cash: You okay?

Hannah: Yes, and no. Pick me up and drive me home?

Cash: On my way!

A slight smile crossed her face when she read his response; realizing how much she missed everything about him, despite the circumstances, made her excited to see him again. His cocky smile, unkempt dirty blond hair hanging in front of his Oakley's, was just what she needed to take the chaos temporarily away that she was now experiencing.

Cash's music could be heard before his Jeep was even in sight, but as he pulled up in front of the hospital entrance, he turned it down. Hannah hesitated before climbing in. With the door ajar, staring at him, she told him how much she loved him and how happy she was to see him at that exact moment.

"Damn! You just made my day!" He winked at her, told her he loved her too, and added, "Are you getting in or what?"

Capturing everything about his expression at that moment, Hannah took a mental photograph of his face. She'd never felt that way before, in love, and except for her mom, couldn't think of a single person in the world she needed right then more than him. Pulling herself up into the Jeep, she leaned over, kissed him on the lips, and buckled up.

"Man, I've missed you!"

"Me too, you," she replied. "It's been crazy."

"I can't even imagine."

His gleaming dark browns told her he was genuinely pleased to see her as much as she was happy to see him. He held her hand the entire way, even while switching gears, never once letting her hand slip out of his.

"I was getting worried about you; I'm so glad you wanted to slip home for a bit." Hesitating, he asked, "How's she doing?"

"Right now, it's hard to say, but none of it is good." Hannah had trouble saying the words. "I heard the words *stage four* for the first time today, and even I know that isn't good." Staring out the window, she added, "They don't know how long she had this before her initial diagnosis, but they think it must have been a long time, and all of these complications stem from it."

"Wow. Did your mom know, I mean, that she had it?"

Hannah shrugged her shoulders. "I dunno."

Shuddering, Hannah blocked the conversation with the doctor out of her mind. Cash, not knowing how to respond, didn't say a word. Squeezing his grip around Hannah's hand was all he needed to do—silent reassurance. After a few minutes, Hannah tried to approach the conversation about the box with Cash.

"I need to pick up some overnight things from the house that I forgot to ask Kathy to grab, and there's something I need to do or find. I don't really know." Glancing at him, she could tell by the look on his face that Cash was waiting for her to explain.

"Well, that sounded vague in a weird sort of way."

Cash gently squeezed her hand. "What are you looking for?"

Hannah shook her head and shrugged her shoulders. "Honestly, I don't know." Running her hands through her long blond hair and wrapping it up into a messy makeshift bun on top of her head, she looked confused as she fumbled her way through what her mom had tried to ask her to do. Her big blue eyes, dull, looked sad and distant, and it pained Cash to see her that way.

"I don't even know if this box exists," Hannah whispered. "Honestly, I don't even know what I'm looking for yet. It's just something my mom was going on and on about; something she said I had to find, and it's supposedly a box that belongs to me located in her closet."

"Well, I'll just wait for you in the Jeep if you like, if it's personal."

Hannah kissed the top of his hand. "No. You can come in with me." Taking a deep breath and exhaling, "I need you to come with me; I'm not sure what I'm looking for."

"Only if you want me to."

Drained, Hannah half-heartedly smiled. "Honestly, I do. I think I'm supposed to take the box to her, but I'm not sure because she's kinda confused. She was rambling and kept saying it was for me. I'm telling you, the whole thing was so weird!"

"Sounds like it!"

"I've never heard her talk about this box or *a* box like this before, like ever. And I'm not even sure if it's real. It's possible she's delirious because of all of the meds."

Hannah paused. "Seriously, though, the nurse did say she could be delirious at times."

Cash pulled up to the complex, entered the code, and parked in front of Hannah's apartment.

"Well, let's go find this box, then!" He grinned. "Or you can, and I'll chill in the kitchen."

"Let's do it!"

The apartment felt weird. The atmosphere was oddly still and semi-stale. No air circulating or activity had been going on in there that day or evening, and it was apparent. Gloria, a stickler for conserving electricity and energy in general, turned everything down or off unless they were home. Nothing, not even a lamp, had been turned on while they'd been gone. She must have managed to either instruct Kathy or turned everything off before she'd collapsed. *Good grief,* thought Hannah. Flipping on the kitchen light, opening the fridge, and grabbing a couple sodas, Hannah handed one to Cash before proceeding down the hallway in such a manner that he knew not to follow.

"Holler if you need me," he yelled, and sat down at the kitchen table.

"Thanks," she replied, marching straight into Gloria's room and flipping on the light. The bed was unmade, but she couldn't help noticing that everything else was still neatly in its place. Nothing out of order. Gloria's heavy sweater lay on the foot of the bed, and Hannah picked it up to inhale the scent of her mom's perfume. The closet door, which was mirrored, was half opened and Hannah caught a glimpse of herself. She stared at her mom's sweater held up to her face. Hannah inhaled her mom's scent again for good measure before placing it exactly where she'd found it. She was her mother's daughter, everyone said so, but in the reflection in the mirror, she didn't feel as if she looked as beautiful as her mom had always seemed to her. Her eyes scanned the room, and in the eeriest way it felt as if she was looking at it for the first time. A photo of the two of them, Hannah was eleven, sat on Gloria's dresser, along with a picture of the three of them, little Hannah, three or four maybe, Hank, and Gloria, and the one of Hannah by herself in her pirate costume. Hannah picked up the photo of her and her mom, admiring the two beautiful people in the frame—was that really them? No one would have recognized either of them! Hannah all grown up, and that lady, she looked so different today. Hannah realized at that moment that her mom hadn't looked like herself for quite some time; in the photo she had a full face, a big smile from ear to ear, sparkling eyes, and glowing skin. That lady, right there in her hands, looked nothing like the woman lying ill in the hospital bed. The one gasping for air, thin, pale, and sickly. Gloria had been settling in these days by 7:00 unless she had a night shift. She was constantly exhausted, and always picking at her food. Now admitted to the hospital, Hannah wondered how long her mom had really been ill, and why on earth hadn't she noticed before now? The signs had surely all been there! Putting the picture back where she found it, straightening it to be sure it was exactly how her mom had left it, she turned to face the closet on the other side of the room.

Reaching out for the handle, Hannah hesitated.

Gloria's words resonated, reverberating as if bouncing around her brain and ringing in her ears. *Sorry, Hannah. I'm so sorry. Sorry.* Hannah froze. Shaking her head as if that would make the sound of her mom's voice go away, she found the courage to reach out and put her hand back on the closet handle door and began to slide it open. Slide it right or slide it left? It made no difference; she'd have to search both sides. She opted to push the door left and search to the right first. The closet was narrow but long. Unlike Hannah's, it was organized, though packed. Sweaters, just like her mom had stated, were neatly folded and piled underneath sweatshirts and pullovers on the top shelf. Reaching all the way to the ceiling, some as old as Hannah, the pile of clothes stretched and Hannah couldn't help but wonder if the woman ever threw anything away. She didn't find a box of any sort to the right hand of the closet, corner, or center. Everything appeared to have a place and seemed to be where it was supposed to be. Stepping out of the closet, Hannah slid the door to the right and began her search of the left-hand side of the closet. Nervously she poked around under each pile until her hand finally brushed up against the side of something hard pressed against the closet wall.

"Everything okay?" Cash yelled from the kitchen.

"Yeah, good. Turn the TV on, if you like."

Within a few seconds Hannah could hear what sounded like a commentator discussing a basketball game. Her hands fumbled underneath the mysterious box, cardboard, and nervously, she slid it out from underneath the sweaters. Her heart was pounding so hard that she could easily count each beat in her chest. It was heavy, but not so heavy she needed help. Upon closer examination, she could tell it was beige, tattered, and worn. It looked like an old shoe or small boot box, and the lid, now loose, had been secured by a thick rubber band. It had apparently been something that her mom had kept up with for many years, and must have been moved from home to home without Hannah's knowledge. Hannah carefully lifted down the box and placed it on the floor so she wouldn't spill the contents. Kneeling in front of the box, she stared at it for a few moments before nervously removing the rubber band. Snapping, it popped her on her bare skin as soon she tried to remove it from the lid, stinging her hand.

"Fuuuuuuuuuuuu!"

She caught herself before the F word flew out of her mouth, but the red mark that the rubber band left behind on her hand was a nasty reminder of why she was about to lose her cool! Though her mom asked her to retrieve the box, it felt as if she were invading her mom's privacy. Weird, since Gloria kept insisting it was her box in the first place. Contemplating what to do and what the contents of the box held, she kept running through the multiple possibilities: mementos maybe, or even her childhood projects from school, photographs, a will? *Just open it!* she instructed herself. Taking a deep breath, she flipped off the lid, catching sight of the contents for the very first time. She wasn't sure exactly what she was looking at. Envelope after envelope filled the box, all the way to the brim. Letter after letter, all handwritten on faded yellow, thinning, worn-out paper, stared her in the face. Eyes huge, Hannah's hands dug in between the envelops and she pulled them out, glancing at them one after the other, and one thing remained the same: they were all stamped, addressed, and mailed to her! Trembling, she read the names one by one: Hannah Gunner, Hannah Gunner, Hannah Gunner, addressee, Hannah Gunner!

"Wait... what?"

Every single one of them was addressed to Hannah Gunner c/o Gloria Gunner. Shock consumed her, chills ran up her spine, and her blood ran cold as her eyes darted to the left-hand side of the envelopes and she caught sight of the return address line. RETURN TO SENDER: HANK GUNNER—FOLSOM STATE PRISON.

Some of the letters and cards were opened, and some surprisingly were still sealed. The muffled sound of the TV in the background had been drowned out by Hannah's racing heartbeats pounding through her chest. Questions banging around in her head, too many to answer, and who would she ask right then anyway?! Frantically rummaging through the box, her fingers landed on an envelope, which had been opened, and a photograph fell out: a little girl dressed in pink and white pajamas, wearing a handkerchief tied around her head, and holding a wooden sword. She was smiling. A smile so huge it practically crossed her entire face. In the background stood a man. Hannah gasped and held the photograph close to her eyes, peering at it in awe, as if seeing the image of the man for the first time in her life.

"Captain," she whispered. "It's the Captain!"

Hands trembling, she stared at the faded ink on the letter that she held in her hands. It was still legible. A nervous, panicky feeling overwhelmed her as soon as she realized a ghost from her past had revisited. Sitting in a crumpled pile on her mom's bedroom floor, she read the letter that she now held in her hand through blurry, tear-filled eyes.

Dearest First Matey,

If you could only see me now, you would not be happy with me! It's safe to say I have quite a black spot on me soul! They say dead men tell no tales; remember when we even used to say that?

Well, Matey, I feel as if I'm already dead without you, my little pirate, at my side! There has no doubt been a mutiny, but you knew that from my last letter. Our scallywag, turned tyrant, is really cross with me, but that said, rightfully so!

Don't worry; I will do my best to make it up to both of you, and will be home soon. Promise to be a good lass, or should I say First Matey! But above all, please, please, please don't forget how much I love and miss you!

Yes, Hannah, I remembered. Exist as a pirate to survive, and always remember, sweet little Hannah, you are our greatest treasure of all!

Captain

Letter after letter all addressed to Hannah: birthday cards, Christmas cards, and even a few Easter cards.

Ripping them open and reading them through tear-filled eyes, she didn't hear Cash enter the room. Startled, she jumped when he gently laid his hand on her shoulder and crouched down next to her. She lost it completely. Feeling as if he'd just walked into something he shouldn't have, Cash suddenly wished he hadn't entered the room at all. Eyes darting between Hannah and the paper-filled box, he knew something was amiss. Crying uncontrollably into his shoulder, with no explanation, she couldn't stop herself.

"May I?" he asked, reaching for the letter that Hannah now held in her hands.

Without saying a word or acknowledging his question, Hannah handed him one of the letters.

Dearest Hannah,

They say time flies, but in here it stands still! I miss you and your mom so much! The silence is deafening; not a word, a single word, have I read or heard from you or that tyrant, your mom. (Please don't tell her I said that.) She is already very angry with me! I know this, it's important you understand she is a great mom; though admittedly, she's a terrible ship-hand. :-)

Truthfully, I bear her no ill will. This is all my doing, but I will fix it, and make it right. Trust me! Please, please ask her to let you write. Have her help you or even by now you could write me a letter yourself, maybe? Just a line or two, and tell me how you're doing. I think about you and your mom every single second of every single day. I hope you will forgive me, even if your mom can't, and even that I understand. Please, Hannah, please, drop me a line. A single line will do.

Daddy, & if you can remember, you called me the Captain!

Cash read the handwritten words scribbled on the page twice.

"Your dad is the Captain; the one in your dreams?"

Hannah nodded.

"I swear at times I thought I imagined him."

Cash read another letter and asked her a question she should have expected, but was shocked and unprepared when she heard him say it.

"Have you seen these before, the letters?" he asked. "Is this the box your mom was talking about?"

It was as if a blanket of shock washed over Hannah's porcelain skin. Struggling for words, she dug into the box and pulled out another letter.

"It is the first time I've seen this box." Staring at the pile before her, and what seemed like hundreds of letters, if not more, Hannah added, "And no, I had no idea the letters existed." Running her hands across her face in frustration, she asked him a question.

"Cash, why would my mom keep these from me?" She held up a letter. "Why?"

Cash shook his head; he had no clue nor response that he could think of that would make any sense. "I have no idea; you know your mom better than me. Maybe there was more between them, history, than you know; think about it, you were little." Cash didn't have any answers nor did he dare try to make up an excuse. He kept his mouth shut after that!

A large tear glided down Hannah's cheek and landed on one of the letters that she was still holding in her hand. Frantically she wiped it off before it bled the faded ink, or worse, made a hole in the aged paper.

"I swear, not even as a kid have I ever seen these letters or this box before. This I know I would have remembered!"

Cash dove back into the box and pulled out another letter and read it, slowly this time, and out loud. They took it in turns, reading a few lines from different letters and cards to each other. It became clear that some were written when Hannah was very young, and some must have been written when she was in her middle school and early teen years. Sharing such a personal moment with Hannah, especially over someone else's privately written words, was both intimate and bonding for the two of them in a way that neither would have ever imagined. Cash leaned over and softly kissed the top of her head, before putting the letters that were scattered on the ground back into the box.

"Well, as much as I hate to bring it up, it's getting late, and I guess we'll be getting some answers for you soon." Sticking out his hand, he offered to pull her to her feet.

Hannah nodded and reached for his extended hand. "Should I ask her about it? Now, I mean."

Cash bit his bottom lip and rolled his head from side to side; that was all the answer she needed, but he added his thoughts anyway. "I don't think that's a good idea right now; she's going through so much and needs her strength, not twenty questions, you know what I mean?" Hannah didn't respond, but she knew he was right; her mom had more significant issues on her plate than a box full of old letters. There would be time for all of this, answers to her questions when the time was right. For now, Hannah would wait.

A text message from Kathy reminded both of them it was time to go; people were tracking them down. Hannah looked worn out, and she hadn't even had time to jump in the shower; the hospital shower would have to suffice. Grabbing a few of the letters, she stuffed them into her backpack, placed the lid back on the tattered box, and placed the box in her room. Cash stood by, watching, but never said one word. Grabbing her phone cord, her brush, and an extra body spray, Hannah shoved everything into her bag and locked up. They drove back to the hospital in silence, Hannah lost in her thoughts, Cash nervous about what she might say to her mom, but hoping for Gloria's sake and Hannah's that she would put it off until the time was right.

"You know, I could've written to him so many times."

Cash carried her bag on one shoulder and held her hand in his as they walked toward the hospital elevator.

"Right," he answered. He tried to change the subject. "I wonder if Kathy needs a break? I can pick y'all up some food; bet she hasn't eaten yet."

Hannah hadn't heard a word he'd said. "Seriously, and I'm not kidding, for years I thought I was going crazy; thought I'd made up the Captain, dreamt about that beach, treasure, ship, and playing pirate games for years." Cash kept walking and pulling her along with him. "I mean, let's face it, I knew he was there once, but then he was gone and Mom never really talked about him." Pushing the elevator button, she kept talking. "Then as a kid, when he did leave, it felt like he'd left me. It got super complicated, super fast, and I guess I quit asking what the hell happened." She laughed, but it wasn't a real laugh. "Don't get me wrong; Mom did tell me he'd ended up in prison, some fight, after losing his best friend." Stepping off the elevator, she casually mentioned, "And that's about the time I found out he'd died, the prison part, and that period for me kinda all ran together." Stopping in the hallway, she looked up at Cash. "I guess because I was little at the time my head must have merged all the events together, blocking my dad out, but keeping the good stuff in."

"Captain Fin?"

"Yep, him, Captain Fin." Hannah blew away a single strand of hair that had fallen across her face. "Captain Fin did bring me a lot of joy as a kid; that I do remember."

Cash wrapped his arm around her neck and started walking, forcing her to do the same. "Guess at that time in your life you liked being a pirate better more than a kid."

"Yeah, I suppose so," she whispered. "He made it really fun."

"Do you remember your mom talking about him when he was gone, at Folsom State Prison?"

Hannah thought about it for a minute. "I don't remember her speaking badly of him, or saying negative things to me about our situation in regards to him, you know, moving all the time. In fact, come to think of it, she never really mentioned him at all."

'She never remarried," Cash noted. "Did she ever date?"

"No, and I've never known my mom to see another man or bring one home for that matter."

"Well if you ask me, and I know you didn't," Cash chuckled, "it sounds like she never got over him." Pulling her closer, he opened his mouth to say something, closed it again as if he shouldn't say what he was going to say, and then blurted it out anyway. "You could look at it this way," he smiled. "She did tell you about the box; better late than never, right?"

Hannah agreed. Her mom wanted her to have the box. She needed her to know that her dad had loved and missed her, but right now they needed to focus on her mom's health and get her well enough to at least come home. Hannah kissed him goodbye at Gloria's hospital door, dismissing him; he still didn't want to leave, but he went home. Gloria was still sleeping, and Kathy was reading in the chair when Hannah entered her mom's room. Hannah kissed her mom on the cheek before planting herself on the tiny couch, which was squeezed next to her aunt's chair and the wall.

"Any change?" Hannah asked, looking toward Gloria.

"She was awake for a little bit, not long, and she's resting now." Kathy set her book down in her lap. "Hannah, she was asking for you. I don't want to scare you, but between the medications and the pain meds, she's delirious." Kathy lowered her voice. "I couldn't make heads nor tails of what she was saying."

The two settled in for the evening; Kathy read her book until her eyes could take it no longer, and fell asleep in the chair. Hannah texted Cash and Lindsey before pulling out the handful of letters shoved in her bag. She read them over and over until she practically knew every word written on the faded yellow paper by heart. So many questions! But Hannah was well aware that before Gloria could explain a single thing about her past, or clarify the questions that raced through her mind, her mom had to get better first.

Chapter 24
Prepare Yourselves

Don't break my heart!
Let her stay.
I need my mom
Just go AWAY!
~ Hannah Gunner ~

There was no such thing as getting any rest that night for Hannah or Kathy. Nurses were popping in and out every other hour it seemed to check monitors, administer fluids, check Gloria's blood pressure, temperature, and run tests. Though they were all courteous and pleasant, it was impossible to sleep. Gloria managed to sleep on and off due to being knocked out by drugs. The reality of how severe her condition was had hit everyone. The morning couldn't roll around fast enough. Fresh coffee and an explanation from her mom's doctor, the oncologist, who was supposed to drop by, which was at the forefront of Kathy's and Hannah's minds. He showed up a little after 9 a.m. He was strikingly handsome and awfully young; too young, Hannah thought, and wondered if he'd been doing this long enough to know exactly what he was doing! An exchange of pleasantries between all of them took place, Gloria—who was actually awake, lucid, and alert—included. After reading his notes, checking her heart, lungs, and the latest lab and test results, the news that he delivered wasn't what they had expected.

"You're just not working with me here, are ya?" He winked at Gloria.

"I'm trying," she managed, but everyone noticed her voice was weak.

Staring at Hannah, as if evaluating her age and maturity, he hesitated before asking if he could speak candidly with everyone present in the room. Gloria didn't object. His tone never changed—monotone, but not unpleasant. And he talked to them as if they knew what he was saying. Thankfully Gloria spoke up.

"Could you repeat the last part mostly, but in layman's terms, please? My daughter and sister aren't going to understand what you're saying, and I don't have the strength to interpret for them."

Hot doctor half smiled and winked. "Sure."

Hannah moved closer to her mom and sat down on the edge of her bed. Kathy pulled out a pen and paper to jot down everything he was about to repeat.

"We're slipping into the accelerated phase of the CML. In other words, from stage three to stage four and, as you can imagine, that's not good. It's the reason your white blood cell count, indicating infection, is still so high and, despite the antibiotics we're trying, they aren't going down. The platelet counts will vary, could be high one day, and could be low the next. The new chromosome changes in the cells are taking place, and unfortunately, this is all due to the CML." He searched their faces for questions, but they were numb. Gingerly he forged ahead. "Patients with CML at this stage, accelerated, often experience the symptoms that you're having, such as fever, lack of appetite, and weight loss."

Hannah knew her mom hadn't been eating normally lately and felt ashamed for not mentioning it. Pulling a chair up next to Gloria's bed, the doctor sat down, crossed his legs, and continued to discuss the information with them. Hannah sat in silence and listened. Kathy, exhausted, put down her pen and dabbed her face with a tissue for fear that Gloria would see her tears.

"Long story short, if you throw this nasty pneumonia in the mix, the complications are tenfold. And well, there's no easy way to say this, but you're in bad shape right now. Your immune system, already jeopardized, is struggling to fight off the infection that is in your lungs, and the fluid you have in them isn't helping." Sighing, he added, "Typically patients in this phase, because it's so accelerated, do not respond well to any treatments. And any illness complicates the situation in the chronic phase—even something as simple as a common cold, let alone pneumonia.

"So there is another phase?" Kathy asked.

"The blast phase, also known as the blast crisis phase. The blast cells often spread to tissues and organs beyond the bone marrow. Depending on the complications, response to treatment, and complications of secondary infections, it can be one of the last phases."

He stood up and put the chair back in the corner. "But let's not talk about that right now. Let's discuss your treatment plan for fighting this nasty pneumonia."

He turned to his scribe and had a discussion with her, then turned back around to finish his conversation with Gloria.

"Well, aren't you just a barrel of sunshine," Gloria chuckled. "Yes, please, tell me what's next!"

"Yeah, sorry about that! I hate delivering this type of news, but we do have to discuss what needs to be done next, and you're not going to like it."

Hannah's ears perked up, and she leaned in so she could hear every single word he said. "What do you have in mind?" Gloria asked. "And can I handle it?"

"You can handle it, but you're not going to like it."

Hannah's eyes felt as if they were piercing right through him as he stood over her mom, seeking answers, a solution, anything that would keep her alive and allow her to fight this thing that he had diagnosed her with in the first place.

He continued to speak freely. "Given the circumstances, at least until we get you stable, I'm strongly suggesting we move you into ICU. Sterile environment and, of course, no visitors." Before Gloria could object, he added, "That will allow us to tackle the pneumonia head on, and then worry about continuing your treatment for CML."

"For how long?" Gloria asked. "ICU."

"As long as it takes, three days, a week maybe."

"When?" Hannah asked.

"Now." Avoiding Hannah, his eyes met Kathy's. "It really is for the best."

The color drained from Hannah's face right before the doctor's eyes.

"Can we spend some time with her first?" Kathy asked.

"Make it quick. The sooner she's isolated, the better for her, and that's what we all want."

Kathy put her arm around Hannah as if to comfort her, but Hannah noticed she was steadying herself. The situation had gone from bad to worse overnight. The constant beeping noise of the monitor attached to her mom was a great distraction, but as the alarm sounded, the nurse rushed in and offered Gloria pain meds. "Your blood pressure is going up, and I'm betting it's because you're due your next round of pain meds." Smiling, she continued, "I'm going to administer through your port, doctor's orders, just letting you know." She finally took a breath. "Do you have any questions?"

Gloria shook her head. "Hannah, do you mind sitting with me for a few minutes? I'm not sure how much time I have before my temporary confinement." Forcing a smile, she lifted her hand and Hannah grasped it and placed it in hers.

"Leave it to you to be so dramatic! Gotta go to ICU to get away from me!"

"Never," Gloria whispered in between breaths. "I want to come home with you." She held Hannah's hand as tight as she could, but her grasp was weak. "Did you find it? The box?"

Hannah couldn't believe that was still on her mind, but she nodded. "Don't think about that right now; it's not important." Kissing the top of her mom's hand, Hannah added, "We'll talk about it later."

The nurse administered the pain meds through the

port as they spoke. "You'll feel better in a few minutes."

She winked at Hannah, checked everything one more time, and left the room. Gloria's grip loosened completely as she mumbled *I'm sorry, Hannah. Soooooo sorry*, and started to doze back off. Murmur after murmur, none of it making any sense. Kathy and Hannah couldn't make out a single coherent sentence that Gloria said except for *Hank, forgive me*, and *Hannah, I'm sorry*. An orderly reappeared with a nurse at his side. They checked her chart, her wristband, and tried to confirm with Gloria where they were supposed to be taking her. She couldn't answer, so they verified with Kathy and Hannah on her behalf.

"Understandable; it's the pain meds. We're headed to ICU. Can you confirm the patient's name, date of birth, and why she's here?" Hannah interjected and gave them the details before kissing her mom goodbye. Gathering up their things, they walked solemnly to the car.

"Yours or mine?" Kathy asked. "I'm open."

"Do you mind if we go home, to ours?"

Kathy shook her head. "No. Figured you'd want to be close to home."

"Great! There's something I'd like to show you."

Chapter 25
Doesn't Add Up

Betrayal
Lies
Deception
And fear
I'm losing my mind
Yet, the Captain is right here
~ Hannah Gunner ~

Cash took off his ball cap, pitched it across the room, and watched it land on Hannah's bed before settling in, opposite Hannah, on her bedroom floor. The only thing separating them was the infamous box filled with letters. They'd agreed to set it aside and go through it together, and finally Saturday had rolled around. He could sense her nervousness, as if scared to death of something she may or may not find, written in between the lines of the letters that she was about to read. Noticing how naturally beautiful she looked without a stitch of makeup, in her oversized shirt and sweats, he couldn't help but stare at her; she never noticed. Absorbed in the handwritten words on the faded yellow paper, she had no idea he was taking in every detail at that moment about her. To say he was head-over-heels about her would be an understatement. Resisting the urge to say something stupid, Cash hesitantly dipped his hand into the box; she still never raised her head.

The first letter Cash pulled out happened to be a handwritten birthday note. It was short and to the point, but he could tell a lot of thought had gone into it. *Guessing they didn't have access to Hallmark cards in prison,* he thought, *not bad for improvising.* The man had even drawn a picture of a cake, a pirate sword, and signed off with a heart! He set it aside and pulled out another envelope. Hannah was tearing through them faster than Cash. Pulling letters out of envelopes, scanning them, pulling out another, going back and reading the previous letter as if she'd missed a clue of some sort in the prior letter. The scent of musty, aging paper filled the room. Kathy popped her head in the door.

"I'm shocked that your mom hid those from you for all of those years, but I'm certain she must have had her reasons." Taking a deep breath, as if not knowing what else to say, Kathy stared at the box in the center of the floor. "I'm going to head over to the hospital just in case they'll let me see your mom. She's coming out of ICU today, and I want to be there to greet her." Unable to resist the urge, she bent down and picked up a letter. Reading it, she smiled, and put it back in the envelope. "I can hear your dad's voice when I read these."

"Why don't you just call?" Cash suggested. "To see if she's coming out of ICU today for sure, and if so, if they'll let you see her."

Kathy shook her head. "I can't sit still. I feel helpless and need to kill time; running up there does just that."

"Do you think I should be there as well?" Hannah asked. "Just in case she does get out of ICU?"

Kathy thought about it for a second, then assured her waiting would be fine. "I'll call you as soon as she's settled if they put her in a regular room. She might want you to bring her something from home when you do visit her." Eyes wide open, daring not to jinx her sister, she added, "Wouldn't it be something if they let her come home?!"

"Right! That would be something," Cash grinned. "Wishful thinking maybe, but it would be great."

Kathy left the two teens sifting through the scattered letters all over Hannah's floor. They stacked letters and cards in piles, which they set aside, and put them in the best chronological order that they possibly could using the stamp dates. They poured through every detail that they thought was important or relevant to establishing a timeline. Suddenly, startling Cash, Hannah squealed out loud and frantically grabbed his arm and started to read a letter out loud.

Sweet Hannah,

I'm assuming by now you're too old to be my First Matey, but in my head, you're still a little pirate to me! When I close my eyes, all I can see is a mass of dark blond hair, running around her bed in the middle of her bedroom, pretending to swim to the beach. Do you remember the beach we used to visit, the real one? You were so little, I'm not sure that you do; but it's crystal clear to me.

I remember that you used to love the water, the beach, and when I'd take you to work with me, kinda, to the docks to see the freighters come in. I miss you so much, but I'm betting by now you do not even remember me.

I think I write these letters now more for me than you. I can't believe today is the day you become a teen!!!!!! Thirteen. Oh how I wish I were there to see. If by chance you can find it in you to drop me a line, a quick hello, please do.

Love always, Dad

One look at Hannah's face and Cash thought she must have figured out what he'd already realized as well... THE DATES... they didn't add up to what she'd been told. None of it was making any sense. Cash was right! He knew precisely what was running through her mind; he could see her wheels turning, and his eyes darted to the stack of letters that he had neatly placed in a pile beside him. Praying she'd say it first, he waited; he didn't have to wait long.

"What the hell?! None of this shit adds up. Someone LIED!"

Chapter 26
Out of Time

Oh God, please no!
~ Aunt Kathy ~

The phone felt as if it was burning a hole in Hannah's hand. She wanted to reach out to Kathy, but every time she dialed, Kathy's voicemail picked up. Frustrated, she left message after message. Cash reached over and gently took the phone out of her hand; Hannah didn't object. He sat down on the edge of the bed and pulled her down next to him. Together they separated all of the letters into significant events in Hannah's life: birthdays, holidays, moving, each grade level, and even into her teen years. Hank had referenced them all. Scooting closer to Cash wasn't a problem; he smelled good, looked great, and the warmth of his body made her feel safe. She wanted to stay right there, on the edge of the bed next to him, listening to him read and theorize for as long as possible.

"Let's call the nurse's desk and check to see if Kathy's in the patient lounge or something," Cash suggested. "If she's taking this long, she might be getting updated."

Despite not wanting to move, she dialed the hospital, and a cheerful voice on the other end picked up. Hannah identified herself and asked about her aunt.

"I think she stepped out for some air or maybe coffee; let me take a look real quick, the patients' area is right around the corner. I do know she has been waiting to talk to your mom's doctor."

"Thank you so much!" Hannah replied.

The nurse returned, apologized, but there was no sign of Kathy.

"She's been here a while this morning. It's possible she's already spoken to your mom's doctor, and I didn't see her. We get pretty busy around here, especially during shift change."

Hannah thanked the lady for her time, but right before she hung up, she asked the nurse a question.

"Do you know when my mom will be out of ICU or able to have visitors?"

The nurse banged away on her keys, mentioned it looked as if they were releasing her mom to a regular room that day, but they were waiting for her doctor to sign off on that.

"I'd say late afternoon, early evening, shouldn't be an issue, but if not by then definitely by tomorrow a room will be available."

Hannah smiled and gave Cash a thumbs-up. They'd head down after a while, stop and visit her mom, and try to get some answers from Kathy. Cash put his arms around Hannah, kissed the back of her neck, and inhaled the scent of her shower gel.

"You smell very tropical," he grinned. "I kinda wanna

eat your hair."

Hannah playfully nudged him. He hadn't seen *that* smile in a while. Leaning in, he kissed her lips. To his surprise she didn't object but kissed him back; long and slow, it was nice. Like it was supposed to be and had been in the past, but then she gently pulled away.

"I must look a mess. No makeup. Hair looks like this!" Pointing to her hair hanging in loose unkempt waves over her shoulders and down the middle of her back.

"You must not realize how good you look; you look amazing!"

She could feel the heat rushing to her cheeks; any compliment he gave her made her blush. Pecking him on the cheek, she looked at him in a way that she rarely did.

"What? Did I do or say something wrong?"

He sounded sincere, but something was weighing on her mind other than the inability to accept his compliment.

"Do you think she knew?" Hannah asked inquisitively. "Kathy? That my mom was hiding all of those letters and acted surprised to cover for her?"

"I was actually going to ask you that question when the time was right, but I'm not sure if there would have been a right time, so I'm actually glad you asked first."

Cash haphazardly placed his ball cap on top of his head. It was crooked but cute. Nervously he asked her a few questions he'd been putting off.

"That would mean your Aunt Kathy lied for your mom. You don't suppose she would lie for your mom, do you?"

Hannah thought about it for a few moments before answering. She honestly didn't know. Being an only child, she had no idea if that kind of bond between sisters was real. They were sisters and seemed really close since they'd moved back, but that was a major lie and would have meant they'd hidden the truth from Hannah for practically her whole life! Hating to speculate and not knowing how she'd feel about her aunt if the answer were yes, Hannah shook her head. For a second she felt as if the two women she loved the most in the world were strangers. It was a sick feeling, knowing the closest person in your life had betrayed you; the possibility of the lie being an actual conspiracy between more people than one was too much for Hannah to comprehend. Too many unanswered questions! Why had her mother hidden the letters? And the most obvious: why did she tell her the Captain was dead when at that time he was clearly writing to her?

"I just don't know." Hannah held her head in her hands. Her hair hung down and covered her face. "I honestly don't know anything anymore!"

Blinking tears away, pretending that she wasn't unraveling, Hannah gasped for air. She could feel her chest tighten as a wave of anxiety rushed over her body, reminding her that she was about to cave in and lose control of her ability to breathe.

"When did Hank, the Captain, my dad, really die?"

Tears she'd been fighting to hold back filled to the brim of her eyelids and finally spilled over, leaving wet trails running down her flushed cheeks.

"I don't think he bailed on us, but I just don't know

what in the hell really happened."

She wiped her tears with her sweatshirt sleeve. Her sparkling blue eyes held an icy, distant stare. "If they conspired to lie to me... why?" Hesitating. "Cash, how the hell do I trust them?"

Cash didn't dare speak for fear of saying the wrong thing; inching his way toward her, he reached out his arms and wrapped them around her body. Pulling her gently toward him, Hannah buried her head in his shoulder. For the first time ever in front of her boyfriend, Hannah sobbed uncontrollably until she could cry no more. Stroking her hair, softly kissing the top of her head as her whole body shook, Cash held her trembling body in his arms and never said one word! His silence spoke volumes. Neither one of them heard the unlocking of the door. Kathy, wide-eyed, stood in the doorway of Hannah's room. She stared at the two teens, locked in each other's arms and looked down at the floor. Cash finally made eye contact with Kathy and pleaded with his eyes, asking for a minute longer to allow Hannah to compose herself before he stepped aside. As Kathy backed away from the door, turned on her heels, and headed toward the living room, she wondered what in the hell else had gone wrong! After a few moments, Cash gently pulled away from Hannah and with his hand moved her now dripping-wet hair from her face, placing it to one side.

"Babe, maybe we can get some answers if you're up to it. Kathy's back."

Hannah raised her chin and looked around the room. "She's back?"

"Yeah. She just walked in the door." Cash leaned forward and kissed her forehead. "Take a minute, splash some water on your face, and I'll meet you in the living room. Okay?"

Hannah nodded.

Kathy was sitting in a chair in the corner of the living room, staring at Gloria's recliner still draped in her blanket. Cash sat down on the couch and waited for Hannah to enter the room. As soon as she walked in, she perched on the edge of Gloria's chair and nervously started playing with the fringe on the blanket as she prepared to gather her thoughts. Neither Hannah nor Cash, being so caught up in search of answers of their own, had noticed how pale Kathy was when she'd entered the apartment. Hannah started rattling off dates, questions, and mentioning Hank and Gloria in the same sentence, and talking about things that Kathy didn't understand. She heard most of the words that her niece was saying, but didn't comprehend what she was talking about or if there was a point that she was trying to make. Hannah suddenly jumped up out of the chair and ran into her room. Instinctively Cash started to follow her, but before he could reach her bedroom door, she reappeared, holding multiple letters in her hand.

"I'm talking about these. What the hell are these about, all of these letters?"

Kathy's head was spinning; in despair, she raised her hands in the air.

"Hannah, stop!"

"Stop what?" Hannah snapped.

Hannah unknowingly took a few steps backward

toward Cash. "Let me start over. Maybe I'm not making any sense, but I will if I explain it properly." She took a deep breath. "It starts with the box and the letters that mom wanted me to find."

But before another word could pop out of her mouth, Kathy yelled, "Hannah, STOP!"

Alarmed, Hannah jumped. Her heart suddenly felt as if it had crawled into her throat. The warm touch of Cash's hand as he reached out for hers made her feel better. Hannah lowered the letters that she now held in her hand and closed her gaping mouth. The two waited in awkward silence.

"Hannah. It's your mom. It's not good. She's taken a turn for the worse, and we need to get you to the hospital."

Her face was pale, and for the first time, Hannah and Cash realized that Kathy was shaking, her eyes were red and swollen, and she must have been crying.

"Hannah, it's bad."

Hannah couldn't think. Nodding, she rushed to the door. Cash grabbed her arm, glancing at Kathy as if asking for permission to speak. Kathy's eyes were empty. Her energy completely depleted, she had nothing left emotionally to support or guide them at that moment one way or the other.

"Babe, take a second and throw a few things in a bag. You may be up there for a while."

Expressionless, Hannah rushed into her room and started shoving miscellaneous items into an oversized bag: shirt, shorts, sweatpants, sweatshirt, underwear, makeup wipe removers, moisturizer, her makeup bag, ponytail holder, brush, an extra phone charger, iPad, and for some reason, she picked up her mom's id. Cash grabbed her a few bottles of water, a pack of peanuts, and an apple.

Cash turned to Kathy. "Would you like me to drive? I can stop by your place, and you can pick up a few items, unless you have stuff here you need."

Kathy wiped away the tears that had trickled down her face. Exhaustion, the unknown, and the shock of the latest news had set in. Thanking Cash, she assured him she had enough items at the apartment since she'd been staying with Gloria so much on and off lately, more so than they had all realized. Excuses of a *girls night, movie night, novel, sip and wine night,* seemed just like that now—excuses for Kathy to stay over with her mom! There was no time to discuss that right then, either, if the two women Hannah loved most in her life had indeed covered up her mom's health issues. A familiar dinging notification sound came from Hannah's room. Cash nodded and without saying a word ran back into her bedroom and picked the phone up off the floor. Tempted to look at the text, he purposely turned the phone the other way as he handed it over to Hannah. Instinctively, Hannah announced Lindsey was checking in.

Lindsey: Love ya. Thinking of ya. Miss ya. Let me know if ya need anything!

Hannah: Same. Thank you! Headed back to the hospital. Things are bad. Talk later. Love ya.

Lindsey: Is Cash with you or should I come?

Hannah: Cash is here. Thank you!

Lindsey: Okay. Love ya. Let me know if you need

anything at all. Tell Momma G. I love her.

Hannah: Will do.

Kathy held the door open; a silent cue to hurry up. Cash and Hannah climbed into his Jeep, following closely behind Kathy. A sick feeling filled the pit of Hannah's stomach as soon as they pulled up to the hospital entrance. Nausea. Nerves. Fear. And helplessness. The sliding double glass doors opened, and the familiar smell of the hospital made Hannah want to gag. The cool air immediately gave them all chill bumps. Cash swung her bag over his shoulder, reached out and grabbed her hand, and pulled Hannah closer toward him. She was trembling. Kathy put one foot in front of the other, but it felt as if the corridor would never end. Finally checking in at the nurse's station, they requested an update and asked if it was possible to see Gloria.

"Let me check with her doctor," an energetic yet sympathetic nurse responded.

She pointed them to the patient lounge, and the waiting game began. It felt like an eternity, but in reality, it was less than fifteen minutes. A middle-aged, good-looking man appeared at the entranceway of the lounge. Popping his head in, he peered around the room, stopping and staring at Kathy.

"May I have a word, please?"

Kathy, white as a sheet, nodded and stood up.

As he glanced at Hannah and Cash, Kathy intervened. "It's okay. They're with me."

"Right. Well, then, let's chat in here."

Pointing to the sofa, Kathy sat back down, and the doctor sat in a chair catty-corner to the door. *Quick escape?* Hannah wondered, just in case patients were too emotional at times like this when *the bomb* was dropped.

"Well... where shall I start?" the doctor asked, already knowing there was but one thing to discuss. Time. And what was left of Gloria's.

Chapter 27
Death Sentence

Death
Loss
Somber
Soul
Heartbreak
Shattered
Leave me alone
~ Hannah Gunner ~

His voice was soft and kind, but it didn't take the sting out of Dr. Krane's words. Numb. His words trailed off as Hannah zoned out. All she could do was stand frozen in one spot, like a trembling child, as Cash steadied her with his arm wrapped tightly around her waist. Kathy's face was drained of any color that she possessed, white as the walls that surrounded them, hearing the doctor's words but comprehending none of them.

"It's not unusual for patients to move from the chronic to accelerated phase quickly, just like Gloria." He glanced at Hannah. "Your mom did; it happens if they don't stabilize within a certain amount of time. Add the additional complications, weakened immune system, and being nonresponsive to treatment and it's almost inevitable." Looking down, he continued, "But we were still hoping to slow down the process at least for a while.

However, I don't believe it will be possible for her to have a bone marrow transplant. She's not strong enough, and it's pretty advanced."

Hannah's eyes darted toward Kathy. "Bone marrow transplant?"

Pausing, he glanced at each one of them, Cash included, checking to see if he could continue. Doing that doctor thing, he moved right along. His voice was even-toned as he continued his speech, not unkind, just business as usual. But it wasn't business as usual for Hannah or Kathy, or in that moment even Cash. Hannah's mind was swirling around and around. This was her mom, her family, only family, that he was talking about!

"Unfortunately, between the complications with pneumonia, and the constant infections that we've been battling due to her not responding well to her treatments, a bone marrow transplant is out of the question. We struggled to prevent one of her lungs from collapsing, but she's now stable in that regard."

"Wait. What? Her lung was collapsing?" Hannah lunged forward toward Kathy. "What is he talking about?"

Suddenly realizing that Hannah did not know the severity of her mom's condition, he waited as Kathy interjected. Her voice was barely a whisper, but she managed to speak up.

"I was trying to tell you, but I just didn't know how." Holding Hannah's hand in hers. "There was so much going on; her lung, that was merely a part of it."

Cash reached out and gently tugged Hannah's arm;

code for *I'm here*. He leaned forward, whispering in her ear, "Be gentle, babe; she's upset as well."

Hannah understood, and slid down quietly and sat down next to her aunt.

"Should I go on?" the doctor asked.

No one spoke, but a silent nod confirmed he should finish what he'd come to say.

"We couldn't contain the CML in the accelerated stage, and it's moved rather quickly into what we call the blast phase."

Cash squeezed Hannah's hand, but he noticed immediately that her hand was lifeless in his. Was her mom's death sentence being delivered? Suddenly, an overwhelming desire to vomit swept over Hannah. Her skin flushed as she felt an all-consuming heat rush to her cheeks. The room started to spin, and she couldn't breathe. Her chest felt as if it had a hundred-pound weight sitting on top of it; gasping for air, she realized she was about to have a panic attack. Cash jumped up and ran to get her a drink of water. Dr. Krane grabbed her hands and instructed her to breathe slowly, deep breaths, in and out, and put her head in between her knees. Hannah recomposed herself before a full-fledged panic attack overwhelmed her, but she was barely hanging on.

"Maybe that's enough for now," Dr. Krane said softly.

"I think I'd rather just get it over with, if you don't mind."

Glancing at Kathy, looking for approval, which came in the form of a nod of the head, the doctor continued, choosing his words very carefully.

"If kept in the blast phase, which is twenty percent myeloblasts or lymphoblasts, the symptoms are manageable. Not curable, but manageable. They're similar to those of acute myeloid leukemia and because of that we can keep Gloria relatively comfortable."

Unable to contain her emotions any longer, Kathy dabbed her cheeks with her sleeve as tears poured over her eyelids and rolled nonstop down her cheeks.

"I really think we should take a few minutes?" Dr. Krane suggested. "Regroup."

Cash nodded but Hannah shook her head, and Kathy even managed to say the word no in between her sobs. Treading as cautiously as he could, the doctor continued.

"We've entered phase four or the blast crisis phase of her illness. She's anemic; her white blood cell count is off the charts despite the antibiotics that we continue to try. Her platelet counts are low, and the blast cells themselves have spread outside her blood and bone marrow and are now affecting other tissues and organs. She will likely continue to battle a fever, lose even more weight as she still has no appetite at all, and despite what we're doing, it continues to get more aggressive and wear her down."

"Are you saying what I think you're saying, that there's nothing else you can do?" Kathy asked.

Dr. Krane's eye softened, and his voice was filled with kindness.

"Keep her comfortable. Once she's able, if at all possible, we'll let her go home and arrange hospice care to help. I'm not making any promises. It's possible due to the turn that she has taken that she may not bounce back as well as we'd hoped."

"What exactly does that mean?" Hannah snapped, already knowing deep down inside what the doctor was trying to say. Her mom, her best friend in the whole world, was going to die.

"Sorry for being rude," Hannah managed to say in between her tears.

"No. That's quite all right. Difficult times." Dr. Krane sat on the arm of the chair, eye level with Hannah. "I would say it is possible that we may have to keep your mother here for a little longer than we had thought. Fingers crossed I'm wrong, but we want her to remain comfortable while we see if she can handle the treatment. If her fever breaks, she may go home. But either way, prepare yourself for the worst." Standing up, he said something before he left that Hannah would never forget. "You have a short amount of time left with your mom. Sometimes she will be coherent and conscious and sometimes she will not; that said, make what time you have with her count."

Stunned, Hannah wrapped her arms around Cash. "My mom was just handed her death sentence!"

Cash held her tightly and searched Kathy's face for help, but as soon as Hannah looked toward her, Kathy buried her face in her hands and sobbed in a way that Hannah had never heard her aunt cry in her life! Wrapping her arms around Kathy, the two of them held each other as they cried. Fighting back the tears, Cash quietly left the room and pulled out his phone. His first text was to Lindsey.

Cash: It's bad. Hannah needs you. Text her asap.

Lindsey. So scared and sad!!!! On it!

His next text was to his mom.

Cash: OMG, Mom, you're not going to believe what the doctor just said.

Mrs. Parks: Everything okay?

Cash: No. Everything is not okay. She's going to die.

Chapter 28
Answers

Can't breathe
Want to die
Heart is breaking
While I cry
World is shattered
What have you done?
Why are you taking her?
She's not the one
~ Hannah Gunner ~

A gentle tap on the door woke Hannah up. It took her a second to remember where she was, but a beeping monitor was a quick reminder that she was in her mom's hospital room instead of the ICU or her own room. Both Hannah and Kathy's faces lit up as they recognized a familiar voice and face. They both jumped up to greet Lindsey barreling toward them, arms extended, offering much-needed hugs. Kathy grabbed her first, embraced her, and then stepped aside so Lindsey could wrap her arms around her best friend in the same welcoming way. Glancing at a sleeping Gloria, Lindsey didn't dare ask the obvious. Sweetly she kissed Gloria's cheek and moved once again out of the way to let Hannah sit back down in the chair closest to her mom.

"I brought you some real food; you don't have to eat

it, but in case you're hungry, here ya go."

Holding up a couple bags of In-N-Out Burger, *real food*, made Hannah smile.

"Thank you!" She peered into the bag. "My favorite! I'll definitely give this a go in a bit."

Handing a bag to Kathy, Lindsey said, "I didn't know what you liked, so I stuck with a combo number one; who doesn't love a number one?"

Hunger had left both Hannah and Kathy a few days ago, but Kathy thanked her, sipped the Coke, and forced herself to nibble on a French fry so she wouldn't seem ungrateful. Noticing how frail Hannah looked, she tried to encourage her to do the same.

"You need to eat something, Hannah; keep up your strength for your mom."

Hannah nodded, but made no attempt to take a bite. She stood up, stretched, and pulled Lindsey by her arm toward the door.

"I really need some fresh air and to stretch my legs. Do you mind if we leave for a few minutes? We'll be right back."

Kathy waved the girls out the door and repositioned herself in the chair closest to Gloria.

"Where's Cash?" Lindsey asked.

"I sent him home. He's been here for hours, and he needs to shower, sleep, and eat." Hannah grinned. "Trust me, he needs to shower."

"How are you holding up?" Lindsey asked, concerned. "I know it seems like a dumb question, but I have to ask."

"I'm not," Hannah responded. "I'm a mess. I thought

I was, but I don't know how to act or what to say. I don't want to believe what I'm hearing, and I don't want my mom to worry when she's awake, but she does."

Hannah dug her hands into her jean pockets. Her voice barely a whisper, she continued. "Cash has been great. Honestly, I don't know what I would've done without him these last few weeks, but of course, I love you too!"

"Again, boyfriend goals!" Lindsey replied, rolling her eyes and laughing. "I know what you mean, don't worry about me. He's a keeper!"

Lindsey wrapped her arm around Hannah's shoulder and squeezed her tightly. She felt weird saying what she was about to say, but felt as if she should say it anyway. It just seemed so serious and out of character for them, even though they were best friends.

"I won't tell you it's going to be okay, because I don't know that it will, but I will tell you that I am here for you if you need anything." Hesitating. "Or wanna talk."

Hannah couldn't respond; sadness consumed her as the seriousness of her mom's outcome weighed heavily on her mind. Facing Lindsey, she squeezed her back and assured her that she knew her intentions were heartfelt, and most importantly, well received. Against Hannah's will, the teardrops that had trickled down her pale cheeks turned into sobs. Sick of crying, Hannah scolded herself and the whole damn situation.

"I'm just so pissed off, confused, and sad! Angry, which is ridiculous, because no one could have predicted this; certainly not my mom."

Hannah laughed, but it wasn't a genuine laugh. It

was a sad, tormented laugh, Hannah's outward display of the emotional tornado that she'd just got caught up in! Taking a deep breath, embarrassed by her outburst, she tried to finish her rant calmly.

"Anyway, I think that just about covers it. It sucks!"

She hung her head, as if in shame, and sniffled. Shakily, she told Lindsey about the box and the letters from her dad.

"I don't want to feel any of these things; numb is so much better, because it doesn't hurt. I want to focus on my mom and help her get through this, and whatever's next. I want the questions that I have to go away; to quit running around in my head; that way I'm not worried about finding out any damn answers. I can't stand it when my mom is laying there, sick, and a question pops into my head about, of all things, those damn letters, *the Captain,* or *my dad,* I should say, and what the hell is really going on around here?" Hannah took a deep breath, exhaled, looked down at her feet, and added, "Because even I know this isn't the damn time or place to bring that shit up!" Frustrated, Hannah spoke and Lindsey listened. "And it makes me feel like crap because I don't want to think about anything but my mom right now. She's *all* that matters! But can you believe I can't seem to get that through to her no matter what I say? She won't listen; not to me, Kathy, or anyone." Blinking her eyes as fast as she could so that her tears wouldn't fall again, Hannah tried to cover up the shame that she felt inside for the words that kept tumbling out of her mouth. No matter how hard she tried, she couldn't stop the thoughts running through her head from competing with the pain in her heart, and the whole thing was torturous.

"I don't want to care about my past, about those damn letters, or my dad, but I know that she has the answers that one day I will need. And during all of this mess, late at night in the silence of that damn hospital room, those freaking questions sneak back into the corners of my mind, reminding me of what a crap daughter I am for thinking about the past instead of her! And honestly, Lindsey, for that, I absolutely one hundred percent *hate* myself!!"

Lindsey shook her head. "You're being too hard on yourself; it's human nature to contemplate, wonder, think, hell, even imagine, you know that! With everything that's going on, don't beat yourself up so badly."

Pulling the JUUL from her pocket, Hannah took a long draw. Exhaled. Drew again, exhaled, and offered it to Lindsey. Lindsey took a drag herself and handed it back. It smelled sweet. If you didn't know better, you'd think they were eating a big ol' bag of cotton candy. Hannah stared at the tiny device in her hand that her mom hated so much, took another hit, and in disgust shoved it back in her pocket.

"My mom hates this thing; I really need to work on quitting, for both of us!"

Hannah perched on a retaining wall in front of the hospital doors. The cool air felt good, refreshing, and she dreaded going back into her mom's stale room. Lindsey leaned on the wall next to her, but knew, today, that her friend needed to talk more than she did. Pulling out a

JUUL of her own, she smoked in silence and just listened.

"It's ridiculous, really."

"Oh yeah, what's that?" Lindsey asked.

"Well, she keeps asking me to forgive her, my mom, and I do because she wants me to, but she doesn't need my forgiveness. She's freaking delirious all the time. All she says over and over and over is *please forgive me*, and *Hannah, I'm sorry.*" Hannah discreetly took a hit off her vape and stuck it back in her pocket. "When I first found the letters, I was consumed with knowing why she hid them, and let's be honest, if she could tell me that would be great, but with the state she's in," Hannah shook her head, "I doubt I'll have the answers I need. But she still doesn't need forgiveness from me. Not over hiding a box of damn letters. I know enough to know she must have had her reasons."

Brushing her hair over the back of her head, Hannah sighed. "Maybe one day someone will tell me why in the hell everyone lied!" Laughing, she added, "I still haven't had the nerve to bring it up with Aunt Kathy, you know, the whole 'did she know why' thing."

"Is it important anymore?" Lindsey asked.

Hannah shook her head again. "No. It's not. Right now, I don't even freaking care who lied or why; I just want my mom to come home, and I don't know if she ever will."

Hugging in the chilly air before making their way back upstairs, Hannah looked as if a weight had been lifted off her shoulders. Talking it out was sometimes the best way to get everything off your chest and out of your system, and Lindsey was convinced that was exactly what Hannah needed! Hesitating, she bit her tongue and decided to hold off saying what had popped into her head as Hannah had vented. The hesitation must have been written all over her face as Hannah suddenly asked her a question.

"What were you about to say?"

"Me? Nothing."

"Yes, you were, what is it? Just say it. Feels good." Hannah actually managed a smile, and the last thing Lindsey wanted to do was ruin it, but Hannah kept insisting.

"Well I don't want to say it, Hannah," Lindsey said softly, "But it might be good to prepare yourself for the possibility that you may never get the answers you need."

Hannah shrugged her shoulders and jumped off the wall. "Like I said, I don't care anymore."

Staring mindlessly across the concrete parking lot, counting the tops of the cars for absolutely no reason at all, Hannah thought about the possibility of her mom not coming home. Her memories of them together, despite being a teen, were good ones. Even though at times admittedly she'd likely blamed her inadvertently for her dad not being around. She felt terrible about that now; especially knowing there was more to the story. Looking back, through the eyes of a shipmate, her memories were solid, remembering so clearly the laughter that had filled her early years. But it did start with her mom, the truth. She was the keeper of secrets or so it seemed.

Hannah's phone vibrated, a text from Kathy:

HURRY BACK, Gloria's frantic and asking for you.

The girls rushed back to the room as fast as they could, receiving dirty looks from more than one of the hospital staff members as they darted around orderlies and nurses. They slowed down once they entered the critical care floor unit, and even then they were walking as fast as some people jog. Gloria wasn't aware the girls had entered the room. She didn't seem to be mindful of anyone around her, but kept repeating Hannah's name over and over again. Lindsey slipped quietly into the corner of the room, hoping that she wouldn't impose, knowing something was terribly wrong. Kathy and Hannah gathered around the hospital bed. Recognizing Hannah's face, Gloria reached out for her. Hannah held her hand and sat down on the bed as close to her as she could get. The crispy sound of the linens, and the crunching sound the hospital mattress made as Hannah moved radiated throughout the room and stuck in her head. Kathy stood by Hannah's side, a look of concern washing over her face.

"Can we get you anything?" Kathy whispered.

Noticing the confusion on her sister's face, she added, "You've been moved to a regular room. You're sleeping quite a bit, on and off due to the meds, and you may not remember being moved or where you are right now."

"I can't hear you," Gloria snapped at Kathy. "Speak up!"

"Sorry. Do you need anything?" Kathy asked again, thinking her sister scolding her was a good sign. "Hannah's here as well."

"I can see her," Gloria replied.

Hannah's heart was racing, knowing something was wrong as the monitor alarms alerted the nurse's station that her mom needed assistance. Gloria was pale, and her eyes were dark and sunken.

"Mom, I'm right here."

"I love you," Gloria whispered.

"I love you too," Hannah responded, but as soon as the words rolled off her tongue, tears dripped down her nose and onto the sheets.

"Hannah."

"Yes? I'm here." She wiped away her tears quickly, hoping not to concern or scare her mom as the nurses tended to her.

"Hannah. Don't hate me."

"I could never hate you! Don't even say that!"

"He's alive." Gloria tried to grip Hannah's hand, but her grasp was weak. "Alive."

"What?" Hannah whispered. "Who's alive?"

Agitated, Gloria tried to shake her hand in Hannah's. "Alive. He's alive." Her eyes were glassy, crying, but her tears struggled to fall. "Forgive me, Hannah, and please don't hate me."

Hannah stroked her mom's hair, held her hand, and sat unresponsive in shock. Her mom was delirious and at times it was scary. But Gloria, becoming even more agitated, kept insisting, and alarms attached to her started to go off.

"Hank is alive!"

Scared and not knowing how to calm her mom down, Hannah tried to console her by leading her to believe she understood the urgency of her message. "Oh, wow! Okay, the Captain's back, Hank is alive." She continued to listen to her mom's incoherent dialog, nodding and squeezing her hand, hoping Gloria would drift off to sleep and get some rest. "Please, close your eyes and try to get some sleep. You need to rest; your body needs rest."

Gloria's eyes were distant when they were open, her breathing was shallow, and her skin looked grey. It wasn't the time to quiz her about anything, including her bizarre claims. Hannah was sick of hearing about Hank. She didn't care about him right then; she wanted her mom to quit worrying about it as well, and stay with her, present, and in that moment. Any questions that she might have had didn't have the same urgency that they had days ago, as Hannah watched her mom's health decline. Her eyes flashed toward another monitor that had started beeping at her mom's side. Within seconds a nurse appeared, readjusted a sensor on her mom and reset the machine.

"No signs of settling down yet?" the nurse asked, and Hannah shook her head.

"Your doctor said you could have a sedative to help you rest. I'm going to get that for you; it should help you sleep."

Gloria, too weak to fight, didn't object. Her blood pressure erratic, a sedative was administered to help her relax and sleep. As they prepared to leave the room, Gloria called out to her sister, but her words were barely audible. One of the nurses closest to her said that she had asked that Kathy watch over her daughter.

"What did she say?" Kathy asked.

"Watch over her daughter, that's what she said." The nurse smiled. "Her exact words were, 'Watch over Hannah,' but I think she's drifting off now." After delivering the message, the nurse went about her day as if it were business as usual; and for her, it was.

Kathy couldn't hide her own grief, knowing her sister was making arrangements for her daughter. She stood motionless, grasping for the right words to say; there weren't any. Lindsey, stuck in between invading their privacy, trying to help, and not knowing how to gracefully exit without being noticed, stood in shock. Kathy walked toward the door, and Lindsey, with Hannah trailing behind, grateful to leave the room, followed her. Lindsey had never been so grateful in her life to see her best friend's boyfriend, Cash, as she was when he turned the corner. Hannah felt the same way, and a minute alone with him was exactly what she needed! As soon as he reached Gloria's door, Hannah looped her arm in his, spun him around, and asked if they could step outside for a moment. Glancing over his shoulder, he pointed to Gloria.

"Your mom is calling your name."

Hannah nodded. "I know, she's delirious right now, but I can't breathe in here." Peeking over his shoulders, she added, "She's sedated, she should be drifting off to sleep any second. She's exhausted!"

Gloria faintly called out to Hannah again; her voice barely a whisper, as if speaking under her breath, weak, shaky, and barely audible. Hannah, at that moment, made a split-second decision which would haunt her the rest of her life!! Grabbing Cash's hand, pretending that she hadn't heard her mom's whispers at all, she pulled Cash toward the elevator. Her mom's earlier anguish, crazy delusions, confessions, and her decline in stability were just too much for the teen. The air in the hospital was stale and Hannah couldn't take it anymore! Head spinning, needing to be alone to talk to Cash, she pressed the elevator button at least five times before the wide doors finally opened. Even the stark white walls of the hallway felt like they were suffocating her. Disgusted that her mom thought she could actually hate her, Hannah wondered, as a daughter, what she could have possibly done that made her mother think her love for her could so easily be tossed aside!

The crisp air hit her in the face like a splash of ice water, completely opposite from the stuffy, oppressive air inside the hospital ward. Deep breaths. Hannah forced herself to fill her lungs and exhale slowly multiple times before asking Cash if he would hold her for just a minute longer. Nodding, he strengthened his grip and softly kissed the side of her face. Knowing it wasn't a good time to stay away for long, Hannah tugged at Cash's shirt, indicating she had pulled herself together.

"Can we take the stairs?" she asked. "Just give us a few extra minutes before we get there."

Nodding, he grabbed her hand and led the way. One by one Hannah counted each stair that she climbed, a momentary breather, before she sat and waited in the ominous patient lounge. Stepping out of the stairwell onto her mom's floor, it never once occurred to her that something else could go wrong, until she turned the corner that led to the corridor of her mom's room. The normal smells of the hospital, disinfectant, food, bedpans, people, made her nauseous on a good day, but for some reason it hit her hard as soon as she approached the nurse's station. Noticing a lot of unusual activity happening on the same floor, people rushing around, equipment being rolled down the hallway, Hannah started walking faster, so fast that Cash had troubling keeping up. She had an overwhelming sinking feeling in the pit of her stomach that something was wrong with her mom! She was right. Kathy and Lindsey stood outside her mom's room, both inconsolable. Rushing past them, Lindsey reached out and grabbed Hannah's arm.

"Wait."

Hannah couldn't speak. Frozen in place, a nurse physically moved her to one side. The nurses who were working inside the room were solemnly going through the motions of what was expected of them, conducting their duties, turning off alarms and disconnecting equipment. Hannah's throat felt as if there was something suddenly lodged in it; gasping for air, she realized what had just happened! Rushing past the attending nurse to her mom's side, she screamed and begged Gloria to wake up. Gloria's lifeless body never moved, and the disturbing masked expression on her face would be forever ingrained in Hannah's mind.

Pericarditis and cardiac tamponade, resulting in a massive heart attack, linked to complications due to her original diagnoses, was the official cause of death. Hannah hadn't been there; she hadn't made it back in time, and even worse, she'd left her mom's side in the first place! A tiny part of her was grateful that she hadn't witnessed her mother die, and another part of her was overwhelmed with guilt that her mom was without her, alone, her daughter and sister removed from the room. The doctors assured them that they had done all they could do, worked for as long as they possibly could before calling it. The date and time had been recorded.

"She didn't slip away!" Hannah screamed. "She wasn't peaceful, and it wasn't her time! It shouldn't have been her time."

One of the doctors was trying to explain what had happened, how fast it happened, and how Gloria would have felt minimal pain, but they found no comfort in his words.

"No. No. I should've stayed. I should've been here. I should've been here!" Hannah sobbed inconsolably. "I'm so sorry, Mom. So, so sorry!"

Dropping to her knees, head in hands, Hannah's heart shattered. Physical pain, pain she'd yet to ever experience in her entire life, pierced her heart and consumed her whole body. The tables had quickly turned, as within minutes the only words that could be heard in between wails were Hannah's.

"Please forgive me, Mom. Oh my God, please, please forgive me, Mom!"

Weeping without taking a breath, gasping at times for air, her sobs echoed off the hospital walls and sent chills down Cash's spine. Tears of his own dripped down his face. Wanting to hold her, but not daring to approach her, he waited until she glanced up and looked for him.

Through tear-filled eyes, no words exchanged, he reached out and pulled her onto his lap right there on the hospital floor. Lindsey and Kathy, embracing each other, sobbed together, until a doctor asked Kathy's permission to give Hannah a sedative to help her calm down. Once the sedative had been administered, Kathy and Hannah went back into Gloria's room. Cash and Lindsey waited outside. One arm over Lindsey's shoulder, Cash braced himself for what Hannah might need from him. Lindsey cried quietly behind Cash's back, as they watched Kathy lovingly stroke Gloria's hair and Hannah lay over her mom's body, crying and crying, until two people arrived and Kathy knew they had come to tend to Gloria.

"Sweetheart; its time. They have to take her now and we have to let her go."

"I can't! I just can't." Hannah, still stretched across her mom, never once looked up. "I didn't mean it. I didn't mean to be gone that long," she sobbed. "I shouldn't have left. I shouldn't have left her! Kathy, I heard her call my name."

Had she only known that time was not on her side that day, she never would have left her mom's side. Kathy knew that, and she was certain that Gloria would have as well. Hannah would've sat and listened to her mom ask for forgiveness she didn't need a hundred more times if it brought her mom peace of mind and if Hannah could have had a few more minutes with her!

"Hannah, she wasn't herself; it was all the medication. I bet she didn't even know you weren't by her side. She probably felt your presence with her even though you'd stepped out for a second."

"But why today, and why now?"

Cash slipped into the room, put his hand gently on Hannah's shoulder, leaned over and kissed Gloria's cheek. He never spoke. The loss Hannah was feeling was too great; his words would have seemed empty. Gutted, even the sedative didn't help; Hannah could contain her grief no longer. Her whole body trembled as her heart broke right there in front of everyone. Tears flowed nonstop, as if the floodgates had been opened. Grief, shock, and guilt, all at the same time, and to make matters even worse, the *what if's* were plaguing her mind. *What if she'd just let her mom ramble? What if she hadn't felt so frustrated?* And the biggest one of all, *What if her mom didn't know how much she really loved her?* **Had she told her mom that she loved her before she'd died?** Panic swept over Hannah as her mind rushed with battered memories of that day. Trying to retrace the things that she had said, she couldn't remember if she'd told her mom she loved her before she died! A vile feeling of regret, guilt, and loss consumed her, knowing that it was quite possible that the last words she may have spoken to her mom were in pure frustration! Nausea swept over her and vomit rushed up her throat. Grabbing Cash's arm, she motioned toward the door, but the vomit had already pooled in her mouth. As soon as he realized what was going on, he tried to pull her toward a nearby sink. It was too late; vomit projected all over Cash, Hannah, and the floor. Disgusted with herself, Hannah hung her head in shame.

"It's okay, babe, it's okay," Cash whispered, as he

took paper towels and blotted her face, shirt, and cleaned up the floor.

"It's not okay, I'm not okay, nothing's okay!"

A piercing wail, signifying the internal pain Hannah was feeling, forced Cash to drop to his knees and gather Hannah up in his arms and rock her like a rag doll. His tears flowed, as did Kathy's and Lindsey's, as they watched the pain Hannah felt.

"I let her down," Hannah whispered. "In every possible way a daughter could!"

Words would bring her no comfort, no matter what any of them would say. They sat on the floor, Kathy stroking Hannah's hair, and whispering in her ear, "Sweetheart, we have to go. We have to let them take her away; it's time for all of us to let her go."

Cash wrapped his arms tightly around a shaking Hannah.

Lindsey, still in shock herself, assisted Kathy with Gloria's things.

Kathy squatted down and put her arm around Hannah. "I want Lindsey to take you home, and Cash and I will meet you there, at the apartment."

Cash kissed Hannah on the cheek, gave Lindsey a hug, and asked her if she was okay to drive. She assured him that she was. He stood by Kathy's side and watched the girls walk down the hallway.

"She gonna be okay?" he asked. "I'm worried about her."

Kathy hesitated. "It's not going to be easy."

Gloria didn't have that much to pack up at the hospital, but Kathy didn't want Hannah to have to deal with it. Cash packed her things away, and Kathy filled out all the necessary paperwork.

"What about, you know, the arrangements?" Unsure of where to start, let alone worrying about burying her sister, Kathy wasn't sure what to do.

"You don't have to worry about any of that stuff right now. I think you probably need to rest for a day or even two first, as well." He hesitated, not knowing if it were even his place to mention anything. "They do have people, here I mean, who can help with that or at least point you in the right direction."

Kathy's tear-stained face stared at him, her eyes looked straight through him. "Thank you, that's not a bad idea! It's not like we had our own church or anything."

"Are you ready to go?"

Kathy nodded, reaching for her car keys.

"I'll drive you." Cash repeated. "We'll pick up your car later. I can even come back with my dad, if you don't want to leave it up here, but for now I'll take you home to Hannah."

Shooting a quick text to Lindsey, Cash confirmed that Hannah was in the car and holding up as well as could be expected. She wasn't talking, and Lindsey wasn't pushing her.

Cash: The apartment?

Lindsey: Headed there now, but haven't made it yet.

Cash: Let me know when you do.

Lindsey: K

Cash: Right behind you.

Within minutes of the car door shutting, Hannah

had buried her face in her hands and sobbed without taking a breath. It didn't take long before she couldn't breathe at all and a full-fledged panic attack set in. Lindsey opened the windows, allowing the cool air to blow across the back of Hannah's neck. Then Lindsey pulled the car over and gently rubbed her friend's back.

"Breathe. Calm down and breathe. In and out, slow, deep breaths."

"I can't, I can't breathe, I can't breathe."

Hannah's chest felt as if it were caving in. Her heart racing, she gasped for air. Lindsey rubbed her back and continued to speak softly to her, talking her down. Finally, Hannah's breathing returned to normal. Her tears had wiped away any trace of makeup she had applied earlier, and Hannah suddenly looked younger than her teen years. Lindsey struggled to hold back tears of her own as she grasped Hannah's hands in hers and held them as tightly as she could. There were no words of comfort offered, none needed, they'd already been said, but Hannah knew Lindsey was grieving as well. Shallow breaths assured Lindsey that Hannah's breathing had returned to normal. Still holding Hannah's hand, Lindsey pulled away from the side of the road. They drove in silence for a while until cautiously Lindsey brought up the first time she'd met Gloria. To her relief, Hannah smiled.

"Hey, remember when you first brought me to your house?" Lindsey asked, not expecting an answer. "She thought we were going to get in so much trouble. 'Thick as thieves,' she'd call us."

"'Cause we are!" Hannah managed the slightest

smile. "I'm really glad she moved us back here."

Hannah remembered the day they had moved her back to San Francisco.

"I'd love for you to spend time with your aunt Kathy, you know, get to know her the way I do. That way, you'll have more than just me for a family."

"Nothing wrong with *just* you!" Hannah had replied, a big grin spread across her face.

"Thanks! But you know what I mean, right?"

"No." Hannah smirked. "But I don't care; that's fine by me if you want to go back to San Francisco. I remember kinda liking it there anyway as a little kid."

The car rolled to a stop at a red light. A cool breeze blew through the opened windows and Hannah caught wind of a terrible smell—her shirt. The air shifted and whipped back through the car and the stench of the hospital sticking to her like glue made Hannah gag. Hospital smells, so specific, sick people, bedpans, disinfectant, hospital food, and body odors all together in one terrible combination. Hannah could barely walk into the hospital as of late without feeling violently ill herself; now the hospital stench was wrapped around her.

Struggling with what had just transpired, and the realization that half of her life had been a lie, Hannah sat in the passenger seat, shaking in absolute shock. There'd been a lot of lies floating around apparently for the past, say, most of her life! Sitting in the seat, she tried to process three things: why exactly did her mom keep all of that from her, was her dad—the Captain—really alive, and what the hell was she supposed to do now? She pulled a tattered yellow piece of paper out of her sweatshirt pocket and stared at it.

"What's that?" Lindsey asked softly.

"Something I need; but not sure I want."

Hands trembling she moved the worn-out paper, a faded handwritten letter, quickly to one side so that a massive teardrop didn't splatter on it and ruin the words that were hard enough already to read. The fact that they were faded and worn wasn't the problem; the problem was as she read them to herself, Hannah didn't recognize who had written them. The voice that reverberated back to her as she read the words out loud seemed foreign and didn't match those of the voice that she recognized. The voice that was so familiar, the Captain's, that lived with her in her head. The voice of the man who supposedly wrote the letter that she held in her hand was a stranger, dead. His voice—the man whose hand wrote to her—didn't match that of the Captain in her dreams, the one that had held her together for all of those years. The man who had played with her for hours at a time, her dad, Captain of their ship, who made sails from her bed sheets, that man was dead!

Chapter 29
Lost

Numb
Going through the motions
What's next?
Why bother
~ Hannah Gunner ~

The service was well attended, considering they hadn't lived back in town that long. Gloria was liked at work, had a few select friends, and even some of Hannah's and Cash's friends came to show their support. Kathy slipped Hannah a Xanax to help her cope, but it didn't help. Hannah was already numb. She heard the words as the minister started to speak, but her mind couldn't grasp why a paid stranger would talk about her mother in such a beautiful way. He didn't know her. He didn't have a clue about the things written down on the piece of paper that he was saying about her mom. *Borrowed minister*, Hannah thought. *What do you know about my mom? Not one thing except what Aunt Kathy scribbled on that piece of paper that you're holding in your hands!* Her mind drifted to the last time she saw her mom alive and the last words she had said to her. Haunting her, the words were neither of comfort nor of understanding, but of a promise that wasn't fulfilled.

"I'll be right back."

"Your mom loved you." Cash whispered, tightening his grip around Hannah's hand.

Grateful for the distraction, Hannah wiped a dripping tear off the tip of her nose and nodded.

"She did. I honestly can say I know that she did."

Cash prodded Hannah and directed her to the front of the church. Aimlessly she followed her aunt, but couldn't for the life of her figure out why she had to stand up front and thank people for witnessing the worst day of her life. One after another, people stopped by Kathy and then her; not knowing what to say, Hannah leaned on Cash.

"Thank you for coming," he responded, over and over.

Emotionally drained and exhausted, Hannah felt utterly lost. Finally, she felt Cash's arms around her, leading her toward his Jeep.

"You need some rest; I'll take you home."

"Will you stay?" Hannah asked.

"I'll let my mom know, but you have to promise that you're going straight to bed." He squeezed her hand. "I think that couch has a permanent indention of my ass."

A slight smile, just for a second, escaped her as she climbed up into the passenger seat. Sleep was a gift. If she was sleeping, she didn't have to feel or think. Bring on sleep!!!

Chapter 30
Missing Links

How
How do I go on?
How do I go on without her?
How do I go on without my mom?
~ Hannah Gunner ~

Exhausted, Hannah fell asleep almost as soon as her head hit the pillow. Cash peeked in on her periodically, as did Kathy. She slept all night without making a peep and didn't even stir when Kathy and Cash were making breakfast in the kitchen.

"You need to eat something, Cash. Toast, cereal, something."

"Thanks, but coffee is good."

They sat at the table, Gloria's table, in silence, sipping their coffee. It was surreal. It wasn't long ago that they were all there together chatting with her, discussing their plans for the day, and now they felt like intruders in her home. Cash broke the silence as he looked around the kitchen and toward Hannah's door.

"What will you and Hannah do now?"

Placing her mug on the table, Kathy tightened her robe around her.

"Hannah will move in with me; she won't have to

change schools, it's the same district. I received a letter stating that Gloria has paid the rent here for three additional months. I'm certain that's so we can take our time packing in between school and work."

Running her hands through her hair, Kathy sighed and shook her head.

"I think she knew this was going to happen."

Cash's eyes darted toward her.

"What are you talking about? Like a premonition?"

Kathy half-smiled. "No. Like before she moved here, back home. I think she had this diagnosis before she moved home. I knew she was ill... but I think she already knew she was terminal."

She reached across the table and grabbed Cash's hand. "I don't know why I feel as if Hannah shouldn't know that, but something tells me it would only hurt her if she did." Letting go of his hand, she added, "Besides, that's just what I think. For argument's sake and not to put you in a difficult position, let's just say it's a thought and not a fact."

Cash nodded. It would make sense if Gloria knew that she was terminally ill; besides, he was glad that she had brought Hannah back. As far as he was concerned, Kathy was expressing her grief and nothing out of the norm had been discussed.

"She's been out for nearly fourteen hours now; I'll peek my head in and check on her," Cash offered. Kathy nodded.

The sun was pouring through her window, and Cash realized she hadn't drawn her curtains the night before. Even with the sunshine bouncing off her cheeks, she slept peacefully. Her long hair was scattered all over her pillow and her face. Tiny features peeped out between the strands of her hair: the tip of her nose, part of her chin, and he could see a portion of her ear. Desperately wanting to push her hair to one side and wake her gently with soft kisses, he knew she was mentally exhausted as well as physically and needed all the extra rest. As he gingerly backed out of her room, one step at a time, his eyes caught the tattered box in the center of her floor. So many missing links to Hannah's life were likely held in that box.

Pouring himself another cup of coffee, he sat back down at the table with Kathy. She was lost in thought, but his presence back at the table was a comfort. Wrestling with the idea of asking questions without Hannah by his side, Cash tread carefully and fired away.

"Can I ask you something?"

"Sure."

"Did you know it was possible that Hank was alive?"

Her eyes flashed toward him as if he had said something wrong.

"I'm just asking; I don't mean anything by it, honest!"

Hesitating, she apologized. "I'm sorry, Cash. It's not you; it's Gloria. I didn't know, and I can't believe I didn't know..."

The silence was awkward for several minutes until Kathy spoke again.

"I'm her sister. I thought we shared everything, especially back then. I don't know if she fooled me. Lied to me. Tried to protect me, like I know she must have for

Hannah, or what she was thinking!"

She stood up, pushed her chair into the table, and threw her coffee out in the sink.

"I don't know why she would lie and say Hank was dead when he was in Folsom this entire time! But I do know, that despite her reasons, her intentions must have been good and she would have thought she was doing it for Hannah."

Cash walked over to the sink and wrapped his arms around her. Kathy was confused, hurting, and was as upset as Hannah.

"I think we may find clues in the letters, but I also think Hannah will have questions for you." He stepped back and looked Kathy straight in the eye. "Will you answer any questions that she may ask?"

Chapter 31
Dive In

Ahhhhhhhhhhhhhhhhh!
Help me!
~ Hannah Gunner ~

All three of them sat on the living room floor around the box and stared at it as if it would bite. Cash nudged the box toward Hannah and waited. It wasn't as if they hadn't looked at some of the letters before, but they were searching for answers this time.

"You've read some of them, just keep going."

Hannah knew Cash was right, but a sick feeling in the pit of her stomach was holding her back.

"Go on. Just dive in—grab one and start reading," Kathy suggested. "And if you like, fire away; I'm certain you have questions."

Hannah glanced at her in such a way that Kathy prompted her along.

"If while you're reading the letters memories are triggered, and you have questions, just ask. Honestly, anything, ask away."

Hannah hit her with a question right away.

"Did you know my dad was alive?"

"Hannah, I swear I did not know that your dad was

still alive! I thought, like you, he had died in prison."

"How is that possible?" Hannah asked.

"Your mom had moved out of state when she supposedly got the news. When I called and asked if she was coming home to tend to the arrangements, she said that they had already been taken care of."

"What does that even mean?" Hannah raised her hands. "Wouldn't there have been a service or funeral arrangements?"

"Well, I thought so too, but he was in prison. And what did we know about the rules and regulations of prison?" Kathy answered. "I came to visit. Do you remember? Your mom really grieved. Looking back and knowing what I know now, I think she was grieving the end of her marriage, the relationship as she knew it, and from what we can tell here," she glanced at the tattered box, "hurting Hank."

"Yeah, you could be right," Cash agreed. "That's a lot of trouble to make sure a kid believes it. Moving. Hiding every letter that's delivered. She'd have to watch for the post or get the mail every single day. But it is interesting how she didn't mind discussing him if Hannah asked, correct?"

Cash turned toward Hannah for confirmation. She nodded. He was right. If she'd asked about her dad, her mom would discuss him or answer her question, never expand, mainly yes or no answers, and over the years she had never volunteered information. Hannah never had, until that very moment, ever wondered about that before. Looking back, she even remembered a day when she'd asked about where he'd gone; that must've been when the lie initially started.

"Your daddy had to go to a place where children do not go; but they are taking good care of him." Years later, Hannah remembered pressing Gloria once more about him. This time she wasn't only uncomfortable with the question but irritated that Hannah had asked, and she had snapped at her.

"I told you, Hannah, he passed away! It was a terrible fight in prison, but it's too painful to discuss. Can we please do this another time?" There wasn't another time; Hannah quit asking.

Hannah blew her aunt a kiss.

"I believe you and thank you for being so open about it; I'm sure it was a shock to you, too."

Kathy nodded. That was an understatement. She thought her sister had been hallucinating with all of the meds that she was taking in the hospital. Hank alive? Impossible. But the dates on the letters confirmed her lie.

"I guess we're both figuring out this thing together. Why my mom felt she had to lie."

"Hey, what about me?"

"I meant all of us," Hannah grinned. "You're included."

"Okay then... dive in!" Cash laughed. "Grab another letter!"

They read letter after letter, searching for clues. Many of the letters hadn't even been opened, still sealed, and thrown into the box with the others. Some were short and to the point, others were odd ramblings. All begged Hannah not to forget him and, when she was able, to write him back. Every letter was sealed with love.

"Oh my God!"

"What?" Cash asked.

Hannah addressed a letter that she held in her hand.

"He believes I purposely didn't write him back. He states right here that he's given up and he'll quit bothering me. Listen to what he wrote."

This continued silence, especially after all these years, confirms my worst fears: you have, without a doubt, forgotten me!!! The Captain, as you so often preferred to call me, rather than Daddy, has been erased from your memory.

Do you even remember me at all? You may have forgotten our past, understandably after all these years, and moved on with your future, but I am saddened it is without me.

You know where I am, and how to reach me if you choose, but Hannah, I will not bother you anymore. The silence, even after all these years, is too painful. I will think of you daily, and know that I will love you and forever think about the person you surely must have grown up to become.

Dad

She pointed to the tattered paper in her hand.

"He says that I'm old enough to write back to him if I wanted, but since I'm not responding to his letters, he's gotten the message. Oh my God, Don't you see? He has no idea I didn't know... he doesn't know I never received a single letter!"

Kathy took the yellowed paper out of Hannah's hand

and reread it over and over again. She could hear Hank's voice in her head as she read. Surreal, hearing her old brother-in-law's voice after all this time, if only in her head.

Frustrated, she sat down in Gloria's recliner.

"Your mom loved Hank. She loved him. He really was the love of her life. I just don't understand what happened."

Glancing around her sister's living her room, her eye caught Gloria's bedroom door. She jumped up and ran into Gloria's room, returning a few seconds later with the photograph of their family in her hand.

"Look at this photo, Hannah. Who's in this picture?"

Hannah didn't need to look at the picture; she'd seen that photo her entire life.

"You know who that is."

"I'm asking you. Who is it?"

"Kathy, this is stupid. You know its Mom, Dad, and me."

Cash reached for the photo and examined it carefully.

"Oh my God! Were you the cutest kid or what?!"

"Don't you get it; your mom still loved him. She never brought men around, right?"

Kathy was right; she knew that Hannah had never seen her mom bring guys into their house, either as friends or dates. She remembered her mom playfully arguing with a friend when the friend was threatening to set her up on a double date. They weren't friends for very long after that; her mom never went on that date or any date, period.

"Well, technically, she was still married," Cash added. "But I see what you're saying and so I'll shut up now."

"Right, she was married, but no one knew that she was married, and legally because he was in prison she could have gotten an uncontested divorce." Kathy took a sip of her coffee. "She never did. She'd told everyone she was widowed, and she still didn't keep the company of other guys. We talked almost daily and not a single mention of any men, ever."

"Well, what's your point?" Cash asked. "She didn't like men after that?"

"No!" Kathy grinned. "She loved Hank, never stopped. This, whatever it was, whatever happened between them, wasn't ever about them!"

Puzzled, Hannah asked, "Then what? What is this all about?"

"Whatever her reason, it all revolves around you!"

"Whoa!" Cash responded. "I hadn't really looked at it like that."

Kathy continued. "Hank was serving time for involuntary manslaughter. I'll explain that in a minute if you have anything else you need to know regarding it. But something went down, and there was a fight. Whatever happened at that time, that fight and this mess we have right here involving Hannah, caused Gloria to make a decision that changed all of your lives. It was that decision, the one about Hank, which caused her to believe she needed your forgiveness. And it was the same decision that she made that caused Hank to believe you had abandoned him." She pointed to the letters. "Does any of this make sense?"

"Kinda. Well, yes, but either way, I know exactly what I have to do!" Hannah stated calmly.

"Oh yeah, what's that?" Cash asked.

"I have to meet him. Hank. Oh my God, that sounds so weird." She took a deep breath and said the words out loud again. "I have to visit my dad, formerly known as the Captain."

Cash grabbed her hand and kissed the top of it.

"I'll go with you or at least drive you."

"I don't even know where we're going."

"I do," Kathy announced.

"Where?" Hannah asked, surprised.

"Well, if I'm right, judging by these letters, we're headed to Folsom State Prison."

Chapter 32
What Do We Do?

"Have no idea what to say. I'll shut up now."
~ Cash ~

A tap on the door startled Kathy. Cash was making plans with Hannah in the kitchen and Hannah hadn't mentioned she was expecting anyone. Barely cracking the door, Lindsey, grinning from ear to ear, popped her head in.

"Coffee anyone?"

Handing Kathy a cup, she kissed her on the cheek, brushed past her, and immediately headed toward the kitchen. Watching Lindsey making herself at home, just like she always had when she visited Hannah, brought Kathy a feeling of hope that life for Hannah would get back to normal one day. Half-filled boxes were starting to appear around the apartment. A sense of unknowing was an unspoken feeling around there; normalcy would be a welcoming vibe in Hannah's world again, especially since she'd be living in yet another new home.

"Brought you two losers coffee," Lindsey scoffed.

Hannah jumped up from the kitchen table, grabbed Lindsey, and hugged her as tightly as she possibly could.

"I've missed you!"

"Me too, you."

Cash took the cup holder from her hand and placed it on the table.

"Thanks, Linds!"

"No problem, but honestly I guessed on yours." She smiled at Hannah. "I got you the usual."

"So what have I missed?"

Hannah filled her in. The secret revolving around Hank's death, the lies, and the fact that her dad was actually still alive in prison, and he had no idea that she hadn't received any of his letters. Cash also mentioned that Hank had written Hannah one last time, saying he wouldn't bother her anymore, and they figured that's when he'd quit writing.

"That's when the letters must have stopped. I guess I must've been about thirteen or fourteen."

"Wow!" Lindsey was stunned. "That's not that long ago."

"Right," Cash replied.

Kathy joined them in the kitchen, perched against the sink, and listened to the teens talk about the past, the letters, and what her sister had supposedly done. Her heart sank. *How had she not known what her sister was going through?* Gloria must have been desperate to make such a terrible decision. Maybe she could have talked her out of it had she known the truth, but there was no way of knowing now and no point in second-guessing what Gloria might have done.

"That must have been a huge burden that she carried with her for all of those years," Kathy whispered.

"She didn't act like it though, but I guess." Hannah

felt guilty for saying it.

Kathy, lost in thought, remembered the days when Hank and Gloria used to bring Hannah over to visit her. They'd sit and talk, laugh, and eat. Family. They were a close family. She also recalled when she'd pop over to visit, and Sandy and Nathan were often there, all sitting around that same kitchen table, laughing and doting over Hannah.

"Kathy, you Okay?" Cash asked, bringing her out of the past, her memories, and back to them and their conversation.

Her face stern, eyes crystal clear, as she spoke with such certainty, Hannah wondered if they'd probed too soon into Kathy's past time with her sister. Kathy continued to insist that Hank and Gloria were close, and everything about the box, the lies, and the secrets revolved around Hannah. Kathy suddenly blurted out another statement about Hank and Gloria's relationship.

"I'm telling you, those two, your mom and dad, were inseparable. People don't find relationships like theirs every day, they just don't, and I'm not kidding when I say that your dad loved his family... you and your mom!" Her voice cracked. "And your mom absolutely adored your dad. He was it for her. Her one! For her to lie like that, and I'm not trying to make excuses, Hannah, but she must have had a damn good reason. That's all I'm saying."

She turned around to the sink, poured out the coffee from her mug, and took a sip of the coffee that Lindsey had handed her. Contemplating adding one more thing, she opened her mouth to speak and then closed it again, as if scared to upset anyone or say anything out of line.

"What were you going to say?" Hannah asked. "Honestly, just say it; we're all just talking."

"Well, I'll say this one last thing, but I have no proof, and it makes no sense."

"Best kind of coffee talk conversations are ones like that," Cash replied.

Kathy smiled and sat down with the teens.

"I think that she felt guilty, regardless of why she made that decision, and that she carried that guilt around for all of those years and it wore her down. I think it was too much for her and none of us knew. I'm not saying it caused her illness, but it sure didn't help."

Thinking that she'd cried every teardrop that her eyes could ever hold, another tear started to roll down her cheek. Kathy quickly brushed it away, not wanting to ruin Hannah's day.

"I don't know why she lied to you or hid his letters, and I'm not saying she handled it right, but I can tell you that the decision she made revolved around you and wasn't based on her and Hank. It definitely took a toll on her. Looking back, especially now knowing that Hank was always alive, I can honestly tell you that whatever the reason, in her mind she was doing what was best, but looking back, she was never the same after that!" Kathy hesitated. "I thought it was grief. Loss of her husband, but it was this, this lie."

"Never the same; wow!" Cash took the last swig of his coffee and shook his head. "That could do it to you, I guess, something this big."

"No. Never. She lost something, part of herself,

maybe?" Kathy dipped her head. "She was sad after that; she didn't have the same tone in her voice, wasn't as happy when we spoke. Again, of course, I thought she was grieving, and I guess in a sense she was. That day, for whatever reason, she'd technically ended her family."

Hannah tried to listen with an open mind. Feelings of sadness, loss, curiosity, confusion, and fear overwhelmed her. What didn't, surprisingly, was anger. The anger had ceased once the reality of losing her mom had kicked in. It didn't seem nearly as important anymore; holding on to the anger she had once felt was now overridden by her own grief. At least now she was able to retrieve the answers that she needed, or at least she hoped that was true!

"We should be able to get the answers from Hank, my long-lost dad!" Smirking and throwing up her hands, she sarcastically added, "Surprise! Remember me?"

"I'll be happy to take you." Kathy offered. "I'm sure because you're a minor you'll need an adult to sign you in."

Hannah smiled and thanked her.

"I'll research and see what we need to do, but we'll all go together if you like, extra support." Kathy glanced at the kids sitting around the table. Who would've thought they'd be discussing visiting a dead man in prison!

Cash and Lindsey knew they couldn't go in to see him. Truth be told, they weren't even interested, but were glad they'd been invited to drive with them to support Hannah before and after the visit. Who knew how the visit was going to go? After all, he thought she'd been ignoring him for years. Kathy hugged each one of them and gathered a few things to go home and check on her house. She had to make preparations to start back to work, and she reminded the kids they had to go back to school that following Monday. Groans could be heard from all around the table. That was definitely a sign of normalcy!

Googling Folsom Prison, the teens found it was only four-and-a-half hours away, totally doable, especially on a Saturday.

"What do we do first?" Cash quizzed Hannah.

"I guess we need to find out when we can visit, visiting hours. Did they post a schedule?"

Hannah grabbed the phone. "I've never had to visit anyone in prison before, let alone my long-lost dad. Isn't there a dress code, you know, like on TV?" Laughing, she searched the website and poked around the links.

The whole thing was so surreal! The man who lived in her dreams, the one she remembered, took her to the beach and on board a ship, not a state prison. Running down a sandy beach, jumping in the tips of the waves, he'd chased behind her, as his gruff voice read the map while they looked for treasure. Didn't every little girl have a treasure map under her bed? If she dreamt long enough, she could hear the seagulls flapping around her, waiting for the scraps from their sandwiches that the scallywag, turned tyrant, had packed for them to take to sea. Her heart sank as soon as she thought of the scallywag... she was so perfect, that scallywag, turned not-so-evil tyrant, after all!

"Earth to Hannah. Helllllllloooo." Lindsey giggled. "Where did you go?"

"Hey, babe," Cash reached over and placed his hand on her cheek. "You okay?"

She could barely answer him; her words stuck in her throat.

"A picnic at the beach, and a game we used to play, me and Hank when I was a kid."

"Oh, yeah, the pirate game. You've mentioned that a time or two."

"Something trigger a memory, Hannah?" Lindsey asked softly.

She nodded.

"Yeah, I guess so. We used to go to the beach with picnics that my mom had packed for us. I must've had a great imagination, because those memories somehow managed to slip into my dreams. I never forgot the games we played." Staring at her friends, a smile crossed her face and it was as if she'd had a lightbulb moment.

"You know, as a kid my dad, the Captain, always put me to bed and I treasured that bedtime ritual. Acting out the pirate story turned into a game that lasted years. Mom, even though we called her a tyrant, let us have that, not once saying a word about being included, or excluded I should say. But I caught her once..."

Hannah took a deep breath. "She was laughing so hard. Hank had pulled out his imaginary telescope and commanded that the ship go to the island where he'd seen an unidentified monster. I remember jumping on the bed, reaching for the telescope, begging to see." Hannah's voice quivered but she kept telling them the story. "When he finally said yes, he grabbed me and threw me over his shoulder, pretending that he was going to feed me to said unidentified monster!" She managed a smile. "It was one of my stuffed toys, an elephant, on my bed. But he twirled me around and around, and I remember laughing so hard I thought I would die, my sides hurt so bad, and that's when I saw her."

"Who?" Cash asked. "Your mom?"

Hannah nodded. "She had one hand covering her mouth, and I know she was trying not to laugh. In the other hand, she held her glass of wine. She was perched against the wall, on the floor, right outside my bedroom door listening to us play, just listening. But even back then, as a little kid, I knew she was enjoying it as much as we were."

"Awe, Hannah, I can so see Gloria doing that!"

Lindsey held out her hand, and Hannah placed her hand in hers.

"I can't help but wonder how many years she had done that each day, watched us play."

"Your mom loved you. Let's go get some answers!"

They located the visitor's application for Folsom Prison. The form looked intimidating, but the information seemed understandable. However, the policy of **SUBJECT TO SEARCH** was terrifying. Visitors entering the facility were subject to search of their person, vehicle, or property. There were several other policies, but that one freaked Hannah out as soon as she read it out loud.

"Surely they don't mean strip search, right?"

"Gawd! I hope not, for your sake!" Cash shrieked.

"Once you submit the form, they'll perform a background check to see if you're approved for a visit. If so, they'll ask the prisoner if he wants to see you." Lindsey pointed to the form. "Look."

Hannah, now sitting in Cash's lap, suddenly squealed. "What the hell!"

"What does it say?" Cash asked, wrapping his arms around her waist and kissing the back of her head.

"I have to state I'm his daughter and he has to agree to see me."

Hannah's face dropped.

"It says on the Department of Corrections Visitation Questionnaire that they will notify the inmate that I've filled out this form, and the inmate has to sign and approve my visit." Hannah put the phone down on the table.

"What if he doesn't approve it?"

Cash pulled her up out of her chair and into his lap. Arms wrapped around her waist, he placed a lingering kiss on the back of her neck. It sent the sweetest shivers down her spine, and instantly she felt calmer than she had seconds before.

"Stop worrying. Who knows what he'll do, but why wouldn't Hank want to see you? It doesn't matter, anyway; you have to do this for you! So finish filling out the form."

Realizing how much she had missed his gentle touch,

knowing he was right, she turned toward him and kissed him on the mouth. He didn't hesitate to kiss her back.

"Seriously you two, come on!" Lindsey playfully rolled her eyes, got up, and left the kitchen table.

Laughing, still seated on Cash's lap, Hannah kissed him one more time before continuing to fill out the application. Lindsey rejoined them at the table and read through the policies for visiting an inmate.

"They have a strict dress code. No shorts, denim, crop tops, halter-tops, see-through garments. Really? See-through, people would actually wear that? The list is endless."

"No jeans, seriously?!"

Cash, picturing Hannah waltzing into prison wearing short shorts, a halter-top, or a see-through garment as listed on the list, started to laugh. He couldn't help but whistle out loud. Hannah playfully tapped him on the arm and shook her head.

"What am I supposed to say once I meet him?"

"Well, that depends on how you look at it, babe. It's all up to you. Do you want to get reacquainted with your dad or do you just want answers?"

"And make sure you really want the answers," Lindsey added. "Not saying they'll be bad or a big mystery or that he'll even have them, but just be prepared in case he gives you answers that you don't want to hear."

"You've got time to think about it. That form has to be approved first, and once it's approved, you can still decline to visit."

"You're so sure I'll be approved?"

Cash grinned. "I'm not even wasting my breath answering that question. Let's get out of here. Go for a drive and get some fresh air. Lindsey, you in?"

"Yeah, and thanks for the invite!"

"Wanna drive so me and Hannah can..."

"Oh my God, shut the hell up, and no! Hell no!" Lindsey laughed. "Gawd!"

"Just kidding. C'mon, y'all!"

Hannah signed the form electronically, took a deep breath, hit send, and they all headed for the door.

Chapter 33
Open It

Can I
Should I
Will I
Dare I
What if I've changed my mind?
~ Hannah Gunner ~

Walking down the school halls should have felt familiar, but suddenly it seemed foreign to Hannah. Yes, she had been in and out of school due to her mother's illness and sudden death, but she'd been at this high school for a while now. Suddenly she felt as if every eye was upon her; the thought that everyone knew her dad was a criminal, an inmate in prison, and people were staring at her, consumed her. It didn't help that she was called out of class during the quietest time possible to visit with the counselor for no apparent reason at all.

"We're aware of your loss and wanted you to know if there's anything you'd like to talk about or anything that you need, we're here for you."

Hannah sat opposite the woman who had barely spoken to her before and who had never been there for her a day in her life until this mandatory meeting and stared at her, speechless. What was she supposed to say to that? *Thanks for being there for me. I'd like an A in chemistry because it sucks that I can't focus right now?* The woman persisted.

"Well, are you doing okay?"

What kind of question was that, really? Hannah wondered. *How was she really supposed to answer that?* Surely the woman didn't think that she was doing okay in any way, shape, or form.

"I'm good. Thanks," Hannah responded.

Every single thing about Hannah's body language screamed, please, just let me out of here!

"Okay, then. Well, let me know if I can help."

"Right. Thanks."

Grateful that Lindsey was by her side for most of her day, and Cash sent constant Snaps and messages, they made going back to school bearable. Every now and then she even managed to see Cash during passing period and that, without a doubt, was the highlight of her school day.

Hannah had submitted the visitation application and then purposely shoved it out of her mind. They were living mostly at Kathy's house, but were still packing and had miscellaneous items still at the apartment. Hannah stopped by the apartment every day after school to check the mail and pack another box. Her heart sank every time she walked through the front door. All of the rooms looked desolate and strange. Scattered boxes, some half-filled, had been left around the apartment. There didn't seem to be any organization to their move; not like when Gloria had packed up a house, organized, planned, proficient, and easy to recognize what went where when you unpacked. Hannah threw the mail down in the center of the living room floor and walked to Gloria's bedroom. It looked and felt strange. No furniture. Boxes. Empty closet. She sat down in the center of her mom's room. It was almost cleared out. Nearly everything donated. Some items, precious only to Hannah and Kathy, had been saved and packed for the move.

A box spilling over with a burgundy garment in the corner of the room caught Hannah's eye. Immediately she ran to the box, opened it up, and pulled out Gloria's oversized, worn-out cardigan. Holding it next to her face, smelling the scent of her mom, the grief and loss she felt came rushing back. Emotions she thought she had already dealt with surfaced again. Sobs, the deepest heart-wrenching sobs, echoed through the empty apartment. Falling to her knees, face buried in the cardigan, Hannah rocked back and forth on her knees and let her tears fall. Wailing and barely being able to catch her breath, Hannah's sobs continued until she felt a hand touch her on her shoulder. The subtle touch turned into a pair of arms wrapping around her, right there on the empty apartment room floor, as her aunt Kathy held her close to her chest and cried as silently as she could. Hannah gripped the cardigan for dear life. Exhausted, the tears finally stopped. Unable to breathe through her nose, still sniffling, and eyes puffy, Hannah stood up. Still gripping the cardigan, she reached out her hand to help Kathy to her feet.

"Let's go home," Kathy suggested.

Hannah nodded.

She walked out with the cardigan and never once looked at the mail she'd retrieved that day. A hot shower, a bowl of soup, and a text from Cash seemed to fix everything. Plopping down on the couch, Hannah reached for the remote.

"Anything you want to watch?" Hannah asked as she flipped through the channels.

Kathy shook her head. "No. But I picked the mail up from the apartment that you'd grabbed today, and you have a letter."

Hannah's head whipped around.

"From Folsom State Prison." Kathy placed the letter on the coffee table in front of Hannah. "Open it."

Hannah's heart suddenly started pounding, beating so hard that she could count each beat. Her palms were beginning to sweat, and she noticed that her hands were shaking. Holding them out, she showed her aunt.

"Oh my God! Look at my hands; I'm shaking!"

Kathy jumped up and sat down next to her on the couch.

"Do you want to wait until Cash and Lindsey are here? You can open it tomorrow if you like."

Staring at the letter, Hannah knew what she had to do. Open it. After all, it was just an approval or denial; it wasn't like it was from Hank, her dad. Slowly she reached for the letter. Hannah Gunner was the addressee. Carefully she opened the seal, trying hard not to rip the entire envelope. One by one, she began to unfold the papers.

"Well, what does it say?" Kathy asked.

Hannah read the letter and reread it again to be sure

it said what she thought it did.

"Hannah!"

"It says I've been approved."

"And?"

Hannah stared at the paper that she held in her shaking hands.

"Hannah, you're killing me here! And?"

"He says he'll see me."

As if in shock, Hannah repeated the words.

"Hank, I guess my dad, says he'll see me."

Chapter 34
Bucket of Nerves

I have her eyes
His nose
Her smile
His... what?
~ Hannah Gunner ~

Hannah stared at herself in front of the mirror. Her long hair hung in waves around her shoulders. Her eyes, surprisingly still bright blue, were slightly sunken but she did notice tiny black circles under them. Lack of sleep, no doubt. The longer she stared, the less she recognized herself. Would he remember her if even she didn't know who she was anymore? An empty feeling swept over her; as bad as she wanted to meet him, she wanted everything back to normal more than that. Her kind of normal, before her mom got sick and her life fell apart. Gloria sticking her head in her room to see if she was awake. Hannah pretending she wasn't so she could sleep a little longer. The smell of cheap coffee filling the air and wafting through the apartment, instead of the sound of a loud grinder, waking up the entire house, as it ground the fresh beans. Heavy heart, stomach flipping, Hannah forced herself to pull back her hair and start her morning ritual. Her new room didn't feel like hers yet, but at least it had its own bathroom. Now that the day had finally arrived, she felt nauseous. Her phone vibrated, startling her, and that's when she knew she had to pull herself together.

Cash: Love you. See ya soon!

Hannah: Love you too. Nervous.

Cash: Don't be. You've got this! Love you.

Standing underneath the hot water in the shower, Hannah didn't fight back the trickle of tears that ran down her face and blended with the hot water running over her body. It felt like a relief to let them out. Not sure what the tears were for in that moment, Hannah shook it off. She chose an outfit that followed the rules and was basic: bra, underwear, socks, black pants since she couldn't wear jeans, sweatshirt, and converse. Leaving off any jewelry, including earrings, Hannah even removed her watch. Most teens her age didn't wear watches, but she'd been fascinated with watches since she'd learned to tell time and Gloria had bought her a new watch. She'd received a new watch nearly every year since her mom discovered her love of them. Taking off the last watch that her mom had ever gifted her, Hannah kissed it before laying it on her dressing table. A part of her felt as if she was betraying her mom, but she pushed that thought aside, out of her head, and reminded herself that it was Gloria who insisted she know about Hank.

"Are you decent?" Lindsey asked, tapping on her bedroom door.

"Does it matter if I am?"

"Guess not."

Lindsey slowly opened the door and peeked in. Hannah was sitting on the edge of her bed, dressed, flipping through her phone. Lindsey pointed to the door.

"Kathy wants to know if you're coming to eat breakfast."

The thought of food made Hannah's stomach turn. She shook her head.

"I honestly don't think I could eat anything right now."

"I brought donuts." Lindsey smiled, trying to entice her friend.

"Jelly?"

"Of course!"

Kathy poured coffee for the girls as they dove into the box of doughnuts. Cash was on his way. It would be time to leave shortly after he arrived. Hannah's nerves were trying to get the best of her despite the distractions. Kathy, pulling together Hannah's birth certificate and her custodial paperwork, wasn't helping. Seeing the paperwork made everything real. She was under Kathy's care until she was eighteen and then what? Would Kathy let her stay until she was on her feet? No time to think about that at this moment. Heading to a state prison was a daunting feeling.

She wasn't allowed to take anything into the prison such as gifts, or supplies, but Hannah instinctively grabbed a few photos and a couple of letters. Kathy drove. Lindsey sat up front with Kathy, and Cash sat in the back with Hannah. Holding her hand the entire way, he continually whispered words of encouragement in her ear. Signs started to appear on the side of the road.

APPROACHING FOLSOM STATE PRISON. KEEP YOUR DOORS LOCKED. PRISON ZONE. FOLSOM STATE PRISON AHEAD. The color drained from Hannah's cheeks as they came closer to their destination and she read each sign. Kathy barely said a word. Struggling with the thought of the man that she knew, Gloria's husband and Hannah's father, behind the walls of the facility that they were about to enter, didn't fit with the man they had once known and loved. Though she didn't dare pretend to understand what her sister might have been going through, she had a better understanding than before. Gloria must have felt sick each and every time she made the drive to visit her husband.

"Oh my God, this is it!" Hannah buried her face in Cash's shoulder. "I don't know if I can do it. I'm not sure I can go in."

Cash gently ran his hand up and down her back. "Look, we're not here to make you do anything that you don't want to do. It's up to you if you go in or not, but you have come all this way."

Kathy stopped at the gate and gave the guard her driver's license. She politely answered all of his questions, and Hannah gave him her ID to be checked off the list. Cash and Lindsey sat quietly and assured the guard that they were there merely for support; he couldn't care less one way or the other. After a few uncomfortable minutes, he waved them through and directed them to a visitors parking area. Kathy parked the car, took a deep breath, and realized just how nervous she was for Hannah.

"I feel like I'm a bucket of nerves. I can't imagine how you must feel right now."

Hannah tried her best to force a smile, but no matter how hard she tried, she could barely turn up the corners of her mouth.

"Cash is right," Kathy added. "We're behind you one hundred percent, whatever you decide to do, we are here for you no matter what!" Rushing toward her, Kathy held Hannah in her arms. "Sweetie, this may be the only way to get the answers to the questions that you're looking for, true, but it's possible no one knows why Gloria did what she did." Stepping back and looking her niece head on, she continued, "My sister wasn't well, and evidently for a long time."

Hannah nodded, reached out and squeezed Kathy's and Cash's hands, then reached for Lindsey, and did the same to hers. "I get it, I do, but like Cash said, we came all the way here for some answers." She took a deep breath, smiled a crooked smile, and said, "Let's do this!"

Chapter 35
I Remember You

I remember you
Don't you remember me?
We used to play that game
The one when we're at sea
Sand in between my toes
Laughter ringing out
How could you have forgotten?
What we were all about?!
~ Hannah Gunner ~

Cash grabbed Hannah's hand as they walked toward the gate. The simple gesture meant more to her than he realized. Her nerves were taking over. Not only was the prison intimidating with its cement block walls, topped with barbed wire, lights, and guard posts just like you saw in the movies, but she had no idea how her dad was going to react to his long-lost daughter suddenly showing up. IDs and paperwork were rechecked, everything was in order, and to her relief, Kathy, Cash, and Lindsey were allowed to wait with her in the actual visitor's area until she was called back to visit with Hank. There was only one condition: they all had to agree to a security check before entering the building. Thankfully no one objected.

"Women to the right. Guys, or guy I should say, to

the left."

Cash leaned in, kissed Hannah on the lips, and went through the metal detector before being escorted by a guard down the hall for another security check in a room on the left.

"Who's the visitor?" asked a guard.

"Me. I mean, I am," Hannah managed.

"Come with me, please."

Hannah's face turned white as a sheet as a female guard instructed her to walk through another security checkpoint before escorting her to a room on the right. Another female guard was waiting for them inside the room. Fear swept over Hannah as the thought of a strip search taking place ran through her mind. The second guard patted her entire body down and scanned every inch of her body with a hand-held metal detector before asking her a series of questions. Digging her hands in Hannah's pockets, the guard pulled out a folded letter and a photograph. She threw them in a basket on a nearby table for the other guard to examine.

"Do you have any illegal substances on your person?"

"No. No, ma'am. Not illegal, just a letter and photo, those, from my pocket."

Hannah motioned to the letters and photos that the guard had pulled out of her pocket with her eyes.

The guard examining the items nodded to the guard standing next to Hannah and handed the items back to her.

"Clear."

"Sorry," Hannah responded nervously.

"No, that's okay. Those are allowed," the guard

escorting Hannah responded. "Your first time?"

Hannah nodded.

"You may join your family and friends; they'll let you know when they're ready for you to go back."

Nervously, Hannah thanked the guard and walked quickly toward the visitor's room. Cash stood up as soon as he saw her, hugged her, and made a place for her to sit next to Lindsey.

"Everything okay?" Kathy inquired.

Hannah nodded. "Yeah. No problem."

Being in the prison, sitting in visitor's area, was surreal. The regular visitors acted as if this were the most normal thing in the world, visiting an inmate in state prison, but Hannah was so far out of her element she didn't know how to act. She looked like a newbie, and she knew it, which only made her feel worse. It was pointless making small talk because there wasn't anything left to say, and when Hannah's name was eventually called, everyone froze.

"Gunner. Hannah Gunner," a voice boomed across the room.

The moment had finally arrived, and Hannah couldn't move. Her body felt as if it were anchored in one position, bolted down to the chair, making it impossible to move. Kathy spoke on her behalf as she pointed to Hannah and tugged at her arm to help her take a step forward.

"Here, right here."

Finding her feet, Hannah shakily walked toward the guard. Her face was as white as the whitewashed walls and her whole body was trembling. The guard assigned to take her back to visit the inmate spotted her as a first-timer immediately.

"First visit?" He asked.

Hannah nodded.

"You'll be all right. Just keep your head down in the hallway and if you do pass any of the inmates, don't listen to them, or take anything they say personally. They try really hard to make visitors feel uncomfortable."

Hannah nodded, too scared to speak.

"You said Gunner?"

"Yes."

"You're only the third visitor Gunner's ever had in here. Not sure why that is, but I do know he doesn't talk a whole lot."

Hannah managed a slight smile. Third, huh. *Wonder who the second was*, she thought as they walked toward the inmate visitor area.

"Take a seat on the end slot."

The guard pointed to a red phone. "When they bring him out, just pick up the phone and you can talk to him through it."

Hannah nodded and pulled the letter and photo out of her pocket. She placed it on the ledge in front of her seat and tried to smooth out the wrinkles from the folds. It didn't work. Each one had lines all through them, but the faded writing could still be read, and the image of her as a little girl and her dad was still visible. The guard stuck his head back in.

"Oh, by the way, you've got one hour."

"Thank you."

"Don't thank me, thank the Governor of California."

A green light lit up above the door on the opposite side of the glass. Hannah's pulse quickened as she realized that was the door the inmates would soon walk through. She took a deep breath as the door started to open and tried to compose herself. Three inmates were escorted in. Watching them closely, she waited to see which one of them would sit down in front of the glass opposite her. The khaki jumpsuits all looked alike, but the men couldn't be more different, and then she saw him. Her dad, the man she called the Captain, the man from her dreams, plain as day, walking toward her. The years had undoubtedly taken a toll on him, but that was to be expected. Seeing him brought unexpected tears to her eyes, but she blinked them away. Her trembling hands reached for the red phone. She picked it up as she waited anxiously for him to sit down and pick up his.

His dark brown hair, which used to spill everywhere, had turned to salt-and-pepper grey. His dark eyes had lost their shine and were sunken in, lost and distant, not the eyes that she remembered. Those eyes were so dark and bright that she could see her own reflection in them when he'd spin her around. There wasn't a single trace of a smile; in fact, it didn't look like he had smiled for years. But then again, who could blame him? There couldn't be that much to smile about in prison. Lines, thick lines, were engraved in his forehead, but Hannah couldn't study his entire face as she'd hoped. She saw him briefly, long enough to soak in but a few details. To her horror, just like her worst nightmare, he glanced her way, took one look at her and turned to walk back toward the door!

He never sat down, let alone picked up the phone. Reaching out his hand to knock on the door that he'd just walked through, Hannah lost it. Jumping to her feet she banged on the glass with both of her hands, and a guard immediately rushed over and scolded her.

"You can't do that, ma'am. You'll be escorted out."

Pleading with him, she begged the guard to reason with Hank.

"Make him wait, please, stop him! Make him wait! I've come all this way!"

The guard did nothing, though the look on Hannah's face and the fear in her eyes made him curse Hank Gunner's name! Hannah never took her eyes off the man who had given her so much comfort in her dreams, the Captain, Hank, her dad, whoever he was these days as he walked away from her. Desperate, she stood there praying he would turn around and look at her... just look at her!

Struggling with demons of his own, Hank, against his better judgment, slowly looked over his shoulder and stared at the young stranger whose face was pressed against the glass. Her fists were clenched, and in one hand she held a wad of paper, and in the other hand, she slammed a photo against the glass. Tears trickled down her cheeks, and she was mouthing words that he couldn't make out. The door that Hank stood in front of swung open, and the guard asked him if he was done. Hank hesitantly shook his head.

"Don't do that again, Gunner. Next time your visitation will be over!"

"No, sir!"

Reluctantly, he walked back toward Hannah and sat down. She was finally face to face with her father again. They stared at each other for the longest time. Hannah pointed to the red phone, mouthing the words, *pick up.* Finally, he reached for it. His voice was cold and monotone, certainly not the kind, gruff voice that she remembered as a kid.

"Yes."

Yes! What kind of greeting was that? Unsure of where to start, worried about rambling, Hannah just dove right on in.

"It's, um, me!"

"Who?"

Taken aback that he didn't recognize her, Hannah put the photo of them together and placed it back against the glass. Leaning in, he peered at it closely, stared at her, and then examined the picture again. His facial expression gave nothing away. If he was feeling anything at all, she didn't know it. Not even a flicker of emotion in his eyes.

"Hannah. I'm Hannah." She waited for a response, anything, but she received nothing. "Your daughter."

Expressionless, he sat opposite her, irritated, and he may as well have taken a knife and ripped out her heart when he finally bothered to respond.

"I don't have a daughter."

A pain so sharp shot through Hannah that she physically felt it, but she wasn't about to let him see that he had hurt her. Right now, he didn't deserve it.

"Wow! Guess prison changes people, huh?"

He didn't respond.

"Well, that's a lie, Hank Gunner, because you do have a daughter, and you know very well that you're looking at her! Yeah, that's right, it's me... Hannah!" Fury spewed from her lips. Anger from her mom's death, lies, betrayal, loss, and knowing she was opposite an asshole she'd admired in her head for so long. "You don't remember me? Really? Evidently not," she added sarcastically. "Well, guess what; I remember you or should I say, lack of you!"

She pulled out the letter and held it up to the glass. "Do you remember these? Did you even write them? How about we start there!" Her tone was bitter and hateful. He had heard it change within seconds. "Did the prison fairy write them, since it wasn't you and all?"

Throwing the letter back down on the ledge, Hannah leaned back in her chair. "I have letters, tons of them, you wrote to me for years and years, and guess what? They all came from Folsom Prison! I can read this one to you if you like... if you've forgotten how to read as well, since you've forgotten a lot of things over the years, you know, like a family."

"Kind of a smart ass, aren't ya?" He chuckled, but Hannah wasn't amused.

Hannah didn't stop. She started reading his letter. Hank never acknowledged that he wrote it. Staring at his hands, scared to look into her big blue eyes just in case he fell head-over-heels in love with his little girl all over again, only to lose her once more. He cut her off before she could say another word!

"You know what, Miss Smartypants, none of that

right there," he pointed to the ledge in front of her that held the letter and photo that she'd brought with her, "or the fact that you showed up here out of nowhere, matters anymore. The decision to bust up what was left of our family, not letting me talk to you anymore, moving without telling anyone where you were, abandoning me in here, was made by one person alone a long time ago, and it wasn't me!" Rolling his eyes, throwing up his hands, he struggled for words. "Letters forwarded, but no more phone calls, but the worst crime, by far worse than anything I ever did, was not letting me talk to my own little girl! Do you, YOU, have any idea what that was like?" He pointed at Hannah, who was speechless.

Merely inches away from each other, and he still wouldn't look at her. Watching her last chance slip away before her eyes, she tried desperately to reach out to him before he hung up the phone. Everything he had just said didn't make sense to her. Why would her mom do that to them?

"Please, just listen for one second, please. I didn't know. I didn't know about the letters, the phone calls, the moves, any of it. I didn't know you had no idea where we were or that any of that was going on."

His eyes flashed toward her. "What do you mean you didn't know about the letters? You didn't think it strange your dad stopped calling you for no apparent reason?"

Hannah shook her head.

"What the hell are you talking about, girl? Spit it out!"

It wasn't as if he couldn't see her anguish, because he was witnessing it right before his eyes. Fear was written all over her face, worried that she'd run out of time and lose him all over again. After all, what was an hour to repair all of the damage, the betrayal, which neither of them could understand? Hannah took a deep breath, and though her voice was trembling, she threw down a bombshell that she knew was going to change both of their lives. How? That depended on how he received the information that she delivered. Forgiveness or bitterness, love or hate, maybe a combination of both was about to be dealt. Fearing for the worst but hoping for the best, fighting back her tears so she wouldn't appear weak, Hannah shared with him the ugly truth.

"Because I didn't even know that you were alive."

"What in the hell are you talking about?" Hank's face changed in an instant. Shock, not anger, swept over him. "How is that even possible?"

"I thought you were dead." Hannah was visibly shaking. "I was told you were dead!"

"That fucking bitch!" Hank, holding the phone with one hand, threw his other hand in the air. "What the hell was that woman thinking? Bitch!"

Hannah cringed.

"Don't. Don't do that!" Hannah snapped. "Please. Don't do that... "

"She had no right! She had no right to do that to YOU or ME!" Hank bellowed so loud that Hannah jumped in her chair, and the guards warned him to calm down.

"NO RIGHT! Do you hear me?"

Hannah sat motionless in the chair, red phone still in hand, unable to say a single word. Hank continued to rant as if unaware his daughter sat opposite him.

"No fucking right!" Hank said, head hung in hands and fist clenched. "I had a life, not in here, but out there with my so-called family, and she ruined my reason to get up in the morning and do it for one more fricking day!" As if the wind had been sucked out of his sails, Hank continued to talk to himself. "Gloria took away my reason to fight," he said, staring at Hannah. "YOU! You were my reason, and she took you away."

Hannah didn't dare move or speak. Hearing his words but barely listening, she sat in the chair as he rambled.

"And I dare say, if you were honest with yourself, that bitch ruined your life on some level as well!"

Hannah fought back her overwhelming desire to fight back on her mom's behalf. On some level he was right, but on another level, she believed he HAD to be wrong. Hank went on and on.

"She destroyed our family and that was her choice, not mine or yours!"

Hannah sat, numb, too scared to speak until he was through with his rant. She looked just like her mother, big blue eyes and all, and at that moment those eyes were both a blessing and a curse. It was a terrible place for Hank to be, in love with someone you hate. His anger toward Gloria was eating him alive, but loving her was killing him even faster. As he spoke, he managed to make eye contact with his daughter.

"I used to call the house begging her, *begging her*, to let me speak to you. I swear I have no idea to this day how she could be so cold, abandoning me and stealing you."

Hannah's eyes glossed over, but she never said a word as he described how painful it was each time he called home.

"Let me talk to Hannah. Please, Gloria, let me talk to Hannah, please."

Blinking away his tears, he placed a finger on the glass and pointed directly toward her; it was chilling.

"Do you know what that cold-hearted woman would say?"

Hannah, a blank expression on her face, shook her head.

"Nothing. Not a goddamn word! Nothing. That's right. Not a word." His voice was cold and angry. "She'd let me beg. Told me it was for the best, insisted it was for you and your protection, and then that bitch would hang up the damn phone."

They sat in silence for a few minutes. Hannah had no idea what to say next; she was starting to think she would never find the answers she needed. Hank didn't appear to have them, and her mom had made no sense. Grasping for straws, Hannah asked him what seemed to be a ridiculous question.

"I was hoping you could fill in some blanks for me. I have clouded memories, and I'm confused by the choices my mom made."

"Hell, you're confused? You're preaching to the choir! Join the club."

"Why don't you ask her and give her a message for me while you're at it. Tell her I want a damn divorce. That she's a cruel bitch who doesn't deserve a beautiful kid like you."

Hannah hung her head. "Please stop."

He didn't apologize.

"She's not perfect, far from it, but she is my mom." Hannah looked him square in the eye and with confidence said, "And I love her!" She took a deep breath, wondering if he was going to say something nasty, but he didn't, so she forged ahead gingerly. "Looking back, I know that she did her best. I wasn't always an easy kid, but what I don't know is why she told me that you were killed in prison." Hannah proceeded cautiously. "I was hoping you could help me figure that part out and we could rebuild our relationship."

His eyes grew huge, but a slight spark was triggered when he heard the words *rebuild our relationship.* Had Hannah really sought him out to do such a thing, and was it even possible? The timing couldn't have been better!

"You have to understand, Hannah, that she betrayed us both! She took you from me, and me from you, blowing up our entire family. Did you know I was up for parole, again, but after she walked out on me and took you with her, I didn't even care anymore."

"But didn't you get into a fight that blew your parole? The one that caused an injury so bad you supposedly, but clearly not, died."

Feelings of anger, resentment, and hate were starting to surface. Hank tried to respect Hannah's feelings and calm down, but recalling every time he begged to talk to his little girl, sitting before him now a beautiful young woman, infuriated him all over again.

"A second parole hearing, and are you blaming me for this mess, not seeing or speaking to you?"

Hannah shook her head. "I don't know who to blame, if there's any blame or what the hell's going on, but I need some answers."

"Watch your mouth!" Hank shook his finger at her. "Your mother teach you to talk like that?" He grinned for the first time, and his face softened. "She promised to stand by me, your mom, but she didn't. Did she tell you that?"

Hannah didn't respond. Her blank stare told him she was evaluating, though not yet convinced he was telling her the entire truth.

"A phone call, Hannah, a freaking phone call, I couldn't even talk to you. Then, wouldn't you know it, without a word she up and moved, taking you with her, and it took forever to get a forwarding address. But a lot of good that did me, considering she didn't give you any of the letters I wrote." His fists were clenched, and his jaw tightened. "Evil bitch!"

Hannah couldn't take the insults anymore. Clearing her throat, she prepared herself to drop the bombshell that her mom was dead. The words formed in her mouth and she realized it was the first time that she had actually said them out loud. She couldn't think of a nice way to say it, and hearing his insults still angered her. Despite her desire to be tactful, the words just blurted out of her mouth.

"She's dead!"

Hank looked at her in disbelief, chuckled, and didn't acknowledge the words that she had delivered into the universe. Something about the way Hannah's big blue eyes turned cold, and her stare shot right through him, told him she wasn't kidding. An awkward silence consumed them for a few moments, but it felt like an eternity. It indeed wasn't the news that he had been expecting. It was easier to be angry, mad, and to resent the woman who he had so desperately loved and missed than to feel grief and sadness for her. The sense of loss that swept over him was confusing; she had, after all, betrayed them. The news was a reminder of how much he had loved her at one time or maybe he really still did. Hannah broke the silence.

"It went pretty fast, but the doctors thought she must've had it for some time."

"How?" Hank asked, his voice barely audible.

"Cancer."

"What about you?" He dipped his head. "What are you doing?"

"Mom must have known she was ill and moved us back home, to be near Kathy, and I'm living with her now. Well, we're almost done clearing out our place."

Hank raised his head and looked up at Hannah. His eyes were glassy, and Hannah could tell the news had shocked him.

"How is Kathy?"

"Fine," Hannah responded. "She's actually here; she brought me to see you."

"I didn't know." Hank hung his head. "I didn't know about your mom. Wow. I didn't know."

"No one did. Mom kept it to herself for as long as she could; she didn't want anyone to worry, but that was who she was; maybe you never saw that side of her."

He shook his head. "No, you're wrong. I did. We had several good years."

Hannah hesitated, and Hank could see the wheels spinning in her head. He likely wouldn't believe her, but she felt the need to tell him that her mom was a good person, kind, and loving.

"She loved you, right up till the end. She kept a photo of us; all three of us, by her bed, and never once went out with other men.

"Well, we were married!"

"Yes, but who would've known that?"

He nodded. Hannah was right about that. More than halfway through the visit and Hannah hadn't once mentioned the games that they used to play, the ones that had kept her going as a child. Nervously she brought him up, the man who kept her safe, if only in her head.

"I remember him, the Captain."

"Who?"

"Captain Fin."

She giggled, but Hank sat sad and stone-faced as he observed every inch of her face as she smiled and flipped strands of hair away from her face with her hands.

"You wouldn't know this, but my most vivid memories as a child are of the pirate game that we always played."

The tiniest smile crept across his face as Hannah recapped some of her memories. Chasing the waves, looking for treasure, pulling up the sails, she had tons of them buried in her memory bank.

"Treasure Island, searching for hidden treasure, our ship, walking the plank, and you even promoted me to First Matey." She laughed so loud it made him smile. "I'm not kidding, over the years my memories and the game became blurred. Focusing on the game as much as I did, in my dreams, daydreams in school, and when I had free time to play, I started to think that maybe I had made most of it up or my dad was really a pirate."

Laughing out loud when he heard those words—really, a pirate—Hannah recognized for the first time the sound of his voice. He was hanging on to every word that she said, waiting for her to tell him more, but she was doing the very same thing! She told him about her prized possession, the one that she had packed so carefully and moved with her everywhere since the day he had given it to her, the conch shell.

"You still have that thing?"

"What? Did you just ask me that?"

His eyes pleaded for more and Hannah didn't disappoint. "My magical shell; the one you gave me with instructions, to boot!" She grinned. "Whenever I was sad, missed you, or if mom was crying, I'd go into my room and pick up my magical conch shell, place it by ear and disappear to the ocean."

Hank's eyes lit up. She'd missed him, just like he had missed her.

"Can't believe you still have that thing."

Hannah grinned. "That *thing* has been my comfort for years."

Cupping her hand, she placed it against her ear. "I remember the day you showed me how to listen to the ocean. I've escaped to my imaginary beach ever since."

The years had flown by so quickly, and he had missed everything! She had grown into a striking young lady, but sitting here, right now in front of him, talking about that stupid shell, she was acting like his little girl all over again.

"I'd fall asleep every night knowing you were going to find me and put me right back on the ship." She rolled her eyes and laughed. "Of course, I mean to bed."

Hank motioned for her to go back to something she'd said earlier; it took her by surprise.

"You mentioned that Gloria cried." His voice had softened. "Did she cry a lot when you were growing up?" he asked sympathetically.

"I think probably more than the other moms. I didn't know that then, but I do now."

"What about?" he asked.

"Well," she leaned forward on the edge of her chair, placing her head on hands, propped on her elbows. "I was hoping those were the answers I could get from you."

"How can I tell you what that woman cried about? I didn't even know who she was anymore. The woman I knew wouldn't have done what she did. Hannah, she wouldn't have abandoned our family like that, wouldn't have abandoned me."

Hank examined his daughter's face for the longest time. After not seeing her for years, he couldn't take his eyes off of her. She had so many of Gloria's features, but a few of his stuck out.

Running his hands over his face and through his hair, shaking his head, Hank finally came up with an answer that was believable.

"YOU. You were the reason!" Hesitating, he finally added something else. "And me."

They were finally getting somewhere. Afraid she'd say the wrong thing, Hannah sat patiently and waited for Hank to take the lead.

"Gloria didn't want you to visit me in prison, here, at Folsom. You were just a little kid back then, tiny really for your age, but smart! She'd done some kind of research, she'd said, read some studies that at the time had said it was detrimental to kids' development to visit parents in prison." He took a deep breath, and Hannah thought he was blinking away tears.

"I begged her and begged her to reconsider. Truth be told, I probably pressured her to bring you up to see me. Telling her that studies change all the time and that you can't believe everything you read, and kids are resilient and you'd probably forget anyway."

Hank hung his head.

"I think she was starting to come around. You probably don't remember, but I was still calling you and talking to you both, but then I was jumped and got into a fight, or another fight, I should say. An officer was assaulted during the chaos; he accidentally took a swing intended for someone else." Hank took a deep breath. "But anyway, I lost early release or any chance of a parole hearing."

It was starting to make sense; there had been more to the story than Gloria just pulling Hannah away from him.

"It wasn't the first fight in here for me, and I think

she knew it might not be the last, and it wasn't, but the day I got shanked put me in medical for a long time. I almost didn't recover; I think that's when she'd had enough and left with you."

His hands were shaking, and his voice was trembling; finally, his words sent chills down her spine. "I did this to us. Ruined our family, but it was easier for me locked up in here all these years to blame her."

Speechless, Hannah sat opposite her dad, hoping her presence was enough to comfort him. She had no words, and no idea what to say anyway.

"Seeing you like this, Hannah, tells me that Gloria was right about one thing."

"Oh yeah, what's that?" Hannah managed, though her voice was barely a whisper.

"This isn't a place for you. I guess your mom did know best. Don't come back here; I'll write."

Hannah shook her head.

"Mom, at the end, was frantic and upset, hating herself for keeping us apart for so long and for not showing me the letters. Dad, she wanted me to have the letters, know you were alive, and for us to forgive her. I choose to believe that mom lied for all the right reasons and handled it all the wrong way."

As soon as the word *dad* popped out of Hannah's mouth, Hank's ears perked up. He didn't argue, but hung onto that one word, *dad*. A buzzer sounded, indicating it was time for the inmates to be taken back and for the visitors to leave.

Hannah stood up, red phone still in her hand.

"I'll come back as soon as I can."

"Please don't. Don't do that; I promise I'll write."

"Up until now I thought my dad was dead and the Captain was a dream in my head. I'm not settling for a piece of paper now. You're going to have to see me or leave me sitting in the waiting room. It's your choice."

She smiled and blew him a kiss.

"Kinda hard for the First Matey to report to duty when the Captain refuses to get on board!"

Grinning, Hannah responded, "Aye, aye Captain! Oh, how I love that man—Captain Fin is back!"

Hank wiped his eyes as he proudly watched her prepare to leave. But she turned around and quickly picked up the phone and pointed for him to do the same.

"I'm your third visitor. Mom was your first, who was your second?"

"What?"

"Gunner. Hang up the phone. Time to go." The guard nudged him to hang up.

"One second. Please. Just one, promise, that's my daughter."

He had no idea why she was curious about his visitor but he rambled off the name anyway.

"Nathan's brother, Nigel. He visits me on behalf of Nate, Nathan's son. He's his uncle. A paralegal. Like family."

Hannah grinned. "I've met Nigel, Sandy's brother. Nice guy."

Chapter 36
Nigel

Will you listen to me, please?
We must right this wrong.
~ Nigel ~

Something about the call he'd received, from an inquiry he made, nagged Nigel as he drove home from the office. Running the conversation over and over in his head, he finally decided to make the call.

"Hey, it's me."

"Hi, Uncle Nigel. Did you find some more stuff out?"

"I did. Let me fill you in."

Nigel looked just like Nathan—same build, hair color, and his voice even sounded like his—or the way it used to sound. Nate looked like both his parents; he had traits from Nathan and Sandy, the best of both, everyone always told him. Nigel talked with his nephew for a few minutes, filled him in and gave him most of the information he had gathered that week. After a few minutes, he asked him to put his mother on the phone.

"Put your momma on."

He heard Sandy in the background asking him who was calling, and he couldn't help but laugh when Nate refused to tell her. He used to hate it when Nathan used to do that to him when they were growing up and they would fight over answering the phone.

"You'll see. Answer the phone."

He knew the look she was likely giving him and the lecture that would follow once she got off the phone, but hopefully, she'd calm down once she realized it was just him on the other end.

"Hello."

"Sandy, it's me."

"Hey, what's going on?"

"How far do you want to take this project of Nate's?"

"What do you mean? I'd like him to know what his father was really like, why it was important for him to be there that day, involved in the talks about the pending strike, and what an incredible man he was, not to mention it would be nice if he got an A. Why?"

He stopped at a red light but didn't realize it had turned green until the cars behind him started honking. Sandy heard the other vehicles and asked if he was okay.

"Yeah, I'm fine."

"Well, call me when you're not driving. You don't sound fine."

She went to hang up the phone.

"Sandra, hang on!"

Her name, Sandra, rarely used, especially since Nathan's death, and the sound of his voice startled her.

"What's going on?" she asked nervously.

"I'm coming over. See you in a few."

Nate had already eaten, showered, and was hanging out in his room when his uncle arrived. Earbuds in, way into the game on his device, he didn't hear the doorbell ring. Sandy walked into the kitchen, poured a glass of wine, offered Nigel a beer, and sat down at the table. Pulling out a chair he joined her, slammed half the beer, took off his jacket, and thought about how to say what he was about to reveal.

"Are you going to tell me what this is all about?" she asked, dying to know what was going on that he'd drive all the way over just to talk.

"Let me ask you this..."

"Okay... ask away."

"When you asked me to help Nate research the events of the night that Nathan was killed and find out what happened during and after the trial, I thought it was going to be cut and dry."

Sandy nodded. "Yeah. And?"

"Well, it's not!" He took another sip of his beer. "I dug a little deeper, followed everyone involved that night, and asked around about what happened the following weeks after Nathan's death."

"Go on."

"And that's where it suddenly got complicated."

"It shouldn't be complicated. The murderer was convicted, the trial, newspaper clippings, you're losing me."

"That part's fine; it's after Nathan's death and Hank Gunner's trial where things get messy."

If looks could kill, Nigel figured he'd be a dead man. Sandy took a swallow of wine, checked the hallway for her son, Nate, and in a firm, muffled voice asked Nigel what in the hell he was talking about.

"God, I hadn't heard that name in years, and now I

seem to be hearing it all the time. Hannah's return, Gloria's passing. What does Hank have to do with Nate's project for school about his dad?"

"Well, that's the complicated part."

"Spit it out, Nigel. What is it?" Her voice was nervous and sharp.

"That depends on how you feel about Hank."

Frustrated, Sandy threw up her hands. She hadn't thought about Hank, Gloria, or Hannah in years until the funeral, and that wasn't her doing. Gloria had moved, and after one move too many, they didn't talk as much, even though she had tried on multiple occasions to contact her and stay in touch.

"I don't know how I feel about Hank," she replied. "I haven't thought about Hank for a very long time."

Nigel grabbed another cold beer out of the fridge, opened it, took a swig, and leaned against the countertop. He waited for Sandy to calm down and speak first, contemplating how to tell her what he'd found out.

"Why are you even talking about Hank, anyhow? This project was supposed to show Nate, and his class, how his dad stood up for what he believed in. Give them the historical facts, the truth, and let everyone know that he did it for the right reasons, the talks, the negotiations, the pending strike, and that his life was robbed from him. That the murder was the crime, and not the pending strike."

Nigel nodded. He remembered, to the day, receiving the phone call and rushing to the hospital. Crying and screaming out promises to his brother that he would watch over his son, and he had, every single day of

Nate's life. Always checking in on them, making sure they had everything they needed, and being the family that Nathan would have wanted. Nigel pulled out a chair and sat opposite Sandy.

"I remember Hank," Nigel said. "And what Hank meant to Nathan; he looked up to him."

"He did. He loved him, truly loved him, like a brother." She reached over and squeezed Nigel's hand. "He loved you more because you were his brother, but Hank was like his older brother, just like he was your older brother." Taking a sip of wine, thinking back to those days, Sandy added, "Hank looked out for Nathan; he was good to him, and truth be told, we all loved or love him still." Blowing her hair out of her face, she added, "Seems so long ago, but I guess in a way he'll always be a part of our family. I loved the Gunners."

"I get it. That's why I'm asking you how *you* feel about Hank."

"Why? Why do you need to know that?"

Nigel shook his head. Having no idea where to begin, he downed his beer for extra courage and reached for another.

"Damn, must be bad!" Sandy stated.

"It's not good, but it's what we decide to do with it that could be a game changer and change everything."

Topping off her glass and placing the wine bottle in the middle of the table, Sandy kicked off her shoes, put her feet up on the empty chair next to her, and prepared herself to listen to what Nigel had to say. By the look on his face, she could tell it was important, but she had no idea the information that he had could change Hannah and Hank's lives forever.

"Go ahead, Nigel, fill me in. What's going on?"

Chapter 37

Hannah

Now I've found you
What to do
Will you love me
Like I love you?
Do you miss her
She missed you!
~ Hannah Gunner ~

It had been a little over two weeks since Hannah had visited Hank in prison, but she still replayed their conversation over and over in her head. Analyzing every word that he'd said and wondering if he'd really leave her sitting in the waiting room when she visited him next. There was only one way to find out: schedule a visit and wait and see. Planning a visit to the state prison was going to have to wait for a couple of weeks. Hannah had to unpack and get settled in Kathy's house, and even she knew that was a priority. Standing with Cash in the empty apartment that she and her mom had once called their home, she could almost hear her mom's voice.

Be kind, Hannah. Don't leave that out, put it away. Did you put your dishes in the sink? Her mom's voice seemed to radiate through the empty rooms as Hannah walked through each one. Her presence felt, though she was clearly gone. Cash stood behind her and slipped his arms around her waist. She could smell his cologne before she felt his touch. Kissing her sweetly on the cheek, he whispered and asked if she were okay. She wasn't. Standing in the middle of the living room, surrounded by the memory of the woman she loved the most in the world, realizing all of the mistakes her mom had made, and believing deep down inside of her that Gloria had made those decisions for all of the right reasons, still she didn't feel okay. Feelings of guilt consumed Hannah for having such thoughts, and a sick feeling was pushed down in the pit of her stomach as she finished her walkthrough.

"Leaving here, I feel as if I'm abandoning my mom, and I know that's ridiculous because it's just a building." She wrapped her hands around Cash's as he held her. "But despite all of our moves and what she did or didn't do, she was happy here, really happy, and so was I."

Cash hugged her tightly. "I know she was, you could tell, but part of that I think was because of you. You were happy, and that made her happy."

Hannah grabbed his hand and pulled him toward the hallway of the apartment, batting away her tears, trying not to cry. She asked Cash if he would walk with her.

"Go with me, please? As I say goodbye to each room and the memories of my mom here."

He nodded. "Of course." But it was the saddest thing he'd ever heard his girl say.

Hannah recalled a different memory she'd shared with her mom in each room while they lived in the apartment. Nervously she put one foot in front of the other and walked into her mother's room. Being in that place gave her chills; it was as if the room knew she was leaving. Cash kissed the back of her head and left the room, allowing her a minute with her thoughts and her mom. Empty, the room had an eerie feel to it, but the memories were fresh in her mind, and Hannah knew that she had to say goodbye to this place.

"I'm so sorry if I let you down, Mom, if you felt as if you couldn't trust me, the part where Hank was still alive. I would've shared that burden with you, I promise I would have, and I would have listened to your reasons." Her hand ran across the walls as she walked around the room. "Did the lie grow so big it was too big to retract?"

As soon as the words left her mouth, she wondered if Gloria felt as if there was no turning back.

"I would have listened, tried to understand, and worked with you." Tears rolled slowly down her cheeks as she spoke her goodbyes to the empty room. "I would have understood; I'm sure of it, the illness, the secrets, none of it matters. But I'd give anything in the world if you were with me now, anything, and I'm certain we would have worked through this mess together."

Slapping herself on the forehead, she snapped herself out of the emotional downward spiral where she was headed. None of it mattered anyway. Her heart heavy and head pounding, she moved onto the next room. Entering her bedroom, her thoughts switched to memories of Cash and Lindsey sitting on the bed talking, music playing, and holding the conch shell against her ear in her bed when she couldn't sleep.

"We had some good talks in here." Cash laughed.

"And, almost, well, you know."

"Stop. Don't say it!"

Hannah's smile indicated that was a great day.

"When we're ready, then." Ruffling his hair as she walked past him, she added, "We'll go there, that, you know."

His eyes lit up. "The that, that, that, the BIG that?"

"Yeah, that," she smiled. "When we're ready."

Pulling her toward him, she kissed him first, and he kissed her back. The past six months had been crazy; too many real-life tragedies going on in Hannah's life for two teens to be themselves. One thing it had proven to Kathy, Hannah's new guardian, was that Cash was sticking around, he did love her, and she was just as crazy about him. Would they last? Who knew? Time would tell, but they definitely had a solid foundation.

"I love you; you know that, and it's when you're ready, 'cause I'll wait."

Hannah's face glowed, showing him how she felt without saying a word. Standing on her tippy toes to kiss him again, he picked her up as if she weighed nothing. They kissed for almost a moment too long, but long enough to know that they were head over heels in love with each other.

"I love you too. But you know what that means now, don't ya?" Hannah grinned.

"What's that?"

"You'll have to get acquainted with the man behind bars."

"Whoa. I forgot about that part, but for you, I can do it. In fact, for you, I could do just about anything!"

Chapter 38
Help

I don't know where to begin
But I do know it could be life-changing.
Are you in?
~ Nigel ~

Nigel fidgeted nervously as he sat opposite his boss's desk. Michael E. Daniels, Family Law. What was he supposed to say? *I helped my nephew with a school project, took it further than it needed to go, and discovered a terrible injustice had been committed?* Saying it in his head didn't sound that bad; it was, after all, the truth. Jessica, the office administrator, stuck her head in.

"He's on his way in. Did you need anything while you wait?"

"Nah. I could go back to my desk, but I'm afraid if I do that I'll lose my nerve."

"Something I can help you with?" she asked inquisitively.

He shook his head. "Not this time, but thanks."

The one-attorney law firm was located in a mediocre part of town. Nigel had worked as a paralegal for Michael, Mr. Daniels, for four-and-a-half years now. He felt comfortable talking to him about most anything, but for some reason, this felt as if he was crossing the line of work-related and friendship boundaries. Nigel convinced himself that all Michael had to do was tell him he wasn't interested. Or worse, that he was wasting his time. Either one of those statements would likely shut him down, at least for a while. What he hadn't expected was Sandy's cooperation and willingness to help. Her belief in justice was sincere, admirable, and Nathan would be so proud of her and the son he never met, Nate.

The door swung open and Nigel, lost in thought, jumped.

"Hey there, Nigel, what can I do you for?"

A disheveled Michael, with his friendly voice and happy persona, bounced into the room. Looking down at his shirt, he laughed.

"Don't say a word! I've already heard it from Mary Beth. I grabbed one that hadn't been pressed because I felt like wearing this color today. Purple. It feels like a purple kind of day!"

Nigel grinned. Purple it was.

"Did you file the Harrington case at the courthouse by 3:00 p.m. yesterday like I asked you to?"

"Yes, sir," Nigel responded.

"Good. Then did you need to see me?" He laughed out loud. "Well, of course you did, you're sitting right here in my office."

He walked back over to his door, stuck his head out, and hollered.

"Jessie."

"Yes, sir."

"Two coffees, if you don't mind, please."

He threw his jacket over the back of a chair and sat down next to Nigel instead of behind his desk. They made small talk until their coffee arrived and then Michael asked him the question.

"So what's really going on?"

Nigel set his coffee down and nervously wrung his hands. Not knowing where to start, he struggled with an opening sentence.

"You're not in trouble, are ya?"

"No sir, it's not me."

"Well, just start from the beginning and tell me what's on your mind."

Nigel took a deep breath and did just that; he started from the day Nathan stood side by side with Hank and the others during the strike. He voice cracked as he described the fatal shooting and his brother's death.

"I'm so sorry about Nathan, Nigel. It was tragic and never should have happened. That pain is real, and you don't have to be afraid to feel it."

Nigel nodded. It was definitely real. Every time he watched Nate score a basket, he thought about Nathan. Every time Nate brought home a great grade, he thought about Nathan, and every time Nate asked about his dad, his heart broke all over again for all of them. Finally, he stared Michael straight in the eye.

"This is the part where it gets crazy." He hesitated. "And where I ask you for your help, if you're willing."

Michael knew better than to make a promise he couldn't keep. He didn't answer one way or the other but kept listening with an open mind.

"Well, why don't you go on and finish your story. I don't know yet what you're trying to ask of me, so I can't honestly say if I can help you or not."

Taking a deep breath, hoping he could persuade Michael to join a cause he had no business getting involved with, Nigel finished telling him about the unusual predicament he found himself in.

Chapter 39
Borrowed Time

Think.
Let me think for a minute.
Your boy's in trouble.
~ Michael ~

Michael stood up and began to pace the floor. The wheels were spinning in his mind, Nigel could tell. He always had a peculiar look on his face when he was in deep thought, thinking, planning, trying to work issues out in his head. Nigel sat motionlessly. Scared to death that bringing this to Michael's doorstep was a mistake.

"You know this is out of the realm of family law." He walked over to the door, pulled it ajar, and asked Jessica to bring in more coffee. "You need a criminal lawyer."

Nigel shook his head and opened his mouth to speak, but before he could get the words out, Michael was flipping through his address book on his desk.

"I know a couple of good criminal attorneys, good guys, who would be a great fit for this type of case. In fact, this would be right up their alley. Here are their numbers."

He was scribbling their contact information on a piece of paper, talking at the same time, and hoping that

Nigel would accept the names and numbers.

"This isn't something we do here, hell, all we're known for in this town is handling nasty divorces, you know that." He sat down behind his desk. "Your boy in there needs a divorce?"

His forced laugh indicated that he knew Nigel hadn't found his joke very funny, and he was right. Nigel shook his head and stared at the paper he now held in his hand. Maybe he didn't sound sincere enough, or perhaps the case didn't seem important enough, but how could that possibly be after he'd just laid out the facts the way that he had? Granted, he wasn't an attorney, but even as a paralegal Nigel knew this could be an open-and-shut case.

"Give Doug a call first, he's likely not as busy as Randall, but still a good attorney," Michael insisted.

Shaking his head, Nigel declined.

"No time. Forget the money, which there isn't any, time isn't on our side." His face was filled with anguish. "We've got the last man alive who can tell us word-for-word exactly what happened that night, the fight, and a witness to verify his account, and he might not live long enough to give a sworn affidavit."

Leaning over to the left side of his desk, Michael pulled out a small bottle of bourbon. Taking a swig right out of the bottle, he held it up to Nigel. Wanting to decline, Nigel changed his mind, reached for the bottle and took a shot of the bourbon as well. It was smooth and went down with ease. Michael took another shot before shoving it back in his drawer. His brow was wrinkled, and Nigel could tell he was struggling within himself.

"I want to help you, I really do, but this is out of my area of expertise."

"Mike, look at the facts, just like you always say to me. This should be, should be, an open-and-shut case!"

Nigel stood in front of Michael's desk, leaned over, looked him in the eye, and made one last plea.

"The man's going to die before anyone hears what he has to say, but what he has to say could affect the lives of so many people, including a man who has spent the better years of his life behind bars."

"Shit!" Leaning back in his chair, Michael gave him the answer that he had hoped to hear. He would help him. "Damn it! You're lucky these sons of bitches are happy in this town! Divorce court is light right now."

Relieved, Nigel stood up to start preparing the necessary paperwork to begin the filings. Knowing what he knew, he prayed the court system would work with him since time sure wasn't going to.

"When can this guy come in? What's his name... Studer, Stodder?"

"Mr. Stockton. It's James Stockton, and he's not going to be able to come in. We'll have to go to him. He's literally counting down the days. Hospice care; any day could be his last, and no one knows which day that will be."

Taking in a deep breath, letting it out slowly, Nigel described his first meeting with Mr. Stockton.

"Man, it was tough! Prepare yourself, seriously, because the first thing I noticed was the smell, and it wasn't because the house was dirty or gross or anything like that, it was like a sickly, someone-in-here-isn't-right kinda smell."

"Well, like you said, he's dying."

"Yeah. You're right. It's that death smell, but he's still here."

Nigel shuddered, and it was visible. Michael pretended he hadn't seen his friend so squirmy, but he couldn't deny that his description was making him feel nervous as well. Being around sick people wasn't exactly his cup of tea.

"He wears this breathing equipment, 'cause he can't hardly breathe, but takes it off to talk. Puts it back on in between sentences."

"What you're saying is no small talk then, right?" Michael smiled, but even he knew it wasn't funny.

"And he gets tired super quickly. So we have to move fast. Know what we're going to ask him. Be direct and get it done."

"So there's no way he's going to be able to come here?"

Nigel shook his head and rolled his eyes.

"Did you hear a word I said?"

"I heard ya!" Michael threw his pen down on his desk, spun around in his chair to stand up, and replied, frustrated, "Ah hell, I hate creepy house visits!"

Dialing his cell phone as he gathered paperwork, Nigel placed the call to Sharon, Mr. Stockton's daughter. The phone went straight to voicemail. Disappointed, and with a sound of urgency in his voice, he left a detailed message.

"Call me as soon as you get this, it's urgent!"

Sharon called back within the hour, agreeing to allow them to visit that afternoon to speak to her dad and try to get a sworn affidavit, if he was up to it. Right before they hung up, Michael nudged Nigel and handed him a piece of paper. He read it and then asked Sharon the question that Michael had posed.

"Sharon, we really appreciate the time with your dad this afternoon, especially on such short notice. Given the sensitivity of this case and your father's declining health issues, do you mind if we also videotape the interview?"

Dead air.

"Hello, Sharon?"

"I'm here."

"Would that be a problem? It is for a record for the court only."

Still, she never said a word.

"Unless, of course, you'd like a copy. If so, then one would be provided."

"I have a request."

"Sure. If possible, I'll try to see if we can make it happen. Of course, I haven't heard the request yet." He chuckled, but she didn't laugh.

"When you introduced yourself, you know, before, when you explained why you needed his help."

"Yeah," Nigel responded hesitantly.

"Well, I think... I think... um... it's kind of a weird request, but I think I'd like to meet the family that he ends up helping." There was silence on the other end of the phone, and just when Nigel was about to say something, she spoke again. "Do you think that would be possible?"

Nigel nodded his head. Realizing she couldn't see him on the other end of the phone, he quickly responded.

"I'm sure they'd love to meet you."

"All right then, see you at one."

Chapter 40
Scared to Death

Fear will no longer consume me
Death is knocking on my door
~ James Stockton ~

Michael drove to Mr. Stockton's house while Nigel searched online for a case that had been overturned that was similar to the one that they were about to take on. Technology, it was a wonderful thing, especially when you were on the go, low on funds, and out of time!

"That's it." Nigel pointed to a beige duplex on the left.

It wasn't in a bad neighborhood, didn't look rundown, and if you didn't know any better, you wouldn't have a clue that a man inside the walls of the average-looking house was, in fact, fighting for every breath he took and was deteriorating by the minute. Sitting in the car for a moment, gathering their things, each one silently wondered if they were doing the right thing. Was it even their place to get involved? After all, it had been years since anyone had mentioned that night. What if no one even cared? To his relief, his boss eased his fears.

"You know, I have a feeling that, like most stories, there's more to this story, and it's about to unravel. It's probably a good thing that we're here; the story may never have been heard in its entirety if you hadn't have pursued this angle on behalf of your friend."

Nigel put his hand on the car door and started to open it. "Well there's only one way to find out; let's do it."

A pretty lady answered the door, but Nigel discreetly shook his head and averted his eyes, indicating to Michael that this was not Sharon, Mr. Stockton's daughter.

"Hello." Nigel politely introduced himself and Michael. "We're here to see Mr. Stockton and Sharon, his daughter."

He pointed to his friend and then to himself. "Michael Daniels and Nigel Nichols; they're expecting us."

"Can you give me a second, please?"

She half closed the door and walked back down the hallway. Muffled voices could be heard, and another lady appeared at the door.

"Sharon! Good to see you again." Nigel immediately stuck out his hand.

"Come in, come in! Sorry about that, you know Nancy, the nurse? If not, that was Nancy." Her smile was warm and her voice welcoming as she stepped out of the way to let them in. "Please, he's expecting you."

Nigel hadn't exaggerated about the smell. The house was small but clean, neat and tidy, and you could tell everything was in its place. But lurking behind the smell of antiseptic and air fresheners was a smell that anyone who had been around a decaying body could recognize. It was a distinctive scent. And despite their best efforts to disguise it, the odor had lingered and penetrated the fabrics, walls, and air of the house. Nothing worse than watching the ones you love dying in front of you, watching them decay from the inside out. Cancer was a terrible disease! Michael felt sick to his stomach but tried his best not to breathe through his nose. Nigel felt sadness for Sharon, who spent each and every day with her father that she could, but likely hadn't given herself a second thought in a long time. Wishing he could tell her how much he admired her, but knowing that now wasn't the time, he recognized they had to move fast. Her father could literally pass at any time. The realization of what ran through his mind prompted him to move swiftly.

"May we speak to your father, please?"

Sharon nodded and pointed toward a bedroom door.

"He just wasn't up to getting out of bed today; he did try."

"No worries," Nigel responded as he pulled out the camera and walked into the room.

Introductions were brief. Nigel set up the video camera and pulled out the document that would eventually become his sworn affidavit.

"When you're ready, Mr. Stockton."

"James," he mumbled. "It's James, and nice to meet you both."

"Yes, sir. James."

Nigel repositioned the microphone.

"I'm going to state the day, date, your name, and location, and you'll confirm. After that, tell us everything that you can remember from that night. Start from the beginning, and try to recall as many details as you can. Where you were, what day or year, if you can remember, who was there, and most importantly, what exactly happened."

"Do you have any questions before we get started?" Michael interjected.

James shook his head.

"Once you've told us everything you can remember, we'll question you, if we feel that there are details missed and see if we can jog your memory. Okay?"

He nodded again. "I'm ready."

Closing his eyes and allowing his mind to drift back to when he was working on the docks, the union, and that night at the pub, the Shamrock. For a second, Nigel thought that between his illness and the medication, James might actually drop back off to sleep. Thankfully after a few moments, which felt much longer, James started to retell his story. The account was ten times more sordid than Nigel had previously heard and he'd heard multiple reports, a few of them hearsay, but from several sources.

"I wished I'd never gone into the Shamrock that night, but like the others, I did."

Nigel, pen in hand, took notes and continually made sure the video was recording as James spoke.

"You already know the part about your brother, Nathan, being shot earlier that week."

Nigel nodded, and though Michael didn't say a word, he reached over and patted Nigel on the back. James took two deep breaths with his oxygen mask placed firmly over his mouth before he continued.

"We'd gone there to have a pint in honor of Nathan, but Hank was already there sitting at the bar. It didn't seem like he wanted to be bothered, and he never talked much anyway. You could tell he just wanted to be left alone."

He pulled the oxygen mask down a tad and went on with his version of the story. "That's about the time he came in, Tom, just mouthing and being his usual loud self, but no one paid him no mind. Well, until he started making a toast for Nathan."

Nigel interrupted.

"Mr. Stockton, excuse me, James, for the record, who came into the Shamrock that evening?"

"Tom O'Halloran." He took another hit of his oxygen. "But he didn't come alone; there was a whole group of his friends, or I should say his followers, with him." He took a couple of breaths in between his sentences. "They wanted him, Tom, to take Hank's spot as one of the leaders in our group down on the docks. It wasn't an official position, but Hank had leadership skills among the workers, and they listened to him." James drifted off in thought for a second. "Influence, you know, like he could make others see things his way."

Nigel and Michael nodded.

Coughing and spluttering interrupted the recording session. A sip of water, a five-minute break, and they were able to continue. Sharon stood nervously at the edge of the bed, worrying that the interview was taking too much out of her father.

"Can you go on?" Michael asked. "If not, we'll stop."

James was having trouble breathing. Each breath was shorter than the last and all involved were fearful it could be his last. Sharon begged him to slow down.

"Take deep breaths, and your breathing will return to normal. Put your oxygen mask back on for a few minutes."

James's monitors started beeping as his blood pressure rose. His heart was beating faster, and his hands were shaking. Stressed. Scared. A panic attack was about to set in. Nigel, worried they wouldn't get the entire story, backed off.

"Let's take a few minutes."

James whispered. "No."

Anxious and frustrated, he belted out a request.

"I need to tell you something first." His eyes were full of panic as he repeated his request over and over to start his story at the very end.

"Can I do that? Just in case we don't finish. In case I croak or something." He tried to laugh, but no one laughed with him.

"Can I? Can I tell you the last part first? I need to tell you why, because it's important."

Having no clue what he talking about and fearing being so upset might actually kill him, Nigel nodded and confirmed.

"Sure, James, no problem. You can tell us whatever you want, okay?"

Nodding, he pointed for his water. Nervously

everyone waited as he took a couple of sips. With a shaky, weak voice, James began to speak. It was the first time in over eleven years the truth had been discussed at all, let alone with strangers, and now it felt as if it were indeed part of his last and final confession. His words stunned everyone, including Nigel, who had not heard this part of the story until now.

"We were scared. Scared to death, more like it!" Tears filled his eyes but never toppled the lids. "Me and Lewis were grabbed from the street corner, beat, beat damn near unconscious with sacks over our heads before we were thrown into the back of a truck. I can't speak for Lewis, but I think I must have passed out because I can't remember anything but hitting the truck bed. I woke up to find myself in an empty warehouse with Lewis laying at my side." He took a hit of oxygen. "I didn't know if he was dead or alive since he wasn't moving and I couldn't hardly move myself to check on him. I know now that warehouse was one that no one used on the very docks where we all worked."

Sharon put a hand over her mouth, sat down on his hospital bed, and held in her cries. The room grew deathly quiet, and every time James moved, the sheets crunching beneath his mattress sounded ten times louder than they were. Placing his hand in hers, she squeezed it, giving him the encouragement to go on.

"A cold, steel pistol was held to our heads."

You could have heard a pin drop. It sounded like something movie scripts are made up of—kidnapping, beatings, and guns. No one said a word; all eyes and ears were on James.

"Tom's allies—thugs—wanted him to be the one that the ILWU leaders confided in, and were grooming him to be that person. Really they were anti-union and wanted inside information to use against them to sway the men. Hank, being well liked by everyone, was the ILWU and the men's go-to guy. He helped with negotiations for both sides; peacemaker, they called him. Tom's people had a deal, under the table of course, with dirty leaders. They needed their people influencing both sides. Being anti-union, they were only going to appear to work with them."

Coughing broke out, and Sharon insisted that they all let him take a few minutes to breathe. Fearing he'd forget where he was in the story, Michael begged her to let him finish.

"If he's up to it, may we continue? Will you ask him?"

Hesitantly she agreed, and the interview went on.

Shaking, James took another sip of water, spilling it down his chest. Embarrassed, he tried to wipe it up, but his hands were too weak.

"I got it. No biggie." Nigel dabbed the wet spot, acting as if he hadn't even noticed it at all.

James closed his eyes, and the others in the room feared he was drifting off to sleep or worse, but he was forcing himself to go back to the warehouse again. The memory still burned in his mind, haunting him to this day. It was the day he destroyed an innocent man's life, and shame consumed him. Remembering the look on Hank's face as James lied in the witness box shattered him. Unable to control the guilt and shame he felt, the tears in his eyes now flowed nonstop down his face. All he could do was apologize over and over again.

"I'm sorry. Sorry. So sorry."

Nigel spoke carefully and softly.

"We're going to fix it. Fix this. Hank has a daughter, just like you. And you and Sharon want Hank to have his family back. It can't make up for lost time, but you can help mend a wrong." Wrapping his hands around James', Nigel added, "James, you can help reunite them for good. You can fix this wrongdoing."

Watching her father so distressed broke Sharon's heart. She wanted them to take a break, but she fought through, hid her tears and, wanting to hear the truth just like everyone else, she sweetly asked him to continue.

"It's okay, Daddy, tell us what happened."

"After the fight, everyone scattered. The police took accounts from a few that were on site, but they all said the same thing."

"What did they say?" Michael asked.

"Most said that Hank had pushed Tom over the bridge during the fight, but others weren't clear what had happened, and I think at that point no one knew exactly what had happened, except that it was a terrible accident."

He hesitated. "Until Tom's people got involved, got a hold of Lewis and me, and then not only did they have enough witnesses, they had star witnesses, eyewitnesses."

"Okay. Let's back up for just a second. Okay. Where were you?" Nigel asked.

"We left, like everyone, ran. Got out of there as fast

as possible. We were headed to another pub, local, near the Shamrock, and that's when we were grabbed."

He stopped. But everyone could tell he was back in his head, digging for details, wondering if he was retelling the story exactly how it had happened.

"I do remember one of the guys in the warehouse used to go by the name, nickname, Chance."

"How long after you scattered was it before they grabbed you and Lewis?" Michael asked.

"Not long. An hour maybe, two at the most, the police had accounts from several people who had already done what Tom's thugs had asked, pointed to the person that they'd been told to identify as the one who pushed Tom over the bridge."

"And for the record, Mr. Stoddard, James, who did they force you and the others to identify as the person who had pushed Tom O'Halloron over the bridge, that night of the fight, that caused him to drown?"

James never batted an eye. "It was simple, and I'll never forget those four words because each one came with a smack upside the head with that pistol I was telling you about." He put the oxygen mask over his mouth and took in three large breaths.

"Four words. Hank Gunner did it. Hank Gunner did it! They hit us. Hank. Hit us. Gunner. Hit us. Did. Hit us. It. Hit us. I think we passed out. And if that wasn't enough, for a final emphasis, they pulled back the hammer of the pistol and released it four times. We had no idea if the barrel was empty. Hank. Click. Gunner. Click. Did. Click. It. Click. But on the fourth click, they grazed our heads one last time for good measure."

Trembling hands placed the mask over his face again, and he hung his head in shame.

Nigel patted the top of James' hand.

"You did good! We've just got a few gaps to fill. Okay. Can you go on?"

Nodding, a single tear rolled down his cheek.

Michael walked over and stood by James's bed. Leaning over, he spoke softly.

"Nigel's right. You're doing great and we're almost done here, but we have to get to the rest of that night. We know why you didn't tell, understandably, and that Hank was framed. But James, for the record, can you tell us what it is that you haven't told the court or anyone else since that night?"

James nodded.

"Okay, good. We're working backward but don't worry, we'll still build a case. Okay." Michael sounded as if he were speaking in code to Nigel.

Nigel knew what he meant and would put things in chronological order when he wrote up his report.

"James, I'm to ask you a question now for the court. Could you please, for the record, tell us who pushed Tom O'Halloron over the bridge or Hank for that matter, the night during the fight?" Michael asked.

Nigel knew the answer. Sharon did not, and Michael had heard it from Nigel. But hearing the truth out of the mouth of someone who was actually there that night was absolutely chilling.

"I did. It was me."

Sharon gasped.

"It was an accident, but the last hands that touched

Tom O'Halloron were mine, and I was the man who pushed him off my body when he fell on me, into Hank, and they both went flying through the cracked top rail of the bridge."

"We should stop. Take a break." Sharon insisted, but her father shook his head.

"Finish. Finish it."

Michael continued working backward.

"For the record, one last time. You were in the Shamrock, Hank was at the bar, and Tom O'Halloron came in with his friends. What started the actual fight? Can you tell me why they threw down in the first place?"

James knew exactly why the fight went down. Tom wouldn't leave Hank alone. He just kept pick, pick, picking at him, determined to get on his last nerve. Insulting his friendship with his best friend, whom he'd just lost. Questioning his loyalty to Nathan, but the final straw had put Hank over the edge.

"What, for the record, was the final statement that put Hank over the edge and started the fight?" Michael asked.

"It was after the toast that Tom had made in honor of Nathan. Hank didn't raise his glass."

"What happened next?" Michael asked.

"Tom delivered a low blow. Stating Nathan would be alive today if it wasn't for Hank. That Hank had cost his best friend his life."

"And, again, for the record, what happened next?"

"Hank got up. Tom got up. They were kinda face-to-face in the middle of the bar. Pete, the owner, was begging them to sit down or go outside."

"And then what happened?"

"Hank walked toward the door, but they started fighting. Bodies into bodies at first, and then fists flying."

"Please state for the record who threw the first punch."

James hesitated. "That I don't know. I really don't know. I think I had taken a drink of my pint at that exact time."

"Okay. No problem. What happened next?" Michael forged ahead.

"They ended up outside. Pete shuffled them toward the doors, and they burst out into the street."

"Is it true that a large crowd had gathered around them?"

"Yes."

"Where did the fight end up next?"

James pointed to his water, took a sip, and continued.

"The bridge to the left of the Shamrock. It was cold. And the street was icy. I remember because Hank slid into several of us during the fight."

"How did they end up over the bridge?"

"People were gathered around them, like you said. They would push them back and forth into the circle as they were fighting if they wandered out. At some point, they landed on me. I pushed Tom, who grabbed hold of Hank; they were holding on to each other. When I pushed Tom off my body so I could breathe, the two fell onto the railing, which was damaged, and it gave way. It was then that they both fell over the bridge."

Nigel pumped his fist in the air. They had everything they needed. He'd even managed to obtain a signed statement from Lewis, who was in a nursing home due to a debilitating injury but was still of sound mind. Michael congratulated James.

"Congrats, man! You've certainly given us the best shot to clear an innocent man's name. Hopefully, because of time already served, he'll be out sooner rather than later."

A feeling of relief swept over James. Knowing that the burden he'd been carrying around with him for all of those years had been lifted, the truth finally out in the open made him feel as if he was the one who had been set free. It was almost too much; sobs overtook him.

"I'm going to die; I know that, but at least now I can die with a clear conscious. Please, please, please, for me, tell Hank and his family that I'm sorry."

It had taken over five and half hours, in between oxygen breaks, coughing, water breaks, medication being administered, and a few sessions of James dozing off, but they had finally obtained a recorded video account and a signed sworn affidavit. Put that with the signed statement received from Lewis, and Michael believed that anyone would consider overturning Hank's conviction and releasing him for time already served. A quick text to his colleague, and Michael secured a criminal attorney for their team. Didn't hurt to have a circle of friends that happened to be lawyers.

As they said their goodbyes, the men knew they would never see James Stockton again. By the time the official filing had been made, the case read, and it actually went before the judge for the hearing, they knew he would be deceased. Never in his life had Nigel felt such a sense of urgency; without James Stockton's testimony, Hank would have spent several more years in jail. The best years of his life already come and gone, but at least now Hannah had resurfaced. Maybe he couldn't ever get that time back, but he could start a new life with her from right here and now.

"You weren't kidding," Michael stated.

"What's that?" Nigel asked.

"We were on borrowed time."

Michael cracked his window, allowing the fresh air to blow over them as he drove. The air in the house had seemed so stale; a reminder of life slipping away. Taking deep breaths, the chilled air burned his lungs. It was a feeling that had a different meaning after that day. Watching James struggle to breathe was an image he couldn't erase from his mind for quite some time.

"Thanks for making me do this, trusting me enough to bring it to me, and making me see it through. I do believe it's the right thing to do. And I think your brother would be proud of you."

Nigel hung his head, grateful for his boss's words. He thought of his brother, Nathan, and how much he knew that he loved Hank. Nathan was a good man; loved his family, loved Hank, but Hank was a good man too, and Nathan had known that. Nigel thought Michael was right; he would have been pleased.

"Thanks, man. I appreciate that!"

"You know what to do with those, right?"

Michael pointed to Nigel's satchel on the floor.

"Yes, sir."

"Great. Let's get it wrapped up and filed. We'll start preparing first thing in the morning."

"I'm on it!"

Chapter 41
Hannah

Yellow paint
Warms my heart
Lifts my spirits
And fills the void
Hear her voice
Inside my head
Missing link because she's...
And I still won't say it unless you force me...
~ Hannah Gunner ~

Covered in overalls, an old shirt, and wearing a ball cap, Hannah stood with a paintbrush in her hand, prepared to tackle her new bedroom walls. Lindsey, wearing a large shirt, old jeans, and a ball cap, pried the lids off the cans of paint with a screwdriver and began pouring the paint into trays that Hannah had set in front of her. Cash, standing on a ladder, proceeded to apply painter's tape between the ceiling and the wall.

"I'll get the baseboards next."

"Do you want me to start those?" Hannah asked him as he carefully smoothed out the tape above his head.

"Nah. I've got it."

Cash flashed her a smile, blew her a kiss, and continued his task.

Kathy tapped on the door and popped her head in

the room.

"Looks like you guys know what you're doing. Do you need anything before I head out?" she asked.

Hannah couldn't count over the years how many rooms she'd painted with her mom. Every time they moved, if the place wasn't as nice as Gloria had hoped, she'd insist that they put a fresh coat of paint on the walls. *Fixes just about everything,* her mom would say. Moving into Kathy's had been an adjustment for both Hannah and Kathy, but when Hannah asked if she could decorate and paint her new room, Kathy didn't object.

She chose a soft yellow, not quite lemon, not as light as vanilla, but a lovely pale yellow. Trimmed with the typical white, the room wasn't going to look the way Kathy had envisioned Hannah would decorate her room. Needless to say, Kathy had been pleasantly surprised by Hannah's color pallet.

"I'll send over a pizza delivery at noon, and I've left the money for a tip on the countertop. I'll pay when I order."

Kathy's head motioned toward the kitchen.

"Ah, Kathy. You don't have to do that... I could whip up peanut butter and jelly sandwiches for all of us."

Pointing toward Cash, she called him out. "Cash."

"Yes, ma'am."

"Money's on the counter."

"Yes, ma'am. Thank you."

Lindsey applied the paint first as Hannah stepped back and watched it roll across the wall. She couldn't hide her big beaming smile. Her mom would've approved of this color. Delicate. Soft. Not the usual bold colors that she'd typically pick. The girls rolled, and Cash followed behind, filling in the corners and the edges with a paintbrush.

"One coat or two?" Lindsey asked.

Cash grabbed Hannah, knocked her hat off, and pulled her toward him, wrapping his arms around her waist and spinning her around to face the walls.

"So, Chief, what do you think, one coat or two?"

The can stated that only one coat was needed, but as she inspected the walls, every now and then the white paint underneath had bled through. Pointing to the whiter spots, she wondered if it would dry unevenly if they went back and applied paint on the thinner areas.

"It shouldn't matter," Cash assured her. "And if necessary, we'll repaint the whole room again. It's not a big deal."

"Well, let's just hit the thinner areas, then. Touch them up with what we have left. When it dries, if we need to repaint the entire room, I'll just buy more paint."

"Sounds good to me."

Cash kissed the back of her neck, picked up his brush, and started painting right out of the can.

They painted a while, music turned up, before a knock on the door alerted them that the pizza had arrived. Cash, still holding his brush and can, told the girls to go on. Hannah answered the door covered in yellow paint splatter, took the pizzas, tipped the guy, and followed Lindsey toward the kitchen.

By the time Cash had washed up and joined them, the girls were already deep in conversation about Hank.

"Do you think the awkwardness has been addressed,

getting that first meeting over with and all?"

Hannah finished chewing the pepperoni pizza, swallowed, and washed it down with a swig of water. She nodded. Surely her next visit couldn't be that bad. Hank pretending he didn't know her, calling her mom names, getting ticked off that she wouldn't leave, and asking her not to come back. She declined to share any of that information with a soul. Cautiously, Cash asked her when she was going back to visit or if she wanted to go back at all. Hannah looked at him, shocked.

"Why would you ask me that?"

"What? When you're going back?"

"No. The 'if you want to go back at all' part?"

Taking a huge bite out of his pizza, Cash stuck his finger in the air, motioning for her to wait while he chewed his food; Hannah sat and waited for him to swallow. Pissed, she eyed his pizza as if she'd throw it in the trash if he dared to take another bite.

"I'm waiting," Hannah blurted out.

"What was the question?"

"You ass! Why would you say that?"

"Oh yeah, that." Setting the pizza on the plate, he fidgeted with his napkin. "Because you couldn't get the answers that you were hoping to find, about your mom telling you he was dead, and you'll never get them because no one seems to really know."

"Well, I know what he said and she said, but I just don't know if I buy it."

"Why?" asked Lindsey coyly. "Is it truly so hard to believe that your mom couldn't stand the thought of you, a little girl, visiting her dad in prison? She panicked and told the first lie: officials said you weren't allowed to visit him. After fighting with Hank over the phone, she got scared and told the second lie: he'd died in prison. Which, as you know, became problematic due to the letters. Dead men can't write."

Hannah sat silently. This was not the way she had expected to spend her day.

"What point are you trying to make, Lindsey?" Hannah asked.

Lindsey glanced at Cash. He nodded, indicating she should proceed with whatever she had on her mind.

"Just that maybe there wasn't a great big conspiracy. No cover-up. It was a lie, yes, but told with good intentions that got way out of hand and ruined lives, multiple lives, including yours, Hank's, and your mom's."

Hannah knew all of that was not only possible but was likely. She understood that most moms wouldn't want to take their kid to prison for visitation. What she couldn't wrap her head around was that her mom ruined everyone's lives while walking away from hers.

"Damn! Y'all know how to ruin a paint party. Feel like I need a shot of whatever's in there right now to lighten the mood."

Cash jumped up and pulled a beer out of the fridge.

"Want me to crack open a cold one?"

Managing a smile, Hannah shook her head. "Put it back; Kathy will know."

"You know there's an upside to this situation, I mean other than finally meeting your dad, which is great... though I'm not sure that I'm ready for it." He grinned. "Just kidding!"

Hannah stared right through him but never said a word.

"The upside to all of this is that even though you don't accept the things we've just discussed and you learn to live with the fact that you may never know why your mom chose to do what she did, you can take comfort in knowing that she regretted all of it. That she saved the letters that ultimately reunited you and your dad, and that she did everything in her power, literally, during her last moments on this earth, to put this situation right before she died."

Reaching across the table, he grabbed her hands and held them in his. Trying to hide her face, she'd allowed her hair to fall down and cover it.

"Look at me. Babe, please look at me."

Slowly her hand swept the hair from her face and pushed it behind her ears. Looking Cash in the eyes, while Lindsey looked on, he finished what he was trying to say.

"She gave you back your dad. Right, wrong, or indifferent, you now have the man you've always called Captain only a few hours away. She tried her best to fix it. You can honor your dad, if you choose, by mending and rebuilding the relationship that was robbed from you both."

"Sometimes your delivery sucks!" Hannah playfully stared down Lindsey and smiled at Cash. "But I'm lucky to have you both, and I'm going do it, rebuild my relationship with him, whether he likes it or not!"

Sighing, Hannah wondered if her opinion of her dad would have changed had she known he was locked up.

Cash was probably right; let the reason go and focus on the future and not on the past. They had to plan their next visit to Folsom. If that meant she sat in the waiting room because he refused to see her, then so be it. They had a lot of making up to do, and she was determined to see it through!!

Chapter 42
Hank

I do not dare allow myself to dream such things!
If it happened—I wouldn't need anything else for the rest
of my life.
~ Hank Gunner ~

The meeting was brief. Nigel could barely contain his excitement, and Hank could hardly take it all in. After all this time and losing hope of any possibility of a life other than what he had behind those prison walls, Hank finally had someone on the outside looking out for him. Rapid-fire questions were thrown at Nigel, and one by one he answered every one of them.

"I don't even know a James Stoddard."

"That doesn't surprise me," Nigel responded. "He worked night shift."

"What exactly does this mean... I mean, really mean?" Hank asked. "What are the odds of me getting out of here now?"

Nigel threw his pen down on top of the yellow legal pad that he had placed in front of him. Leaning toward the glass panel, he spoke to Hank through the red phone he held in his hand. Hank waited patiently on the other end of the receiver.

"Well, it should go like this since we've already filed the appeal. Once we get the date, the judge will listen to our appeal based on the testimony of the witnesses that we've collected, but primarily the sworn affidavits of James and Lewis. We'll also present the recorded sessions and video. Michael, the attorney I work for, will ask the judge to overturn the original conviction because you're innocent of the actual charges. He's being guided by his buddy who's a criminal lawyer."

Hank was listening intently, though the expression on his face never changed.

"We'll ask that the judge release you based on time already served, effective immediately."

Hank's eyes lit up.

"Immediately." Stammering. Searching for the right words, Hank didn't dare get ahead of himself.

"Do you think he'll do that? Let me out right then and there based on the time I've already been in here?"

Nodding, Nigel tried to ignore the sick feeling in the pit of his stomach. He couldn't imagine any more time robbed from Hank's life or how much time one man was supposed to give for something he hadn't done.

"I can't promise you this, but I wouldn't be surprised if the state wasn't obligated to pay back some kind of retribution on your behalf for the mistake they made."

"Like a reimbursement, monetary payoff, to make up for the time that they robbed from me?" Snickering, though he didn't think it was funny, Hank nodded. "I lost my life. My wife. And being there for my kid."

"You did," Nigel answered. "But you have the

opportunity to grab a second chance; it's not perfect by any means, but Hannah's there, and she wants to get to know you, build that relationship again."

Hank nodded. She was the only reason he wasn't angry. After all the years he'd spent in prison, giving up on getting out and living a normal life, now handed a second chance and an opportunity to rebuild his life with his daughter almost seemed too good to be true! Daring not to believe it at first, he quizzed Nigel over and over again, until he finally thought that Nigel and Michael might actually have a shot at getting him out.

"I wish we could say we were doing you a favor, Hank, but we're not. Just trying to right a wrong, that's all, and I'm sorry it wasn't done sooner. Nate will be happy, and at least now you can spend time with Hannah."

"Yeah, I can, can't I?"

Nigel packed up his things and stood up to leave.

"Hey, Nigel."

"Yeah?"

"Thank Nate for me." Hank smiled, his first genuine smile in years. "Until I meet him in person and thank him myself, which I will, thank him for giving me a shot at a real life again." Fighting through his tears, his gruff voice breaking up, he stopped Nigel in his tracks one more time. "And thank you for everything. Coming here. Sitting with me. Listening, and for this, a chance to mend things with Hannah. Ah! Speaking of Hannah."

"Yes."

"I need you to do me a favor."

"Sure. Anything." Nigel spoke into the phone softly,

as if afraid someone would overhear their conversation, even though he knew they were being recorded.

"What do you need?"

Chapter 43

Sit Tight

One second, please.
It will change your life.
~ Nigel ~

Kathy and Hannah had just finished supper when a gentle tap on the door interrupted their evening.

"You expecting anyone?" Kathy asked.

Hannah shook her head.

"Cash is at work, and Lindsey is studying for a chemistry test."

Throwing a tea towel across her shoulder, Kathy walked toward the front door. Putting the safety chain across first, which made Hannah smile because she always forgot to do that, she unlocked the deadbolt and cracked it open. Standing in front of the door was a tall, slender, dark-haired, good-looking, familiar-looking man wearing a pair of black-framed glasses. Familiar, yet she couldn't put a name to the face. Peering at the gentleman, she waited for him to speak, but when he failed to answer within the first few seconds, she talked to him.

"Can I help you?"

"Yes. Kathy?"

The stranger knowing her name startled her.

"Um. Who are you?"

The man held out his hand, placing it between the cracked doorframe and Kathy. Hannah appeared behind her aunt, listening to the interaction between the two, phone in hand in case she needed to call the police.

"I'm Nigel, Nathan's brother and Sandy's brother-in-law. Sandy and Nathan used to be best friends with Gloria and Hank, years ago. I think I met you over at Sandy's and Nathan's, my brother's, a long time ago." He hesitated. "Sorry for your loss, Kathy."

Kathy stood in the hallway stunned. That's why the man looked familiar. She suddenly felt as if she were looking at a ghost; the man was the double of his brother, but she hadn't thought about Nathan in years.

"Is Hannah here and, if so, may I speak to her?"

Kathy started to close the door to remove the chain. Nigel put his hand on the door, thinking she was closing it to end their conversation.

"I have a message from Hank."

Realizing he thought she was shutting him out, Kathy quickly opened the door.

"Nigel, yes, I remember you. Please, come in."

Hannah stepped out from behind her aunt. As Nigel walked past Kathy, he stopped and stared at the beautiful blond-haired, blue-eyed teen. Sticking out his hand, only to instinctively grab her in his arms as soon as her hand touched his, he held her as tightly as he possibly could.

"You must be Hannah! Oh my God! You must be

Hank's little girl!! How you've grown." After a couple of seconds, he loosened his grip.

Hannah didn't exactly hug him back, but she didn't pull away, either. Kathy, in shock, watched them both.

"This hug is from Hank. This is for Hank. And this is a hug for both of you from me!"

Finally, he released her and stepped back to take a good, long hard look at her. His eyes had glossed over, and his face had lit up. Beaming was the best way to describe him. Kathy broke the awkward silence that followed.

"Please, come on in. May I get you something? A drink maybe?"

"Yes. Please, that would be nice. Water, please. And thank you!"

Hannah led him to the sitting room, where they sat down. Kathy returned with a tall glass of water. Nigel took a sip. He placed the glass on the coffee table in front of him and glanced around the room.

"It's a little unorganized because I'm still moving in, but usually it's spotless," Hannah stated as she watched him search the pictures for familiar faces.

"I'm sorry. I'm trying to soak in visuals to take back to Hank. He's missed so much of your life, as you know."

Unsure what the visit was about, Kathy asked if there was something that Hank had sent him around to pick up of Gloria's.

"Did Hank want a photo or memento of Gloria? Is that why you're here?"

Nigel picked up his water and slammed the whole thing down. Setting the glass back on the table, feeling

Hannah and Kathy's eyes on him, he figured it was time to start talking.

"First, again, condolences on your loss."

"Thank you," Kathy and Hannah said in unison.

"I'm really not sure where to start here, so if it's okay with you, I'm going to start from the beginning, and once I've concluded the story, all the way up to where we are right now, I'll answer any questions that you may have... does that sound reasonable to you?"

Unsure of what they were about to hear, Hannah and Kathy nodded. Nigel started from as far back as he could remember; even to the day he dropped by the house, and Kathy had been there visiting at the same time. Hannah was only three or four years old. Kathy couldn't help but smile as she recalled the day clearly as well.

"You have changed!" She laughed.

"You really haven't," Nigel responded.

They went over the strike, the shooting, Nathan's death, the funeral, and how devastated Sandy was when Gloria lost Hank as well.

"Technically, that day, Gloria lost her husband, too."

Kathy grabbed Hannah's hand and held it tightly in hers. Nigel continued. He told them about Nate's project and Sandy asking Nigel to help him find out every single thing, good or bad, about his dad.

"He never knew him. Gone before he was born. The project became an obsession between us, my nephew and me, but once we got to Nathan's death, I thought we'd wrap it up."

"But you didn't?" Hannah quizzed him.

"No. Because we couldn't."

"What do you mean?" she asked.

"We talked to so many people surrounding the night that Nathan died, the fight after his funeral at the Shamrock, and everything that led to the cover-up story. The cover-up story is or was, I should say, the big story we uncovered, which involves Hank."

Hannah pulled her hand out of Kathy's and sat on the edge of the couch. Her blue eyes, now huge, fixated on Nigel, as she listened to every single word that he said.

"There was a cover-up involving my dad?"

As carefully as he could, Nigel retold the story. Tom O'Halloron, the toast, Hank's despair, the fight barreling into the street and then winding up on the bridge. The people who had gathered around Hank and Tom, forming a circle around them as they fought, pushing them from person to person, cheering them on and encouraging the fight. He told them about the top rail being damaged, and finally, he told them about James Stoddard being the person who pushed Tom and Hank off his body as they fought with such a force that they fell into the broken railing, and both toppled over the bridge and into the water below.

"What?" Kathy managed, trying to process what she had just heard.

"Are you saying what I think you're saying?" Hannah asked. "Are you saying that you know another man, this James guy, I think you said, who was the person who pushed both of them over the bridge?"

Nigel nodded his head. "But there's more."

"How could there possibly be any more?" Stunned, Hannah waited.

"Oh but there is... " Nigel raised his empty glass. "May I?"

"Of course." Kathy jumped up, grabbed the glass, and refilled it.

"There were multiple witnesses, false witnesses, on site, who were Tom's friends or friends of people in high places. In other words, enemies of Hank; Hank was respected by his co-workers, peers, and representatives of the ILWU, and Tom's people wanted their man in Hank's role to control all sides."

"How?" Hannah asked.

"Hank was fair. Their rep wouldn't be fair, if you know what I mean. Anyway, they needed to seal Hank's fate with a couple more witnesses. Have Hank take the fall for Tom's death."

Horrified, Kathy asked how.

"They took the one person who could rat them out; the guy who really did it, Stoddard, who accidentally pushed the men over the bridge, and Lewis, his buddy who was standing next to him at the time. In short, they kidnapped them, terrorized them, and if that wasn't bad enough to drive their point home and to show that they meant business and Hank must take the fall, they held guns to their heads and threatened to kill them. After what they'd been through, there was no reason not to believe they wouldn't be killed."

Stunned, Hannah and Kathy sat speechlessly. He'd been innocent for all those years.

"I need to see him," Hannah insisted. "Kathy, will

you take me?"

Nigel raised his hands. "And that's why I'm here; there's more. You can't go see him."

A pin could have dropped, and you could've heard it. Silence filled the room for the first time since Nigel had arrived.

"We're appealing this case, and we believe we've got a good, no excellent, chance of getting your dad released immediately. Or once it's overturned."

"That's great!" Hannah's face lit up. "Even more reason I need to see him. He probably needs something. Clean shirt? Shoes? I don't know. Something?"

"He doesn't want you to go."

Feeling as if her heart just got stomped on, again, she couldn't hide the disappointment she felt. It hurt Nigel to see the look on her face and immediately he realized what she was thinking.

"It's not what you think!"

"You don't know what I think."

"Okay. Hannah, it's not because he doesn't want to see you or want your support."

She was listening.

"It's because he believes Gloria, your mom, was right... and he's sorry he fought her on that—prison isn't for kids or teens."

Hannah rolled her eyes. "A little late for that, isn't it?"

"He said he didn't want you to visit in prison, respecting Gloria's wishes, but that doesn't mean you can't attend the trial." Nigel watched her eyes dart toward him. "He has no issue with that; look, if we have

CAPTAIN FIN

it our way, he'll be out soon, and you'll be able to rebuild what was robbed from you both."

Hannah nodded, grateful for the opportunity her dad was being handed.

Kathy didn't reach for Hannah's hand, try to hug or comfort her, or sit closer to her, but the words she spoke touched Hannah and sent shivers through Nigel.

"Hannah, for me, honor your mom this one last time. She spent her life keeping you away from that terrible place. How she did it, right or wrong, is now irrelevant, but for whatever reason, Hank now agrees with her decision. Can you please do as they ask? Honor their wishes this one last time, and stay away from the prison that inflicted so much pain on your family and required Gloria to sacrifice so much?"

The words Kathy spoke, along with the tears that threatened to spill over her eyelids, touched Hannah. Something about her mom and dad seeing eye-to-eye on the very point that had driven them apart sealed the deal. Hannah nodded. She'd stay away from Folsom.

"Am I able to call him during this next phase?" she asked.

"Yes, absolutely! In fact, he said that he'd call you this week."

Nigel assured them both that he'd notify them as soon as the court date was set. They promised him that they'd both be in attendance. Smiling, he reached and shook Kathy's hand. He'd expected nothing less. Instinctively, he leaned in and hugged Hannah, and she hugged him back.

"Another one from Hank and from me!" Gathering

his coat, he thanked Kathy for the water. Turning to Hannah, he complimented her again. "You have grown into a lovely young lady, and Hank has every right to be proud of you."

Hannah's face lit up.

"He's proud of me? Did he say that?"

Nigel nodded. "Always."

It was a lot to process, but Hannah was excited. As soon as Nigel left, her fingers typed ninety miles an hour as she tapped away on her phone, filling Cash and Lindsey in about the pending court date, the potential of her dad's conviction being overturned, and the possibility of him getting out immediately for time already served.

Cash: Babe, this is unbelievable!

Hannah: Right!

Cash: Have you talked to your dad?

Hannah: Not yet.

Lindsey: OMG! This is crazy!

Hannah: I know. Still can't believe it.

Later that evening, Hannah sat on her bed, conch shell in hand, and read one of the letters from the tattered box. For the first time, the Captain's voice sounded like her dad's. Placing the letter on her chest, she flopped back on her bed and put the shell against her ear. The familiar sound of the air swirling around the inside, reminding her of the ocean, once again brought comfort and also joy. A knock on the door startled her. Kathy popped in her head, and asked if she could come in. She had an unusual look on her face, and Hannah had no idea how to read her. Kathy tightened the blanket that she had wrapped around her and sat down

next to Hannah on the bed. Hannah waited. Kathy
looked as if she was struggling for the right words to say,
but finally, she pulled out a photograph of Gloria that
Hannah hadn't seen before. Gloria was all smiles. Hank
had his arms wrapped around her waist, and Hannah
was perched on Hank's shoulders.

"Oh my God, look how little I was!" Hannah giggled.

Kathy smiled and looked closer at the picture she
held in her hands.

"You were a tiny little thing; I think I'm the one who
took the picture that day. Anyway, I found this among
your mom's things. It was one of many that she
cherished."

Hannah sat and listened.

"She loved him, you know, and she loved you.
Finding out that Hank will be exonerated of the crime
that ruined all of your lives would have made her so
happy!"

Kathy's voice was barely a whisper. Picking up
Hannah's hand, she studied her face. Hannah's eyes, so
big and blue, looked like her mom's. Kathy could see her
sister in her niece. Grateful for that, she finished talking
to Hannah.

"I think Gloria's reasons started out to protect you,
but then she became defiant over an argument that
they'd had, her and Hank. Ultimately, she got in too
deep, the lie, the moves, and the angry words; there was
no way to turn back. But I guess what I'm trying to say
is this..." Kathy took a deep breath as she wiped a single
teardrop that had trickled down her cheek away. "She
would truly be thrilled that you are getting him back in

your life. Happy for both of you, and I think if she were still here with us, she'd spend every moment trying to make it right. And if she couldn't, she'd encourage you to spend every second you could to get to know your dad again. He's a good man. And, again, she did love him."

Hannah hugged her aunt, and though neither one of them acknowledged it, they cried together, tears of loss, hope, and apprehension.

"Do you think he'll be exonerated, for sure I mean, the conviction really overturned?" Hannah asked.

"Based on everything Nigel told us, I do. I really do."

Kathy walked toward the door. Stopping, she turned back around and asked Hannah a simple question.

"Do you feel helpless right now?"

Hannah hadn't thought about that, but yes, she did feel helpless, knowing that all they could do was wait. Nodding, she confirmed.

"Do you want to change that?"

Waiting for Hannah to answer, Kathy could see Hannah's wheels turning in her head as she wondered how she, a teen, could do anything to help. But yes, she was definitely in!

"What do I have to do?"

Chapter 44

Are You Ready?

Peace
Peace and quiet
This I crave
Settle my nerves
Still my mind
Heal me
~ Hannah Gunner ~

Hank sat nervously on the edge of his bunk; after all, this could be the day that changed his entire life. His favorite guard appeared at his cell, opened the door, and handed him a suit.

"Here, your attorney told me to give you this. Put it on, and you can meet with him before you leave for the courthouse."

Hank took the hanger and thanked the guard.

"No need to thank me. I didn't buy it."

The suit was a tad too big, but Hank pulled it off by tightening his belt and rolling the bottom of the pants underneath by a couple of inches and securing them with tape acquired from the guard.

"What you really need is a few safety pins, but you know the rules. I'll see if I can swipe one, might not work, but I can try."

"Thanks, it sure can't hurt!"

A few minutes a later, the guard reappeared.

"Are you ready? Let's go."

Hank was escorted to a small room that had one table and two chairs. Michael and Nigel were waiting for him. Greetings and handshakes were exchanged before they sat down and got to business.

"I don't expect this to take long," Michael told Hank. "Once we present the appeal based on testimony from all of the witnesses, including James and Lewis, I'll ask the judge to overturn your conviction and release you for time already served."

Hank, for the first time in years, was trembling.

"I don't expect you to have to take the stand at all, but it is possible that the judge may ask you a few questions."

Hank nodded. Answering a few questions shouldn't be a big deal. Michael continued as Nigel furiously scribbled notes and tapped away on his iPad. Hank didn't know what Nigel was writing.

"Are you ready for your overdue day in court, Hank?"

It took him a second to answer; images of Gloria and Hannah from a lifetime ago flashed before his eyes. It had all gone wrong, so quickly, so many years ago, but he would have given anything if Gloria were going to be there waiting for him today.

"Hank, are you ready?"

"Sorry. Yes. Yes, sir, I am. As ready as I'm ever going to be, I suppose."

Nigel signaled the guard that Hank was ready to be escorted out. He was cuffed and taken to the waiting dock for a van to arrive that would take him to the courthouse. Nigel and Michael discussed the details of his case on their way to court. Receiving a text message that Sharon, Mr. Stoddard's daughter, was on her way pleased them both. If the judge needed to question her, they wouldn't have to track her down.

Hank rarely left the prison grounds. Riding in a vehicle didn't feel familiar to him anymore, and he couldn't help but notice his knuckles were white from holding onto the armrest too tightly. He had given up hope of being paroled early, let alone released early. Forcing himself to think only of that moment, he tried to clear his mind, but it was impossible. His freedom, yet again, was at stake and there was nothing he could do about it.

His attorney's car pulled up to the courthouse several minutes before the prison van arrived. Shocked by what they saw, Michael grabbed his cell phone and started filming the crowds that greeted them and instructed Nigel to do the same.

"That's, that's Hannah!"

Nigel pointed to the slim teen standing on the courthouse steps chanting something he couldn't quite make out yet. She was holding a sign up above her head. In fact, just about everyone who had gathered at the courthouse was holding some sort of sign.

"How many people do you think are here?" Nigel asked.

"I don't know, honestly, a hundred maybe? A hundred fifty, if not more?"

The signs read all kinds of things from RIGHT THE

WRONG, FREE HANK! to WRONGLY CONVICTED! WHO'S THE CRIMINAL NOW? The media was on site, and multiple reporters were trying to grab an interview with Hank as soon as he arrived. Hannah spotted Nigel and made her way down the steps toward him. Cash and Lindsey were by her side.

"Is he about to be here?"

Nigel nodded. "This is amazing! How did you do it?"

"What, this?" Hannah smiled. "It was Kathy, Cash, and Lindsey, really, who helped me. Phone calls, Twitter, Insta, Snap, you name it, we were spilling our story everywhere."

"Well, it worked!" Nigel reached out and hugged her. "It worked! The community is on his side, and that can't hurt. Well done!"

The crowd suddenly started to cheer, clap, and broke into a chant *free Hank, free Hank, free Hank,* indicating that the prison van had finally arrived. Staring out the window in disbelief at the support that he had received from what was left of his family and total strangers, Hank, shaking and holding back his tears, couldn't help but break down. The guard assigned to escort him laid a firm hand on his shoulder. No words were exchanged. He sat in place for a few minutes and gathered himself. Taking deep breaths, wiping the stray tears away with his hands, he stood on trembling legs and made his way to the door of the van. Slowly he stepped off the steps and onto the concrete. Nigel grabbed Hannah's hand and led her over to the side entry. For the first time in over eleven years, Hank came face to face with his daughter, no glass barricade between them. A guard stood between him and Hannah. The crowd spotted them and once again started chanting, but this time the chant sent a different haunting message. *Wrongly convicted, robbed! Wrongly convicted, robbed! Wrongly convicted, robbed!* The guard showed zero expression on his face as he stepped to the left and let Hannah look into the eyes of her father for the first time—no glass between them— since she was a little girl.

Cash slipped his arm around her waist, as he watched her nervously take three steps toward Hank. Hank, still cuffed, looked his daughter up and down. How tall she was now! How beautiful she had become, a true young lady. She had Gloria's nose, her little chin, and there were those big, beautiful blue eyes. His heart was pounding in his chest and he wasn't prepared for Hannah as she suddenly lunged toward him and wrapped her arms around his neck. The crowd, which had been chanting nonstop, suddenly went silent. The reporters crowded the pair as Hannah burst into tears.

"I can't believe it's you. You're here. You're really, really here."

Hank could barely hold his emotions intact as the years flashed before his eyes. Here stood, right before him, his First Matey, that pirate child still somewhere inside those blue eyes. Wanting to reach out to hold her, he raised his cuffed hands, but Hannah kissed his cheek and whispered in his ear.

"Don't worry about that now, Captain, those damn cuffs will come off inside."

Michael tapped her on the shoulder.

"It's time, Hannah. We have to go."

Hank's hands, cuffed together, reached up and touched her face. She was truly there, standing in front of him, and it wasn't a dream. They led him up the concrete stairs as the crowd once again started to chant his name. Reporters tried to ask him questions, but he ignored them as he tried to speak to Hannah one last time. He yelled her name, but she hadn't heard him over the crowd. Frantically, he yelled it again.

"Hannah. *Hannah.*"

Cash and Kathy cleared a path for her as she ran up the stairs before he entered the courthouse.

"Cap. Right here!"

"I just want to say," he started to say, but struggled to find the words. "I just want to say, well…"

"I love you, Dad!" Hannah said.

"I love you too," he managed before they pulled him inside the door.

Chapter 45

This IS It!

Grief turns to joy
Pain turns to love
New beginnings unfold
Gifts from above
Life left to chance
Is no life at all
I'll choose my destination
~ Hannah Gunner ~

Much to Michael and Nigel's delight, the courtroom was packed. Michael had ensured that Hannah, Kathy, Cash, and Lindsey had seats directly behind the council's table where Hank was seated in front of the judge. Hannah had been added as a character witness, as had Sandy, Nathan's wife. As soon as Hank spotted her, he was overwhelmed with emotion. Cupping his mouth with his hand, he gasped, and mouthed her name: *Sandy!* She spotted him immediately, as soon as he looked in her direction. Placing one hand over her heart, she blew him a kiss with the other, signaling that, despite the loss of Nathan, she was going to stand up for, by, and support him. Sandy slipped Nigel a note with Hank's name written on it.

We'd give anything if this had never happened! But it

did, and now we have to make it right. We're on your side and always have been! Can't wait for you to meet Nate.

Hank read it twice before turning back around and mouthing the words *thank you.* He noticed that all of the seats in the courtroom were filled, and reporters lined more than a few rows. That could be good for him— public support for his case. Hank looked over his shoulder one last time, stealing a glimpse of Hannah talking with Kathy. He still couldn't wrap his mind around the fact that she was a mere foot away; all he wanted to do was reach out and hold her! A poke in his ribs startled him, followed by an announcement from the bailiff as the judge entered the courtroom.

"Please rise. The Court of the Judicial Circuit, Criminal Division, is now in session. The Honorable Judge Cardiff presiding."

The sound of everyone shuffling to their feet bounced off the walls, as people stood up and waited for the next round of instructions before the trial got underway. Hannah reached over and grabbed Cash's hand. She was visibly shaking, but Cash tried to reassure her by gently squeezing her hand in his and softly nudging her with his body. Lindsey stood as close to Kathy as she possibly could, and nervously the four waited as the judge addressed the courtroom next.

"Everyone may be seated except the defendant. Mr. Payne, please swear in the defendant."

Hank remained standing as everyone around him sat down. After Hank was sworn in, the judge asked Hank's counsel and the prosecution's counsel to step forward. After a couple minutes, they were dismissed to their tables, and the judge made another announcement.

"Ladies and gentlemen, this is a unique case. We do not have a jury, but we do have a list of character witnesses. I'm going to ask that all character witnesses for the defendant please rise. We will swear you in all at once at this time."

Hannah—feeling nervous—stood, along with Kathy, Sandy, and a few others. The bailiff asked them all the same question.

"Please raise your right hands. Do you swear to tell the truth, the whole truth, and nothing but the truth?"

In unison they all answered, *I do*. The bailiff addressed the judge again.

"Your Honor, today's case is Gunner versus the State of California."

"Is the defense attorney ready?" the judge asked.

Michael stood up. "Yes, Your Honor."

"You may be seated."

"And the prosecuting attorney?"

"Yes, Your Honor."

"Be seated."

Judge Cardiff gave the defense permission to proceed. Nervously Hank sat in his chair, helpless, and listened to every word that Michael carefully told the judge. His opening statements were strong and carefully crafted to deliver maximum impact.

"Your Honor, the State of California has committed an incorrigible crime against Hank Gunner. We're here today to ensure that the original conviction for involuntary manslaughter is overturned and that he is released immediately, based on time already served.

Robbed of the best years of his life and serving time, a sentence that he didn't deserve for a crime that he did not, I repeat *did not,* commit! This terrible injustice has cost him years of his life that can never be recouped! He cannot wish them back, and even the monetary retribution that we're asking for here today cannot buy back those years that he wrongfully served in Folsom State Prison. Those years, wrongfully convicted, not only cost him his personal life, it cost him his family. Not to mention precious time with his wife, who became ill and has since passed. For reasons beyond his control, brought about by this wrongful conviction, he wasn't even able to attend her funeral. And we haven't yet discussed the years that he'll never recoup—in any way possible—to retrace the time and get back the days with his then-elementary-aged daughter so he could watch her grow up. Her first day of first grade, reading on her own, first and early years of school plays, first dance, first boyfriend, first kiss... the list goes on and on. Now she's a teenager, and she'll be graduating high school soon!"

Whispers broke out among everyone sitting in the galley, and the judge asked everyone to be quiet. Hank hung his head in shame, knowing he hadn't been by Gloria's side for most of Hannah's life, or when she had needed him most. Michael continued to narrate a story that grabbed the crowd in the courtroom and delivered the maximum amount of emotional impact that he possibly could before he presented all of the evidence. The prosecution for the state, wanting to object, held their tongues and waited to see what else Michael and his team had to present to the court first. Nigel handed notes and files to Michael as he pressed onward, and eventually, he got to the part where he started to bring in the witnesses. He asked to bring up Lewis first. His nurse, from the nursing home, wheeled him in and asked him if he needed anything before he answered the attorney's questions. He didn't. Lewis answered Michael's questions one by one. The prosecution then cross-examined, but their cross-examination, thankfully, wasn't as brutal as Michael and Nigel had feared.

"Hi, Lewis."

"Hello."

"You nervous today?"

"Yes, sir."

"It's okay to be nervous. It's not every day that you're in a courtroom."

Lewis nodded. "No, sir."

"Now, you said that you hadn't come forward before now because you were scared, correct?"

"Yes."

"Then why would you speak up now? What I mean is, are you sure that the threat is gone, if you were so scared and all?"

Hank watched Lewis as he spoke, and Lewis glanced in his direction. Guilt consumed him as he answered the question.

"I'm a coward. I was scared. But when I had the chance to speak when James did, well, I took it. Things have been quiet for years, on the docks and all, and I don't work there anyhow. I'm in care and don't reckon I've got that much time left anyway. Maybe I do, maybe I

don't, but I do know that what happened to Hank ain't
right. And I hate that I was part of it, even if it wasn't by
choice."

Surprisingly, the prosecution accepted his statement
and left him alone. After the judge dismissed him, his
nurses got him ready to return to the nursing home. As
he left the courtroom, he yelled out Hank's name.

"Hank!"

Hank turned his head, and they made eye contact.

"I'm sorry. Sorry," Lewis said as his caregivers
wheeled him out of the courtroom.

Hank, numb, watched them take him out of the
room. Hannah leaned forward and whispered something
that he held on to for the entire day.

"Daddy... it's going to be okay."

Next Nigel stood up and asked if he could approach
the bench. He was allowed and presented the judge with
James Stoddard's affidavit. The judge permitted a thirty-
minute recess while he read the document and informed
everyone in the courtroom that afterward, the judge, the
attorneys, and their teams would watch the videotape.

"After recess, we will watch the recorded session
with Mr. Stoddard."

"All rise."

The bailiff took Hank to a small meeting room away
from his supporters, including Hannah. Unable to relax,
she paced the floor outside the courtroom. Reaching for
her JUUL, she headed toward the door.

"Stay inside. It's chilly out there. Please."

Cash held out his hand toward her; she placed hers
in his and walked back toward the courtroom. Lindsey

met them halfway and handed her a Dr. Pepper.

"Here, sip on some sugar."

"I don't think I need the sugar, but I could do with the caffeine. Thank you!"

It didn't take long before the court was back in session. The judge acknowledged to the entire courtroom that both the prosecution and the defense had agreed that the affidavit was compelling evidence and announced that he would allow all those in attendance to view the tape as well. A court assistant set up the equipment, and within minutes the lights were turned down and the video interview with James Stoddard was reviewed.

Hannah, along with the entire courtroom, was stunned. During his explicit account, he openly admitted that he was the last person to lay hands on Tom O'Halloran. Even under cross-examination that day of the interview, he admitted on his own accord that he had pushed Tom and Hank over the bridge. The rest of his testimony—the threats, kidnapping, and the gun that was held to his head—matched Lewis's story. He spoke clearly, and the video and audio quality were excellent and admissible. The judge acknowledged that it had not been edited and must have been taken in one sitting. He also noted that the guilty party, Mr. Stoddard, had not in any way, shape, or form been led by the attorneys present that day. He acknowledged that Mr. Stoddard was asked and answered direct questions, seemed emotional at times, but sincere and demonstrated guilt. He called both the prosecutors for the state and the defense to his bench and all agreed the video was solid evidence. The prosecutors, at that point, felt completely defeated.

Judge Cardiff proceeded to order the attorneys to prepare any character witnesses testifying on Hank's behalf. Kathy was called first. She felt nervous as she took the stand. She told the court how she had met Hank, what her sister's relationship with him had been like, and she purposely stuck to the years prior to Gloria stating that Hank was deceased. She also answered any of the rapid-fire questions that were directed at her with finesse and confidence. She was a phenomenal character witness, and Hank was grateful. Sandy did just as well. She explained how Nathan had loved Hank as a brother, and dodged any questions indicating that Hank had anything to do with Nathan being in the wrong place at the wrong time that caused his death.

"Hank absolutely had nothing to do with Nathan's death. He did not pull the trigger. He did not put a gun in the hand of the murderer who killed my husband, and he did not force my husband to join him that day. I find this type of questioning disturbing when we're supposed to be talking about how much my husband admired Hank."

The judge agreed with her and told the prosecutor to tread carefully. He had no more questions for her after that. Hannah was called to the stand next. Legs wobbling, hands shaking, stomach doing flips, she managed to walk to the front and take her seat. Michael gently led the questioning.

"Hannah, do you recognize the gentleman sitting to the left of you at the table over there?"

Hannah instinctively turned and faced her dad. Smiling, she nodded.

"For the court please, Hannah. Do you recognize him?"

"Sorry. Um, yes. He's my dad."

"We all know why we're here today, so as best you can and in your own words, could you please tell the court what it's been like for you all of these years without your dad?"

It was so quiet you could literally hear a pin drop. Hannah had heard that expression a million times, but for the first time she knew what it felt like and meant at that moment in a room full of people waiting for her to speak. She opened her mouth to begin and didn't recognize the sound of her own voice. It was raspy and shaky, but she dug deep into the back of her head and pulled out memories of how it felt when her dad had left.

"I didn't know what was going on when he left, because none of it made any sense to me. He went from putting me to bed every night, reading my favorite book and turning it into a game that we'd play literally every night, to never coming home."

Tears had pooled in her eyes, but she blinked them away, focusing on the things that she knew she needed to say. Hank's eyes were filled with tears as well, as were Kathy's, Sandy's, Lindsey's, and even Cash had to fight his back.

"I had a little white stool, I think my dad actually made it for me." She glanced at Hank, who was nodding; he had made that for her a long time ago. "Every day before supper I would put it by the back door in the kitchen. That door was half glass, and I'd wait for him to come down the path, but of course, all of a sudden he never came. My mom tried to comfort me and distract me, telling me how much he loved me and let's read and she'd put me to bed."

Hannah wiped the tears off her cheeks with her hand but didn't dare look at Hank for fear she'd burst into sobs and cry harder. "Looking back, I know that I was really horrible to my mom. I was such a bad daughter back then, mean to her, all because I didn't want her to read to me and put me to bed. I wanted my dad, the Captain, to do it, just like he'd always done."

Michael interjected. "Hannah, you weren't a bad daughter, you were five! Can you tell us why you didn't want your mom to read to you, and why it meant so much to you that your dad spent that time with you?"

Hannah, remembering how her mom had tried to cope, hung her head in shame.

"Because I needed my dad. That was our thing—our time and our game. I wanted the Captain to come back. I knew my mom couldn't read and play the pirate game with me like that, and my dad was always the Captain, until one day he was gone, just like that!"

"And then what was life like?" Michael asked.

"Where to start? We kept moving because we couldn't afford to stay in our home. Mom always tried to get higher-paying positions in her field, and we moved each time she did. I didn't have friends to speak of because we moved so much, but I always escaped by losing myself in the games that we used to play—imagining in my mind's eye that I was still playing them with him." Hannah half-smiled and pointed to her dad. "That pirate game got me through many years of loneliness. It allowed me to wander beautiful beaches when I was scared, lonely, or sad, you name it, but my mom, she struggled. She didn't have her husband by her side, and she loved my dad. His picture was always by her bed, and it remained by her bed until the day she died." Looking at the judge, Hannah added, "I guess you could say the state took away our whole world."

"I think we get the picture Hannah, thank you, you may get down," Judge Cardiff said kindly.

"Everything we have seen, heard, and read here today is indeed compelling evidence that Hank Gunner was wrongly convicted of a crime. But I would like to speak with James Stoddard myself. Please arrange for him to be brought to my chambers or a court representative to visit with him."

Michael jumped to his feet. "Your Honor, may I address the court?"

"Go ahead."

"Mr. Stoddard passed away two days ago. Stage-four cancer. We've been working against the clock."

The judge put down his pen. "Well, that answers that and complicates this... um."

Hank's ears perked up, as did everyone else's in the room. The judge requested that Hank take the stand and tell his side of the story. Hank proceeded to tell his side of what happened the evening Tom O'Halloran fell over the bridge, clutching his jacket, pulling him over the railing with him. Reporters scribbled away and checked their recording devices continually to ensure they were capturing everything that was said. As soon as he was finished, the judge asked him to sit back down.

"I see no reason for you to be questioned or cross-examined, Mr. Gunner. I just wanted to hear your account for myself." Turning to the courtroom and the attorneys, he said, "Since the actual accused, James Stoddard, who confessed both in a court affidavit and recorded video, both admissible, is deceased, it does complicate things. However, in regard to Mr. Gunner, I believe the defense has proven that Hank Gunner was wrongfully accused, prosecuted, and convicted. The motion to overturn his conviction has been granted and will be overturned. The request for immediate release based on time served, which is eleven years, and good behavior for the last few years, has also been granted."

The judge addressed Hank directly.

"The State of California will award retribution, the amount to be determined once your attorney files suit, and whatever they award you, in my humble opinion, will never be enough. I might add you have our sincere apologies, and condolences on the loss of your wife. I hope you can begin to rebuild your life and spend what time you have left with your daughter. Though she is growing up, she still needs you."

He looked at the defense team.

"Defense?"

"We're good, your Honor. We agree with your decision, and unfortunately it would seem it's been long overdue."

"I couldn't agree with you more, counselor!" Judge Cardiff signed a document placed in front of him and addressed Hank.

"I can't begin to imagine what you and your family have endured over the years, and I know that nothing that we can say or do will turn back the hands of time. I hope that the compensation that you'll be awarded, which as I said, in my opinion, will never be enough, will allow you to make a fresh start and rebuild your relationship with your remaining family. I understand it will never replace what was stolen from you. I sincerely hope from this day forward you find some peace."

A nod of his head, acknowledging the judge's words, and Hank finally realized he was going to be a free man.

"Thank you, Your Honor!" he replied. "Thank you."

"That's that, then. Good luck!" He turned to his bailiff, indicating they were calling it a day and dismissed his court. "Court dismissed."

"All rise," instructed the bailiff, and Hank was a free man!

Chapter 46

Captain Fin

Hope is a gift,
Love is a treasure,
And FAMILY is forever!
Hank and Hannah Gunner together at last!
~ Lindsey Rawling ~

Ribbons and balloons filled the hospitality room at Hannah's and Kathy's apartment complex. A cake placed on the center of a table was surrounded by finger foods, punch, beer, and wine. Hannah, Kathy, Cash, Lindsey, Nigel, Sandy, Nate, and Sharon were among the guests crammed into the room.

"They're here!" whispered Hannah excitedly. "Hurry. Turn off the lights!"

Giggles and whispers were all you could hear as people unsuccessfully tried to hide in a room with limited places to do so. Michael opened the door, and Hank followed him into the dimly lit room.

"Surpriiiiiiiise!" everyone yelled.

Hank studied every face of those present, recognizing most, but unfamiliar with a few. How he had aged and missed so much over the years. Hannah approached him with Cash by her side. Beaming, she held out her hands and in it was the conch shell that he had given her so many years ago.

"I told you I still had my *magical* shell!" She giggled and placed it by his ear. "It still works—hear the ocean, Captain?" Hannah laughed. "I couldn't resist!"

Laughing, he reached up and took the shell out of her hands. He held it firmly against his ear and listened as the air swirled around and around. She was smiling, just like she used to, and he couldn't believe this beautiful young lady who now stood before him used to be his little girl. Wrapping his arms around her frame for the first time in years, he hugged her as tightly as he could without hurting her. To his relief, she hugged him back. Tears ran freely down his cheeks as he buried his face in that mass of hair, and he felt no shame in being so emotionally overwhelmed. No words were exchanged; there was no need. Hannah held on to him as if she was afraid he would be taken away once again, and he held on to her as if he was scared to let go. Cash stepped back a bit and let them be, while Lindsey pulled out her phone and snapped a photo of the two. Posting it on her story, she captioned the touching moment: ***Hope is a gift, love is a treasure, and FAMILY is forever. Hank and Hannah Gunner together at last!***

"There's someone I'd like you to meet," Hannah whispered. "Please be nice."

Hank's eyebrows rose as he waited for the introduction. Hannah reached out and pulled Cash toward her.

"Dad, this is Cash." She turned to her boyfriend.

"Cash, this is my dad."

Reaching out to shake Hank's hand, Cash waited for a firm death grip to intimidate him. Pleasantly surprised when a strong but normal handshake reciprocated his, he finally relaxed. The vivid memories that Hannah had shared of the Captain popped into his head as they spoke and, despite trying not to picture him with a sword in his hand, Cash was struggling not to see a pirate standing before him.

"Nice to meet you, Cash. An unusual name that, Cash."

"Yes, sir, it is. It's a nickname. Grayson Parks is my given name."

"Ah ha! Nice to meet you, Grayson!"

And there it was! Cash could've sworn he heard the Captain, the one Hannah had so often described. Trying to focus on what Hank was saying as they spoke, Cash continued to make small talk. Noticing that Hank always had an eye on Hannah throughout the entire evening made Cash a tad nervous.

"Can I have everyone's attention, please?"

The room fell silent, and Nigel made a toast to honor Hank and his release. Hank raised his beer, which tasted unbelievable after all those years, and made another toast to his legal team.

"I can't begin to thank you, Nigel, for taking on Nate's project and talking Michael into helping you help me—for free, I might add." Everyone laughed.

"I will, however, make a substantial donation to your firm as soon as you obtain my funds from the state!"

"We're on it!" Michael laughed.

They cut the cake, had a few more drinks, and started to say their goodbyes for the evening. Hannah had insisted that he stay with them, but he had convinced her that the nearest hotel would be best until he was on his feet.

"That's not fair to Kathy," he'd insisted. "And, this might not make sense to you, but I don't think your momma would approve."

"What?" Hannah laughed. "That makes no sense at all!"

Hannah's heart skipped a butterfly beat as soon as he referenced her mom. Shaking her head, she let him say his goodbyes, and he even accepted Cash's offer to drive him to the hotel. Kathy hugged him, as did Hannah, before he climbed into the Jeep. Lindsey waved goodbye.

"It was lovely meeting you, Mr. Gunner."

"Thank you and likewise. But you can call me Hank."

As they were about to pull out of the complex, Hannah tapped on the hood of the Jeep. Cash stopped the vehicle and half-wondered if she was about to hop in.

"Tomorrow. What do you want to do tomorrow?"

Hank was solemn, but he answered immediately.

"If you don't mind, I'd like to say my goodbyes, properly, to your mom." Hesitating, he asked her if that would be okay. "I understand if it's too painful for you, too soon to go back, but I didn't get a chance to make things right, and I need to say my goodbyes."

Taken off guard, Hannah's shock was written all over her face. She hadn't visited her mom's grave since they'd buried her.

"No. I don't mind at all. I'd like to do that with you."

"See you in the morning, then."

"See ya."

Hannah waited in the lobby for Hank to come down. She held a hot cup of coffee in her hand from her favorite coffee shop. Each time the elevator doors opened, Hannah searched for him, but he never stepped out among the people getting off the elevator. There was no point in checking her phone, since Hank didn't have a cell phone yet. Nervously she paced the lobby.

"Hannah."

Whipping around, her dad was standing behind her. He had a new look about him, and she couldn't quite figure out what it was; rest maybe, refreshed, and the knowledge that he was free had made a difference this brand-new morning.

"Where did you come from?" she asked. "I brought you coffee."

Handing him the cup, she pointed to the door.

"I've got creamer and sugar in the car because I had no idea how you take it."

Smiling, he reached for the cup and said, "Good morning."

He took a sip and added, "Black is good! And I took the stairs. Enjoying being able to walk where I please these days."

The cemetery was less than forty minutes away.

Finally having her driver's license, Hannah drove Kathy's car. She had initially climbed into her mom's car, but couldn't bring herself to drive it. Climbing into it earlier that morning had sent chills down her spine. Feeling sad and depressed, she begged her aunt to switch vehicles for the day. Kathy reluctantly switched keys.

"We could sell or trade the car and get you something else. Just a thought, but think about it," Kathy suggested.

Hannah wasn't sure if she wanted to do that, either. She rarely needed to drive, and there was so little left of her mom that wasn't packed away in a box. At least each day when she walked past the car she was reminded of Gloria and the adventures they had shared, good and bad, moving from town to town in that damn run down, piece of crap car!

"Ready?"

"Whenever you are," Hank grinned. "Can we stop at a flower shop, please? You know, the cemetery and all."

Hannah nodded, disappointed she hadn't thought of that. Hank pointed out different landmarks, shops, and parts of town that he remembered when they had all lived there, and ones that had changed since he'd been gone. Hannah hung on to every word.

"That's the park I wrote to you about, do you remember? I told you we'd go hike and have a picnic there, likely bury our treasure." He laughed out loud. "It's Dolores Park, doubt they'd let us dig."

Hannah giggled. "You know, I read every one of those letters once I had them in my possession, every one of them! And I remember playing our game just about every night." Laughing, "Mom must've hated that game."

"Nah. She didn't hate it." Hank rolled down the window, and the cool breeze filled the car, carrying the smell of the sea-salt in the air.

"She'd sip her wine and sit outside your bedroom door, listening to us play. Once you were settled, almost asleep, we'd talk about what had made you laugh during the game that day. Was it the seagulls pecking at your hair? The buried treasure you could never find? The imaginary waves tickling your feet as you jumped over them on your bedroom floor, or even navigating the ship—you know, your bed." Hank smiled. "Gloria, your mom, loved to hear you laugh, and you might not believe this, but she loved when I was at home playing that game with you. Why?" He chuckled. "Because it made you laugh."

He laughed again, and Hannah noticed that the deep lines on his brow seemed to have softened, and his eyes were no longer dull.

"It's my fault you thought she didn't like it. I used to call her a tyrant, but I was only playing because it made you laugh and I liked it when you laughed."

Pulling in to the cemetery had an effect on both of them; the mood changed from jovial to somber instantaneously. It took Hannah a few minutes to find Gloria's gravestone, but when they did, Hank approved. Reading the words on her headstone over and over again, as if memorizing them, Hank crouched down next to her.

GLORIA YVONNE GUNNER.
LOVING WIFE, MOTHER, AND SISTER.
GONE FOR NOW, BUT NOT FORGOTTEN.
WE'LL SEE YOU SOON.

"I never meant those angry words that I said about her before, in Folsom. I never meant 'em. I've loved this woman, seems like most of my life. Damn sure the best parts of it."

Reaching around him, Hannah placed her arm around the back of his waist and leaned her head against him. Realizing he was praying silently, she stood up and gave him some space. His gentle hands were shaking, voice trembling, when he finally spoke again.

"I never knew she was sick. I didn't know."

"No one did," Hannah whispered. "She didn't want anyone to worry."

"Sounds about right," he managed, but Hannah knew he was trying to hold it together for her.

"Things got so out of hand so fast. The fighting. The arguing about bringing you up there to visit me, the phone calls, me getting into fights and ruining my parole. The entire situation turned into a huge mess. Gloria panicked. And though I'm angry that I didn't get to talk to you or see you for all of those years, and I am upset about that, I think I understand how she felt that I forced her hand."

Fighting back tears, afraid of scaring his daughter, Hank took a step back. He couldn't look at her at that moment.

"If you go back to the very beginning, none of this

would have happened if everyone would have come clean in the first place. The rest of the mess I take accountability for. Don't blame your mom, blame me."

"How about we don't blame anyone?" Hannah took the flowers out of his hands and placed them on the grave.

"How about we consider today and every day going forward a gift? I've got my Captain back, after all." Hannah smiled the way she used to, and looped her arm in his. "Captain Fin is back!"

"You make me laugh!" Hank pulled her into his arms, kissed the top of her head, took her by the hand, and walked her back toward the car.

"I make you laugh! At a time like this; why do I make you laugh?"

"Yes, you make me laugh!"

"Explain yourself, Captain Fin!"

Laughing, Hank shoved her playfully as they walked. "That, that right there... *why* do you insist after all these years on calling me Captain Fin?"

"What?"

"Captain Fin, Hannah. Why do you keep calling me that?" He laughed out loud. "Me and your mom laughed about it every time your tiny voice said it."

"What are you talking about? Captain Fin! That's who you are, to me, my whole life! You know, you, you're the Captain, Captain Fin, and I'm the First Matey. Hell, mom was the scallywag turned tyrant." Hannah let go of his hand and shoved him as they walked. "Why you gonna mess us up like that?"

Leaning against the car door, all smiles, Hank shook

his head. To tell her or not to tell her, tell her or not, that was the question. It was too funny not to inform her of the truth, not to mention it was time to lighten up the mood.

"Hannah."

"Yes."

"There never was a Captain Fin."

"What in the helllll are you talking about? Explain yourself!"

Laughing so hard he could barely speak, Hank tried to pull himself together long enough to explain. "The book that I read to you every night when you were a little girl, which turned into play-acting, was *Treasure Island*. My dad used to read it to me, and his dad to him. The pirate in the story was Captain Flint."

"Na uh!"

"Yep! Flint. Captain Flint. The story goes, Jim Hawkins' father owned the Benbow Inn. Jim realizes that Billy Bones, a lodger at the inn, is in hiding. Anyway, later in the book, Jim cares for Bones and Bones tells Jim that he was the mate of the late and notorious pirate... Captain Flint."

"Well, I'll be damned!" Hannah burst out laughing. "I feel like an utter idiot; all these damn years I used the wrong damn name!"

Grabbing her in his arms, he swung her around. "Well, me lass, not completely wrong. Ye used to have me swagger, right?"

His stance, like a pirate, made her howl. His voice, gruff and thick like a pirate, was the one she remembered that had brought her so much laughter as a kid. Standing in the cemetery parking lot, within seconds Hannah was whisked back in time as her dad became the pirate of her past. Opening the car door, he instructed her to dive in and take the wheel so they could grab some grub.

"I'm craving seafood, not just any seafood mind you, fresh seafood." Hank pointed out the window. "Let's go to the bay, lass. Find a cook."

"All right, knock it off! I get the picture," she laughed. "And I do know a great seafood restaurant."

Chatting about memories, mistakes, the future, and letting go of the past, Hannah and Hank enjoyed their lunch. Having no idea how involved Hank would be in her life, one thing was for sure: Captain Fin, regardless of the incorrect name, wasn't going anywhere. He'd been her salvation when she was scared. Her sweetest memories even when she thought he was a dream. A voice that connected her to her past that turned out to be her closest remaining family, and Captain Fin was even the connection to her future with her dad. Tucked away in the corner of her mind, Captain Fin would remain with Hannah forever.

"Now, start talking."

"About what?" Hannah asked, startled.

"Cash. Fill me in on this boy—everything. What are his goals, colleges he wants to attend, what his family is like. I want details."

Grinning, Hannah set down her fork. "Cash. Um, where to start! Let's just say I do love that boy, and I wouldn't be surprised if one day, not anytime soon, I wouldn't consider marrying that boy!" Grinning, she added, "But gawd, Dad, don't tell him I said that!"

Author's Note

I'm so excited to share CAPTAIN FIN with you! This novel has been a labor of love for me, the novelist, and for Kevin, the screenplay and feature scriptwriter. Usually, a novel is written first, and a script is written afterward, but once Kevin approached me about writing a novel based on his screenplay, I fell in love immediately with the life that both the young Hannah and the teen Hannah could have or would have lived. Her character is a beautiful soul, and I believe could step into another novel of her own with her friends, and of course Cash.

It would mean so much to us if you took a picture of your book and posted it anywhere, Facebook, Instagram, Twitter, and tagged us. Let us know what city and state you're from @AmandaMThrasher and @KevinONeill5. Also, if you like the book, please leave a review on Amazon and tell your friends about it. If you'd like to chat about the book, have any questions, or would just like to visit, you can find my contact form at amandamthrasher.com.

Thank you so much and enjoy!

About the Author

Award-winning author Amanda M. Thrasher was born in England, moved to Texas, and resides there still. She's the author of picture books, middle-grade chapter books, early readers, and young adult pieces. Additional work includes a graphic novel for the Texas Municipal Courts Education Center, Driving on the Right Side of the Road program (DRSR), titled *What If... A Story of Shattered Lives*, which was adapted into a reader's theater.

She is the recipient of multiple Gold Mom Choice Awards for young adult, general fiction, and early reader chapter books, a Readers' Favorite International Book Award for young adult social issues, an NTBF award for young adult and general fiction, and she was awarded a New Apple Literary Award for young adult and general fiction.

The Mom's Choice Awards® (MCA) evaluates products and services created for children, families, and educators. The program is globally recognized for establishing the benchmark of excellence in family-friendly media, products, and services. The organization is based in the United States and has reviewed thousands of entries from more than 55 countries. Around the world, parents, educators, retailers, and members of the media look for the MCA mother-and-child Honoring Excellence seal of approval when selecting quality products and services for children and families.

As Co-Founder and Chief Executive Officer at Progressive Rising Phoenix Press, she assists other authors with their work and shares her writing process and publishing experience with them. She continues to speak and share her work with children and adults of all ages, conducts workshops, writes a blog, and contributes to an online magazine.

For more information, visit the author's website at: www.amandamthrasher.com.

Titles by
Amanda M. Thrasher
www.amandamthrasher.com

Captain Fin
Bitter Betrayal
The Greenlee Project
The Ghost of Whispering Willow
Mischief in the Mushroom Patch
A Fairy Match in the Mushroom Patch
Spider Web Scramble (A Mischief Book)
There's A Gator Under My Bed
Sadie's Fairy Tea Party
What If... A Story of Shattered Lives

Coming Soon – *Book 4 of the Mushroom Patch Series*

Progressive Rising Phoenix Press is an independent publisher. We offer wholesale discounts and multiple binding options with no minimum purchases for schools, libraries, book clubs, and retail vendors. We also offer rewards for libraries, schools, independent book stores, and book clubs. Please visit our website to see our updated catalogue of titles and our wholesale discount page at:

www.ProgressiveRisingPhoenix.com

CPSIA information can be obtained
at www.ICGtesting.com
Printed in the USA
JSHW010748140220
4228JS00002B/13

9 781950 560011